DAUGHTERS OF SONG

Daughters

OF

Song

PAULA HUSTON

Random House

NEW YORK

Library of Congress Cataloging-in-Publication Data
Huston, Paula.
Daughters of song / Paula Huston
p.   cm.
ISBN 0-679-41969-1
I. Title.
PS3558.U8124D38   1995
813'.54—dc20   94-22683

Manufactured in the United States of America on acid-free paper
24689753
First Edition

For my father

Remember now your creator
       in the days of your youth,
Before the difficult days come,
And the years draw near when
       you say,
"I have no pleasure in them":
While the sun and the light,
The moon and the stars,
Are not darkened,
And the clouds do not return after the rain;
In the days when the keepers of
       the house tremble,
And the strong men bow down;
When the grinders cease
       because they are few,
And those that look through the
       windows grow dim; . . .
When one rises up at the sound
       of a bird,
And all the daughters of song
       are brought low . . . .

"Vanity of vanities," says the
       Preacher,
"All is vanity."

—Ecclesiastes 12:1–4; 8–9

ACKNOWLEDGMENTS

I am grateful to the National Endowment for the Arts for its support during the final draft of this novel. I also wish to thank Binky Urban and Kate Medina for their unwavering encouragement and excellent editorial advice, along with Gretchen Steer, Gail Westberg, Ron Dahl, Solveig Dahl, Al and Lynne Landwehr, John and Mary Kay Harrington, Pat Grimes, and Hunter Lillis for their patient and multiple readings. In addition, I wish to express my deep appreciation to those friends and musicians who helped with research or checked facts—Anne Campbell, Ken Walker, Greg Barrata, Cathy Harvey, and John Hampsey—and especially loving gratitude to my sister, Christina Dahl, and my husband, Mike Huston; without them there would be no book.

PROLOGUE

The city never sleeps, but now, four hours before dawn, the streets are as quiet as they ever get. Streetlights shine down on cold sidewalks; filthy water moves in sluggish rivers deep beneath the pavement; the winter grass crackles in the cold. In small parks, ringed by black wrought iron, red squirrels sleep in their tree-hole nests while all around them tall narrow houses lean into the mystery of the night. Here and there a cone of yellow light descends from a second-floor window: a mother in bathrobe and slippers moves down a long hallway toward her coughing child.

Deep in the heart of the city someone is practicing Beethoven, a difficult piano sonata with somber chords.

The alley men, huddled in the doorways, do the best they can. Sometimes, when it is really freezing, they make fires in the trash cans—crackling, leaping demons that sear their eyebrows and bring out the police. Tonight, however, it is not freezing, it is not storming, it is just cold and dark, and so instead they drowse and pass wine and tell each other lies.

The tide changes; the black ocean seeps into the bay.

At the conservatory the sonata comes to an end, and soon the last student leaves the building, glances at her watch under a streetlight—it is shortly after 2:00 A.M.— and hurries down the city blocks toward home. Inside the old many-storied school where she has been playing Beethoven, the building now makes its own music: radiators hiss, iron stairways clang, walls settle.

Outside, a cat shadows past sleeping cardinals. Three cars meet at an intersection and quietly move on. An ambulance wails. A jet passes over, thirty thousand feet above the city.

Across the Atlantic, the sun is already rising.

Book
ONE

How beautiful it is to live one's life
a thousand times.

—*Ludwig van Beethoven*

CHAPTER ONE

Sylvia stands on the broad ledge of the fifth-floor practice room window, gripping the sill on either side of her and wondering what someone below might think if he glanced up to see her there. Would I look brave? she thought. Or suicidal? Or maybe just crazy?

The first time she'd done this—climbed up onto the windowsill and leaned out, suspended in air over the sidewalk—was of course with her friend Peter; he'd been the one to do it first. He had stood there, broad and solid and silent as Buddha, looking out over the city, showing her it could be done.

She climbs up onto the sill as often as she can, hoping to conquer the great vague fear that shadows her wherever she goes.

Below her, Baltimore is spread out under a brilliant blue sky. Clouds of a dense silver purity and whiteness scud across it toward the harbor, toward the cold winter water of the bay. The wind whips against Sylvia's pants' legs; they flap around her thin calves, and she braces herself on the window ledge. Out in the harbor, beyond where she can see, great ships creak against their ropes, nosing out patterns in the water. Floating trash, wheeling seagulls, crabcakes at the Lexington Market: She imagines the lunch mobs, their heavy coats steaming in the heat as they herd into the Market, pushing and shoving to get to the counters, calling for beer. She thinks (guiltily, for there is no *point* in thinking these things) that if it were not for her talent, she could be one of them, one of the nameless hungry lunch crowd, some anonymous nineteen-year-old with no obligations to her parents or to her famous teacher or to Beethoven. An uncomplicated, happy girl in an old gray thrift-shop coat.

Her talent. She winces, thinking that in the long run, her talent has become nothing more than a curse. Miss Selkirk, of course, always called it a gift. You have the gift, my dear child, she would say sternly, gnarled hands folded across her thin voile dress. You have been blessed. . . . As though she saw such enormous and early promise as the sure sign of holy favor. What would she think, Sylvia wonders, if she could see me now?

The buildings of Baltimore look old and fragile, the color of tobacco and smoke. She imagines children playing with blocks in high narrow rooms; she remembers herself as a child, the books she used to read, her bed with the yellow canopy, her black patent-leather shoes shining nose to nose on the closet floor of the house near Minneapolis. She had been a serious child, with music in her head. No playmates, of course. Instead, a trio of intense adults—her mother Anne, her father Ross, her teacher Miss Selkirk—devoted solely to the care and feeding of her talent.

Of course, she has talked to Peter about this. You're lucky, he says bluntly. In my family, nobody gave a damn about music.

But you don't *know*, she tells him, you just don't know how hard it is to have everyone's . . . *everything* riding on your shoulders.

Who's everyone? he asks her.

You know, Peter. My *father*.

Somewhere in the city, cooks are singing in the kitchens of French restaurants. Waitresses lay out roses and white linen. In the air floats the rich heavy steam of Sicilian pasta—hot, herbed, pungent. Young boys call to each other in the streets, and Sylvia listens, aching. If she were a young boy running loose in the streets. If she were a French cook singing.

Your father's not everyone, Peter tells her.

Yes he is, she says—he *is*. And what's going to happen when Toft finally drops me?

Across the park is the brownstone apartment, three floors up, that she shares with Marushka and their clutter of plants and sheet music and instruments. She has lived with Marushka for a whole year now, ever since they both left the conservatory dormitories. Marushka is not always an easy roommate; she can be fierce and unyielding, but she is also the strongest person her own age that Sylvia has ever met. And funny; it was she who taught Sylvia to laugh. Their apartment is dark and cramped—nothing like the spacious and light-filled house on Cedar Lake where Sylvia grew up with Anne and Ross—but she must admit she has grown to love it; it is the one thing, in fact, that she truly and without reservation loves about Baltimore. The deep, rust-stained bathtub, the single bulb in the narrow hallway, the charcoal-colored rug . . . the tiny, darkly cheerful kitchen, and Jessye Norman on the stereo: the place is hers in a way that nothing else has ever been truly hers before.

The second movement—the arietta—of Beethoven's Opus 111 still lingers reproachfully in the air behind her. How beautiful it is in Toft's recordings; she cries every time she hears him play the last long trill on G, the ethereal triplets in thirds and sixths, that sudden swelling up on the descending scales . . . she has never heard anything so haunting and so strange. She loves it but cannot possibly play it; she falters, in the fourth variation, over the syncopated disintegration of the melodic line; she cannot handle the meter shifts between the first and second and third variations; she can't even play the repeat of the first eight-bar phrase correctly—she blunders through the delicate bass line like an elephant. Worse than her technical gaffes, however, is the fact that she goes blank before the beauty of the music. She stands before it in helpless awe, as though someone has handed her a chisel and told her to recarve the ankle-bones of Michelangelo's "David." During her lessons, Toft glowers as she desecrates this most exquisite of sonata movements, and she has nothing to say to him . . . the work is simply too difficult for her, both technically and emotionally.

This is how she fails with the movement she *loves;*

how much worse she is with the first movement, which seems to her both frightening and ugly, with its thunderous bass, its music constantly torn out of key.

Beethoven's last sonata: What in the world is she doing playing late Beethoven? Neither Miss Selkirk nor Mr. Binder would have ever allowed it—she is much too young—but Cornelius Toft . . . well, in spite of the fact that he gets visibly enraged whenever he hears her play it, he continues to insist that she perform it for her April recital. He must be hoping she will fail—why else would he be torturing her this way? He wants her to fail so he can finally drop her.

She looks down. A woman is towing a child across the cobblestoned street; the child's hat, tied beneath her chin, has blown off and is battering her small back like something crazed.

The sidewalk is directly below Sylvia's windowsill. It's a long fall—five stories—and she wonders for a moment how it would feel to float like an angel in the cold air above the hard ground, everyone gazing up in horror and fascination.

You're being dramatic again, she tells herself nervously. Stop it.

But she is so worn out with constant anxiety that her muscles ache; she lies awake night after night, brooding, wondering how much longer Cornelius Toft will put up with her. She may have great talent, as everyone has always told her, but she is clearly not living up to her promise. In the two years since she has been Toft's student, she has suffered from memory lapses onstage, once during Schumann's *Carnaval* and once during a Brahms intermezzo—sheer nerves—and, worse, has several times gone simply dead. Her strength as a performer, in spite of how thin and shy she is, has always been her passionate engagement with the music; she can be an exciting pianist when her confidence is high. With Toft, however, she has no confidence at all and so she has begun to switch off subconsciously, cut her own nerves, sometimes in mid-performance.

It's like going numb, she tells Peter. My hands keep on, but I can hardly hear myself playing.

It happens to everyone.

No it doesn't. Don't lie to me, Peter.

I don't lie.

She wonders what she would do without Peter these days. How she ever lived without such a friend. She's only known him for two years, a little longer than she's known Marushka, but beside the two of them she feels very young and inexperienced, though they are all quite close in age.

I think I need to grow up, she says to him.

Well yeah, he says. Good idea, Syl.

Music is pouring out into the cold afternoon air: Bach and Scarlatti, Liszt and Barber and Schumann, Mozart and Debussy. Practice room windows open to the chill January wind. Schubert and Ravel. Rachmaninoff. Scriabin and Haydn. A massive confusion of Steinways and Baldwins; damp, high-ceilinged rooms smelling of dust and sweat. Colette, Peter, Brandon, Jan—all the hopeful young pianists, room after room, door after door. She sighs. In spite of everything, a slow reluctant joy is rising once again. I'm sorry, Beethoven, she says, hoping for forgiveness, but instead his glowering face thrusts itself before her, as disapproving as Toft's. She pushes it away, and eases herself backward off the sill and down to the floor.

The window is immensely tall, ceiling height; everything in this place, she thinks, is high drama.

At the piano, she rubs her fingers, warming them. Where will she start? Where *can* she start, after once again mangling the arietta? She doesn't do many scales—she hasn't since she was a small child, for Miss Selkirk taught her instead to concentrate on the chords, to open up her hands until they quiver. To stay on a chord until she can feel the stretch. And later, after Miss Selkirk died, Mr. Binder showed her how to keep her wrists low and her fingers close to the keyboard, as though she is part of the piano.

So—chords it will be, with one hand pulling the other open if she has to. Her hands are small; she is still very young, and she cries too much. Well, that is just the way it is, Mr. Toft. She tries to think the thought with some ferocity.

CHAPTER TWO

Peter sits at the table, smoking his one cigarette for the day. The light in the room is pearl-gray; his smoke rises silently, disappearing into the dull silver of the light. Outside, late morning; the sky has gone a darker pewter with the coming storm; the wind has begun. Sylvia can hear old newspapers sliding over Peter's front steps and, somewhere, the barking of a dog.

From her place on the floor, she watches Peter as he smokes; she is fascinated, as always, by the way he regards the cigarette so carefully before he lifts it to his lips, the way he inhales with his eyes closed, the way he sighs, smiling to himself, as though never in his life has he experienced greater pleasure. She once asked him about his daily cigarette: It's my tea ceremony, he told her, laughing.

She knows it is no use talking until he is finished—the ritual of the cigarette requires absolute concentration—so instead she tries to gather her own senses together by focusing on Peter. His coarse black hair is tied back today in a long ponytail that falls almost to his waist. His broad face is tilted slightly, his narrow eyes closed; if she did not know him better, she would think he was sleeping.

Behind him are the empty walls of his studio apartment and the single window facing the storm. His kitchen is small and clean; on one counter sits a birdcage with his blue lovebird, Fred, pacing back and forth along the dowel perch and cocking its head at Sylvia; on the other is a radio/cassette player. Though they listen to music all the time, neither of them owns a stereo.

He has two chairs for his table; his living room is empty except for the dull black grand piano that takes up most of the space and the futon on which he sleeps. When Sylvia visits, she sits cross-legged on the rug with a pillow in her lap. Their visits follow a pattern that sometimes includes his daily cigarette, but always a cup of tea for her, many minutes of the silence that she finds so strangely calming, desultory talk, music, one or two startling moments in which something that has been troubling her finally comes clear, and then a final chat with the lovebird before she goes back to the chaos of her life. Why are Peter and I friends? she thinks. What can he possibly get out of me? She is always slightly shamed when she has been with him for an hour—his serenity opposes her nervous energy like a judgment—but she has never before known anyone like him, and she is drawn back to him over and over again.

Finally, with one last pleased sigh, he sets the still-burning butt on the edge of a saucer and turns his face toward hers. He's readjusting, she thinks. Getting ready to deal with the problem child.

"So what's up, Syl?" he asks. "How's the Beethoven coming?"

She laughs up at him, shaking her head. Her mass of light curls lifts and settles. "You're great," she says. "You never give up on me."

He turns the saucer with one finger, smiling. "How's the Beethoven?"

"Horrible."

"Why?"

"If I knew why, it wouldn't be horrible."

"Don't think. Tell me fast."

Sometimes Peter does this—fires questions at her—and she has to answer as quickly as she can. At first it upset her; she was too shy—her tongue was tied. Every time he asked a question, she blushed and went silent. Now she finds it exhilarating; she feels her lungs filling with cold air, her mind expanding.

"I don't understand it."

"What's to understand?"

"Why he wrote it. What it means."

"Why *did* he write it? Fast, Syl."

"He wrote it because . . . because he was deaf and he was thinking about dying?"

Peter watches her, smiling.

"Am I right?"

He shrugs. "Maybe."

"*You've* played it before, Peter—what do *you* think?"

"I've never performed it."

"But you're *great* with Opus 106."

"The *Hammerklavier*'s a different thing. What I know about that isn't going to help. It's what *you* know about 111 that's important."

She drops her head, feeling as though she might begin wailing. "But that's the point—I don't know *anything*. All I know is that I'm scared of the first movement and the second is incredible and I don't get either one. And Toft makes me feel like an idiot. He just stands there huffing and snorting—he can't *stand* me anymore, Peter."

She *is* wailing now—as usual, she thinks—and Peter gets up without answering and goes to the cassette player on the counter, where he puts in a tape. What will it be? she wonders in the midst of her misery. Something cool—something detached. And sure enough, he has called upon Thelonious Sphere Monk to settle her down; "Misterioso" lifts into the air. Jazz from another planet. She had never listened to *any* jazz before she met Peter; Miss Selkirk, had she been even slightly religious, would have characterized jazz as the work of the devil. In spite of an initial distaste—jazz is not beautiful, Sylvia thinks stubbornly, not like Chopin or Schubert—she finds that it haunts her. When Peter takes her to a jazz club (for Christmas a year ago he got her a fake I.D.), she is quiet for several days afterward, going over what she has heard, the image of the piano player or horn player or drummer lingering in her mind. Playing jazz is different from what she does, what she struggles through with Toft, but she has not figured out yet exactly what the difference is—and of course Peter will not tell her. You'll get it, he says. One of these days.

They sit listening, Peter standing at the window, and when the piece is over he switches off the tape. "Go play me some Chopin," he says. "Anything you want."

She looks up, startled; his face is turned toward the deep lavender of the storm clouds outside. He is going to listen; she is going to play. Okay, she decides. I can do that.

She stands up, her knees cracking, and stretches. The *Raindrop* Prelude is already in her mind. She loves Chopin as much as she loves her parents, as much as she has loved anybody in her life—more. She has been playing Chopin since she was eleven; Miss Selkirk put no restrictions on her when it came to Chopin. She knows every nocturne, every prelude, most of the waltzes. His B-flat Minor Sonata, which she played for her high school recital. The E Major Scherzo, which she submitted to Toft on her audition tape.

She runs her fingers over the top of Peter's piano— what an old friend it has become—and then seats herself at the bench. She can hardly play Chopin without melting into the beauty; she turns warm, then cool, then warm in waves; she is lifted out of herself. She does not think when she plays Chopin; she has never needed to, once the pieces were learned. He is as natural to her as sleep or breath, her old friend who knew what it was like to be alone, to be frail and weak, to be shy and dominated by others.

She plays and Peter listens. Tears rise and spill over while she is playing, but they are not sad tears—more the result of an aching she cannot contain. When she is done, she puts her hands in her lap and looks over at him. The light has grown so dim she can hardly see; he is still in profile beside the window; the storm is hitting the glass with bullets of rain.

"Play Beethoven like that," he says finally. "Simple."

She clears her throat, still tight with the ache, and tries to laugh. "Beethoven isn't Chopin, Peter."

"I mean get out of his way, Syl. The way Monk does with the music. The way you just did with that prelude."

She thinks about this for a few moments, almost but not quite understanding what he is telling her. Peter does this to her often—gives her a half answer that she can't complete. While she is still struggling to comprehend, for she *knows* this is important, she *knows* she needs to get it, she thinks of Toft, his fierce old face, his piercing, simian eyes, and the fear comes over her once more. She shudders. The room, vibrating now with purple stormlight, suddenly feels icy. "This is going to be a big one," she says shakily, pointing toward the window. "I heard we might get snow."

Peter turns and smiles at her. "Let's go for a walk."

"*Now?*"

"Why not?"

She stares at him, feeling a grin coming on. Of course. A big storm—just the place for them to be. Why not? It's like standing in the practice room window, or sneaking out for jazz performances knowing she has early classes and Toft would kill her if he found out. It's like using her fake I.D.

They wrap themselves in layers of clothes, then Peter cuts holes in a couple of big trash bags and they drape each other in plastic. They look like worms—dark green worms. Sylvia is laughing when they go out the front door and into the wind, remembering the jubilant barking of the dog. What would her mother think? Poor Anne. To her, Sylvia will always be a straight-A student with a long, thick braid swinging down her back. A cherished daughter, ever obedient and good. A child to shield from the force of her husband's will.

Bare-limbed winter trees, black with wet, are thrashing in the cold rush of air from the Atlantic. Sylvia lifts her face, already red and stinging from the pelting rain, and feels the water streaming down her neck and into her sweater. They will be soaked, trash bags or not. She raises her arms and whirls along the pavement, a wild green worm in a Chopin mazurka. Peter, behind her, ambles along, strands of dark hair, blown loose from the ponytail, plastered across his face. No one else is on the sidewalk; lights glow in brownstone windows. "Where are we going?" she calls back to him.

He lifts one hand, his trash bag billowing. A lone car creeps along beside them on the cobblestones, headlights shining on the black puddles, capes of rain blowing back over its hood. She spins for the sake of the driver, whom she can just make out hunched darkly over the wheel behind the windshield wipers. Somebody trying to get home before it snows. The car creeps past; he doesn't even see her. She waves and whoops, the rain filling her mouth. In all her years of childhood, she can never remember deliberately going out into a storm. At home, storms meant hot chocolate with whipped cream on top. Storms meant Ross piling on logs in the big stone fireplace, Anne in the kitchen stirring soup, muffins in the oven. Storms meant heat and light and both parents temporarily united against the fury outside.

For a moment she feels a deep stab of homesickness, a condition that plagued her for months when she first came to Baltimore, but one, she suddenly realizes, that has been diminishing slowly, without her even being aware of it, in the past year. What a surprise. She stands still in the middle of the tossing rain for a moment, pondering this new fact, then feels Peter's hand on her shoulder. She turns; he is pointing; she looks down into an alley.

Against the brick wall is a dark shape covered in wet newspaper. The alley is narrow, the rain somewhat blocked by the height of the buildings on either side, but whoever it is must be soaked and freezing by now. Sylvia shudders; she has a horror of the homeless men who populate the alleys around the conservatory. Sometimes they are sleeping in doorways when she walks to school early in the morning; sometimes they are lying on the iron benches in the little park. They are filthy and gravel-voiced and smell like rotted hay. Often they stare at her as she hurries past with her canvas bag of music.

Peter heads into the alley. She pulls at his arm, but he ignores her, dragging his plastic trash bag over his head. What is he doing *now*? she thinks, but she follows him obediently.

Between the two walls the storm is quieter, but the wind calls hollow-voiced from the mouth of the alley and Sylvia stays close behind her friend. He stops in front of the huddled shape. She can see shoes, thin ankles with no socks, frayed cuffs ruffling in the wind; even in the rain, the thick dank smell of wine and filth and body odor rises up around them. Peter waits. The man stirs, then lifts his head slowly, peering at them, and Sylvia is startled at the vicious intensity of the dark eyes in the grizzled face. He looks like an *animal*, she thinks, ashamed of herself. Without speaking, Peter hands him the trash bag. The man takes it, studies it, shakes it out, and pulls it over his head, all in one swift motion, and then, before she quite realizes what has happened, she and Peter are back on the sidewalk, walking.

Once again, the full blast of the storm is in their faces; Sylvia's hair writhes around her head like wet snakes. Why did you make me do that? she wants to ask Peter. What was the point? She is even a little angry; they could have been attacked.

Instead, she follows him for three more blocks, until they reach the White Tower, where he pulls open the outer door. "Time for something hot," he says.

Later, as they sit steaming in their wet clothes, coffee mugs in their hands, he adds, "You were scared, but you did it."

"The man?"

He nods, sipping.

"I never would have gone into that alley in a million years without you there."

He shrugs. "You did it. Don't analyze everything to death."

She turns the mug between her hands. There is something here she is supposed to get, but she's not getting it.

The serenity she always feels at Peter's house is already fading; now she is close to home, where at any moment the telephone could ring, with her father on the other end. How's everything with my favorite girl? How's the recital program coming along? And, unspoken: What does Mr. Toft *really* think of you, Sylvia? Is there something I should know?

Peter says, "Are your parents coming for the recital?"

She sighs. "Of course."

He picks up a fork and taps it gently against the edge of her mug. "Next time you play the *Raindrop* Prelude," he says, "what's going to be different?"

She stares at him. His black eyes are somber, but crinkled at the edges; she's seen this look before—he's holding back a smile. What does he want her to say?

"Quick, Syl."

"The rain," she says. "The rain's going to be . . . wetter. Colder. More dangerous."

The smile breaks through. The waitress pours them more coffee. They sit on in the light and the steamy warmth while the storm rages outside.

CHAPTER THREE

*T*he conservatory library rises in six ornate tiers beneath a small old-fashioned light-filled rotunda. In spite of the high windows, the floor lies in shadows. Wooden ladders hang from big brass hooks; a librarian moves slowly along the rail on the third tier, searching for a title. Outside it is morning, cold and clear; inside, it is duskily warm. Sylvia can hear the throb of the furnace in the basement as she sits in her wooden alcove under the warm yellow light of the desk lamp. In the back of her throat she can taste the thick must of cracked leather and faded gold leaf.

She is reading about Beethoven. Opus 111 is certainly not the only piece on her recital program—she is also playing three finger-bending Scarlatti sonatas, Ravel's *Sonatine*, and Schumann's *Fantasiestücke*—but it has become the test.

In front of her is a stack of books and a small pile of scrap paper. She is not sure what she is looking for, but she is determined to read until she finds it. You'll know,

Peter is always telling her, as though wisdom is something that lurks just beyond the limits of her ability to see. But how can she be so blind? She has always been a good student, capable and efficient; she has always done her homework in a neat and diligent way. She has made her parents proud—but it is beginning to seem that the older she gets, the less she knows and the more often she is destined to fail.

She has been looking at portraits of Beethoven all morning, hoping to see something in his face that will help her with his music. Miss Selkirk, of course, had a bust of Beethoven near her piano, so Sylvia has grown up with a certain heroic picture in her mind; the manly chest of white marble, the white marble face with wild mane and staring eyes. What she has learned so far from the paintings has surprised her; he is not heroic at all, aside from a few portraits clearly meant to flatter; he is short and broad, with disheveled graying hair—not a handsome man, but compelling. She does not think she would want to have him for a teacher; he glares from under his eyebrows the same way Toft does. His chin is cleft, his nose strong, his wide mouth almost always frowning.

She turns to the Ferdinand Waldmüller portrait, dated 1823. She likes this one the best so far; he looks . . . not exactly kindly, but not cruel either. Tired, somewhat irritable, with a touch of sadness around the eyes and mouth. His gray hair does not bristle around his head, as in so many of the other pictures; his hairline actually recedes. He is fifty-two, hopelessly deaf by now, but still he seems to be listening intently. It seems to her that he has other business on his mind that is more important than sitting still for a painter; he may get up at any moment and leave the room. What is he listening to? she wonders. Could it be Opus 111?

She checks her notes: No, 111 was published in 1822, a year before this portrait. What else could it be? She turns pages, reads intently. This is *her* era, this portrait. At some time very close to the day he sat being painted by Waldmüller, he wrote out the score that she has studied for so many months. Opus 111—his last piano sonata, dedicated to his friend and patron, Archduke Rudolf of Austria. No—not just his patron: his *pupil.* And then he had stopped writing for the piano, saying that it was, after all, "an unsatisfactory instrument." Though later, of course, he couldn't resist Diabelli's challenge and had written the longest set of piano variations in existence, not to mention that last set of bagatelles . . .

She circles back to Archduke Rudolf, his pupil. How did the irritable Beethoven teach? Like Toft? She shudders, and reaches for another book. Beethoven as a teacher, a teacher . . . she turns pages, scanning. Letters to countesses, snatches from his famous conversation books, quotes from his students, from Czerny, Ferdinand Ries . . . here it is, a quotation from Ries: "If I missed something in a passage or incorrectly played notes and leaps which he wanted to have consistently accurate, he seldom said anything." She stops, writes this down on a scrap of paper; she'll hang it on her bedroom wall to give her courage. She returns to the page and reads, "Only if I showed a lack in expression, in *cre-*

scendi, etc., or in the character of the piece, did he become aroused, because, he said, the former is an accident, the latter a lack of knowledge, feeling, or attention.''

Knowledge, feeling, or attention. Well, here we have it, she says to herself. She puts down her pencil, rubs her neck, stares up at the morning light in the high rotunda. At this moment she would like nothing better than the chill air in her face, the sun falling in patterns through the bare tree limbs. At this moment she wishes more than anything to be a child again, a prodigy whose talent is so rare, so startling, that all she has to do is play and everyone is thrilled. But I'm not a child anymore, she thinks. And this is hard. And my father doesn't have a clue about any of this—all he wants is for his daughter to be another Moon Ja Koh, another famous Toft protégée.

So—do I lack knowledge?

She thinks of her friend Marushka, only two years older than she is, and the sly wisdom Marushka seems to have about the world. How many times has she said to Sylvia, Didn't you notice the way Jan was staring at you? The way Miss Haupt caters to Toft? The way David smiles at that girl? And Sylvia is always surprised once again at what she has missed; she has never been on a date, never kissed a boy, never even thought about love. So, yes, it appears that she lacks at least a certain kind of knowledge.

What else? She glances again at her notes. Ah—feeling. Am I lacking in feeling? That, at least, seems wrong. She *feels* more than anyone she knows. She cries for everything and for nothing. She embarrasses herself, over and over, with her overwhelming emotional reactions to music. She cannot look at beautiful things without breaking down. Isn't *that* feeling?

Perhaps it is the wrong kind. She takes a strand of hair in her hand and twists it slowly, then lets the curl unwind. What kinds of feelings does she have, after all? Does she feel joy? Well, rarely, unless she counts her peculiar reaction to beauty. Does she feel satisfaction? She ponders for a moment. No—never. She has never felt satisfied with herself—only that strange aching yearning that goes on and on. Does she feel . . . at peace? She thinks of her sleepless nights, the anxiety that haunts her, the great vague fear that dominates most of her actions.

She looks back at the portrait of Beethoven: Is he afraid? She cannot see it, though he must know he is going to die soon—he'll be dead within four years. What *is* he hearing in his head, at this very moment the painter is catching him in the windowlight? Perhaps it is his magnificent Ninth Symphony—yes, of course. It *has* to be the Ninth—the culminating work of his life. What else could he be thinking of? He's left the piano behind and he is thinking of something greater than himself, greater even than fear. How often, she thinks, am I *not* afraid? How often do I forget my fear and simply play as I should?

What's left? She reads from the scrap of paper: attention. Do I lack attention? she wonders. Do I pay attention to what Toft is telling me? Do I really *listen* to Peter? Do I concentrate on the music instead of myself?

Her head is aching. She has never thought of questions like these before. She has never thought much at all; she has not needed to. Her parents, her teachers have always made the decisions for her. And now here she is in this shadowy warm place with the furnace pounding in the basement and two hundred years of ghosts roaming the tiers—here she is in this place, alone, with just herself for company.

Late afternoon and she is back in the apartment with her stacks of Beethoven books. Her eyes ache; she sits at the small round table in the kitchen eating crackers and tomato soup. Her throat is sore, her sinuses tender; she is either getting a cold or suffering the aftereffects of the book dust in the library.

How easy it is, she thinks, to slip into self-pity when I don't feel good. To fantasize about home.

But no matter how she pushes them away, the images are vivid today: the wide green lawns, the dark pines, the sun flashing on the lake. She can see Ross down at the old wooden dock, tackle box open, rod and reel propped against the silver bass boat. She can see Anne in the wicker chair on the wide porch, sipping hibiscus tea, her long legs wrapped about the legs of the chair. She is wearing a yellow dress; the yellow skirt falls across the white wicker; she turns the pages of her novel, sipping, and Sylvia wants to reach out and stroke the springy hair, the light curls that are so much like her own. They are both so *good* to me, she thinks. Why can't I let myself quit and go home?

Ross looks up from the tackle box. He has heard her; his handsome face has gone ashen; his blue eyes deepen in sudden . . . what? Fear? Disappointment? Shock?

She can never quit. It would kill him.

She sips the tomato soup from her spoon. The back of her neck is stiff, and so is her back, low down. She's been practicing too much, and much too tensely.

The door slams and suddenly the apartment is filled with the thunder of Marushka, her boots on the wooden floor, her bags swinging against the walls. "Sylvia!" she calls. "Where are you?"

"Here."

Marushka rounds the corner, pulling off her red scarf and throwing back her hair. She is a big dark-eyed Ukrainian blonde, handsome as a horse; she brings with her into the kitchen a faint aura of winter cold. "Sylvia!" she says. "You will never guess!"

"You're playing at the White House."

"No!"

"You won the concerto competition."

"No again!"

"Well, what?"

Marushka flops down into the chair opposite Sylvia and pulls the plate of crackers in her own direction. "How is that soup?" she says. "Is it hot? I am very cold—give me a taste."

Sylvia sighs and slides the bowl her way. This is life with Marushka—nothing is sacred. No concept of private property—no respect for secrets. Marushka eats half the contents of the bowl, making little sounds of such pure enjoyment that Sylvia cannot be angry. "Ah," Marushka says finally, pushing the bowl aside. Sylvia waits with her spoon, wondering if her friend will notice, but of course she does not, of course Sylvia must rise and retrieve the bowl on her own.

"Good—thank you," says Marushka. "And now let me tell you my news!" She leans forward against the table, flattening her big breasts against the edge. Sylvia has always been amazed at Marushka's figure; she is only twenty-two but looks like a nursing mother of six. Pierogi, Marushka always says proudly, hefting her chest. I love, love, love to eat—and what is wrong with that?

"Sylvia, I have heard a rumor that David is asking me into the quartet. The quartet! Just think about this!"

"That's *great*, Marushka. Who told you?"

"Brandon! David has been talking about me to people!"

"Well, it's going to be a fantastic quartet—I'm really happy for you." Marushka is one of the best fiddlers in the school; in spite of her flamboyant personality, she works terribly hard at the violin, spurred by an intense ambition that Sylvia sometimes finds alarming. David, though, is a different story—he hardly has to work at it; he's a natural, a darkly handsome young Israeli whom people are already comparing to Zukerman. Of course, he is also a terrible show-off, always doing the big virtuoso stuff, like Paganini and Wieniawski, but he plays with such . . . *enjoyment*. That's it: He's crazy, casual, full of joy, unlike so many music students—unlike *me*, Sylvia thinks—to whom performing has become a matter of life and death. David loves what he does, and he also loves women; he is never without one—they hang all over him shamelessly, and he enjoys them all. Even Sylvia, who doesn't notice such things, has noticed David and his women.

"I am very good in ensembles," says Marushka, her mouth full of crackers.

"You are."

"He would be crazy not to ask me."

"You're right."

"Sylvia, I must ask you a favor."

"Oh, wonderful."

"Seriously. I need you to accompany me in the Philadelphia competition on the tenth."

"In less than two weeks, Marushka? Are you crazy?"

"It will be nothing for you, it will be a snap." Marushka clicks her fingers.

"But I thought Colette was accompanying you in Philadelphia."

Marushka looks away; it is clear that she is uncomfortable.

"What happened?"

Marushka shrugs. "We quarreled. She is much too sensitive, Sylvia. She blames everything on the color of her skin."

"Oh, Marushka—what did you say *this* time?"

Marushka shrugs again. "It was nothing. She took it wrong."

Poor Colette; Sylvia likes Colette, though the two of them have always been too shy to pursue a friendship. But she is fascinated by Colette's reserve and her mastery of the French repertoire. And Colette never has to worry about memory slips; she is an absolute perfectionist at the keyboard.

"Besides," Marushka continues, leaning closer. "You already know the music—the *Kreutzer* Sonata."

Sylvia stares past her, thinking. Opus 111 completely aside, she still has much work to do on her other recital pieces. The Scarlatti sonatas, for example: Miss Selkirk would have had her do them in slow motion for months before she brought them up to tempo. But not Toft—oh no: I do not believe one can discover fingering by playing slowly, Sylvia—that is a cheap myth. And what about the pedaling and hand movements? What are you going to do about them at one third the tempo? Do you see?

She falls asleep at night, *when* she can sleep, with his Do you see? in her ears, along with the glittering upper-register work of Ravel's *Sonatine*, the third piece on her program and one, she thinks, much more suited to a cool, polished player like Colette, who collects French music—Fauré, Poulenc, Debussy, Satie—the way Peter once collected baseball cards.

"Don't you remember what happened last time I accompanied you in a competition?" Sylvia asks.

Marushka makes a dismissive gesture. "I am not worried."

Sylvia sighs; Marushka's faith in her is unwavering and absolute. The first time she ever heard Sylvia play (they hardly knew each other), she came up afterward and said, "In ten years you will be famous."

"So you will do it?" Marushka's expressive face is filled with hope.

Sylvia ponders for a moment. Marushka may be demanding, but she rarely asks for something as important as this—her pride wouldn't allow it. She trusts me, Sylvia thinks. To her I'm not a failure. Besides, accompanying at such short notice without Toft's permission feels like an act of courage, like standing in the window-sill or using her fake I.D. to get into a jazz club with Peter. I *need* to do brave things, she thinks, so maybe I should do this. "Okay," she says finally. "But don't tell anyone. Toft will kill me if he finds out."

"Oh, Sylvia!" Marushka has come around the table, is smothering Sylvia between her hearty breasts. "I will never forget this! You are my friend forever!"

In the middle of the night as she lies awake in bed listening to Marushka's snoring down the hall, Sylvia's mind moves among the portraits of Beethoven, the alley men, her father at the lake, her lessons with Toft—and then she is thinking of Moon Ja Koh, her father's heroine and her own. Miss Koh: Toft's most famous student, the only other woman, besides Miss Haupt, he ever taught; she has carried the image of Miss Koh in her mind since she was only eight and first saw her perform in Minneapolis. She has followed Miss Koh's career around the world, through Europe and South America and now Asia, where Sylvia can imagine her idol sitting alone in a lighted room with rice-paper walls. What is she doing? Is she wearing glasses? Does someone like Miss Koh need glasses? No—she is drinking something from a small cup and she is reading, her black hair falling forward; there are no glasses to be seen, only a mass of white roses in a tall vase on the table beside her.

Knowledge and feeling and attention, Sylvia tells Miss Koh sleepily. Don't forget, or he will be very angry with you. And then Miss Koh, without a piano, is playing Schubert's *Wanderer* Fantasy. How difficult and beautiful it is! Sylvia closes her eyes while the music goes on and on, and then her head is filled with forests and rising mists and a soft heavy darkness that muffles all sound.

CHAPTER FOUR

*C*ornelius Toft stands in the hallway, smoking; he does not do it the way Peter does—gracefully and with pleasure—but pecks angrily at the end of his cigarette. Smoke puffs from his narrow nostrils; he is eighty-four years old but has not given up either his cigarettes or, worse yet, his cigars. Sylvia, waiting fearfully inside the practice room for her lesson, can see him just outside the door.

He has been talking to someone. Now the door bursts open, making her jump, and he strides into the room, trailing smoke. "Tell him he's a fool," he barks over his shoulder. "Tell him I said so."

"Oh certainly, Cornelius," says a woman's voice, sweetly sarcastic—Miss Haupt? Perhaps—the two of them are great friends, anyway, in spite of Toft's long-established reputation as a misogynist. Miss Haupt is old, though not nearly as old as Toft, and she is also a piano teacher at the conservatory. The story is that she often cooks for him. They are both ex-Berliners; Sylvia has heard that Miss Haupt studied briefly with Toft before either of them left Germany. She must be very brave, Sylvia thinks, to tease him that way.

Toft, muttering, marches to the window without glancing at her. She waits at the bench, flushing hot and cold. Whenever she is in his presence, all of Peter's lessons about courage evaporate. Why? she wonders. How can Toft do this to me—make me into nothing just by walking into a room? She is ashamed at his power over her—but she has to admit that her father has the same kind of power, though in a different way; together, they determine what she thinks of herself. It's not me deciding how good I am, or even if I *am* good—it's them. It's always the two of them, Ross and Toft, her father's tense and handsome face, her teacher's glowering looks.

She risks a peek at Toft; he is standing beneath the tall mahogany window frame, one hand cupping the opposite elbow, finishing his cigarette. She is the farthest thing from his mind and she knows it, though this gives her little comfort; all she has to do is blink and he could turn on her, crackling and spitting into blazing life. She cannot relax for a moment.

Schubert's Little Sonata in A Major drifts through the room—Brandon? Colette?—and Toft listens, cocking his head, then shaking it as he tosses his burning cigarette to the street five stories below. Clearly, he is not pleased. Her stomach tightens.

"So," he says, turning. "And what is the news from the clouds?"

Sylvia swallows, touching a key with her finger. What is it about her that disgusts him so? The way she cringes,

maybe? Peter, though he would never say it directly, has
implied as much. She thinks of herself on the windowsill, clinging to the frame. She cannot even do *that* the
way Peter does it; she is too careful, too afraid of being
hurt.

Of *course* she cannot play Opus 111. What has she
been thinking of, with all her Beethoven books, her research? Who is she kidding? The first movement especially, with its enormous, crashing chords, was meant for
Toft, not her—it is pure power, pure will.

But *he's* the one who's making me play it, she thinks.
And he's never even told me why, and besides that, he
isn't helping me a bit—isn't this *his* responsibility too?

The words, however, sound weakly ineffectual and
she knows she will never say them out loud even if she is
right. Cornelius Toft is an institution, as her father reminds her in his intense way. The very best, Sylvia. The
best that money can buy.

Instead of feeling grateful, she dreams of Toft at night,
his querulous nasty voice with the power to freeze her
cold, and then she listens one more time to his magnificent recording of Opus 111 and is flooded with disbe-
lief. I am his student, she thinks. Me, Sylvia. Impossible.

"Are you in love with some longlegs, or what is the
story, miss?"

Here it comes. She forces herself to lift her head until
she is looking directly into his eyes. There is no point in
answering questions like these; she can only wait him
out. Her palms are slick with sweat. Peter, she thinks,
Toft is your teacher too—how do *you* handle him? But
she can't compare herself to Peter. He's too good—he's
in a class by himself.

Toft's eyes are very dark and round and he can make them as hard as marbles when he holds a stare. In spite of her fear of him, she has noticed that there is something monkeyish about the puckered old mouth, those quick eyes in their nest of wrinkles, the blue-veined hoods he can raise and lower at will.

"Ah well," he says, shaking his head. "Come. Let's get on with it. We are already behind schedule."

"What"—her voice breaks—"do you want first?"

He crosses the room to his chair, ignoring her, and she crosses her fingers, hoping that he will ask for Schumann or Ravel or even the Scarlatti sonatas—anything but Beethoven first. If he did not frighten her so, she would find him amazing. In spite of the military bearing, his spine is beginning to cave in; he has to tuck his chin to stand up straight. But his shoulders are broad and he still has the muscular forearms of a pianist. He settles himself, fussing a little with the angle of the chair, then once again bores into her eyes with his.

"Scarlatti."

She swallows. None of the little sonatas are ready yet, though she has been working very hard. "Which one?" she asks.

"Three fifty-six."

She turns back to the keyboard, looking down as though it's the first time she's ever played. Eighty-eight keys, the long sweep from bass to treble. In spite of Toft, she has never stopped loving this big black monster, loving the battle between her small hands and the cold ivory. She still remembers her first lesson with Miss Selkirk, the seven-foot Steinway beside the arched window. She had been ten; she had played Beethoven's

Opus 49, No. 1, for her new teacher—Beethoven had seemed delightful then, a playmate—and Miss Selkirk had been pleased enough to raise the lid so that Sylvia could hear herself from every corner of the room.

She takes a long breath and brings her hands up. Pretend you're Peter, she says to herself. Pretend you are strong.

After the third sonata is finished—Scarlatti always sounds to her like someone breaking icicles with a little hammer—she sits back, prepared for the worst. Her fingering was off in the second, and in the third she was pedaling like crazy, with no earthly excuse for it. Toft *hates* extraneous pedaling, especially in Bach or Scarlatti, where he can hardly accept pedaling at all.

She hazards a look in his direction. His head is down; he is making circles on his forehead with his thumb and his forefinger.

"Do you understand that I am trying to give you something?" he says at last, without looking up. He is speaking very quietly, not at all with his usual snappish forcefulness. This takes her by surprise—he seems so old and weary suddenly, and so honestly saddened. "I am taking a risk, Sylvia—do not make me into a fool."

She swallows, knowing neither what he means nor what he expects her to say.

"Are you familiar with Hegel?" He is staring at her now, the heavy, unforgiving eyelids once more in place.

Hegel? She searches her memory frantically; she cannot think—a composer? A pianist? She knows she has heard the name somewhere . . . is he a philosopher?

"Never mind," he says. "Of course you aren't. You

are too young. And, of course, an American . . ." He coughs, holding the back of his hand to his mouth. His small frame shakes; it's a miracle he is still alive; she's heard that he smokes two packs a day.

She waits.

He says, "You are a talented girl. You know that."

She looks down. "Yes," she answers very quietly.

"It is not that you are not talented." He sighs loudly, a disgusted sigh through his nose, and turns back toward the window. "You simply do not think."

She doesn't think? What does he mean?

"You seem to feel that this should be easy, that having a little fire in your hands is enough. Do you see?"

Fire in her hands? She can feel the skin jumping near her mouth; she is embarrassed beyond words. What if her father heard this?

"You need the ice, too, young woman. The hard cold intellect. Do you know what I am saying to you?"

She is blushing now, deep hot blushes. She looks away from him.

"You must steel yourself to a discipline of thoroughness. In Germany we call it *Gründlichkeit*, what I am talking about."

Gründlichkeit. Outside the window, the sun is on its long slide into evening; the dark waters of the bay slosh in their great bowl. Geese pass overhead, a wavering black arrow into the blue silk of the sky. Someone is leaning on a car horn. A cool wind rattles the panes. For the first time during this lesson, she feels that she really might cry.

"It is probably not your fault," he says, "that you do

not know how to think." He is looking down at his hands, and his voice has gone flat. "Ah well. It was an idea I had—one I've kept to myself for a very long time. I thought perhaps you were still innocent enough . . ."

Someone is tapping at the door. Toft, irritated, turns his head. Brandon is peering through the small window at them.

"Come in, come in," Toft calls gruffly.

Brandon glides into the room, cushioning the click of the door behind him. "Hello," he says to Toft, smiling. He half raises his wrist, glances down at his watch. "I wasn't sure . . ."

"No, no, my boy, you are fine. I am the one who is running behind schedule." He stands, breathing hard, and Brandon moves solicitously to his side. "Sylvia," says Toft. "We are done now, I think. We will continue this later."

"Of course," she says. He is cutting off her lesson for Brandon's sake, but what else can she say? Her father would be very angry; who knows how much he is paying for this? But she doesn't have the courage to tell him. He thinks that lawyers can solve everything, but no lawyer, not even him, can fix what has gone wrong between her and Cornelius Toft. Her throat feels very tight; her heart is racing; she knows she will not sleep again tonight.

"Hi, Sylvia," says Brandon. He smiles at her with his white teeth and runs one hand over his hair. He is very handsome, very preppy. She's heard that he grew up with servants and maids, that he could have studied in Paris or Germany but that his father chose Toft instead. Brandon is quite clearly Toft's favorite. For a passionate moment she hates him—and then even that dissolves into a weak and embarrassed resentment.

"Hi," she says. Her stomach is flip-flopping. Discipline and purity, she thinks desperately. *Gründlichkeit.* That's what I need.

She will wake at 5:00 A.M. every morning; she will read—who was it? Hegel?—or track down his music if he is a musician; she will walk six miles a day and eat only vegetables and grains. She will talk to Peter, ask him for a plan. Something, anyway, to fix her in a path, free her from the chaotic and fearful emotions that have apparently ruined her musical potential and, possibly, her life.

"You're sure I'm not interrupting?" says Brandon. "I can wait."

"No, no, my boy," Toft assures him. Toft is actually *smiling.* The hard cold intellect, Sylvia tells herself. Remember. Think.

Brandon is already shuffling through his music. "There was something I wanted to ask you about in the Bartók—here, in *Night's Music,* do you see where I've got it marked?"

Their heads are bent together over the score; Sylvia has already been forgotten. She begins, quietly, to gather her things, trying not to call attention to herself or her own insignificance. Is this what Toft wants from her, then? Brandon's endless questions? Is this what he means by thinking?

She slips away from the bench and heads toward the door, hearing, behind her, their eager talk. They do not even sound like student and teacher, she thinks. They sound like *friends*. Yet she knows, because she has heard him play, that Brandon is not that much better than she is, especially with Chopin. So why does Toft respect him and not me? Why am I so different?

What is wrong with me?

CHAPTER FIVE

*N*oon.

Moon Ja Koh sits alone in a restaurant on the Ping River eating pla taw and thinking of her concert in Bangkok two days before. She had played Mendelssohn's *Three Fantasies*—they loved "The Trumpeter"—then Mozart's K. 271, the concerto that someone once called his *Eroica*. The orchestra was surprisingly good.

Four bodyguards, provided by the king, wait patiently at the next table as she finishes her meal of tender fish; she should probably not have traveled to Chiang Mai— her schedule is so full—but she has heard about the silver and lacquerware, the silk and cotton weaving, the beautiful ceramics that are to be found in this lovely place. And she needs a break; she has been traveling hard and performing almost every other night.

The tour has been tough. First Auckland, Sydney, Brisbane, Perth, where people clapped for her in a hearty, Texas-style way, and then on to Djakarta, where she thought she would be swallowed up by the hordes on the streets. Never in her life—not in Manhattan, in Paris, in Rome—has she seen so many people shoulder to shoulder, wheel to wheel, eye to eye. Women with baskets on their heads, messengers with caps, slick-looking young men with black jackets, babies, soldiers, Muslims, farmers, housewives—a living kaleidoscope swarming beneath a dense cloud of gray smog. She had been afraid in Djakarta, though they took care of her very well; she had her own car and driver, after all, and rooms in the best hotel.

She glances at the bodyguards. They are smoking and talking, but when they see her looking at them, all four of them smile at her, the wide, sweet Thai smile that she has learned to appreciate so much. They are handsome men, all of them: young and muscular. And their faces are the faces of their Chinese grandfathers. Too bad such gentle men must carry guns for a living. But the king, in his quiet but firm way, insisted they accompany her, as he had also insisted she be taken to the Temple of Dawn on the Chao Phraya River, and to Sukhothai to see the ruins.

What do they think of her, these young bodyguards? What do they see? She straightens in her chair, lifts her chin, tips her head slightly—her most flattering angle. She is wearing yellow silk, and her hair today is especially lustrous. Around her neck is a medal, a hai-huang, handed to her backstage in Bangkok by a well-dressed stranger; on one wrist are multiple strands of pink seed pearls. She is always keenly aware of how she looks; such vigilance is part of her job. For there are thousands of people who can play the piano, her teacher used to tell her, but very few an audience will pay to see. Especially because you are a girl, Moon Ja, and an Asian besides. They won't believe you have the strength or the temperament to handle the repertoire.

But I'm an American! she wanted to shout back. I can hardly remember Seoul.

Nevertheless, her teacher, who could read her mind, invariably responded: To them you will always be Korean, so turn it into a strength.

And she had. She had turned herself, a nondescript L.A. schoolgirl in gray pleated skirts, her hair held back with plastic barrettes, into an exotic woman: Moon Ja Koh, crossing the stage in blue silk. Moon Ja Koh and her flawless skin, her slender legs, her haunting half-smile.

The four men are watching her, quiet and respectful. She is not beautiful—she knows every inch of her physical self; she has charted every flaw—but what she has perfected at age forty is how to create and maintain the illusion of beauty. And it is all to do with mystery, she thinks. What they don't know, they wonder about, and that keeps them thinking.

So for this reason she never laughs. And she is forever elegant, forever gracious, forever remote. And only when she plays does the real Moon Ja emerge—or that is what her audiences think, and that is why they come to see her.

She is very tired. What she would like to do at this moment is simply to turn to the table of bodyguards and point to one of them—you—who would then rise and come forward, her companion for the day. Together, not speaking, they would walk beside the seven-hundred-year-old city walls. They would linger on the bridge over the moat filled with red lotus blossoms and he would watch, smiling, as she pulled back her hair and fanned her warm neck.

Then afterward they would return to her room overlooking the river, where she would strip down to her slip while he closed the shutters against the heat. The sheets would be taut and clean and when she climbed into bed they would cool her hot feet. After her eyes were closed he would come to the bed with a bowl of fresh water and a soft cloth and he would hold the cloth to her temples until she fell asleep. And then he would go to the place he belonged: a chair in the corner under the window, where he would wait faithfully for however many months it took for her to awaken.

She takes a sip of water, hiding a smile. Which one of the four should it be? Does it matter?

A waitress—how lovely she is, Moon Ja thinks—passes by the table with three plates in her hands. Fish and vegetables, the most exquisite glass noodles, some kind of spice that bursts into blossom in the mouth.

She has told no one about her bleeding, which has now gone on for several weeks, and has not yet seen a doctor. No pain, but she feels a little sickish most of the time, a little faint. Perhaps it is only the heat, the unfamiliar food, the enormous and frightening populace. Perhaps it is simply stress. But she still has two weeks in China and then two more in Korea, the first visit since her family left Seoul in 1953. And here in the heart of Asia she is feeling as rootless and disconnected as she's ever felt. What's wrong with you, Moon Ja? she asks herself. Why all the self-pity today?

She inclines her head slightly and the four guards are instantly on their feet. Poor things, she thinks, but what else can they do? This is the country where people crawl on their hands and knees to meet that nice king of theirs. You could probably get used to this, Moon Ja.

She pushes back her chair and rises, thinking of his lovely queen, the brief and gracious conversation they'd had two days before. She gives the men a look and turns as regally as possible toward the door beyond which the ancient city awaits, and the moat of floating lotus blossoms.

Afternoon.

Katerina Haupt sits at her kitchen table before a steaming cinnamon roll, fresh from the oven. This isn't a treat, it's energy, she thinks defiantly, then smiles at herself. Who is around to see her? To whom is she justifying this hot cinnamon roll, smothered in white frosting and butter? But guilty self-justification is the habit of sixty-three years, as is the guilty pleasure she takes in such indulgences. Austerity is not my forte, she thinks. So there, Cornelius Toft.

She lifts her fork, carves out a small piece of roll, brings it to her mouth. In moments her eyes are closed and she has given herself over to the sweet joy of sinful eating. Ah, Katerina, she tells herself. It's a wonder you can play the piano at all, you're such a lazy and self-indulgent creature. She chews thoughtfully and with great pleasure, thinking of her upcoming recital at the

Library of Congress. She rarely concertizes anymore, but once a year at least she is obligated to perform, if only to remind the public she still exists. And also to maintain the respect of my students, she thinks. What would Jan and Colette think if their fat old teacher never played?

The truth, however, is that she hates performing, dreads the necessity of dressing up, the long walk across the stage, the harsh, blinding heat of the spotlights. And, even after all these years, she still dreads most Cornelius's reaction, his severe and unyielding judgment of every phrase she plays. How silly, she thinks. He's my *friend*. Which of course he is—her two closest friends are Moon Ja and Cornelius, aren't they?—but one can never forget *who* he is, or Moon Ja either, for that matter. Both a bit too godlike to feel things the way *she* does. And both a bit daunting in their severe and single-minded devotion to music.

The cinnamon roll is perfect, soft and buttery and hot. She sighs, leaning back in her chair, happy, full, and vowing, as she always does, to go on an immediate diet, to stop getting involved in her students' lives, to take her art more seriously, to overcome her—yes, she admits it—secret and shameful jealousy of Moon Ja. There— every so often she has to confess it to herself, get it out into the light of day. I'm jealous of my friend: Why? Is it because my day has come and gone and I didn't do anything about it? Is it because she's forty and I'm sixty-three? Or is it because she was strong enough to set everything else aside and I wasn't?

I'm *old*, she thinks. It's time to be wise and serene, for heaven's sake.

But, aside from her body, she does not feel old. She feels as young, as curious, as bursting with love and passionate interest as she always has—all fine qualities that have nevertheless kept her from a disciplined life. In a half hour, when she puts on her coat and walks through the late afternoon winter sun to the conservatory for her lesson with Jan, she may pass someone on the street, fall into conversation, make a new friend. She may dart into a flower shop, stop for a cup of cappuccino, linger in front of a bookstore. She never knows, in fact, what she will do next—she bumbles happily through her days, dawdling, wasting time, yet overtaken at times by blinding moments of joy so intense that the very air turns gold. And thus she is a failure—a lover of life, a friend to all, a master of nothing.

I have no willpower, she tells herself for the thousandth time. For her hours at the piano mean nothing; they are but another pleasure; discipline is stern, remote, unforgiving . . . no more crises, she resolves. No more students in this apartment at all hours of the night, telling me their troubles. No more dinners for Cornelius until this recital is over. No more analyzing Moon Ja.

You are a professional, Katerina, she tells herself. You are supposed to be an artist, for heaven's sake. Why don't you act like one?

Night.

In the brownstones, mothers in plaid bathrobes move down narrow hallways to bedrooms where nightlights burn. The doors are cracked; their children lie sleeping, flush-faced, arms outflung; the children lie heated and dreaming. The mothers kneel beside the beds, patient, watchful, amazed by the quiet, the utter stillness of their young at rest. The air smells of milk and sweat. The windows are blind with frost.

Morning.

Moon Ja Koh is looking down at China. Dawn is just breaking over the Yangtze delta and the acres of water below are rose instead of blue. The earthen dikes are thin black lines; she has read that here even the dikes are planted with crops—mulberries and sugarcane. A billion people to feed; she can't imagine such a number even after growing up in a metropolis like Los Angeles.

The shadow of the plane passes like a gliding osprey over the submerged rice fields, teeming with fish. One small cloud darkens the water of a paddy. The sun spreads out over the land.

She yawns behind her hand; she is very tired and beginning to be concerned—the bleeding is not heavy, but it is constant. She turns in her seat so that she is closer to the window. Too bad she never had time to take up photography. She has caught herself over the years memorizing scenes as though for a mental picture album; she has a razor-sharp memory and she can call up the images—Vienna, Prague, Leningrad, Buenos Aires—at will.

Well, she will have to go to a doctor, but not here, not in Asia, where they will give her some kind of herb and tell her to think good thoughts. No, she will wait until she is back in Georgetown, back in her own apartment, where she can best deal with whatever is happening to her. If things get worse, she'll have to call Katerina—put her on alert that all is not well. Katerina is so good about things like this: She'll make the doctor's appointment, show up at the airport, air out the apartment for her. . . . She straightens her shoulders and crosses her legs. A woman, a mother with a young boy asleep in her lap, is sitting across the aisle and shyly watching her every move out of the corner of one eye. Moon Ja is wearing a wheat-colored linen suit, with high heels of bronze-colored leather; she has done her hair in an Audrey Hepburn French roll, very elegant. No one on this plane knows that last night she played Schubert before a thousand people in a place called K'un-ming and that she lay awake half the night afterward, as she usually does, reviewing every note, every arm movement, every motion of her own face.

By late morning they will be in Shanghai, and she will have two days to shop and sleep and practice before her next concert. She has heard that with its river, its bridges, the barges that float beside the pavement, the city looks something like Paris.

Evening.

A poker game is raging in the alley across from the music school. A group of men have drifted over from the little park and are playing for cigarettes. Bellyman, too sick to be in the game, sits against a trash can watching a narrow band of light deepen against the rose-colored brick of the apartment next to the brownstone. He pants lightly, his chest hardly rising. His long black hands are folded in his lap, and an orange cat with encrusted eyes crouches near his feet. The smell of trash is like a thick mist. He can hear, very faintly, a jumble of piano music from the music school and, above it, the sweet soaring of a violin.

He turns slightly, still panting, just as she passes the mouth of the alley, the young girl with the wild light curls who lives in the apartment above. She wears an old gray wool coat; a heavy canvas bag hangs from one shoulder. She walks very slowly, her head down.

"Hey, baby," calls one of the poker players, laughing. "You make my dick happy." She pauses for a second as if struck, but does not turn. Bellyman begins to cough, the harsh, tearing cough that wracks his days and nights. The sound of the violin lifts through the darkening air.

CHAPTER SIX

$\mathcal{R}$ ows of students sit together on the worn green velvet of the concert hall seats. Outside, a delicate snow glitters in the light of the street lamps, falling through the pure dark cold of the night.

Jan, the young Czech who stares at Sylvia (yes, she *has* noticed; how can she help it?), is nearing the end of his program; to her surprise, she finds that she is overwhelmed by his playing. He is doing Liszt's *Dante* Sonata: she watches, enthralled, as he attacks the enormous octaves and arpeggios; his hands are all over the keyboard and the sweat from his forehead is flying, sparkling in the light on the stage.

She could never play like this—this takes *courage*. Everything is so fast and so powerful; a second's hesitation and he will lose it all. She crosses her fingers for him, but he doesn't need her good-luck gesture; he is completely focused, playing from the shoulders; his glasses flash, and then he is bending over tenderly, caressing the keys. The music becomes faint, lovely, poignant, and the tears begin to rise into her throat, both because of the music, how magnificent it is, and because of how he is playing it. There is something unutterably moving about such moments of perfection; she does not know why, but they undo her.

She is filled with the familiar longing—for what, she cannot say.

Her eyes remain fixed on the black piano, on the shy young man she hardly knows who is yearning so over the keys, and then, finally, when she thinks she cannot bear it for another moment, the last chords are hanging in the air and the audience is breaking into long, fervent applause. She lets her breath out in a rush, laughing out loud in delighted relief that he has made it safely to the end. Jan rises and stands facing the crowd; he is serious and embarrassed in the flooding of applause, his thick hair a tragedy of storm damage.

Jan. Although he is always watching her, she has never spoken to him; he dodges away whenever she glances in his direction. She has heard that, like Toft, he does not believe in female pianists. She forgives him for that, she forgives him for staring at her, and she forgives him also his stumbling, clownish exit to the wings, all because of what he just did with Liszt.

Afterward, she walks with Peter and Marushka down the powdery sidewalks toward Miss Haupt's apartment, where there is to be a reception for Jan. The students laugh and kick up thin snow. Sylvia, snug between her two friends, is as happy as she's been since coming to Baltimore.

"He was *great*," she says. "Wasn't he?"

Peter, looking uncharacteristically natty in his long

red scarf, gives her his thinking smile. He is someplace else tonight.

Marushka says, "That Jan is in love with you, Sylvia. You *know* this is true!"

"He's not."

"Oh yes! It is very obvious to everyone but you. Isn't it, Peter?"

"I don't know what you mean," says Sylvia, blushing. "All I know is he almost made me cry."

"Why?" says Peter.

Sylvia looks up at him. He cocks his head at her. He really wants to know.

"Oh, Peter," she says. "You're hopeless."

Marushka stares at Peter as though she has never seen such a creature before. To Sylvia she says, "He does not like Liszt?"

"He *hates* Liszt."

"I don't hate Liszt," says Peter. "There ought to be a law, that's all. Play Liszt, go to jail."

"But Jan was wonderful tonight. How can you say that?" Sylvia is growing angry; most of the time Peter's detachment is soothing, but once in a while it feels like simple coldheartedness. Jan was wonderful; there's no question in her *mind* that he was wonderful; the performance knocked her flat. Which, of course, probably proves nothing more than her own romantic foolishness. "Besides," she adds defiantly. "Even your hero Brendel is getting into Liszt now."

"Anyone can make a mistake."

Marushka laughs. "Oh, this is too funny! Oh, I love this!"

"Shut up, Marushka," says Sylvia, stalking along the

sidewalk. Her cheeks are suddenly flaming; she is ready to smack both of them. Jan *was* great; why are people so cruel when somebody shows a little emotion? Her father, Toft, apparently *everyone* thinks that to be any good you have to be cold, cold, cold as ice. You do not know how to think, young woman. Having a little fire in your hands is not enough, do you see?

"Hey," Peter says gently. "Calm down, Syl. It's just teasing."

"It's *not* teasing," she says. "It's true. I *am* too sensitive. I am *too emotional.* I'm never going to get anywhere this way."

Marushka steps in front of Sylvia, facing her, and before Sylvia can escape, she has been caught up in a passionate hug. Marushka's voluminous blue coat smells of lilies and winter and faint smoky oil from the family kitchen in Kiev. "Sweet girl," Marushka says. "We love you, truly. You are an *outstanding* pianist, isn't she, Peter?"

"And she doesn't even know it," he says. "That's why she's so damn good."

Then they are walking again and Sylvia is feeling as happy as she was when they first came out into the snow, and she wonders, Where did the anger go? How can I be so happy and so mad all in the same five minutes? Toft must be right about me; I don't know how to think. All I do is react; someone pushes my buttons and suddenly I'm scared or angry or happy or proud. . . . I'm like one of those dogs that drool every time the buzzer goes off.

Peter is sorry; he has put his arm across her shoulder,

something he does very rarely. They hardly ever touch, in fact; it is not that kind of relationship. We're brother and sister, she thinks, and that's fine. She has never even *thought* about the other kind of relationship; the whole idea of love seems so mysterious and complicated and fraught with danger that she is not even tempted.

They have arrived in front of Miss Haupt's apartment, but apparently no one has gone inside yet; the other students, murmuring, are huddled together before the front steps, their nervous breath hovering whitely above them in the frigid air.

"What are they doing?" says Marushka. "What is wrong?"

The small crowd parts. Two alley men sit on Miss Haupt's front steps. One of them is asleep or drunk, his head fallen forward; he is wearing an old hat—blue, maybe?—dark with melted snow. The other is enormous and has no hair; his black skull gleams, as do his eyes. He does not speak or move; with one arm he helps support the drunk.

Miss Haupt—she is wearing her red coat and galoshes—says, "Is there anything I can do?"

The big man stares at her silently.

Marushka tugs at Sylvia's arm and motions with her head and Sylvia looks behind her. Handsome David, the Israeli violinist, has joined the group with his newest girl, a dark beauty wearing plum-colored lipstick and a coat with a silver fur hood. Sylvia recognizes her—a soprano. "Somebody should call the police," the girl says in a careless, lilting voice.

The man with the blue hat snores, head bobbing.

David steps forward. "Maybe you should just leave," he offers. "Just get up and go."

"Honestly, there's no need . . ." begins Miss Haupt. She has moved out in front of the group, her key in her hand, and Jan takes her by the arm and draws her back as the big man gets slowly to his feet. He is immense, with heavy shoulders and a thick neck.

Miss Haupt looks confused; she is the hostess, after all, and what will she do about these uninvited guests on her front steps? To Sylvia, she does not look afraid, only puzzled. And possibly a little irritated; her party food, upstairs, will be getting cold. Sylvia has never been to her apartment before, but she has heard there are plants tangling up the chair legs and the place always smells of onion and tea.

"Those men are both drunk," Marushka whispers hotly. "They are disgusting. David is very brave with them, don't you think?"

Peter says into Sylvia's ear, "Be ready if he pulls a knife," and Sylvia remembers the other man, the one he gave the trash bag to during the storm. What is different about these two? she wonders. Why is he nervous about them and not the other one? Try as she might, she cannot read these homeless men; to her, they are all equally terrifying, trolls out of her childhood fairy-tale books.

The whole noisy nighttime city—the radios, the televisions, the blaring traffic—seems muffled under the quiet fall of snow, leaving them alone and shivering on the sidewalk, face to face with the men on Miss Haupt's front steps. The snow slows; the cold intensifies.

Suddenly, Jan steps forward to the very edge of the

circle of light. "Sir," he says with his heavy Czech accent. He pulls his wallet from the inner pocket of his overcoat and takes out a thin roll of bills, thrusting it forward. "Please buy your friend a cup of coffee. We would be honored." He stands very still, his glasses glinting, and Sylvia waits for the pipe to split his skull, for the blood to pour out across the clean and lovely snow.

The big man watches, motionless.

"Please," says Jan. "You must be cold. Please take it."

The smaller man begins to cough, a rasping, hacking cough that goes on for minutes. He crouches forward on the steps, huddled over his own chest, his arms around his knees and his head hanging down. "Oh my," says Miss Haupt softly.

Everyone waits. Clouds of ice hang in the air. Jan's hair and the rims of his glasses are powdered with snow. Then, when Sylvia has begun to feel the night will be endless—the cold, the danger, the dark—the big man puts out his hand and takes the roll of bills.

"Thank you," he says to Jan, and his voice is deep and powerful, a bass, Sylvia thinks. He puts a hand on his friend's shoulder. "Bellyman, let's go. Time to get up, Bellyman."

Miss Haupt's apartment is warm with candlelight; the scent of cloves and cinnamon drifts from the stove, where a huge iron pot of mulled wine sits over a low flame. Students lie on the rug and lounge on the sofas. Everyone is in stockinged feet, including Miss Haupt, who by now—1:30 A.M.—is nodding off in an easy chair.

I *like* her, thinks Sylvia. She's very strange—like a kind old witch, a good witch—but I like her. I wonder what it would be like to have her for a teacher.

The party has been interesting, though Sylvia, too shy to mingle, has stayed close beside quiet Peter in one dark corner of the room. She has been watching Jan, however, as he tries to accept with grace the compliments on his performance, and her heart is aching for him. If anything, he is shyer than she is, staring at the floor in panic when anyone approaches, distractedly patting at his wild hair. He has not looked once at the half of the room in which she sits.

Marushka has managed to insinuate herself into the group around David. Sylvia watches as she tosses her blond hair and gives her wicked laugh, ignoring completely the dark-haired soprano beside him. Francine? Is that her name? She's very good; Sylvia heard her do "Vissi d'arte" from *Tosca*, and she did it straight, very pure and clean. Poor girl. She doesn't even realize yet that she is in Marushka's way, willful Marushka, who, it is clear, will stop at nothing to get into this new quartet. As always, Sylvia is fascinated by Marushka's ability to flatter and cajole and manipulate someone else into doing what she wants, in spite of any obstacle. There is no fear in her, Sylvia thinks. She never even questions herself.

I want to tell Jan how much I loved the *Dante* Sonata.

The thought is in front of her before she is aware of thinking it. Well, I *did* love it, and it might mean something to him, coming from me . . . she blushes, looking around the room, but he's no longer sitting on the arm of the sofa; he's moved off somewhere while she was following Marushka's little drama. Has he gone? No—there he is in the kitchen alone . . . and suddenly she is standing up and moving toward him. What am I going to say? she thinks, panicked. What am I doing?

But then she is behind him—he is very tall—and she is clearing her throat, which feels as though it has become sealed shut. "Jan?"

He whirls—he has been stacking cups in the sink—and looks down at her, clearly aghast. She has never been close enough to see his eyes behind the thick lenses of his glasses; they are the palest of blues, flower-blue, with thick dark lashes and reddened baby-rabbit rims. She is startled at their sad beauty. She thinks, Why—how could I be afraid of *him*?

He fills up most of the kitchen with his eager hunch and the big, knobby expressive hands that dangle at his side. She remembers his sweat sparkling wildly in the spotlight. "I loved your *Dante* Sonata," she says in a rush.

He stares at her, baffled, and then he breaks into a smile. His teeth are large and very white; one of them protrudes slightly, a small happy square against his lip.

"Thank you," he says. "A compliment from you is very fine." He nods and his glasses slip down his nose.

"Why is that?" she asks shyly.

"Because I admire your playing. I am very impressed with your Schumann," he says.

"My Schumann? Really?"

"Your Schumann is very fine. No American accent."

This is not what she expected. She is pressed back

against the refrigerator, her neck tight; she can hear Marushka's big laugh and, from a nearby corner, Brandon, sounding bored. No wonder; nobody here tonight is famous—only, perhaps, Miss Haupt, who has certainly never behaved like a famous person.

"I . . . when did you hear my Schumann?"

Jan looks away. He is quiet for a long time; she thinks he may not answer. Finally, he sighs and looks down into her eyes, shrugging helplessly. "Sometimes I stand outside your practice room listening to you play."

She feels a bit light-headed, a bit off balance. He stands outside her practice room, watching her through the little window. How many times has he done that and she's never even known it? She is not sure whether to be flattered or afraid—but look at those *eyes*, she thinks; how can I be afraid of someone with eyes like that? "I guess I'm surprised," she says. "I heard . . . well, never mind."

"You heard what? That I do not like Schumann?"

She swallows. The kitchen is small and they are standing close to one another. He is shy, but very intense; her stomach feels odd—fluttery, as though it is full of wings. She has never had a conversation quite like this before. And she doesn't want to say what it is she has heard— she doesn't want to hurt his feelings—but some little voice is telling her she must be truthful. Courage, she thinks. She takes a breath and says, "No, I heard that— well—you don't believe in female pianists."

Someone laughs. David, on the other side of the small breakfast bar, is leaning over, looking in at them from under the hanging cupboards; Francine is nowhere in sight. "What did you just say?" he asks. "About pianists?" He is smiling at her; his teeth are very bright against his dark skin; she cannot remember him ever speaking directly to her before.

"Nothing," she says shyly. She can feel the panic rising; where oh where is Marushka?

David is leaning on his forearms; he brings one palm slowly to his chin and settles down into it, still smiling. "No," he says. "It's an interesting question. Should or should not women be musicians?" His eyes are locked on Sylvia's; she cannot turn away.

She studies David's face, confused. What is he doing? Is he flirting with her? She has always thought of him, when she thinks of him at all, as someone in a magazine ad or a rock group—not a real person. He wears his hair long, but not like Peter's. It is dark and wavy, parted in the middle, and he often pulls it back into a short ponytail, as he has tonight. He is very confident for his age, very forceful; for some reason, Sylvia thinks of her father, imagines Ross and David meeting, and she has no doubt that they would take an instant dislike to one another.

"I am absolutely convinced that women can make excellent musicians," says Jan. She glances up at him, distracted, then back at David, who cocks an eyebrow at her. His jaw has a deep blue sheen that she has noticed before.

"What do *you* think, Sylvia?" he asks.

"About women?" She can hear herself stammering. What is he getting at? What game is he playing with her?

He leans forward on his elbows until their faces, almost level, are very close. "Yes, women," he says quietly. She could lean down herself and their cheeks would be touching. And she can smell him, too—something clean and cold, full of male energy.

"Well, of course I think women belong in music," she says. "Look at Moon Ja Koh. Look at Miss Haupt." She stops, unable for a moment to think. "And I'm here, aren't I?" she finishes lamely.

"You are," says David. He is studying her mass of hair, still wet from the snow, though she can feel a lighter halo, almost dry, rising around her face. He tips his head, and then, before she can pull away, puts out his fingers and lifts one of her curls, turning it in the dim light. "Wow," he says. "Wow." He gives the curl a gentle shake, drops it, and slides his elbows back across the bar. "Don't let me interrupt anything," he says before he straightens up and turns back to the crowd in Miss Haupt's living room.

Sylvia gives Jan a quick glance, her cheeks flaming. This is all too much; she has no idea what to say next.

"I want you to know," he says in a rush, "that I think you are a truly fine musician. There are indeed *many* fine women pianists. Why, there is Clara Schumann. And we have Miss Tureck and Miss de Larrocha and Miss Kraus. And Miss Koh and Miss Haupt, from this very school. . . ." His eyes are pleading with her, and suddenly all she wants is to be back in her own apartment, alone in her bed . . . and Marushka, wearing her ratty old burgundy bathrobe, will be perched on the edge, talking, talking, talking. I won't have to say a word, she thinks gratefully. She'll go on and on about the party like I wasn't even there. And none of this will have happened, this strange conversation with Jan, this odd flirting thing with David. . . .

Sometimes in the past few years she has felt haunted, as though there is a little girl, seven or eight years old perhaps, who lives inside her and who is having to run as fast as she can just to keep up. And the little girl loses her breath sometimes and sinks to her knees, tears of fright streaming down her face. Usually, Sylvia is impatient with her, urging her back to her feet, but often enough she has to fight herself not to turn back.

Gründlichkeit, Toft told her. The discipline of thoroughness. She must begin her life anew; she must learn how to think; she must get up at 5:00 A.M., eat only grains and vegetables, learn from Peter. . . .

She says, "I have to go now. Thank you," and backs out of the kitchen before Jan can say anything more.

Book
TWO

Music is love in search of a word.

—*Sidney Lanier:* The Symphony, *1875*

CHAPTER SEVEN

*T*he city is bathed in a cold rose light. The brownstones stand like ruins against the dawn sky. Far out over the Atlantic, the sun is consumed by running clouds and the wind smells faintly of tundra.

Today is the competition in Philadelphia, and Sylvia and Marushka are late for the train; they hurry along the sidewalk in their heavy wool coats, their scarves whipping in the wind; they still have fifteen blocks to go. Marushka, in her cheap black boots, stumbles and nearly falls. "Sylvia!" she cries, but Sylvia does not pause. Both of them are slung with bags; Marushka cradles the leather-fringed case that protects her marvelous Vuillaume violin. The competition starts at three o'clock; first they must check in, then find their room. . . . Sylvia wonders if she is really ready for this—she has been concentrating so hard on Opus 111 that she has not, she is just realizing, given as much time to the *Kreutzer* Sonata as she should have. What if she lets Marushka down again? But she cannot think about the possibility, she cannot let herself dwell on it, for that is when she slips or goes numb.

Fortunately, at least, she does not have another lesson with Toft until Monday, and it is now Friday morning, so if everything goes well—"Hurry up, Marushka!" she cries, tugging at her arm—they will be back on the train by Sunday evening and she can spend a good four hours in the practice room before she sleeps. *If* everything goes well. And if she is *very* lucky, Toft will never even have to know about the competition, unless of course Marushka wins, and then everybody at the conservatory will hear about it, including him—oh, why is my life *like* this? she thinks. I do something brave, and then I die of fear.

The train approaches Baltimore, the girls hurry—four blocks, three blocks—and Sylvia is wondering if she has brought enough money and whether or not she remembered to turn off the bathroom light and if Marushka did indeed lock the apartment door behind them—and then she sees that someone is standing in the middle of the sidewalk, blocking their way.

At first he looks like somebody waiting for a bus. At first she is not even *afraid*—she is hurrying so fast, after all, and it is still hard to see—but then, as they are moving around him, he reaches out almost casually and takes her by the upper arm (three more steps and she would have been out of his grasp) and says, "Over there," motioning with his head toward a nearby alley. His voice is low, calm; he looks like a normal man, perhaps forty or so, in an old blue navy coat and a red stocking cap, except that his face is too pale, his nose too sharp, and his brown hair not very clean; it hangs down, too long, in his eyes, and he shakes it back regularly, as though it bothers him. He is not hurting her, but she knows that if she tries to pull away, he will.

Marushka has stopped six feet away, just out of range, and Sylvia can't read her face. Is she thinking of running? Of screaming? Of fighting him? Sylvia stares at her helplessly. "You too," he says. "Over there," and Sylvia thinks, *Do* it, Marushka! Don't argue with him! Oh please, just *do* it. . . .

Marushka shrugs and turns toward the alley, and he herds them ahead of him, Sylvia hurrying obediently, almost eagerly, with tiny tripping steps like a woman with bound feet. If we just *obey* him, she thinks—if we just don't give him any trouble. . . . He can't hurt us if we're nice to him—just *please*, Marushka, please don't try to *fight him*. . . .

The alley is dark, protected from the faint early morning light by high walls of dank brick. It smells of urine. At the other end are trash cans, overflowing, and at the top of one of the buildings pigeons stir throatily. He herds the girls to one of the walls. "Here," he says. "I want you here." Sylvia turns quickly, obediently, pressing her back against the cold brick, holding her arms a little out from her sides to show him that she has nothing in her hand, she is absolutely no danger to him, she will do whatever he says. She even gives him a small, tremulous smile. She does not dare speak, but she wants him to see it: Look, she is telling him silently, look at me—I'm harmless; I'll do whatever you say. Just don't hurt us.

His voice is soft, almost polite; he doesn't look cruel or crazy. He looks, except for the too-long, dirty hair in his eyes, like almost anyone she might see on the street; he might even have a family. He's probably just . . . well, if I'm kind to him . . . maybe he's just lonely? If I just smile? She tries another smile, a bit more like a *real* smile this time; she tries to make her eyes very kind and reassuring; she tries to let him know how *nice* she is. Why, he's almost handsome, she thinks, if he would just wash his hair. . . .

"Give me the guitar," he says.

Sylvia snaps her head in Marushka's direction; the leather-fringed violin case is clutched against Marushka's chest like a baby, and Marushka, unbelievably, is shaking her head no, is saying the word out loud: No!

Sylvia tries to whisper, Don't be crazy! Give it to him! but nothing comes out, just an odd whimpering noise. What is Marushka *doing*? Is she going to try to fight him after all? Oh but Marushka, she wants to say, you don't understand; he won't hurt us if we just obey him.

"Hand it over," he says, and Marushka answers back in a wobbling voice, "What? Do you have a knife? A gun? Why should I give you my violin?"

At this his hand goes out, still almost casually, and he takes a mass of Sylvia's curls and twists them in his fist so that her head is bent straight back, her neck stretched tight. . . . She stares up at the square of sky over the alley, her vision slowly going gray. "I don't need a knife," he says. "I could do it with one hand." And he passes his other hand slowly over Sylvia's face, a quarter of an inch above her skin, and then down the front of her throat. "One good chop," he says. "Now, give me the damn guitar."

"Let her go first."

For an answer, he yanks harder at Sylvia's hair, and she feels the pressure on the front of her throat, her windpipe swelling. . . .

"Okay, all right!" says Marushka. "Look. I am putting it down."

"Open it!"

Sylvia cannot breathe, she is starting to black out, she feels her knees sagging sideways and still he holds her viciously in place with his hand twisted in her curls. But, she is thinking frantically, I was *obeying* you. Why are you doing this to me?

"Look!" says Marushka. "Here it is on the ground, like you said! Now, let her go!"

Silence, then he gives Sylvia's hair one last hard jerk, almost toppling her, and suddenly her head is free, light, her scalp throbbing, and she goes down on her knees against the hard pavement and stays there, kneeling before him dumbly while he squats to inspect the violin.

The Vuillaume gleams softly in the fragile new light. Sylvia watches, her head still bobbling vacantly, as the two of them crouch over the case like customers at a flea market. "This violin you will never sell," Marushka is saying calmly. "Look here—you see this number? And there is another deep inside, where you can never find it. I'm telling you, this is a museum piece."

He reaches out and touches the violin with one finger—pianist's hands, Sylvia thinks vaguely—and strokes the rosy wood.

"This instrument belonged to my great-grandfather, Jaspar Kubicek, have you heard of him? The most famous violinist in Europe for three years at least." Marushka's voice has gotten louder, more confident. "You think you can steal from a museum?" she is saying. "I'm telling you, man, you will go to prison for life."

He touches the wood again, then rises. Sylvia stays where she is; she could not move if she wanted to. "Get up," he says to Marushka. She ignores him, reaching for the cover of the case. "One chop," he says. "Get up."

Marushka looks up at him, then at Sylvia. She gets to her feet slowly. The century-old violin lies in the open case between them, rich with light. "What do you want with me now?" she asks.

"Nothing," he says. "Just tell me what the fuck good is something you can't sell?" And while Sylvia watches, disbelieving, he steps into the case, crushing his foot down into the center of the amber wood. "There," he says. "See? No big deal."

Marushka wails once, a high thin wail, then rushes at him with her fists; Sylvia starts to rise, to stop her, but before she can, Marushka is slammed back against the brick wall, her head bouncing once, hard, against it, and then, in slow motion, she is slipping down, down to the pavement, her eyes closed, her face empty of all color, to lie crumpled beside the crushed violin.

Sylvia reaches out for her friend, then looks up into the man's face. He is breathing hard now and his pale, almost-handsome face is twisted unrecognizably as if he suddenly hates them both, as if he could kill them without a thought, for the pleasure of it. Oh, Marushka, Sylvia thinks, oh God, why did you have to make him mad?

He shakes back his bangs under the red stocking cap and looks away down the alley for a moment, and for the first time Sylvia thinks, We might die right here under these windows and nobody will ever know what happened. . . . Finally, however, he glances down at Sylvia, a long glance. His green eyes gleam suddenly with good humor. "Fuck you," he says, and turns and disappears into the maze of cold morning streets.

Marushka awakens slowly, her head in Sylvia's lap. Her eyes fly open all at once; she looks astonished and put out; then her eyelids begin to flutter, her eyes to roll, and Sylvia smooths her hair gently away from her forehead. Her left cheek and eye are already beginning to swell. Sylvia croons to her softly, wondering how she will ever get her out of the alley and to the doctor, but finally Marushka opens her eyes all the way and sits up, rubbing the back of her head. "Oh, Sylvia," she says. "I am feeling very sick."

"Can you stand up? Let's try it."

Together they rise, though Marushka is unsteady, and then, after Sylvia has closed the case over the crushed violin and put it under one arm, they leave the alley and walk the last three blocks to the train station, where there is a telephone. They do not talk about the attack; they do not talk about the missed competition; they do not talk about the ruined Vuillaume.

When the taxi comes to pick them up, Marushka insists on going back to the apartment. "No," she says.

"No doctor. I am just needing some sleep." She is the stronger one, so that is what they do.

Sylvia stays in the apartment all day reading in a chair in the living room, every so often realizing that she is shivering. She still has not allowed herself to think; when she does, she is suffused with a sense of shame so profound she can hardly bear it. Marushka snores in her bedroom for hours and then, when Sylvia has almost fallen asleep herself, she hears a crash and runs down the hall to find Marushka bent over on the floor in the bathroom, rubbing her elbow. Her face is a terrifying powdery white, her cheekbone and eye where he struck her a swollen, polished blue. "My head," she is moaning. "Oh my God, my head is hurting so bad, Sylvia."

"I'm going to take you to the medical center at Hopkins," Sylvia says loudly. "Can you get down the stairs?"

But Marushka cannot do anything for herself; she is confused and rambling; she stumbles over her feet and bumps the walls as she tries to walk to the door, and the cabbie and Sylvia must hold her up with their arms around her waist, the three of them tottering slowly down the stairs together.

Marushka is lying on a metal bed, eyes closed, with that hideous blue swelling on her face. Her hair is spread out on the pillow, her hands, on top of the white sheet, absolutely still. Sylvia has never seen her so still, not even in sleep. Marushka is always in motion, always crashing around, pushing her way here and there . . . She looks *dead*, Sylvia thinks. Oh God, she *does*; she looks *dead*.

The doctor, a young resident, is taking notes. "You didn't call the police?"

She shakes her head, guilty tears rising. "I . . . well, I didn't even think of it. Not with Marushka like this—I had to get her home and then. . . ."

"Were you also injured in this attack?" The resident is young and seems angry about something; she herself is feeling more bewildered by the moment. Why *hadn't* she called the police? Why hadn't she forced Marushka to go to the doctor right away? How could she have sat reading in the living room all afternoon?

She feels as though she is just emerging from her own version of a coma. Her whole body aches. "I . . . no. He pulled my hair, that's all."

The resident looks at her over the tops of his black glasses, his eyes traveling over her floating curls as though he has just noticed them, and then writes something on his clipboard. "How are you feeling?" he asks her more sympathetically. "You're very pale. Are you feeling faint?"

She shakes her head again.

"You're her only roommate?"

She nods.

"Well, then, I'm going to go ahead and check her in to the hospital."

She makes a sound—whimpering, pathetic, ineffectual—then clears her throat. "It's serious, then?"

"No, no." He says it almost kindly, and Sylvia watches as he writes down one more thing, then sticks his pen in the top of the clipboard as though he is done for the night. "She's got herself a pretty good concussion, that's all. She needs to be watched for the next twenty-four hours." He sighs, rubbing his eyes, then looks up again at Sylvia, his gaze once again lingering over her hair. "*You* obviously need some sleep. I can give you something if you want."

She shakes her head, crushed once again by an enormous shame, the shame that began the moment *he* tore her head backward, baring her throat to the empty sky above the alley. She had been nothing more than an animal to him, an obedient heifer, rolling its stupid eyes.

"Well," the young doctor says. "You might want to alert her parents. And the school ought to know about this too."

Marushka is in the hospital for three days. On the third day Sylvia calls Kiev, figuring out the time difference first so that she will not wake her friend's parents in the middle of the night. The father's English is deep and halting; Sylvia speaks in short, careful sentences, not mentioning the ruined violin. She can hear the rest of the family buzzing worriedly around the phone, and then the father says, "We are grateful. You are sweet girl, you know? She need to come home, she come home."

The next day, though the doctor finally releases her, Marushka is no better. Sylvia brings her home in a cab, and Marushka goes straight down the hallway to bed, where she stays for the next two days, listless and prone to weeping. She will not eat.

On the fifth day after the attack, Sylvia finally calls her own parents. She has been having nightmares: all she can hold safely in her mind is the house on the lake, the big stone fireplace stuffed with blazing logs, her mother's warm freckled arms around her. If she never

has to see Baltimore again, she is thinking as she dials—
or Toft or street people . . . and then her father is crying,
"Sylvia!" in that half-delighted, half-worried voice he
uses whenever she calls home unexpectedly, and she is
telling him, without her usual censoring, the stark facts.

Afterward, he is quiet, thinking, and then he says, "I'll
be there tomorrow."

"What do you mean?"

"I mean, I'm coming to Baltimore, Sylvia. You can't
handle all this alone."

She holds the receiver to her ear, looking around the
empty apartment. Her father is coming. He will be staying in this place where she has been living alone with
Marushka. She tries to imagine him standing in the living room beside the fake fireplace or sitting at the little
kitchen table, his eyes everywhere, drinking in the details of her life, assessing them, passing judgment.

She longs to see him, if only for an hour. Here, she
wants to say. You can have this part—you can call the
school for me, tell them what has happened to Marushka. You can call the police. You can deal with that
young doctor at the hospital—all I want to do is get back
to practicing and forget this ever happened.

She longs for his strength, his will, the sound of him
striding down the hall in her lonely apartment, but she
thinks for the thousandth time about the alley, the man
in the red stocking cap, his hand in her curls, and the
way she had melted down into fear—become fear. Not
Sylvia anymore, but a thing.

"No, Dad," she finds herself saying. "Don't come. It's
okay. I'd rather . . . deal with this on my own."

He is hurt, she can tell. His voice when he finally hangs up is stiff and wounded. He is not used to being dismissed by her—have I ever? she thinks. Have I ever just told him to back off? What's even more astonishing, however, is that he *listened*. I told him to let me be and he did . . . though when Marushka does not improve, she wonders if she has made the right decision, if she can really handle this herself after all.

And Marushka does *not* improve. After three more days of headaches and insomnia, she becomes weepy and disoriented, refusing to go outside. Sylvia calls the doctor at the hospital, who says, "Her concussion wasn't all that bad. She's probably going through some trauma stuff. She might be better off with her family for a while." He pauses and adds, "How are you doing? They ever catch the guy?" Sylvia remembers his irritation, the way he seemed to accuse her that night—and also how she'd caught him staring at her mass of curls in that speculative way.

"I'm fine," she says. "And no, they didn't."

After she hangs up, she goes down the hall to Marushka's room. The shades are pulled; the room is dim and musty, a convalescent's room. This—the lassitude, the not eating, the constant crying—is bigger than she can handle alone. Perhaps the doctor is right after all. She sits down on the bed beside her friend and pats her knee under the covers. "Marushka," she says. "How would you feel about going home for a while?"

The ride to the airport is long and quiet. Marushka's old suitcases fill up the trunk of the cab. The girls sit in the backseat holding hands like children, giving each other's fingers occasional squeezes. The crushed violin lies in its fringed coffin among the suitcases in the back.

"You *know* I will be back," Marushka says once.

Sylvia nods, though she doesn't believe it. The apartment already looks like someplace else; the bathroom is empty of Marushka's things, the closet in her room vacant, the walls bare of posters. She *is* leaving, Sylvia thinks, and is amazed at how quickly her life has changed.

In another hour, Marushka will be on the plane and maybe, Sylvia thinks, we will never see each other again. It is a shocking word, *never*—a word as difficult as *infinity* or *eternity* or *death*. To think you can live with somebody, as close as sisters, and then, in hours, she is thousands of miles away. And all because of taking one street instead of another—a simple choice, not even thought about, three steps this way instead of that, and suddenly there *he* is, holding her by the arm. This is what shakes Sylvia more than anything else—how random it all seems, how vicious and unfair.

This, and the awful shame she still has not admitted out loud concerning those long moments of utter helplessness. She could have run. She could have flown from the alley—she's a fast runner—and screamed for help. She could have gone for his face, the way Marushka did—perhaps with two of them to contend with at the same time he wouldn't have been able to hit so hard. . . . Instead, she'd been paralyzed, mute, less than worthless. He didn't even have a weapon, she thinks over and over. He might have killed her and I would have just knelt there, waiting like a stupid animal . . .

She squeezes Marushka's hand. They are already

here; the cab is pulling into the airport terminal area. Vans and buses are everywhere; horns honk, people dodge across the street pulling suitcases on wheels. The air throbs with the thunderous whine of jet engines. Sylvia looks at her friend.

Marushka is staring eagerly out the window, as though she can hardly wait to be on the plane. She's dying to go home, the way I was the other day, Sylvia thinks—and how can you blame her? *She's* the one who got hurt, she's the one who had to go to the hospital, it was her violin . . .

Oh, but Marushka is something, even after all this. Her eye and cheek are a mottled eggplant color, true, but her hair is thick and gold, her good eye a snapping brown, her big breasts proud beneath the long green sweater. She looks happy, for the first time in a week, almost like the old Marushka. Sylvia studies her, aware that she is memorizing the lift of her eyebrow, the way she holds her head, the curve of her fingers in her lap. Will I ever see her again? she wonders.

When they hug each other goodbye at the gate, however, Sylvia does not cry. She thinks of the man in the red stocking cap and steels herself, knowing that she must somehow begin to learn courage. Marushka kisses her dramatically on both cheeks and then whispers hoarsely in her ear, "Remember what I said—in ten years you will be famous."

CHAPTER EIGHT

*T*he room, half timbered and robustly medieval, does not look like a jazz club, though it is filled with the usual smoky darkness, the usual laughers and drinkers. Sylvia is twenty tonight—a year closer to the age on her fake I.D.—and Peter has paid for their tickets to see Oscar Peterson play the lacquered black Yamaha that sits in the center of the small stage. They have a table near the piano so they can see his hands. Sylvia, to look older, is wearing lipstick and has released her hair from its usual combs; she is nervously aware of several men glancing in her direction.

She sips at her ice water, which is really mostly vodka smuggled through the door in Peter's small silver flask. "It's your birthday," he explained, "and you need to be a little drunk to listen to this guy." She has never been drunk before, but the vodka goes down so easily that this might indeed happen; the only symptoms she can feel so far are a certain new heaviness to her head, a tightening in the back of her neck, the tendency to sway a bit when she moves.

Peter is wearing his party shirt, a black tuniclike affair with a gold dragon coiled up the front. The shirt makes her laugh; it is so flamboyant, so un-Peter-like—and, amazingly, it does not change his personality in the slightest; he is as calm, as quiet, as measured as ever. She smiles at him. The air is blue with smoke; her throat is already raw with it.

"How's Marushka?" he asks.

"Okay, I hope. She called me a few days after she got back to Kiev. She sounded happy to be home."

"It'll wear off."

"You think so? She's pretty close to her family."

"Once you move out, you're gone. Can't go back."

"Maybe," she says. "But she'll never come back *here*, not after what happened."

Peter shrugs.

Sylvia takes another sip. One of the men in the crowd has rearranged his chair so that he can lean back against his table, facing their direction. He is staring at her frankly, and before she can pull her flustered gaze away, he winks.

She flushes. He could be the same age as her father. For a moment, she feels very strongly the sensation of being caught between childhood and something else; she hears the frantic footsteps of little Sylvia, running to keep up, behind her.

"It wouldn't take much to get *me* home," she says.

"Why? What's there?"

"It's what's not there. No Toft, no screw-ups during performances, no muggers, no street people. . . ."

"But?"

"Well, of course. The But. My dad."

They sit for a moment in silence. She sneaks a look across the room; the man is still watching her.

Peter says, "This guy we're going to see? He's *something.*"

"How old were you the first time you saw him?"

"Oh, about fifteen, I guess. Sometime in the mid-seventies, anyway. He was mostly doing solo performances by then. I'd never seen anybody with that kind of technique. It was like he could hear exactly what was going to happen right before he played it. He was always doing horn lines, making the piano come out with stuff you'd usually only hear on a saxophone or trumpet. He made me want to play jazz."

"Really? You never told me that."

"There's lots I haven't told you."

The man at the other table is eating an olive on a toothpick, still staring. She drops her eyes quickly, touching her hair. The vodka is at work; her skin feels hot all over. "So *have* you ever played it?" she asks.

"Been playing it since I was sixteen."

She looks up at him, startled. Peter playing jazz? Peter, the big Beethoven star? "Does Toft know?"

"What do you think?"

"Will you play it for me?"

"Why?"

Peter and his questions. Why, indeed? She is not even sure yet that she likes it, that the word *like* is at all applicable to what she feels when she watches a jazz musician improvise onstage. *Tension* is the word that comes to mind instead. She feels tension and a helpless empathy for the performer who seems to her to be drifting out in space without a lifeline.

On the other hand, the freedom is alluring; there is nothing like it in classical piano. "Because," she answers Peter, "*we're* so tied to the score, I guess. We're such robots sometimes. Everything always going back to what the composer supposedly wanted. But when I play Chopin . . . well, I feel like I know him, like I know who he was and what he would approve of. I feel like I could change things—not a lot, just some little things here and there—and it would be okay. But that's impossible, right?"

Peter nods.

"So I guess I want to know what the connection *is*. What you can take from jazz and apply to the *Hammerklavier*. Do you know what I mean?"

Peter slips the flask from his pocket and unscrews the top. She watches as he dumps more vodka into her water glass. He takes a swallow himself, then screws the cap on and slides the flask back into his pocket.

I will soon be drunk, she thinks.

"Oh, there's a connection all right," he says. "Where do you think jazz came from, anyway?"

She shakes her head, mute.

"One form of jazz voicing goes straight back to Chopin. And you can see the same harmonic stuff in lots of the other nineteenth-century concertos."

"Even the dreaded Liszt?"

"Play Liszt, go to jail."

She laughs.

"Liszt was a fantastic improviser. So was Busoni—but so was the whole pack before them. Mozart was great,

Beethoven was unbelievable. It's how he composed. Even after he went deaf, if someone wanted to hear him improvise, all they had to do was pretend something was wrong with a note on the piano. He'd go over to try it out, add in a fifth, try another interval, and whammo—he's off and improvising.''

Sylvia rests her head, now grown heavier, in her hand. She's not used to this version of Peter; he rarely talks this much. She smiles at him encouragingly; perhaps for once he'll tell her something straight out instead of making her put it together from his oblique and cryptic remarks. He's animated tonight; his coarse gleaming hair slips over one shoulder, veiling the gold dragon.

Suddenly, he leans forward, looking her straight in the eyes. "Sylvia, where are you?"

She straightens, flustered. "I'm here, Peter. What are you talking about?"

"Where were you? Quick."

She thinks. "I was . . . well, part of me was in the library, reading about Beethoven. I was putting together some things I saw in a book with what you were saying, and I was also thinking about"—she swallows, and then says bravely—"that man over there. The one who keeps staring at me. He's making me nervous."

Peter turns his head calmly, searching the room. She does not have to point the man out—he sees him, she can tell by the way he moves his chair. Suddenly, she wants to burst out laughing; Peter has adopted the exact pose, the exact facial expression of the other man, and soon—in no more than a minute—the starer has gotten hastily to his feet and headed out of Peter's range.

She does laugh.

Peter turns his chair back around and gives her a look. "Next time, say something."

Just then the lights go down and people, one by one, stop talking and shuffle their feet expectantly. Peter leans forward and says, low, "Here he comes. Don't think, Syl. Watch. Listen. That's all."

She nods, and then she is turning toward the stage, where in another minute one of the best jazz pianists in the world will be walking out before them. And there, at that gleaming and expensive instrument, he will sit and sweat, giving back, under the hot glare of the white light, everything he has ever learned. His hands will flash, his body roll, his foot beat out the time—she steadies herself, getting ready. Perhaps there is something here she can learn about Opus 111, something she can't see in the score itself, now set in stone. Perhaps, if she is lucky, she can get a glimpse of what the sonata must have been like in its early stages—young, fresh, brash, and *alive*.

She wants to concentrate so hard that she is hearing the notes like Peterson does—like *Beethoven* did—before he even plays them.

Moon Ja is finally in Korea, the country of her birth, and to her surprise she has been hearing Brahms in her head since she arrived. She has never liked Brahms and rarely plays his music—too baggy, as Cornelius Toft always says. But here in this land of yellow gingko leaves and wind from Siberia, she is thinking, with uncharacteristic moodiness and drama, about death. What is wrong with her these days? Something nasty and hormonal, no doubt. Something that not only makes her bleed but does bad things to her personality.

She has to admit, however, that coming back to Seoul was a real shock, a shock for which she was not prepared. She hadn't seen the city since 1953, after all; she was eight when they left, and all she can remember now is the long freezing winter after the war when she could not sleep because of the cold. There was no running water and by morning what they kept in pans in the house was ice. She remembers having nightmares about dead soldiers in the streets, dreams she has not thought about in years. And she can't even be sure—did she really see those bodies, or are they just part of the legend of the war, drummed into her by her parents?

She does remember the wool army blanket, sewn into jacket and pants, that she wore for months, how it itched and made her cry. She remembers being very hungry, holding her stomach in the night. She remembers bullock carts in the avenues, hauling loads of rubble. And also how it was to leave her friend, a young stoic by the name of Jue Hee, who refused to say a word when Moon Ja hugged her goodbye. Sad, all of it. No wonder she is hearing Brahms.

She hardly recognized the city—the Han River, of course, but the mudflats are now covered with buildings, the winter sky a dirty gray. *Yontan*, the maid at the hotel told her. The smog is from *yontan*—coal briquettes we burn to stay warm, miss.

On her second night in Korea, Moon Ja performed at the Sejon Cultural Center to an enormous audience who listened intently and broke into sustained and passionate applause after Mozart's K. 310, and then again after Schubert's long Sonata in D Major. The piano was very good, for once, and halfway through the performance she had almost succumbed to a rare wave of emotion, thinking of the long years since she last saw Seoul. Right down the street, she kept thinking, is the Palace of Shining Happiness. Such a thing exists.

Now it is morning and she is far from the great city, sitting in the wet grass and waiting for the sun to rise and strike the jewel in the forehead of a sixty-ton Buddha. What in the world is she doing here? She shivers, hugging her jacket closer. This is ridiculous, Moon Ja, she tells herself. This . . . whatever it is. This Korean quest. The dawn air is cold, though not as cold as in Seoul, and everywhere the rice fields cover the valley. The huge statue broods, dark and unblinking. Other pilgrims, farmers' wives and fishermen, wait beside her; no one is speaking. She longs for a cup of hot tea. She is both amused and disgusted with herself, and feeling just the smallest ounce of trepidation. She thinks: What role am I playing now? The good tourist? The good Korean-American, searching for her Asian roots? The good daughter, collecting stories for her family? As if in response, Brahms's B-flat Major Concerto suddenly washes over her in a darkly thunderous, unexpected wave. Flinching, she closes her eyes.

When she opens them again, she is looking directly into the face of the Buddha. The statue is immense; the granite blocks of the shrine are black with moss and age. Below the pilgrims, mist rises in the valley; here and there are the tile-roofed houses of the farms outside

Kyongju, their spines tilted skyward at the corners. All of it a painting, still unreal to her. But hauntingly beautiful, she has to admit it. Like nothing she has ever seen before. To be Korean, her mother once told her, is to come from beauty—never forget this, Moon Ja.

If they had stayed in Seoul, what would her life have been? This is the question, the real question here. What would she have become without America? She sighs. Impossible to know, and the whole line of thought makes her obscurely angry. She would have no doubt become a practical young Confucian, just as she became a young Methodist in the youth group in Los Angeles. They had called her Martha in that group—a suggestion by the middle-aged pastor from Nebraska. A beautiful name for a hard worker, he'd told her, smiling—and easier for everyone to remember. So she'd lost Moon Ja for a number of years—ten, at least. She was Martha at the Methodist church and Martha in school, and it was not until she won the Young Artist Competition that she recovered her name.

It chills her now, this loss, and she wonders if this is why she has never believed in God, not even as a child. Never, in fact, believed in anything outside herself or her own implacable will. She looks up, studying the impassive stone eyes of the great Buddha. If they took away her identity at that church, it was no doubt out of nothing more than misguided concern. And she had complied fully, after all; she'd wanted nothing more than to fit in, to be an American Martha. At bottom, the loss of her own identity had simply made her stronger.

Yesterday she visited Pulguksa. There, in a temple

built twelve centuries before, she watched, rigid and un-
moved, as a barefoot monk in a gray wool robe beat a
gourd to welcome the morning. In the monastery, other
monks still slept in their cells, each a mystery behind his
rice-paper door. A bronze bell rang out once; incense
twisted in the cold still air. The gray-robed monk
chanted and clacked a wooden fish. I should be feeling
something, she thought. This stuff should be in my
blood, but it's not.

The sun is up, the eye of the morning. The shivering
crowd of pilgrims draws closer together, hushed, and
Moon Ja raises her eyes with the rest of them to the
jewel in the center of the Buddha's forehead. Inside her
brain Brahms plays on, the sorrowing slow movement,
now, of the first concerto, a requiem for his friend's ap-
proaching death. She closes her mind to the music but
cannot shut it out. Neither can she look away from the
Buddha. Stasis, she thinks. I'm being stopped in my
tracks. What on earth is going on here?

The jazz performance in Georgetown has been over for
hours. When Sylvia wakes on the train, her ear mashed
against Peter's arm, it is 2:00 A.M. and they are pulling
into the Baltimore station; she is still hearing "Joy
Spring" and thinking of the ebullient, sweating pianist
who, growling happily as he played, kept them mesmerized for an hour and a half.

She struggles to come fully alert. Around them the
passengers stir, shrugging into their overcoats, gathering
up purses and bags and hats; they merge into the aisle
and then the long tunnel, clamorous with graffiti, that
leads them to the lighted depot.

Yawning, Sylvia hangs on to the back of Peter's coat and lets him carve a path through the crowd. She had loved the performance—really loved it this time— though she still has a hard time making the connection that Peter insists is there. Did Beethoven ever bounce and mutter like that when he played? It seems almost sacrilegious to think so; she has been propagandized, no doubt, by the dignity of marble busts and Miss Selkirk's absolute veneration of the masters. But she feels looser than she has in weeks—more purely happy and relaxed. Music for the sheer joy of it. . . .

Peter stops in the big hall and they stand squinting for a moment in the light. Men are sleeping on the wooden benches, men in filthy jackets and stained pants and shoes without laces, and Sylvia, suddenly wide awake and shivering, thinks of the blocks she and Peter still have to walk, the alleys they must pass, the barred windows, the empty streets. Somewhere out there is the man in the red stocking cap.

She edges closer to Peter, and he gives her his usual calm, abstracted look. The alley men are the farthest thing from his mind—but then again, so is she. What is he thinking of? It doesn't matter. He's thinking of Peter things.

He takes out his flask and hands it to her. She takes it but shakes her head. "I've had enough," she says, "but thanks."

He looks at her quizzically. "What's enough?"

"Enough is the right amount."

"When do you know you're at the right amount?"

Here they go again. She is smiling now, and answers, "When you can walk, but not without your friend's jacket to hang on to. When you can listen to Peterson and hear all the notes. When . . ." But she has to stop, stumped, and suddenly her eyes are burning and she blinks hard to keep them from filling with tears, for she's just had a vision—clear, simple, bleak—of what her life in Baltimore would be without him. No one to tell Toft stories to. No one to take her to jazz performances. No one to go to for advice. "Peter," she says a bit shakily. "Don't . . . well, don't ever go away like Marushka did, okay? I don't think I could stand it."

He sighs and looks across the room. "You're tough as they come," he says. "You just don't know it yet." He takes the flask from her hand and slides it into his pocket. "Ready?"

She nods, tucking her purse deeper under her arm. They both take long breaths—the air inside the depot reeks of ashes and stale wine—and then he says in a different voice, a troubled voice, "Don't count on things, Sylvia. Just take it day by day."

She stares at him, surprised, but he shakes his head, so she doesn't ask him what he means. His words, however, go right to the center of her and become a small dull fearful throb, like a bruise she can't remember getting. He smiles at her, and she, hiding the bruise, smiles back at him. Bravery, she thinks. I need to learn to be brave.

Together they shoulder the glass doors open and forge into the night.

CHAPTER NINE

*D*eep night, and a wet cold that drifts up and down the dark alleyways: Sylvia, safe and warm at the bench, is nevertheless aware of the cold fingers at the window, the cold breath that mists the panes. She should quit for the night; she should hurry home in the dark, turn up the radiator, take a hot bath. Instead, she is struggling once more with Beethoven.

She stares grimly down at the keys, thinking over what she has just played. The first movement of Opus 111, the movement that usually frightens her—yet this time (she thinks it over carefully, running in her mind through passage after passage to make sure)—no, *this* time, something had been different. What?

She lifts her hands to the keys, still thinking, and plays the maestoso once again, listening hard. There—something . . . what is it? She starts over at the sixth bar, where the bass is moving upward in semitones while the treble makes it slow diatonic descent, and then hits the two-octave drop into bar 9, which has never made sense to her before. But now . . . yes, it's the crescendo in bar 10, that reaching . . . and then the sudden shocking juxtaposition of G and A-flat—well, what? What is she thinking?

She stops; the chords dissolve in the air around her and so do her barely formed thoughts. She wants to hit the keys with her fist, the first time she can ever remember being so angry with a piece of music. This sonata twists her brain. She can hear Beethoven, that ugly, pockmarked man, laughing at her from behind the shower of wild notes.

I'm only *twenty*, she thinks. How do you expect me to handle a monster like this?

She plays it again, the sixteen-bar maestoso, and then again, and the more she plays it the angrier she grows. Think, Toft told her. Think, Sylvia. A little fire in your hands . . .

She slams at the keys and stops, panting. Things are being taken away from her: her home, her parents, Marushka, her talent, her joy in music. She is all alone in Baltimore, a city filled with evil men.

She plays it again.

The cold seeps through the panes, invisible and bone-deep. The radiator hisses. She pulls her hair up off of her neck, shakes it, lets it fall. She is sweating. Again, damnit.

The very first bar—she plays it, stops, listens to the fading notes. Why did he start on a diminished seventh like that? She can't even tell what key he's going to land on, and the very first formation makes her so tense, so expectant, that she can't settle down through the entire allegro.

She gets up, walks around the room. She feels a little sick. She has never been so frustrated before. Think, Sylvia. She stops at the window, stares out blindly through the misted pane at the grimy old city below her.

And then suddenly she can see Beethoven moving about his messy studio. His ears are ringing violently, painfully. He holds his head; nothing gets through anymore but the ringing, which is constant and cruel. How many years has it been since he heard music that was not in his own mind?

He sits at the pianoforte; he is wearing an old green silk smoking jacket and velvet slippers. Haydn's bust looms down from the wall at him—his old friend, his kindly teacher in the days when he was still a young man convinced he would be the greatest virtuoso in Europe. He shakes his head again—the ringing grows shriller, a nightmare that never ends.

Suddenly, in sheer desperation, he is playing; he watches his own hands from miles away as they move soundlessly over the keys, and the ringing becomes a great smothering blanket between him and the music that is pouring out into the studio. If he could cry, he would—his heart is breaking—but instead, caught in a state of profound and permanent suffering, he plays on into the lonely night.

Sylvia comes to herself gradually, one chilled cheek resting against the moist pane. The streetlights are halos, blurred by the mist. *Poor man;* she shivers, and the maestoso begins once again in her head in all its passionate tension, moving into the powerful bass of the allegro, the conflict between G and A-flat suddenly and inexorably resolving to the tonic. . . .

Slowly, she realizes a new and startling truth: Opus 111 is becoming part of her. She turns in wonder toward the piano, her favorite old black Steinway, with its battered legs. The room is empty of everything but the two of them, girl and instrument.

Again, she thinks. Play it again, Sylvia.

An hour later, exhausted, she lets her hands fall to her lap. It must be nearly 1:00 A.M. by now, and suddenly, her muscles drained of energy, she is chilled through and through. The vision, or whatever it was, has left her; Beethoven cannot help her more than he already has. She will have to come back tomorrow and the day after that and the day after, for all the weeks left between now and April. She will have to play it and think about it and breathe it until she never has to think about it again—until she can play it in her sleep.

She sits for a few minutes, resting, and then slowly begins to gather her music together for the walk home. As she fumbles about looking for her keys, her coat, she suddenly hears clanging on the iron stairs, the tread of heavy feet. She puts her hand to her mouth, barely breathing. Who? . . . It's so late—who else is in the building? Who would be coming upstairs *now*? She feels her newfound courage, a gift from Beethoven, draining out of her; she is once again in the alley; it is dawn; a man has her by the hair and has bared her throat to the pink sky.

She runs to the light switch and plunges the room into darkness. No lock on the door, but perhaps if she stands behind it . . . She flattens herself against the wall, straining to hear if someone is coming down the hallway. Yes—someone is walking quickly, straight toward the room. She feels herself going numb, just as she had on her knees before the crushed violin, and forces herself away from the wall, searching wildly around in the dark for some kind of weapon. At least this time she won't just sit there like a stupid heifer . . . She stumbles against the wooden chair in the corner and swings it off the floor, listening.

The footsteps have stopped. Is he there? Is he standing right there outside the door, peering in at her? Her palms are slippery against the wooden legs of the chair.

The handle turns slowly; the door begins to open. She gets ready to scream, and then a voice says, "Sylvia?"

"Who . . ."

"It is Jan," he says. "Did I frighten you? I hope not."

Quivering, she sets the chair back on the floor. She cannot see him; he, presumably, cannot see her either— or the chair she was planning to brain him with. She says breathlessly, struggling to control her words, "Oh no. I was just getting ready to go home."

"I saw your light," he says. "I was up late working, and I kept looking up and seeing the light. I did not think you should be out walking alone at this hour."

She manages to laugh. She feels like a complete fool. She is still streaming cold sweat.

"Thank you," she says. "That was . . . sweet." Not the word she would have chosen had she been thinking straight, but she is very tired, on the verge of hysteria— he will just have to understand.

"Are you all right?" he asks. "You sound shaken."

"I'm just tired," she says. "And freezing."

"You are cold?"

"I overdid it tonight."

He moves closer to her in the darkness; she can sense his tall presence right in front of her. The cold night air, caught in his clothes, touches her like wings before it dissipates into the room. Her eyes are adjusting to the darkness; she can see the outlines of his face and his hair, standing up every which way, in the dim and misty light from the window.

"If you will give me your hand," he says shyly, "I will warm it up for you."

She stares at him, his faint glowing presence, and she can feel the sudden embarrassed intensity in the room. Dumbly, not knowing what else to do, she puts out her fingers, and he reaches for them in the dark, taking them into his big knobby hand, where he holds them reverently for a moment before he begins to rub.

In spite of the cold air in his clothes, his hands are warm. She closes her eyes, succumbing like a cat to the pleasure of having her wrist stroked. "You are icy," he says at one point, and she murmurs, "Yes," and stretches out her other arm, wondering at the same time what in the world she is doing, how she has come to be standing in the dark holding hands with a total stranger. If he turns on the light, she thinks, I will be so embarrassed—but he won't. We are both too shy.

"Sylvia," he says in an apologetic voice. "Your fingers are still very cold. May I . . . well, what I mean to ask . . . do you mind if I warm them with my breath?"

She blushes and murmurs, "No, it's okay—go ahead."

He lifts one of her hands to his mouth then and blows gently, and she feels his warm breath traveling down her palm, the underside of her wrist, her forearm—his breath flows over her and suddenly she is warm everywhere, even her eyelids. She has never felt this way before; her knees go weak for a moment, and then she is embarrassed at her weakness and the warmth that is flowing everywhere. Such a small thing, his breath on her wrist—why should it have such a large effect? But for some reason she now feels drawn toward him, toward the open overcoat and his thin vibrant nervous body inside it. What would it feel like to have those long arms around her? To rest her head against his chest and listen to his kind heart?

She has actually begun to move closer, a small shuffling, unthinking motion, like someone deaf and blind, when he sneezes suddenly and the strange yearning tension is broken. "God bless you," she says in a shaky voice.

He sneezes once more, a loud whooshing sneeze, and drops her hand. "You make me—how do you say it? Allergic?"

They laugh a little, and then there is a long silence during which Sylvia wonders what happens next. Are they supposed to kiss now? Should she tell him to leave? She thinks of her father, the expression on his face if he could see her here in the dark with a strange boy, and she is suffused with an automatic, irrational guilt.

"Are you hungry?" he asks her finally.

She thinks for a moment. "Well, yes," she says. "I'm starving, actually."

"Let me take you for some breakfast, then," he says. "We can go to the White Tower."

"Marushka and I used to go there all the time. I miss that."

"So," he says. "Where is your coat?"

In the restaurant under the bright neon lights, they are suddenly nervous with one another. His eyes behind the glasses are red and tired-looking; his face is pale, his hair a mess. She wonders if she looks as frazzled. They fumble with their silverware, sneaking glances at one another, and then he grins at her openly, that hopeless, rueful grin of his, and the crooked tooth gleams against his bottom lip. She smiles back, trying to imagine him onstage, sweat flying, but she can't. The image has faded, along with the raptures she felt that night as she heard him play Liszt. Now he is just a shy sweet boy with a way of making her go weak when he looks at her.

"Do you miss your country?" she asks him, for something to say.

"I cannot begin to tell you," he says, "how I long for Prague."

"Me too. I miss my parents, I miss the lake, I miss everything."

"Tell me about your home," he says, and so she does—she tells him about Anne and Ross and the boat dock and Miss Selkirk and Mr. Binder and how she was able to get Toft for her teacher—and a half hour into it, she realizes that she has not talked so much without interruption since she arrived in Baltimore. Marushka was Marushka—not a good listener—and Peter . . . well,

Peter, quiet as he is, directs each conversation. He moves her along to his own ends. Jan simply listens with his chin in his palm—and when their hotcakes arrive, he continues to listen, chewing raptly, his eyes never leaving her face. It feels good talking this way; she finds herself sighing with sad pleasure as she recounts the events of her vanished childhood.

Finally she stops, too tired to continue. It must be at least two-thirty by now; soon they will have stayed up the entire night. "Your father must be a very strong man," Jan says.

"He is."

"He must be proud of you."

She laughs. "More than that. Much much more. You can't even imagine it."

"He loves you oppressively?"

Oppressively. She glances up at Jan, startled. How does he know? Yes, that's it, though she's never thought it before. It is a true oppression, her father's love for her. She feels smothered under the weight of it at times, as though she cannot turn her head without somehow disturbing his sleep in Minnesota. They are connected by a long silken thread, she and Ross, and everything she does, every thought she thinks, automatically travels back along the silken thread, straight to him.

"It must be difficult sometimes," says Jan.

She nods, feeling disloyal for even admitting this.

"Do you ever tell him?" He is studying her face seriously; she is the only thing on his mind, she can tell—not like with Peter when he drifts off into his Peter thoughts.

"Oh no," she says. "I couldn't. It would just kill him."

"Are you sometimes angry with him?"

Angry. She thinks for a moment. Yes, certainly she gets angry. Or perhaps *resentful* is a better word for it; she resents the silken thread, the tugs he makes on the other end, the sense that she is never out of his gaze. "It's like I'm still a child to him," she says finally. "He's never accepted my growing up."

"But you have grown up anyway," says Jan, leaning back against the booth, "and you should be proud. Making your own way in life is not easy with such a father—you must be very brave."

"Me? Brave?" Sylvia laughs incredulously. "I'm the world's biggest coward."

"No," says Jan, shaking his tousled head. "You are filled with courage. I admire you greatly."

Sylvia is astonished; she cannot believe what he is saying. Courage? She, who cringes in Toft's very presence? She, who knelt obediently on the hard ground while the mugger beat Marushka? No—but what had Peter said to her that time? You're as tough as they come, Syl.

"How many weeks are left until your recital?" Jan says.

"Nine."

"Are you ready?"

"Oh no." She laughs, shaking her head. "No—I have a long way to go. Tonight I finally made some progress, though." And she had; she can feel it all the way through her body to her hands, so recently warmed by Jan. She looks at her watch; she should be exhausted, but the longer they stay up, the less sleepy she gets.

"What about your home?" she asks him. "Tell me about that."

He sighs, and she can tell how homesick he must be. "There is a bridge in my city, the Charles Bridge, that is lined with thirty statues. Imagine! A bridge built out of sandstone in the fourteenth century. People walk across it in the snow. No cars allowed, only people. Very beautiful, very majestic. Prague is a wonderful city. Music everywhere."

"Why did you leave?"

He goes silent and looks down at his hands, clearly embarrassed. Sylvia says quickly, "That's all right—you don't have to tell me."

"No, I will tell you, but not tonight. Someday when we know each other better, perhaps."

"Sure," she says. "Don't worry about it. It's none of my business anyway."

They fall into an awkward pause. He pats his hair down; it springs back immediately.

She says, to fill the silence, "Tell me at least where you got your name."

"Oh, it is a common enough Czech name, but I was named in particular for Saint Jan Nepomuk, a priest who was thrown from the bridge in a sack."

"You were named for a saint?"

"Many Catholics are."

"And that's how you were raised? Catholic?"

He laughs. "*Very* Catholic, Sylvia."

"What does that mean? If you don't mind my asking?"

He smiles and shakes his head. "When you know me better, you will understand."

She is starting to feel a bit drunk with fatigue, and thus somewhat bolder than usual. "What do you think about," she asks, "when you play? When you played Liszt that night? Do you ever think about the composer? Do you feel, maybe, that you have some kind of connection with him?" She cannot shake Beethoven out of her mind, the strange vision of his messy studio, his anguished, deaf music.

"Oh yes," he says, nodding. "I have felt this many times, particularly with Liszt. He was misunderstood in many ways."

"Do you think artists are crazy?" This, perhaps, is the question she has been heading for all evening without realizing it. And she is not even sure why she is asking it, except that she is so often out of control, so often dominated by her emotions, that on occasion—standing at the windowsill, for example, thinking about falling five stories—she has worried about her own sanity. How many times has she cried simply because something was beautiful? Normal people don't behave this way—not the kids she went to school with, anyway. Not most of the people she has ever met.

"No," he says. "Absolutely not. To be an artist is a holy thing."

"Holy?" She laughs; she can't help it. What is he talking about, this shy sweet boy who was named after a saint?

"It is a calling, just like in the church."

"What do you mean by 'a calling'? I don't know anything about that stuff, Jan. I've only been in a church two times in my life, when my grandmother took me, and of course that wasn't Catholic."

He makes a tent with his long fingers, thinking, and says. "You will not laugh?"

"I promise."

"Sylvia, can you remember a time in your life when you did *not* know you were going to be a pianist?"

She ponders for a moment, then shakes her head again.

"Who do you think put that idea in your mind? The idea of playing music?"

"I don't know. My parents?"

"But they didn't make you a pianist. They just recognized, when you were very young, that you *were* one. Do you see?"

She nods slowly.

"So where did it come from, this gift of music?"

Gift. Miss Selkirk's words. You are gifted, my child. "I don't know," she says. "I never thought about it."

"God," he says simply. "It came from God. He is the one who called you to it. And that is why being an artist is a holy thing—only God can make one."

She watches him across the table, his tousled hair, his intense pale blue eyes behind the smudged lenses, the spots of color high in his thin cheeks. If she has ever seen a crazy artist, it is him.

"Do you still go to church?" she asks.

"I am at mass every morning. Seven o'clock."

Every morning? She is beginning to believe that she has never before met another person like Jan. "Where?"

"Saint Anne's, on Charles."

"*Why?*" she asks.

He shrugs. "I cannot explain this to you. If you ask me that question, then there is nothing I can say to make you understand. Please do not be offended."

She settles back against the vinyl booth cushion. The two church services she has ever attended did not, quite frankly, impress her. Her grandmother's white wooden prairie church with a stark steeple, floating above a field of corn. Hitterdal farmers with bands of pure white around their foreheads and white fleshy bands below their shirtsleeves. Heavy farmwives with swollen ankles and sturdy shoes, handkerchiefs tucked into the bosoms of their flowered dresses. The summer heat had made her legs stick to the wooden pew; wasps had zigzagged back and forth through the rows of drowsing parishioners. Church every *morning*?

A new awkwardness has fallen over them, and suddenly she feels sad. She thought they were on their way to a friendship, and then this . . . *whatever*-it-is came along. This unexpected gulf.

But suddenly he leans forward, as intense as ever. "Sylvia," he says. "Miss Haupt has a recital coming up soon at the Library of Congress. She is wonderful. Would you like to go see it?"

"*Sure*," she answers, surprised and relieved. "Of course."

"Good, then. I will call you with the details." He nods.

"*Okay*," she says. "That's *great*."

"You did not offend me," he says. "I want you to know that."

She drops her eyes.

"I realize that I am probably different than most of the people you know," he says. "Most of the Americans."

"Well . . . yes. That's true, Jan—you are."

"I do not mind being different. I am used to it."

"Well, that's good, then. That you don't mind it, I mean."

"You are different, too, Sylvia."

"I am?"

He is staring at her solemnly. "Yes, you are. You are special—you have been called to music."

"Well but, Jan—so has everyone else in this place."

He shakes his head. "No, no, Sylvia, that is not true. Look around you. Most are here for other reasons."

"Sometimes, though, I think I'm just here because of my dad."

He shakes his head slowly. "Down inside of yourself, you know why you are here. Do not ever let go of that, no matter what happens."

"What do you mean? What could happen?"

"Suffering. Sadness. The terrible things of life."

She thinks of her vision of Beethoven hunched over the piano, the awful ringing in his ears, and shivers. "You're scaring me, Jan."

"I do not mean to frighten you. But you must take this gift seriously."

Gift. There it is again. The word is becoming as oppressive as her father's love.

CHAPTER TEN

*A*fternoon.

Moon Ja sits between her parents at the oak dinette set, which has been expanded on both ends by card tables; she is surrounded by relatives, everyone crowded close together, elbows bumping. Her brother August and his wife and daughters are directly across from her; cousins and spouses sit to her right. Children, most of them under five, perch under their parents' arms, quietly observing the adults. Auntie Kim presides over one card table, Auntie Lee over the other.

Her mother, as usual, has made her fabulous marinated beef, and though Moon Ja rarely eats meat anymore, she is suddenly ravenous when she smells the spices and soy sauce. This is nice, she thinks. I'm too used to being alone; I'm turning into a real old maid.

"More rice?" asks her mother. She hands over the bowl, and Moon Ja sees that her round face is covered by a sheen of sweat. She was up very late cooking, and though Moon Ja helped for as long as she could, the time change from Korea finally got to her at midnight. She went off to her old room—her mother's sewing room now, with a fold-out sofa—and fell asleep to the sound of her mother's steady chopping.

This house in the suburbs is small, and the area has gotten worse and worse. People have iron grillwork over their doors and signs that announce burglar alarm systems. She has offered, numerous times, to help her parents move, but—she glances at her father, who is sipping soju out of a shot glass and looking bored (these are mostly her mother's relatives)—neither of her parents will even pursue the conversation. "I can afford it," she's said to them. "I'd like to do this for you." Her efforts are useless, of course; this is the old neighborhood, the street they've lived on for thirty years, and they are never leaving a life again.

Finally, the meal is over and the women get up to clear. The men don't even glance in the direction of the kitchen. Most of them are already crowded around the TV, smoking and watching the Lakers.

Auntie Lee, who is eighty-one, is stooped over at the sink, running hot water. "Here," says Moon Ja. "Let me do that."

"No, no, I like to do it. I used to work." She looks up into Moon Ja's face, grinning sweetly. Her eyes have vanished into the smile lines.

"Auntie, here. You dry instead, okay?" Moon Ja hands her a white towel and pulls a chair close to the sink so the ancient little woman can sit down if she needs to. Her aunt takes the towel obediently and steps away from the running water. They work in silence for some time while the other women clear the table and put away the food.

"Moon Ja," says Auntie Lee. "You go to Korea." It is a statement, not a question.

"Yes—for two weeks. I went to Seoul and saw some other places, too."

"You go to Mokpo?"

"No, I didn't get down that far."

"Yosu, maybe?"

"No, Auntie Lee, I'm sorry. But I saw Kyongju—it was beautiful." She thinks of the immense stone Buddha, the jewel in the forehead, the stubborn way she'd waited there beside the other pilgrims, drawn to the shrine against her will and better judgment, expecting nothing, receiving nothing.

"Ah, Kyongju. Ah-ha." Her aunt nods. "Strange place, very strange."

Suddenly, Moon Ja's arms are tingling. Perhaps there was something, after all, that she had missed. "Why, Auntie? Tell me."

"The burial mounds. Like city of death."

Moon Ja had seen them, of course—had even walked through the park that surrounds them—but somehow could not connect them with human beings. They were enormous—full-sized earthen hills in the middle of town; they looked like some kind of natural wonder. Yet she couldn't stop hearing Brahms in that place; she'd never stopped thinking about death. She shudders as that eerie sense of stasis once more takes her over.

"I die soon," says her aunt happily.

"No, Auntie . . ."

"Yes, yes, I am very old. And I go to fortune-teller one time, she say I live to be eighty-two. So next birthday is it. Eight months left."

"A fortune-teller in Korea?"

"No, no, here in L.A. Gypsy lady read my hand. Life-line very long, she say. But stop at eighty-two."

Moon Ja looks down at the old woman, who is carefully drying a spoon. Her hair is very fine and white, a little cloud around her face. She sets down the spoon and picks up a fork. She does not seem at all afraid of her impending doom. Moon Ja thinks of the doctor's appointment that awaits her, what she herself might soon learn. She watches her auntie drying the silverware, piece by piece.

"Moon Ja," says her aunt. "You play the piano in Seoul?"

"Yes. In the Sejong Cultural Center, a big hall."

Her aunt nods twice and picks up a butter knife. "Good," she says simply. "I like that."

Evening.

Bellyman and Tee are awake: the cold, and piano music from the school across the park. The girl with the wild hair must be playing; Bellyman noticed her earlier, hurrying with her canvas bags out the front door of the brownstone and past the mouth of the alley where the two of them sit with their backs against the damp brick, trying to sleep.

For once, Bellyman is quiet, not coughing. He leans up against Tee's shoulder, listening to the girl's music, but he is not really thinking of her. Instead, he is remembering the village and the long walk down the dirt road to the cane fields. It is raining in the village, the streets are mud, but the rain is warm; it bathes his face and soaks his shirt. The sun is coming up over the Blue Mountains and the tin roofs in Siloah are brightening under the rain. His woman is still sleeping, but she will wake soon, and when he comes back from the fields tonight, she will have hot food ready. "Bellymon," she'll say. "I got dese good bean fe you. Eat, mon."

"What dat song?" he says to Tee, whispering so he won't cough. "She always playin' dat song."

Tee takes the cigarette from his mouth and blows the smoke away from Bellyman's face. He's careful about that. "Don't know, man," says Tee. "But I be gettin' *mighty* sicka that shit."

Midnight.

In the brownstones, the mothers sleep against the broad backs of their men. It is the one consolation for their busy days, this sweet skin, this radiant warmth. It is endlessly familiar, endlessly pleasing, this curling together of bodies beneath the blankets, the sleepy turnings, the hand on the hip, the legs fitted together in perfect harmony. Sometimes in the night there are murmurs, urgent stirrings and, half asleep, the mothers fall into deeper warmth, are taken, dreamlike, by the lovers they married. Sometimes in the night, new children are conceived, new visitors from outer space who travel like light from the distant stars.

Morning.

The sun falls through Toft's studio window, falls in a

golden band across the piano, the floor, Sylvia's shoulders. Her back is warmed by the light. She can see, with her peripheral vision, her own lit curls, Toft's black shoes, the shadows thrown by her flying hands. She is playing Schumann's *Fantasiestücke*, the "In der Nacht" section, which she has *always* loved; when she plays it, she cannot help thinking of Hero and Leander.

So far, and in spite of her usual sweaty palms around Toft, she is doing very well. Better, in fact, than she should be; she has been neglecting the *Fantasiestücke* for Opus 111. But "In der Nacht" pours out into the sunlit room as though someone else, someone older and infinitely more confident, is playing it, and she listens intently, wondering why. Is she suddenly getting better—is that it? All the hours of practice starting to add up?

She glances over at Toft's shoes; they are gone. He has moved to another part of the room, somewhere she can't see him. Oh well, she thinks, so much the better. For she simply loves this piece; she does not want to think of Toft at all, particularly since "Traumeswirren," that beautiful finger-crusher, is coming up so quickly, and she will need all her concentration to pull it off.

She finishes "In der Nacht" well and rests for a moment, head bowed, waiting for Toft's comments. Nothing. Instead, she hears the creak of his chair as he settles himself behind her. He is breathing loudly today, the stentorious breathing of a very old man, and, for the first time, he sounds . . . what? Fragile? Mortal? As though he is dying?

She actually turns her head to look at him, to assure herself that he is still there, gripping the armrests with his bony fingers and boring into her sunlit back with his cold simian eyes. Yes, there he is—small, indomitable, irascible . . . but suddenly what she is seeing is her father's face instead of Toft's, her father on fire in a burning halo of sunlight.

"Well, for God's sake, what are you waiting for?" barks Toft. "Do I have all day?"

But still she sits staring at him, forgetting for once to be afraid, her mind turning over wonderingly the revelation she has just had.

"Play!" says Toft, and she hears the frustrated old man's whine in his voice, a whine that must have always been there, though she has never noticed it before. He is so angry with her that his two black shoes are jigging up and down against the wooden floor. By now she should be shaking with terror.

Instead, she asks him gently, "Do you want me to go ahead with 'Fabel'?"

"Of course! What else would it be, I ask you!"

She turns back to the piano, where everything—the keyboard, the stack of music on the floor, the white wall behind the piano, adazzle with morning light—has become somehow different, yet without changing in any apparent way. How utterly strange. What has happened? I have to tell Peter about this, she thinks.

And then she is once more playing Schumann, forgetting, for the moment, everything but the music.

Late afternoon.

Katerina Haupt is at the stove, stirring stew in her iron pot. Rosemary and tarragon and the smell of onions and good beef rise in a steamy cloud around her; she sniffs happily and pulls at the neck of her sweater, giving herself air. One of the distinct disadvantages of being fat: She heats up in the mildest climates these days. Her forehead is actually damp.

The stew, however, is glorious in spite of the fact that she has forgotten the pepper again. Age is not an easy thing: Now her memory is going. She remembers writing it down, not two days ago—PEPPER!—in big letters on a scrap of envelope, which she must have promptly thrown away.

She dips her spoon in the garlicky, oniony mess and turns to the side so that Jan, sitting at her kitchen table, cannot see her sipping. Perfect even without the pepper; she may be a person of no discipline, but she certainly can cook.

"Are you hungry?" she asks him.

"I am always hungry," he says, grinning. She loves his grin, the cheerful crooked tooth that winks at her.

"Okay, then," she says. "March your bowl over here, young man."

Then he is standing beside her at the stove and she is struck, as she always is, by his height, his lankiness, the long shy hungry lines of his young man's body. His wrists are as thick around as her ankle, but without an ounce of fat to them. His shirt is positively threadbare; he owns but one pair of shoes. "Jan," she says impulsively. "You need to eat more. You need to take better care of yourself."

He laughs. He is very easy with her, in spite of his shyness; within two weeks of meeting one another, they

fell into something much deeper than the usual student/
teacher relationship—deeper, even, than friendship. In
some odd way, they are soulmates; not much disturbs
their natural joy. She does not *really* mind her own fat;
he is curiously undisturbed by either his poverty or his
oddness. What is important to each of them is music and
the kind of messy freedom from distraction that it requires. They can't be bothered by silly details—*or*, she
thinks, a lack of pepper in the stew.

When they have carried their bowls to the table and
she has chosen their music—Bach's *Magnificat*—they sit
for a moment in companionable silence, the only family
either of them really has. Yes, she thinks, of course there
is Cornelius, of course there is Moon Ja—but Jan is different. Not a son, exactly, but a child of her heart. "So
what's on your mind?" she asks him gently, for she
knows he has come to talk.

"Miss Haupt," he says. "Have you ever been in love?"

Night.

Sylvia is sitting alone at the kitchen table in her apartment, working on her term paper. The overhead light
falls on the heap of note cards, her pencils, an empty tea
mug, a stack of faded books from the many-tiered library filled with ghosts. She lifts her hair from the back
of her neck and shakes it, yawning. The apartment is
very quiet; she cannot play music when she writes or
she'll fool herself into thinking that whatever she's doing
is wonderful. If only Marushka were in the bedroom
down the hall, quiet too, studying, but at least there.
Solid, warm, full of Marushka passions and petty angers.

Sylvia picks up a note card. The chansons of Dufay and Binchois, song poems about chivalric love. All interesting, of course, but in spite of being a good writer, she's not comfortable with research papers. She finds that she always has too much to say and not enough time . . . and that she tends to stray, following interesting trails that lead her nowhere. She and Jan have talked about this in the last several weeks (he is now walking her home almost every night). He's a natural theorist and loves to grapple with musical arguments, and he seems to think that because she can play Chopin and Schumann, she spends most of her time thinking about music. She is still too shy with him to admit that she does not. She *hears* music, constantly; she rarely *thinks* about it, unless she is forced. Which, of course, is probably exactly Toft's complaint about her.

Why *can't* I think about things? she wonders. In an organized way? Am I that much of a child still?

Her present loneliness is heightened fiercely by the emptiness of the apartment. Nothing stirs. She watches the hallway, imagining Marushka—anyone—emerging from the bedroom, coming out to stand there in the dim light, stretching. How she, Sylvia, would make another cup of tea, pull out a chair, and then there would be someone sitting across from her sipping quietly and humming while she worked on her paper.

Should she call Jan? She blushes. He has been very nice and she has enjoyed their times together in the past few weeks, their discussions, but his eager hovering presence seems to require more. Though they always linger for a while, talking, on the steps in front of her door, he has not yet kissed her—and she has not wanted him to. She has a dim belief, not thought out, that if she kisses him, something else will have to happen. At the very least, some declaration, some commitment that she is not ready to make, will be required. And her life, which has only recently begun to seem like her own, will suddenly belong, in part, to another person, a person she likes very much (she blushes again) but after all does not know well.

Perhaps, instead, she should call Peter? No—Peter will be calmly asleep by now, stretched out on his futon near the covered birdcage. Except for late jazz concerts, Peter keeps early hours; in his balanced Peter way, he sees no point in wasting good hours of darkness by staying up late working.

Colette. She sits up in her chair, surprised. They have never really been friends, but Colette lives alone too and has always, at least to Sylvia, seemed lonely. The only black student in the school, and shy besides—she *must* be lonely. Her father is so famous; it must be hard for her. And none of the other piano students are into French music either; she doesn't have a lot in common with anyone. Maybe she would be interested in sharing the apartment? It would only be for five or six months—Colette leaves for Juilliard in the fall—but by then Marushka may have come back. Something—anything—could happen in six months.

Instantly, hope rises like a gossamer balloon.

She reaches for the phone on the counter.

CHAPTER ELEVEN

Six weeks left until her recital. Sylvia should have practiced longer tonight—she is usually at the bench until at least eleven—but Colette came by to see the apartment, and then they went to the White Tower for a cup of clam chowder, and now it is too late. She yawns. Perhaps, instead, she'll take a nice long bath—though it is hard to relax, knowing she's been neglecting Ravel in favor of Beethoven. She's been neglecting *everybody* for Beethoven's sake—the more time she spends on Opus 111, the less prepared she feels with the *Fantasiestücke* or the *Sonatine* or Scarlatti.

Colette seemed pleased by the apartment. She had been slow and careful, moving from room to room, door to door, studying the enormous claw-footed bathtub like a connoisseur. "This is *nice*," she said finally in her soft New Orleans voice. "You sure you want to do this? Give up your privacy?"

"My *privacy*? Colette, I'm going nuts here all by myself. Please say yes."

Colette had laughed. "Okay, then—yes! If I can get away with two weeks' notice, I'll be in by the fifteenth."

Now Sylvia wonders if she made the right decision; they hardly know each other, after all. And they hadn't exactly burned up the White Tower with their conversation. Long silences—not awkward or unfriendly, but still long. She's very reserved, Sylvia thinks. Like Peter, in a way, but without the self-confidence.

She heads down the hall for the bathtub, still yawning. She'll wash her hair tonight, even though it will take hours to dry, and she'll wash out some clothes, too. Small domestic chores to keep her mind off of Toft, the recital, and the fact that Jan has finally kissed her (sweetly, warmly, in the dark)—and she *liked* it.

In the alleyway, Bellyman lies on his back astonished, knees bent, hands folded across his chest. The night is brilliantly clear; he stares wide-eyed at the rectangle of black sky above the alley, the faint spangle of white stars. He is not cold; he has no idea of how he came to be lying on his back. He remembers coughing, coughing, his hands full of warm blood. He remembers a singing in his head, a choir, and the warm blood dripping between his fingers.

Tee—where is Tee? He remembers Tee holding him, Tee touching his face, Tee walking off into the streets. Be cool, Bellyman, be cool. I be back soon with some help for you. Bellyman isn't frightened, though he is crying a little without knowing why, the way he used to wake from a sound sleep with tears coming down his face.

From across the park comes the sound of a violin.

• • •

The bathwater is already running when Sylvia realizes that something is once again bothering her about Opus 111, something she can almost feel herself working out if only she were at the piano. She looks at the clock, thinks about how dark it is outside and how empty the building will probably be. But inside her is a growing surety that this is important, that she should get herself over to the practice room before she forgets it.

Without thinking any further, she jumps up, goes down the hallway to her bedroom, puts on her shoes, and grabs her coat and bag of music. Outside, the darkness is thick, cold, oppressive. She looks around before she goes out onto the steps, shivering but determined. Ever since Marushka got hit, she's been too afraid of the night. I'll just run, she thinks. I'm a fast runner.

Poised like a deer, she listens carefully, then pulls the door shut behind her, moving into a quick lope as soon as she reaches the street.

At the conservatory, most of the practice rooms are dark. Sylvia makes her way upstairs to her favorite. She can hear Schubert's Duo in A Major going on nearby, and the bittersweet tangle of violin and piano makes her heart ache for Marushka. After the first phone call from Kiev, she's heard nothing. Marushka is not a letter writer and neither, she has to admit, is she.

She sits down at the piano, hardly daring to breathe. Will it come back, that revelation she had beside the bathtub? She closes her eyes, waiting, and after a while, her fingers make their way to the keys and she listens, as hard as she's ever listened, to what the music is saying.

Yes, she thinks, oh yes. She plays the eight measures over and over, and it seems to her that somehow they have become a key, though she has not yet unlocked the entire mystery.

Over and over and over . . . and then, suddenly, she's ready to do the whole thing, to see how it works *this* time, and she begins the first clamorous movement, the movement she's always thought unnecessarily loud and . . . well, *ugly*. So much chaos and passion to get through before the beautiful serenity of the second-movement trills—perhaps that's what's been wrong all along. She's been rejecting the first movement, subconsciously racing to get to the second, and then the second sounds thin and brittle instead of how it should sound—rich and unearthly and full of peace and joy. She feels flooded with some kind of new knowledge, some insight about the music that might evaporate if she's unable to put it into sound *now*, and she leans over the keyboard, playing from her wrists and forearms, concentrating with all her intellect.

An hour later she jumps up, tingling with energy, smiling blindly around the empty practice room. I need an audience, she thinks; I need to hear if I'm right about this. She walks quickly to the window, stares down at the web of streets below, searching for Jan's apartment, which should be blazing with lights at this time of night—he's such an owl—but is not. She can't even find it, in fact, in the dark welter of apartment buildings, shut down for the night. Where could he be? Not sleeping— he never sleeps. She searches the area again—all dark— and then gives up in frustration.

Sit down, Sylvia, she tells herself. Be calm. *Think* about this. What did you just do?

She perches obediently on the bench, closes her eyes, tries to imagine Toft standing before her, wrinkled and suspicious. Maybe, she offers silently, the second movement is like a . . . a *reward* or something? And the first is a kind of tragedy? And you have to concentrate on the first movement the most because if you don't survive it, you don't deserve to play the second? She sits for a long time, eyes closed, thinking this through, and it finally makes a kind of sense to her, though she can't imagine how she, who has never suffered anything but the going away of her best friend, can learn to play the somber first movement without trying to soften it and make it beautiful.

Finally, tired but still charged with breakthrough exhilaration, she looks at her watch—a little after midnight, once again. And Jan, wherever he is, won't be by to walk her home tonight; she told him Colette was coming over to the apartment and she wouldn't be practicing tonight. Well, she'll just have to lope home the way she came.

She starts packing up.

In the alleyway, Bellyman floats beneath the stars. He is warm, transported; he drifts back and forth through a shining pale membrane that flutters like breath. Jimmy, calls his mother. Jimboy! His father is lifting him, high, high. He is no longer than his father's arm. His cheeks are fat, his flesh is firm. He coos, swimming in a sea of light. He kicks, his feet fluttering. He glides like a fish through the lighted air.

He dives down, inches from his father's eyes. They are enormous, bigger than his fists. Enormous and deep-set, dark and kindly. Sweet, says his father. Sweet little mon.

He is kissed on the neck; he squeals, batting at the wide lips, the great cheeks. Jimmy, says his mother. She is smiling. The light shimmers all around him. The world is a shining place. He swims in bursts of terrible energy; he is powerful, twenty-four inches of intensity. He wants everything, all the light, his father's face, his mother's skin. He swims, he beats the air, reaching out, fingers grabbing. Jimboy, they say. Sweet, sweet little mon.

Sylvia edges through the street door and stands for a moment searching the dark park with her eyes. Nothing, no movement anywhere, but she can't see much in the dim streetlights. A block and a half, she tells herself. That's all. She moves to the sidewalk and hoists her bag over her shoulder, breaking into a fast trot, thinking of the man in the red stocking cap, his hand wrenching back her head.

She's breathing hard when she reaches the mouth of the alley, but she hears the sudden terrible sound clearly above her own panting: a descending appoggiatura of moans. Oh my God, she thinks, and without considering what she is doing, stops dead on the street, listening. There—again. Something dying; she recognizes this immediately, though she does not know how. The police, she thinks automatically, and starts to move to her front stoop just as someone enormous and ominously familiar steps up beside her, taking her arm.

She jerks and twists; he is saying something over and over; she strikes out with her other hand, too frightened to scream; he tugs at her arm roughly, saying, "Miss, miss, listen to me, *listen.*"

She stops, staring up at him in horror, her heart twisting inside her chest. She's gasping for air; her knees are collapsing; her eyes are stretched wide, trying to see him in the darkness. His head is shining. Then she recognizes him. The enormous bald man on Miss Haupt's steps that night. The one who took the money from Jan. The moans bubble out of the alleyway. What has he done in there? What will he do to her?

"Miss." He shakes her arm, hurting her. His big bass voice is ragged; something frantic in it catches her attention; she tries to listen to what he is saying.

"My friend in there"—he gestures at the alley—"he need help *bad*. He need to get to the hospital *now.*"

He is breathing almost as hard as she is, big rough animal sounds, and she realizes that he might be crying. She reaches up carefully and pries his fingers from her upper arm, rubbing it where he's probably made bruises. He lets her do this.

"What," she whispers, "do you want *me* to do?"

"He need a taxi. We don't have no money, lady."

"The police?" Her voice comes out stronger this time.

"No!" He takes her by the wrist and shakes her arm, hard. "Nobody, you hear me? No cops, no fire trucks, no uniform shit."

"Okay!" she says quickly, filled with sick terror.

"Okay, it's all right. Just a taxi. I've got it." The moaning is terrible, hoarse and filled with pain. She trembles, touching her wrist and thinking fast. If she opens the street door to her apartment, he could push his way in, follow her upstairs . . . Who knows what he might do? He's desperate, that much is clear, and filled with rage that his friend is dying. Dying. She turns her face toward the mouth of the alley, listening in spite of herself. She's never even been to a funeral—my God!—and surely never seen anybody dying.

Suddenly, she straightens. The violin and piano—were they still playing when she left the school? She tries to think, imagining herself once more on the iron stairway, going down, reaching the first landing . . . yes! She remembers: They'd switched to some Kreisler varia-tions; somebody was still playing; they were very likely still up there . . . "I'll be right back," she says breath-lessly, dropping her heavy bag of music and jerking away. He reaches out; before he can grab her, she has broken into a sprint back toward the school.

"Hey!" he shouts.

"Don't worry," she calls back over her shoulder, but her voice is lost behind her. "I'm going for help."

One of the practice room lights is still on. Sylvia, gasping from the run, bounds up the stairs, dragging herself along by her hand on the iron banister, listening for the sounds of a violin, but everything is silent except for the chiming of the rail. Oh please, she is chanting, please be there, whoever you are. Please don't have gone home, please, please. . . .

Suddenly, the sound of the violin is pouring over her on the stairs, flooding her like warm water with something crazy and Spanish—de Falla?—and she laughs out loud in relief. David—it has to be. No one plays like brash, handsome David, not that wild gypsy stuff, anyway. And if it is David, the piano has to be Brandon—it *has* to, they are always teaming up—and so that means at least two men to help her.

She runs down the hallway toward the light and flings the door wide, panting, blinking, stunned for a moment by the brightness. David, silent, his violin still in position, stares at her over the top of his music stand. Brandon is not at the piano but instead is slouching in a chair that he has tipped back against the white wall. Above him is a wooden clock; the window is open; a moth dives back and forth through the light. She takes in all of this in seconds, and then David says, "Sylvia?"

"There's a man in the alley who needs help," she says quickly, "and I—we need to get a taxi, and someone needs to come back with me if you can." She stops, folding her hands and looking down, shaking, the tears beginning to well. She'd been so *frightened* when he grabbed her arm, all she could think of was Marushka and the mugger and how lucky the two of them had been not to be killed.

David is already packing away his violin, stowing it in the closet at the far end of the room, pulling on his jacket. Brandon tips his chair forward. "Where are you going? What do you think you're doing?"

"You heard her," says David. "Come on, Sylvia."

"Will you call the taxi?" she asks Brandon. "No po-

lice, no paramedics—he'll hurt me maybe if you do—
promise me you won't, Brandon, *please*. Just a taxi,
that's all we need."

David is already out the door and she runs after him
down the hall. They zigzag down the stairs together, silent, their feet crashing against the metal, and then they
are out on the street and running back toward her apartment. When she trips and stumbles on the cobblestones,
he grabs her by the hand, pulling her upright without
speaking, and she flies along beside him through the
dark, glad for her deer legs. Before she can think about
what she is feeling—terror? exhilaration? glory?—they
are at the mouth of the alley. Both of them come to a
confused stop, not knowing what to do; just then the big
man calls to them from the darkness, "Down here."
They stare in the direction of the voice, but there is
nothing to see. The alleyway is hidden to them by a
deep, velvety blackness. Sylvia can feel David's arm jerk
nervously, and she moves closer. "I have a flashlight in
my apartment," she whispers. "And some blankets."

"Okay, hurry," he says, low, and she can feel all
around her the dank fear rising like mist. The animal
moaning goes on and on.

She rushes to the front door, fumbling for her key,
just as the bass says in a terrible, mournful voice, "Bellyman, don't die on me now, baby," and she thinks, Bellyman—of course. The old man with the terrible cough.
Oh my God.

In minutes, she's back downstairs with an armload of
blankets and her flashlight, and somehow in between
she has become calm. Perhaps it was the voice and how

despairing it sounded, perhaps the fact of David's presence, the imminent arrival of the taxi and help, but she is now curiously unafraid. She loads the blankets into David's waiting arms and they move together into the alleyway.

Bellyman has finally come to rest; he has reached the island and the sand is hot beneath him. He bakes in the sun while the light shimmers around him, and he listens hard for the sweet voice of his woman, so long gone away. The trees are thick and green, swaying in the blue air; he can smell cooking fires, blossoms, the deep salty bloodsmell of the ocean.

Siloah, he thinks. She waitin' in de hut, cookin' de beans. She singing' and lovin', all by herself.

He tries to turn over, to crawl down the beach toward his woman, but his arms and legs are soft, like a baby's, and he can't lift them anymore. Her low songs fill his head; he moves his hands like a sea turtle swimming; then she is gone, vanishing into the eye of the sun, and he lies quiet in the deep heat, already forgetting her. The slow water washes over the ragged coral reefs. Something not human is calling to him, a lovely, haunting call; he listens in mounting joy and terror. He waits and listens, stirring his fingers through the hot gold sand.

Around him the green sea quietly rises.

Sylvia and David move through the thick darkness, knocking into garbage cans, the cold stink of the alley in their nostrils. They stumble, and she turns on her light; masses of some kind of paper lie in their pathway.

"Watch out," she says to David, who cannot see the ground over his armload of blankets. "Don't fall." She is trembling but not frightened; she has never felt more alive. She is walking into the wild zone; anything can happen; her skin tingles with cold and anticipation.

Something looms ahead—the big man sitting cross-legged on the ground (she flashes her light over him) rocking a rag doll in his arms. The yellow beam plays against the bundle of rags; she sees a head flopping, the angle of the neck, and then, impossibly strong, the moaning begins again. No, she thinks. Not a doll, not a doll. Something—the smell of sweet decay—fills her throat. Bellyman.

David stops. She moves forward slowly, reverently, not knowing what she will do or say. The big man looks up at her, his face shining wet. His eyes gleam at her in the dark and he hugs the bundle—Bellyman—closer to his chest, rocking, rocking. She lowers herself to her knees and crawls forward on her hands until she is sitting beside him in the cold dirt. "I'm Sylvia," she whispers. "And this is David. We've . . . brought him some blankets. And a taxi. There's a taxi on its way."

Bellyman moans and turns his head. The big man takes a long, shuddering breath. "Tee," he says. "I'm Tee. Time we wrap this little man up."

David is crouching beside them, and together they spread a blanket in the dirt while Tee lowers his bundle onto it. Sylvia rolls another blanket for a pillow, and then, not sure what to do, not wanting to touch the dying man, says to Tee, "Will you lift his head?"

David holds the light and for the first time they are looking into Bellyman's face. My God, she thinks, he looks like he's been beaten. She closes her eyes for a moment, sick, and when she opens them she is looking at the mouth, the parted lips, the teeth dark with blood. And the skin—the skin. An unearthly shade—blueblack faded to gray, translucent, tinged with lavender, the color of rainclouds at twilight. "What *happened* to him?" she says.

"It the sickness," says Tee. "He been coughing blood for a week."

"Jesus," David says, then lays down the flashlight. Quickly, together, they push a blanket beneath the dying man's legs and wrap another over him and then sit trembling, their hands between their knees as he moans softly, turning his head back and forth, back and forth, in the yellow ray from her flashlight on the ground.

A car moves down the street, passing the alley. The minutes tick by. Nobody speaks. Sylvia breathes through her mouth, tasting the peculiar smell of rotting garbage and Bellyman's sickness in the back of her throat, wondering what he can possibly be thinking, what can be going through his mind—if he knows he is dying, and if he is sad.

Finally, David whispers in her ear, "Maybe you should go back and wait on the street—so the taxi can find us. I'll stay here with him."

"No, you go," she says, surprised at the sound of fierce tears in her voice. "I know him." And what does she mean by *that*? That she saw him that one night on Miss Haupt's front stoop in his wet blue hat? That she knows for a fact that somebody—the big bald-headed man called Tee—loves him?

David doesn't answer her, but slips away without the

flashlight. She hears him kicking through the paper, then sees him silhouetted at the end of the alley, peering back toward her. She sits quietly beside the two men, waiting. Once, Tee makes a strangled sound, then coughs to cover it. Her heart wells up for him as they go back to their vigil.

Jamaica is sinking. The weight of the water presses down on all sides. Bellyman feels the ground trembling beneath him. The sun, the sun . . . he can't move, he can't swim, he can do nothing but lie on his back in the hot sand while the sea rises around him. The crushing weight of all the world's water is rising around him, pouring down upon him; waterfalls, warm green cataracts of water stopping his eyes, his breath. He lies still; he cannot move, nor does he try to, and his heart is beating in terror and joy. He will never leave the island again.

But then, just at the last, he cannot help himself; he struggles to move, to breathe, to escape. He cries out for help, for life; he flails against the water; he is caught up like driftwood in the terrible green swirl of the maelstrom.

The old man coughs and coughs, crying, while Sylvia holds frantically to his thrashing legs and Tee props him upright. She can hear a siren wailing through the streets; Brandon must have called an ambulance instead of a taxi, and she's glad that he did, for Bellyman is dying in front of her; he's *dying*. She holds his stick legs, crying, and she feels something warm and wet in her hair, on her hands. Tee is chanting, "No, no, no, no."

And then, when she doesn't think she can stand it another second, there are suddenly huge lights in the alley and people and voices and the clattering of equipment, and she is being shoved aside so that men in uniforms can take over. But, she wants to tell them, astonished, he's already gone. He's gone, can't you feel it? I felt him leave.

She sits in the muck of the alley, shaking, as they tear off his clothes and listen for his heart, then begin pumping his chest. She looks around stupidly for Tee, to tell him about Bellyman leaving, but he has vanished. Don't worry, she wants to say. It was just like breathing out and then not taking another breath. It was peaceful—he didn't hurt right then. Oh, I know he didn't hurt.

Somebody crouches beside her, a thin young man with glasses and a white uniform and soft frail curls like an angel. He is very pale, with two bright red spots on his cheeks, as though in pain. "Be careful you don't get any of that blood near your mouth," he says calmly. She nods at him.

"Do you live close by?"

She points up at the brownstone.

"Good," he says. He lays his hand on her shoulder for a moment and together they watch as two other men push their hands down, over and over again, on Bellyman's silent chest.

But Bellyman has left the island now and is spinning slowly through fathoms of water, slow-spinning with arms and legs outspread. The ocean rises above him, mile after mile. He passes unseen through years of water, through eons of spinning darkness. His eyes are open, his lungs are full; he has become like a fish.

The silence is astonishing. The absolute solitude. It is beautiful, he thinks. The icy elegance of eternity . . . he has already forgotten the world.

CHAPTER TWELVE

*I*n time, when everyone has finally gone, Sylvia and David are left alone on the sidewalk in front of her apartment. Brandon, who arrived with the ambulance, stands with them. The night has been overtaken by a deep predawn chill; she clutches her coat to her throat and marvels at the quiet; nothing stirs now in the neighborhood that was so recently filled with lights and sirens and onlookers in slippers and winter coats.

Bellyman . . . she does not want to think about Bellyman. Or Tee, who is no doubt hiding somewhere close by, watching everything.

"Well, I'm out of here," Brandon says. "You coming, David?"

David, his hands jammed deep in his coat pockets, his collar turned up against the cold, shrugs. Sylvia watches him. He looks young and lost to her. "I guess I'll stick around a while," he says, not looking at her, but motioning with his head in her direction.

Brandon nods knowingly. "Uh-huh. I see. Right."

Sylvia has a hard time forming the words, but she makes herself say them anyway: "Thanks for . . . well, thanks, Brandon. For calling and everything."

"Oh sure. Sure. Gotta go now, though."

Sylvia and David both nod at him somberly; he gives his flirty little wave—toodle-oo—and then (he can't resist) turns and says, "You two be good now, you hear?"

Neither of them responds (David does not even look at her), but then, when Brandon's long, twinkling legs have vanished into the dark, he says quietly, "Can I come up? Just to clean up before I go?"

"Oh, of course," she says. "Sure. And I just want you to know how much. . . ."

He shakes his head again. "No problem, okay?"

The sound of his feet on the stairs behind her is comforting.

The apartment feels unfamiliar to Sylvia; she can't relax. She prowls restlessly up and down the hallway while David showers, and then waits obediently in the kitchen while he makes coffee. They each have a cup, not speaking, and it seems to her that she can hear Marushka, mumbling in her sleep. Peter, she thinks. She sets her cup in the sink and wanders into the bathroom, back out again. She looks at her hands. Suddenly, she doesn't seem to be functioning well.

"Sylvia," says David. "Come here where I can see you."

She heads back to the living room. He is standing by the breakfast bar, finishing his coffee. She holds up her hands for him to see. He studies her in the light. "God," he says. "What a mess." She follows him down the hall-way, sits on the closed toilet seat, her eyes only half open, suddenly beyond exhaustion. He is on his knees on the bathmat. Water thunders out of the spigots; steam rises. She is utterly drained, but when she closes her eyes entirely, strings of lighted beads batter against her eyelids.

"Okay," he says, standing, his hands against his back as though he aches, as though he is hurting through and through with some deep and unfathomable pain that has crushed him, briefly, into a sweet and maternal ten-derness. He looks down at her. "Just take your time—I'll wait till you're done before I leave, okay?"

She stares up at him dumbly and he says, "Put up your arms." She raises them obediently, two thin arms in a baggy sweatshirt, and he takes hold of the sweatshirt at her wrists and pulls the whole thing gently over her head. "There," he says. "Now you do the rest."

She hears him leave, hears the door close, sits on the toilet-seat lid for another few minutes before she can rouse herself enough to get undressed and climb into the tub. What did they just watch? They watched a man die. She cannot stop thinking about it; the skin over her cheekbones is jumping; she has never longed so for the big pines on the wide lawn of the house on Cedar Lake.

The hot water takes her in like a mouth; she floats, boiling herself, turning back and forth as Bellyman's blood melts away and disappears into the clear, deep heat. Once, she rolls over and puts her face under, hold-ing her breath. I won't cry, she says to herself.

Her hair, soaked and heavy, swirls around her; she

opens her eyes underwater and stares at the white porcelain wall of the tub. Somebody died, somebody died,
and I was there. She feels both numb and electrified, as
though she has just touched a spitting live wire. One
minute he was moaning, and then he was gone.

She scrambles to her knees on the hard porcelain,
pulling her heavy hair out of the water, gasping for
breath. My God, she thinks, a person died in my arms
. . . she grabs the soap, scrubs her hot skin over and over,
then pours shampoo over her wet head. The bathwater
becomes white froth, mounds up like meringue, and still
she scrubs away at herself.

Finally, she is calm. She rinses in clear water and rises,
toweling herself dry. David must have found her bathrobe—it is hanging on the door. She combs out her mass
of wet hair, rubs lotion into her clean, pink skin, and
pulls the white robe tight around her waist, tying it.

Tee has been walking for a long time, but he finally gets
to the train yard and stops, looking around him. He has
always avoided this place; there are fights, sometimes,
and knifings. Tonight, however, he doesn't care; all he
wants is red wine and a place to think, far away from the
alley. Bellyman is dead. Sure, he knows that, but he
keeps saying it anyway: Bellyman dead, Bellyman dead.
And what do Tee do now, he asks himself. Where do
Tee go?

He walks and walks along the trains, his eyes blind,
his stomach paining him, and he can't think of any reason to keep walking or to stop, either way. No answer
comes to him. Sometimes his whole face crumples and

he has to bend over for a minute or two, holding his belly, while a storm of grieving takes him over.

Finally, he just stops, leaning up against the hard cold metal of a train car and watching the sky. In a few more hours it will be morning. Everything starting to go gray. And then the sun will come up blazing and everyone will be waking up in their beds, looking around, smiling, stretching, thinking about breakfast. Everybody with someplace to go, something to do. If this was yesterday, he'd be waking up too, yawning, getting himself ready to leave the alley and scrounge up some food for old Belly-man.

The sky is still black. He lets himself slide down until he's sitting in the cold dirt. He never did find the wine, and there are no Dumpsters with any food in them way out here. Get movin', Tee, he tells himself. Nobody's goin' to bring it to you, boy.

But he doesn't move. He only sits in the dirt holding his middle as though he's been stabbed.

David has made a bed for Sylvia on the rug by the radia-tor in the living room. She notices that at the same mo-ment that she sees him, head resting against the sofa back, legs propped against the coffee table, sound asleep. She sits down quietly beside his feet on the edge of the coffee table, watching him. He's a neat sleeper—he sleeps like a cat, silently, with folded hands and closed mouth, his chest rising and falling as though he intends to stay for the rest of the night. His hair is still damp from the shower and there is a rusty streak of blood on his shirt, but aside from the somber, crushed look she saw earlier in the bathroom, he looks the same; he looks like David the rock star, the magazine-ad David who in a million years she could never know the way she knows Jan or Peter or Marushka. He is a sleeping mystery, a beautiful stranger trapped and held, momentarily, by the fact of ugly death outside her window.

She shifts; his eyes fly open, unfocused, terrified, caught in some nightmare, and he makes a sound and sits up quickly, running his hands through his hair. "God," he says, his face in his hands. "What time is it?"

"Late." Her voice is small; they have already become strangers; by tomorrow they'll pass each other in the hallway, headed for their separate practice rooms, and the hissing electric wire they held together in the alley will be dead and cold, a strange, middle-of-the-night fantasy already set aside and forgotten. She moves over to the sofa and sits down beside him. He does not move away, but he does not look at her, either.

"Did you have a good bath?" he says.

"Yes. Thank you."

Neither of them moves. She is shy, but she can't help herself; she is studying his profile like a book, trying to read what is there, trying to decipher the mystery. He's beautiful, she thinks, so he *must* be good. But a deep and joyful terror has taken hold of her; she suspects that she knows nothing, that she is not thinking again, simply trusting in the odd sense of urgency that has taken her over. He might stay; he might as easily leave.

"Well," he says. And then he turns to look at her.

She holds still, though the moment is excruciatingly long. He studies her wet hair, her forehead, cool and probably pale now, her shy eyes, hardly able to hold his, her nose, her shaking mouth. He studies her throat, following its line down into the white robe. And then he looks back into her eyes.

"I feel weird," he says simply. "Kind of . . . sick. What about you?"

She nods, thinking of the bathtub, the way she held her eyes open underwater for so long. The way she had scrubbed herself raw.

"I've never seen anybody die before."

"Me either," she whispers.

His arm lies behind her on the sofa. With his other hand, he reaches out very lightly and touches her cheek with the back of his fingers. "I should go," he says softly.

She holds still, trembling, then closes her eyes. "Don't. Stay."

The stroking fingers grow still against her cheek. He sighs. And then he is moving toward her—she can feel him, that strange male energy all around her in the air—and his mouth is on her mouth and they are kissing and kissing, hungrily, blindly, in the deep, cold recesses of the night.

In one of the brownstones, a mother is rocking her baby. It is three weeks old and she still cannot believe it has gender. She loves it more, already, than her own life. Boy or girl, what is the difference? A round head, the pinkest of scalps, the depression in the skull that flutters with each breath. Eyes of a solid dark blue, dense as marbles, that watch her unceasingly; it maps her hairline, this baby, it charts the slope of her eyebrow like a small cartographer. The tiny hand waves, a feeler testing the dense, alien air. The mouth roots at her breast.

They rock alone in the absolute silence of a sleeping house. Her disparate strengths, her handful of odd powers—these, she thinks, are drawn into perfect harmony at this moment. She has not slept through the night in weeks, yet she watches the darkness with the eyes of a hunting cat, weaving circles of magic around the infant who sucks at her breast.

Beware, she commands. Do not come closer. I would die for this child.

David and Sylvia have moved, somehow, from the sofa to the bed he arranged on the floor. She lies on her back, her lips bruised, her face wet with kissing, the white robe still cinched around her waist but the top open now, loose, like her legs. Like all of her. She lies there loose and decadent and caught in wave after wave of exhilarating warmth as David's hands move inside the furry robe. She drinks him in—his soft clean hair, his hot skin, the petal of his ear against her mouth. And then, with a hard moan, he pulls at the bathrobe tie; it comes apart like yarn; the robe falls open; cool air plays along her belly. She lies there panting, horrified and delighted, knowing he can see all of her, not caring.

He pulls away, standing up, and she starts to cry out, No!, then sees that he is undressing in the dim light and so she holds perfectly still, her arm across her forehead, watching him. His body is beautiful and compact, the body of a muscular young boy. How many times has he undressed this way for a woman? She follows every move greedily, taking him in: the way the hips are knit to the pelvis, the way the knees protrude, the smooth bands of muscle across the back, the deep dimples in the buttocks. She has never seen a penis before; now she will; she studies him in the half light—he is crouching to take off his pants, but he sees her watching him and turns toward her, straightening—and she thinks, How heavy it is! What a secret thing, in its dark nest of tangled hair.

"You've never done this before," he says, standing above her. It is not a question.

She shakes her head, mute.

He squats—she hears his knees cracking—and then slides under the sheet beside her. They lie for a moment, inches apart; they are both breathing hard and she can smell it again—the urgent energy between them. Now that the decision has been made—now that they know what they will do—everything has gone into slow motion; they have, in spite of the surging energy, all the time in the world.

He turns on his hip, propping himself up with one arm, looking down at her. His face is sweet with anticipation, the crushed look gone—he is perfectly happy at this moment, she thinks. I am making him happy, a man I don't even know. With the other hand, he slowly reaches out and begins to stroke her—shoulder, arm, breast, belly, over and over, the gentlest brushing of his fingers against her skin. She smiles up at him, but she is trembling again. I am naked in bed with a man, she thinks. And I'm glad it is him, someone who knows what to do.

She swallows, and reaches out with her foot until she has found his. His toes are warm and blunt, his foot bony. She strokes it with the bottom of hers and he lets himself down—slowly, slowly—against the length of her until they are touching, feet to collarbone. His skin is dry, almost hot; she can feel the beating of his blood. For a moment she succumbs to terror—what am I doing? how did this happen?—and then she is melting into his flesh.

His soft hair in her face; the scent of soap and cleanliness. His lips along her jawline, traveling like silent blind creatures over her throat, her neck. He breathes into her ear and she feels the tip of his tongue, his teeth against her earlobe. He is moving against her gently—in no hurry at all, but absolutely focused on every cell in her body—and she is moving with him. She has never felt anything so beautiful, so pure, and she is astounded; she never thought it would be this way. She feels herself rising out of her body onto some plane where everything is warm and thick and rich with blood. For a moment her father's face looms before her—Sylvia! he is imploring, What are you doing?—but she thinks, How can this be wrong? This is so *beautiful,* so full of love—and we're both such good people. When David breathes, she thinks she can hear words; she tries to hear what he is saying, and then she realizes he is saying her name, Sylvia, Sylvia, Sylvia, over and over.

She feels like crying again—everything is so warm, so kind—but she is aching too, yearning for something more, though she can't tell for sure what it is. Blindly, yearning, she moves her hands from his back, down,

down, to the round, strong humps of his buttocks. She is whispering too—Please, she is saying—and he nuzzles his face into her neck and pushes her legs apart with his knee.

So *this* is how it is, she thinks. Like music. And then David is suspended above her—she opens her eyes and sees him, dark against the dim light—and he is holding himself with one hand, stroking her, up and down, back and forth, in the warm place between her legs; something tells her to rise up to meet him, and she does, arching her back.

His penis, warm and blunt, noses itself inside of her, and she almost laughs in triumph; suddenly, however, there is terrible pain and she cries out, but David doesn't hear her. He is moaning himself—is he in pain, too? Hot, hot pain; she feels seared inside. She turns her head on the pillow back and forth, back and forth, biting her lips. He rocks above her, pushing himself deeper and deeper, a desperate exploration. What is he hunting for? She is almost crying, he is hurting her so badly. What is he doing? And why has she let him inside of her? His face is contorted, he pants, he is like Bellyman in the final agony. Oh God, she moans. What is happening? Are we dying?

He is clasping her, he is pulling her closer and closer. She pants with pain, she is trying not to sob. And then, suddenly, he is calling, he is calling after something disappearing on the horizon; he calls out desperately; she can hear the utter loneliness in his voice. She moves her hands on his back, holding him there. No more dying, no more dying, she thinks. I won't let you.

He is lying on her body like something newborn. His skin is wet, his hair is wet, his breath sings between his teeth in the space beside her ear. She is throbbing deep inside; her flesh is torn; she wonders if she is bleeding. She is quiet, holding him, thinking: What does this mean? She cannot move her legs; the weight of him has pinned her to the floor. They lie this way for a long time and finally the pain subsides and becomes something else—something wet and aching and beautiful.

He stirs. His voice is distant, half asleep. "Did I hurt you?" he asks.

She is quiet. What will she answer? That it was the greatest of pleasures? That it was the worst of all pains? "A little," she says. "I'm okay." A small lie, for his own good. She is still dragging her soul back into her body. She is still searching for a missing person.

"May I stay?" he murmurs into her ear. "It's close to morning anyway."

If Jan comes by to take her to breakfast. If Francine calls looking for him. If anyone sees them leaving the brownstone.

"Well," she says.

He stirs against her. Her skin flutters. "If it's a problem, I'll go," he says into her hair.

She ponders this. If he goes, she thinks, she will wake alone; she will rise in the morning and rub her eyes; she will wake from this fantastic dream. She will be Sylvia. If he stays, however. . . . Who will she be then, if he stays? At least she will have chosen this. At least it will be real.

"All right," she says.

• • •

Sylvia wakes once before dawn, a hard jerk of the heart; she has been dreaming she is falling. She looks around wildly: Whose room is this? David murmurs in his sleep, rubbing his nose against the pillow. His leg is flung across her thighs; the wiry black hair along his shins prickles against her skin. He is as warm as sun.

She turns over carefully, resting her hand on his hip. The sheets smell of sex, the room is a warm cocoon; it is though they have given birth to one another. If I had been alone tonight, she thinks.

A light wind, chill, but smelling of black earth. Seagulls crying over the bay. Bellyman spiraling slowly through endless dark water; Bellyman sounding the bottomless depths.

Book
THREE

He who learns must suffer.
And even in our sleep, pain that cannot
forget falls drop by drop upon the
heart, and in our own despair, against
our will, comes wisdom to us by the
awful grace of God.

—*Aeschylus*

CHAPTER THIRTEEN

"So," says Toft. They have just swallowed the last of their almond croissants—room service—and are sitting uncomfortably in his eighteenth-century chairs, balancing china cups and saucers on their knees and waiting for what comes next: Brandon, Peter, Sylvia— the chosen few.

Sylvia has only been to his suite one time—the day he took her on as a student—and then she was with her father, who of course did all of the talking. Her father wore a tweed jacket that day and an open-necked shirt; he looked breezy and athletic and distinctly non-lawyer-ish. A little bit, actually, like Mr. Binder. Toft looked like Toft—perhaps grumpier.

She remembers the concert Steinway in the corner of the room, and the wall behind it covered in black and white photographs. Also the busts of Bach and Beethoven, the black marble mantelpiece, the heavy white draperies, held back with swags. But the books—she had forgotten how many books. Every wall except for the photograph gallery is a bookcase, and most of the book spines are gilt-edged crumbling leather—first editions.

Toft, in a blue wingback chair, eyes the last of his croissant and sets it back on his plate. "So," he repeats, wiping his fingers on his napkin. "You are here." He shakes the napkin once, folds it, and looks up, giving Peter and Sylvia each a piercing glance.

She swallows; she guessed, as soon as he called this meeting of his students, what this is about—though she finds herself, now that her nightmare is coming true, curiously emotionless. She has been staving off the inevitable for two years, but clearly the moment has arrived; Toft is going to drop her.

Why doesn't she feel anything?

She watches Toft brushing crumbs from his pants, the famous Toft who studied with Schnabel and Godowsky, as her father is always reminding her, and she thinks of how he has terrified her for two long years. Now, it is all about to end; now she will no longer be a Toft protégée—and who *will* she be when he lets her go? No longer a child prodigy, no longer a young girl with great promise; now, she supposes, like so many others, she will simply vanish and go back home a failure. Somehow, however, that horrifying thought, which used to keep her awake hour after hour, has been completely overshadowed by the night with David.

David. It has been two days; she has not told Peter (the first time she has withheld something from him), and she has certainly not told Jan. They know about Bellyman, of course—they know about the death in the alley, the fire trucks and lights—but somehow she cannot bring herself to tell the whole truth of that night. What *is* the whole truth, anyway? She is not even sure herself.

How could she, for example, possibly explain to Jan what she did with David after a mere half hour when she had been unable, out of shyness, to kiss *him* for weeks? No, she can't talk about that night, can't even *think* about it, at least not in any coherent way, and she cannot imagine setting it out in front of other people. What would Toft say if he knew? Her father? It is like a treasure she is hoarding—something secret and powerful that other people would try to take away from her. But it wasn't *bad*, she tells herself. It was beautiful. It has changed everything for me.

She looks at Toft. She has no idea what she *will* do next—if she will have to limp back home in defeat (oh God, poor Ross), or if she will stay on at the conservatory and try to get another teacher—Miss Haupt, maybe? She has not thought yet of anything beyond this moment. She does wonder why he has chosen to do this in public. Why in front of Peter and Brandon? Though she is numb about being dropped, this aspect, at least, is degrading. And how can he do this so close to her recital? How can he do this after all her work on Opus 111—just when she is starting to make some headway? For a moment, she is stabbed with grief, thinking of her long hours at the piano, the grueling, bar-by-bar work she has put herself through in the past months.

"I hope the croissants were satisfactory," Toft says.

"Oh yes," says Brandon. "Excellent. From the hotel kitchen?" He is very relaxed; one ankle rests on the other knee; he holds his china saucer in the open palm of his hand. His hair, the color of butterscotch, sweeps away from his intelligent forehead. Well, *he* doesn't have anything to be afraid of, she thinks. Why shouldn't he look relaxed? Brandon, in fact, is going to compete in both the Kapell and the Bachauer this year, another aggressive protégé of the man who says he doesn't believe in piano competitions.

Peter is very quiet, as usual. He is wearing a red bandanna above his eyes; his black hair falls loose over his shoulders. They listen to Brandon, slanting looks at one another.

"Yes, yes," says Toft gruffly. "An excellent baker, in spite of everything." In spite of what? They wait for the revelation, but Toft is bored with the croissants and stares, for a moment, at the high ceiling with its deep, intricate molding. In spite of herself, Sylvia's eyes rise too.

"I am old," he says suddenly, leaning forward in the chair. He catches her unaware; she jerks the way she sometimes does in bed, half asleep. His hands grip the armrests; his eyes bore into hers. "In my day, I have accomplished some things."

Brandon chuckles richly, the chuckle of a man twice his age. "Boy, have you," he says. "My God." She watches him shaking his smooth head—oh, that Cornelius, such an understated guy.

Toft pushes himself up, using the armrests, until he is standing. He grimaces when he is doing this, as though a shoulder or back muscle hurts in a serious way, and in spite of herself she is briefly moved. He *is* old, she thinks. He's ancient. And no matter what I do, I just make it worse for him. Though something is gnawing at her now, something he said once that he never has explained. What was it? She remembers that it came up, this thing she can't remember, when they were talking about Hegel.

He stands there for a moment, glowering, balancing, then moves off across the silver carpet to the window, with its enormous view of Baltimore. He leans there for a long time, looking out, and then, as though the outdoor air has reached him through the glass, he begins to cough, cupping his face with the napkin he carried from the chair. Brandon starts to rise, but Toft, still coughing, waves him back into his chair. When he is finally done, he uses the napkin to wipe each eye and the corners of his mouth, then folds it in fourths and puts it in his pants' pocket. He looks both pale and angry at life; Sylvia wants nothing more than to be gone from this sumptuous, lonely suite; she wants this awful moment to be over.

"One does not like to think about death," he says, his voice still thin. He is gazing out the window, regathering lost dignity. "One does not enjoy thinking of decay." Outside the glass, the air is very blue, the sun bright; it is the youngest of mornings.

Finally, he turns back to them. His hands, she can see, are still trembling from the coughing. "The important thing," he says, "is that it all goes on. That we do not take ourselves so very seriously, do you see what I am saying? Because you and you and you"—he points to each of them, his finger wavering in the air—"are nothing in the face of history."

She is mesmerized; she cannot help herself. She

thought she had it figured out, why he had asked them to his suite. But this version of Toft—the inspired teacher—is not what she expected.

"You, young Brandon," he says, still pointing with his trembling finger. "You are very good, especially with Bach."

Brandon looks startled—Toft never gives compliments—then drops his eyes with charming modesty. "Oh well . . ." he says, shaking his head.

"Beware," says Toft. "Beware. You are only one of a long line, my son. Alone, you are nothing. Never think you are more."

Sylvia, and Peter beside her, hold very still. What is going on? Brandon is his favorite.

"You are all so young, you cannot possibly see it. But we are worthless, we musicians. Only the music itself— only *this*, do you understand me?" He glares at them; they drop their eyes.

"Ah well," he says, when no one speaks. His shoulders slump forward; he sounds defeated and suddenly bored. "I am very old and leaving this world soon."

"No . . ." Brandon says emotionally, but Toft waves him off.

"I can only give so much these days."

Here it comes after all, thinks Sylvia. Oh God. She folds her hands in her lap, her mouth dry.

Toft sighs. He looks very small standing there in his black shoes on the wide silver carpet. "What do you think I must do? You tell me."

No one says a word. Sylvia feels the tears rising in her throat; he is staring at her; he wants her to be the one to say it. Poor Mr. Toft, I understand. You no longer have the strength to teach an idiot like me. I quit; you're free. But first—first you have to tell me what it was you expected from me.

Peter stands and clears his throat ceremoniously. What is *he* doing?

"This is probably as good a time as any to say this," he begins. "I was going to wait a few weeks, but . . ."

Toft looks confused. Sylvia, startled, turns her head to watch Peter.

"I'm leaving," Peter says simply. "I'm dropping out of the program."

No one says a word. Toft moves to his chair and sits down slowly, groping at the armrests.

"My family," Peter says. He is uncomfortable; she can see it in the set of his shoulders, the way he is holding his head. His black hair ripples down his back. "Well, they've always wanted me to go into law. And they're paying the bills, so . . ." He shrugs. "Anyway. Maybe this will work out better for you, Mr. Toft."

Toft glares at him as though he has been double-crossed. It was supposed to be me, Sylvia thinks. He wanted to get rid of me. And then suddenly it hits her: Peter is leaving.

"I must say I am quite surprised," says Toft in a thin voice. "You have great potential with Beethoven, Peter. A young man who can interpret the *Hammerklavier* in the way you do . . . well, I must say I am both shocked and disappointed."

Peter leaving? Suddenly, her numbness is gone; she wants to cry out, "No!" Toft wants *me* to leave. *No*, Peter, what are you *doing*?

"Well," says Peter. "I appreciate . . . you know. And

I'll miss this place when I'm gone." He tries a dignified smile.

Toft glowers at him. "I'm very tired," he says abruptly. "I must ask you all to go."

They get up immediately, even Brandon, and Toft turns and walks from the room before they are out of the door. In the hall outside the suite, Brandon gives Peter a long speculative look. *"Tough break,"* he says. "I always figured we'd be going head to head someday at the Tchaikovsky, but—well, *c'est la vie,* right?" He shrugs and saunters off toward the elevator, his hands in his pocket.

"Peter," she says, anguished. "What, what did you do?"

He looks down at her, his usual serene Peter look, and her heart feels clenched when she thinks of him leaving her life, leaving her alone in this miserable city with such a miserable old man. "You should have done what he wanted," she says. "You should have let him pressure *me* into quitting."

Peter puts his hands on her shoulders.

"Sylvia, listen to me now. He's a jerk, we both know it." His hands are warm; he shakes her gently. "He's a complete egomaniac. But he's a genius, too. You know that. What, are you going to throw away your chance to study with the great Toft?" He smiles at her. She doesn't laugh.

"But you tried to get me to quit before, Peter."

"Yeah," he says. "You can quit anytime *you* want to quit. Just don't do it for *him.*"

"But how can I stay on with him now? He's going to *hate* me—we screwed up his plan."

He tightens his grip on her shoulders; she closes her eyes; David has just moved through her in a warm flash. "Look at me, Syl," Peter says. "Listen to me. What's more important—Toft's little comfort zone or Beethoven? You're coming along with 111—you're *getting* there. Nothing else matters."

"But what about *you*? How can you say that? You're better than *I* am, Peter, and you're giving it up."

He goes silent, looking away. His fingers bore into her shoulders; she has never seen him so upset, though he is doing his best to hide it. "And that's why you can't," he says finally, in his quietest voice.

Outside, the morning is beautiful. Sylvia and Peter stand on the sidewalk outside Toft's hotel watching an old man across the street painting a small green door. Cars drive by slowly, their windows down. Mothers push strollers along the sidewalk; children run screaming, as though they will take flight, and the blue air billows against them, tossing their hair. People, their legs, in shorts, a shy winter white, hang their rugs from clotheslines strung between the brownstones. False spring has arrived.

Sylvia breathes in the fresh warm air; it is only February 3, but it feels almost like summer. She thinks of home, the lake smells of late May and early June. Fishing in the bass boat with Ross, her hand trailing in the murky water; Anne in the garden stringing up pole beans. She waits for the wave of homesickness to hit her, but the scene slowly fades, leaving no pain in its wake. Home is beautiful, home is safe—so why does she no longer want to be there?

Peter is very quiet. If she didn't know him so well, she would think he looked bewildered. What had he said in there? *I wasn't planning to do this for a couple more weeks. . . .* So perhaps he hadn't even thought out yet what he was going to say, how he was going to announce this thing to Toft, but when he had seen she was in danger . . . "Thank you, Peter," she says humbly.

"For what?"

"You know."

He shrugs. "Just promise I won't ever see you on TV playing Liszt."

She laughs, her throat tight, and says, "I'm starving— I'll treat, okay?"

In the Market, the crowds are thick and happy, drunk on sunshine, the mild air, the first crack in the cold fortress of winter. Coats are lying everywhere, across the backs of chairs, in piles on the grimy floor. The essence of the Market—crabcakes, chowder, Polish sausage; baklava, ravioli, ale—rises in steamy clouds. Cooks in soiled aprons with pencils behind their ears lean over crowded countertops to take the shouted orders. Children wander through forests of legs, balloons tied to their wrists. Mothers lean back in their chairs, hair hanging loose and windblown, sweaters open, knees apart, with cups of cappuccino in their hands. The city dances in the mild morning air.

Peter and Sylvia find a place to sit against the wall, holding paper bowls of fish chowder over their laps. Slowly it is sinking in; he is leaving, just like Marushka. And she will be left behind with Toft, with Jan—with David.

"How long ago did you decide?" she asks him.

"Christmas."

"You never said a word."

"I wasn't sure I would do it."

"Why *are* you doing it, Peter? I'm not trying to . . . I'm asking for myself."

He takes two calm spoonfuls of chowder, thinking. He is slowly returning to his usual self. "To do this—to spend your life on Beethoven or whoever," he says finally, "—you can't let things pull at you. It's all or nothing. You have to cut everything else out and concentrate totally." He runs a napkin over his mouth and sets down his bowl. "But they can't help themselves—they've always been in the background, pulling away."

"Your family?"

He nods. "I told you, they don't give a damn about music. And it's their money . . ."

"Could you stay here and work?"

"Could you?"

"Not and put in six hours a day on the piano."

"Exactly."

"I feel so bad for you, Peter."

"Don't."

"But you're so *good.*"

"Sometimes good just ain't enough," he says. "Things get in the way. Life's tough, Syl."

"Are you taking your piano?"

He smiles at her. "What do you think?"

"When are you . . . when do you have to leave?"

"This has been coming for a while. I applied to Princeton last year—I can start spring quarter, right after Easter."

"Oh, Peter—*soon*."

He nods. "I'm going up to look for a place pretty quick. But I'll be back—can't miss you playing old 111, can I?"

She puts her hand on his arm, starts to say, Peter, there's something I have to tell you, but stops herself. Why does he need to know about David right now? She is so used to bringing Peter her life, laying it out on the table before him, waiting obediently for him to solve her problems. But this is *mine*, she thinks. And it's time for me to grow up, damnit.

"I'm going after crabcakes," she says, before she can make a fool of herself. "Be right back," and she gets to her feet and pushes her way into the crowd, bumping elbows and shoulders.

Katerina Haupt is perishing of hunger. She stands before the open refrigerator searching the shelves under the little yellow light. A bowl of sliced carrots in water, left-over pasta with pesto sauce, three pieces of chicken Kiev—oh was that good—and the last of a blueberry cheesecake. She ponders for some time, finally opting for the dessert, which would go best, she thinks, with a nice cup of French vanilla coffee and whipped cream.

The cheesecake is delicious—it's best on the third day—and while she is eating and sipping her coffee, she mentally reviews her Library of Congress recital program. Cornelius Toft, of course, will hate what she has chosen. Don't forget I'm really Russian in my soul, she often has to remind him; don't force me into that cold German mold of yours.

She is happy, though, with what she will play: a Field nocturne to start (she loves Field, that wild alcoholic in a bearskin cloak), then Busoni's "Variations on a Chopin Prelude" (Cornelius cannot abide either composer), Scriabin's Sonata No. 4 in F-sharp Major, Grieg's Norwegian Peasant Dances, and finally Schumann's F-sharp Minor Sonata. The Scriabin will knock them sideways. They don't imagine I can do triple fortissimos anymore.

Scriabin. She smiles, knowing she will fool them. For nothing about her has ever looked serious—the way she dresses, her coiled gray-blond braids, her confusing apartment, more like a greenhouse than someplace to live. Good old Katerina, they think. They have no idea how many hours she spends at the piano each day, how much she loves to practice—much more, indeed, than she has ever enjoyed performing.

She swallows the last bite of cheesecake and brings the napkin to her mouth. So what if I'm too heavy? she thinks. Food gives me strength.

Moon Ja will be home in less than two weeks; she called Katerina from Los Angeles to say she was cutting short the last leg of her trip. "My mother won't forgive me for leaving early, but I'm beat. And, Katerina, I need to get to a gynecologist. Could you set it up for me?"

"Well, of course. My friend Margaret is excellent. Are you all right?"

"Yes. Though I feel like I've been having an affair with Dracula."

Katerina laughed, but felt an icy shock pass through her at the same time. Moon Ja ill? In all the years they have known each other, she has never seen Moon Ja so much as falter. It's her incredible *will*, she thinks. And she's so disciplined . . .

So now she has two friends to worry about—Moon Ja and Jan, who has fallen very hard, it seems, for Cornelius's little student, the one with the frightened deer eyes and all that hair.

She sighs and goes back to the stove for another cup of coffee. This will all take some thinking.

Peter is sleeping against the wall when Sylvia finally returns, his head resting crookedly against his shoulder, the empty paper bowl cupped in his hands. Around him they swirl, the children leashed to balloons, the mothers, the workmen with their girls. His bandanna has slipped; he looks like a pirate. His eyelashes are a dark, stiff fan against the polished hardwood of his cheek.

She watches him for a long time and it seems that he is sliding, before her eyes, into a great river of children, balloons, bright sweaters; soon his bandanna will be nothing but a tiny red dot on the horizon as he is tumbled with the rest of them into the sea.

CHAPTER FOURTEEN

Sylvia and Colette had talked about getting help—Peter? Jan, maybe?—but then decided they could do the move alone. Colette has few possessions; she is as neat and simple as a nun. "All I've got is this stuff," she tells Sylvia as they stand awkwardly facing each other on the front doorstep of Colette's old place. She gestures behind her at the small pile of bags and boxes on the red rug.

"We can carry that ourselves," Sylvia says, thinking, What have I gotten myself into? I don't even know this person, not really. What if Marushka comes back? What if David wants to stay over again? It has been a week since their night together; he has not called and she is slowly going crazy. And now that she has committed herself to this arrangement—it was she who called Colette, after all—she is wondering if she's made a mistake.

Colette seems, if possible, even tenser than Sylvia; she doesn't say a word during the entire four-block hike. She does not relax at all, in fact, until she has finally installed herself in Marushka's old room, her bags and boxes spread out around her. And then she ventures furtively into the hallway, the bathroom, the kitchen, inspecting everything as though she's never seen it before. Sylvia, in her bedroom, can hear her picking things up and putting them down, opening cupboard doors, flushing the toilet.

From a practical standpoint, Colette's moving in makes sense: Sylvia cannot continue to pay the rent alone, but will not call her father for help; in fact, ever since Marushka was in the hospital and her father threatened to come to Baltimore to "handle things" for her, she's carefully avoided talking to her parents at all. She's noticed that even though she loves them and misses them, their phone calls (particularly her father's) leave her drained. She finds that in spite of their loving encouragement, she is on the defensive much of the time—and afterward, little Sylvia, who these days must run so hard to keep up, lies exhausted in a heap on the floor, weeping.

Now, of course, there are things she cannot ever tell them.

Colette, too, is saving money—for Juilliard in the fall. It's done, Sylvia thinks. Colette has already moved in; stop worrying about it. This is weird, though. Some stranger loose in the apartment.

And then she goes back to thinking about David, thinking about the smooth hard naked chest, the blooming heat of his skin against her arms. *Why* has he not called? She has been almost sick for a week, thinking through every moment of their time together. But it is already going; she cannot feel it the way it was, can only summon a memory now of murmured words and dim light and the way his hand looked resting on her arm. How tall is he, really? And the hair on his arms—is it straight or curly?

"Sylvia, do you know this toaster doesn't work?"

"I know," she calls, and she hears pain in her own voice. David, David, where are you? Why don't you *call* me?

"Are you planning to get another one? I'm used to having toast for breakfast."

Sylvia is silent. A toaster—who cares about a toaster right now? Listen, she almost says, I made a mistake. This isn't going to work.

She looks down at her hands. Her fingers lie quiet and miserable on the rounded caps of her knees. She has not even been able to practice since David left the apartment; she sits at the piano in the drafty practice room, her hands resting on the cold keys, and thinks about him. Sometimes, however, even the thought of David is gone, and then her mind, so recently bursting with Beethoven and Toft, goes perfectly blank—there is nothing within her at all. She is so miserable she has not been able to eat. Her stomach aches quietly; she lies awake in bed at night.

"Sylvia," calls Colette. She is inspecting the refrigerator now; Sylvia can hear jars rattling, and the vegetable tray, which always sticks.

"What?"

"We're out of food."

"I know. I haven't been . . . too hungry lately." She goes back to staring at the wall.

"Why not?" says Colette from the doorway. She

looks shy but defiant, as though she suspects she is intruding but chooses not to care. Her brown eyes inspect the room, every inch, though when she sees that Sylvia has noticed, she drops them sheepishly. "Are you sick?" she says to her feet.

"No, not really." Sylvia looks around at what Colette has found so interesting: stacks of books against the white wall, her term paper on the chansons spread out over the wooden floor, three African violets by the window, the pillows from her bed lying on the rag rug, the Thelonius Monk poster Peter gave her for Christmas hanging over the bed. The white window with no curtains; the red bricks of the building across the narrow alley.

"Are you . . . are you wishing I wasn't here?"

Sylvia looks at her quickly. Colette is still staring at her feet. Her narrow shoulders are set tightly, and Sylvia can see the top of her head with its multitude of cornrows.

"No, no," Sylvia says, putting out her hand. "No, I'm sorry, Colette. Really. I'm just . . . weird right now. I'm having sort of a problem."

Colette looks up. They stare at each other for a long moment. She's beautiful, Sylvia thinks automatically, in spite of being distracted by her aching stomach. She's like one of those polished wood carvings, but smaller and sweeter.

"You're sure?" says Colette. "Because I don't want to be here if you . . ."

"No, honest. It's me—I think I'm going a little nuts right now." Horrified, she feels her eyes filling with tears, the tears spilling over onto her cheeks. She holds her face rigid, does not raise her hand to wipe them away. Maybe Colette won't notice, she thinks.

"Oh," says Colette in a softer voice. "Hey, now."

Sylvia takes a long, shuddering breath. More tears spill over.

"Sylvia, he's not worth it."

She blinks hard. How does Colette know about this? "Who do you mean?"

Colette drops her eyes again. "I'm sorry, I shouldn't have said anything."

"Who are you talking about?" The tears are disappearing; she is suddenly becoming angry.

"Well, David," says Colette simply. "It's kind of . . . around, you know. Brandon's been talking to some people. And then Francine—remember her? David's girlfriend?—well, anyway, she's pretty upset . . ."

Sylvia is so horrified she cannot speak. She just stares at Colette.

"Well, I thought you'd probably heard it, you know. From somebody."

"No."

"Oh, Sylvia, I'm *sorry*."

"It's not your fault. I'm glad you told me." Damn Brandon. Damn Francine. Damn everybody in town. *Everybody*—Jan, Toft—oh God. Toft! She takes another long breath. She might go crazy after all. This is not how it is supposed to be.

"Do you . . . do you want me to make you a cup of tea? Something?" Colette is shifting from foot to foot—she is *so* sensitive, Sylvia thinks—and looks, if anything, more unhappy than she has since she arrived.

Sylvia takes a third enormous breath, lets it out

slowly. What can she do? There's nothing she *can* do—
the word is out, has been out for some time, and she
hasn't even known it. "No," she says, trying to sound
calmer. "No—I really *haven't* eaten in a couple of days.
I'm starving to death. Let's go down to the White Tower
and get some pancakes."

"Pancakes?"

"Yes," says Sylvia, and suddenly she can smell them—
the enormous fluffy hotcakes she had that night with
Jan, soaked in butter and berry syrup. So everybody
knows what she did, that private secret act she has been
hugging to herself so jealously.

"Okay. Sure. I'll get my shoes on." Colette pads away
down the hall, and Sylvia pulls herself off the bed,
searching for her hairbrush and as usual not finding it.
What *if* her father finds out? He could—he knows her so
well, he might hear it in her voice. His daughter, the
brilliant young pianist, sleeping with someone she
hardly knows? Someone who has, as her mother would
say, "been around the block"? She can imagine the looks
on their faces. Ross's hands jammed into his pockets as
he tries to be a modern dad, a with-it parent, who nevertheless wants to kill them both. I'm not paying a fortune
to send you to Baltimore to screw around, she can hear
him thinking. Goddammit.

She cannot find the brush. She pulls her hair together
and ties it at the back of her neck; it floats away from her
back. Stupid hair, she thinks.

Out on the street, it is once again false spring. The air
is mild, laden with the sea, though there are horsetails in
the sky, and sometimes a cool gust of wind. The air is
brilliant blue, the old buildings shining in the bright

light. As soon as the air hits her face, she feels somehow better—cleaner, anyway.

"Minneapolis looks like this," she says to Colette, "in May."

"Minneapolis?"

"Where I'm from."

Colette looks at her sideways, smiling. "I heard," she says, "that there was a music company there with *Gaspard de la Nuit* painted on the outside wall."

"Yes, Schmitt's. My dad used to drive me past it all the time."

"I'm from New Orleans."

"I know."

"Where did you hear that?"

Colette has a skipping walk, light and, it seems to Sylvia, inherently joyous. Why is she always so quiet, then?

"Oh," Sylvia answers, "I can't remember who told me, but I heard that your dad is Jackie Beauchamp and that you grew up with all these famous jazz musicians but that you're still nice."

Colette stops in the middle of the sidewalk. Sylvia stops too.

"You heard about my dad?" Colette says.

"Well, *everybody* knows, I think. Aren't you proud of it? You *should* be."

"It's not that I'm not proud. That's not it—don't ever think that." Colette looks angry suddenly, as though she has been through this a million times. She is staring off at the building across the street, her shoulders once again as rigid as when she first got to the apartment.

Sylvia puts her hand on Colette's arm. "Look," she

says. "I believe you. And I'm glad you're my new roommate, okay? I've been really lonely—you can't believe
how lonely. And nobody to talk to, especially right
now."

Colette turns back to her. The sunlight catches the
planes of her face, her deep brown eyes. "Good," she
says simply. "Let's go eat." Somewhere in the next
block, she adds, "You can talk to *me* if you want. Not
that I know a lot. I mean, about this kind of stuff."

Sylvia smiles at her and touches her shoulder. They
are passing George Washington. She looks up, and suddenly, though she is still smiling for Colette, she is aching all over. Oh, David, David. The way you whispered
my *name*. She thinks of him lying across her, breathless
and sweating, his curls in her face. She looks down the
street, blindly, and gasps out loud. There, down on the
next block, wearing a trenchcoat and carrying a briefcase, dark hair shining in the sun. . . . She stops, her hand
at her mouth, until she realizes it is not him, it could not
possibly be him—David does not carry a briefcase, he
carries a violin.

And will it be like this forever?

Is this is a sickness?

Yes, she thinks. I hate this.

Moon Ja and her mother sit at the kitchen table in the
small house in Los Angeles, drinking coffee. The house
is empty, all the relatives long gone—even her father is
out for the afternoon.

Her mother sips slowly, preoccupied, and Moon Ja
watches her face, the procession of memories and con-

cerns and small disasters that passes over it between
swallows. I came from her, Moon Ja thinks. She was
once young, lying in a hospital bed in Korea, waiting for
me to be born.

She watches her mother with great fondness, studying
the round face, the filigree of lines around the eyes, the
dark hair in its 1940s waves. She loves her mother—her
entire family, really, but especially her mother—with an
unwavering loyalty, a deep and distant admiration.
What a pack of strangers, though. The paradox of her
youth: a close and loving family, herself the foundling,
the crow in the chicken's nest.

I have no family, she thinks. The thought is sobering
but not sad. She has known it in her bones since early
childhood. Nobody in this house speaks music, for one
thing. And nobody is driven with such intensity; nobody
has the iron will she takes so for granted.

Where did I get all this? she wonders, watching the
kind and daily face, the small, hardened hand holding
the coffee cup. Where did I even get my fingers?

For many years when she was young, Moon Ja
dreamed about dead soldiers, true—but once she
dreamed a different, darker dream, in its own way just as
upsetting. In it, a strange woman, tall and with long
hands, carried the tiny Moon Ja through the night, the
wide sleeves of her dress fluttering like enormous moths.
Not another mother—not even a human woman. Someone—some*thing*—however, more truly hers than anyone in the family who claimed her.

"I have to leave early, Mom," she says now, steeling
herself against the small cry of protest, the urgent ques-

tions. "I know you thought I was staying longer, but I've got things to do back home."

Katerina Haupt stands before her window, looking out at the marvelous day. On the stereo Rubinstein is playing Mozart's K. 467, which is one of her longtime favorites, especially the lovely cantilena. She has always loved Rubinstein, his openness and balance, the joy with which he approached the piano. She saw him play in Berlin before the war, but was too young and too shy then to meet him, though his performance left her singing inside for days. It was not until he was nearly ninety, half blind, that she got her chance to tell him face to face what he had meant to her all her life.

A cold March night in New York, an enormous crowd, a brilliant rendition of Schumann's *Carnaval*— and afterward she had gone backstage at Carnegie Hall to greet him. He was wonderful—he'd kissed her hand and complimented her on her old Decca recordings, which he claimed to admire deeply. She found herself blushing—she was fifty-two, for heaven's sake—and wished that she had done this years ago: made the pilgrimage to the feet of one of her gods.

Who are her gods now? Does she have any left? Certainly, Cornelius's best recordings still have the power to move her. And Moon Ja playing Schubert can literally raise the hair on the back of her neck. But neither, it seems to her, is fully human in the sense that Rubinstein was. Neither knows much about joy.

She watches a lean cat flash across the street and dart down the sidewalk. A car rolls over its melting shadow.

Neither Moon Ja nor Cornelius has any idea about
. . . what? What *is* it that is missing in her two best
friends? She thinks hard. They are both highly accomplished, brilliantly talented performers. Cornelius, in
addition, has made an international name for himself as
a pedagogue, while year after year *she* picks up the students he rejects. And when Moon Ja, still stunning at
forty, walks across the stage in one of those silk dresses
of hers . . . Katerina feels the jealous worm begin to wig-
gle. Is she even capable of thinking about her friends
objectively?

It seems to her, however, that what she admired in
Rubinstein was the peculiarly enthusiastic nature of his
playing—his flaws and extravagances as well as his moments of genius. His flair and his willingness to risk failure, even at ninety-two. His profound love of life. He
was clearly a man who *felt*.

Is that it? The ability to feel things? Is love the missing
ingredient in Moon Ja and Cornelius?

Somehow, this answer seems simplistic—but what
else could it be? Has Cornelius ever loved *anyone*? Has
Moon Ja? And how can you know joy unless you love?

Ah, Katerina, she thinks—you are such a romantic.
You are living in the wrong century; you should have
been born while Brahms was still pining away over Clara
Schumann and Liszt tossing back his long golden hair.

Here I am, a fat old lady, mooning about love.

She looks at her watch. Two o'clock—almost time for
a piece of pecan pie and a cup of coffee.

Besides, she reminds herself, *Jan* is in love, and now
there is a new wrinkle to the story, a hitch he will not tell

her about. She sees it, however, in his long silences, his sorrowful eyes, his halting sentences: a joyful young man collapsing under the weight of love. So perhaps she is wrong; perhaps Moon Ja and Cornelius are the smart ones, perhaps one should just throw up a wall, barricade oneself against pain and joy, all at the same time . . .

She has noticed, over the years, that these internal discussions of hers never move in anything but a circular pattern. Round and round she goes, always in the same groove, like blood circulating through the heart. Passion versus reason, emotion versus logic, love versus cold discipline . . . I'm lazy, she thinks. I'd rather just live than think. I'd rather have a piece of pecan pie than go around in this endless circle.

Except for the quiet pull that never ceases, the compulsion that draws her back, over and over again, to the piano in the corner, like someone hunting for treasure.

When Sylvia steps outside, the first thing she sees are the roses, a dozen of them, yellow, lying across the front steps. She leans over slowly and picks them up, searching for a card, but there is none. Instead, she sees that the yellow is already edged in brown, the buds slightly withered. There is an enormous yellow bow around them and white paper lace stained with something that looks like coffee grounds. David? Her heart contracts; she looks up and down the street but sees no one.

Suddenly, she leans forward, sniffing. Yes. The faint smell of decay—the flowers must have come from the garbage can.

She starts to thrust them away from her, but she

catches a glimpse of something out of the corner of her eye. A shadow in the alleyway, someone large, moving back out of sight. Of course. The big bald one, Bellyman's friend—Lee? Was that his name? She blushes, not knowing what to do, then she shifts the bouquet in her arms once more and opens the door to the downstairs entry, carrying her roses up to the apartment.

CHAPTER FIFTEEN

Sylvia floats through her days in a fog, struggling to concentrate during lessons, struggling to focus during practice. She is unusually tired and, at times, feels disconnected from her own body. When she does remember to think about her recital, she imagines it to be a movie, due to open soon, starring someone other than herself.

She never thinks of David anymore—not specifically, anyway—not as David. Instead, she ponders over a time, already long gone, when she stumbled upon perfect beauty and then somehow lost it. What she feels is not a specific grief or longing, but something much more overwhelming and pervasive; she wakens each day to the knowledge that she is undergoing a certain kind of death, a bright, galloping decay of the self. Why? she wonders. Surely not everyone goes through this. And what will be left of me when this is over?

She has forgotten almost everything she had once figured out about Opus 111. She has stopped reading books about Beethoven. Toft has completely lost patience with her. She does not return her parents' calls; soon one or both will be flying to Baltimore to find out what is wrong, but she cannot even muster up enough energy to worry about *that*.

Jan, however, still has the power to break her heart. He is so kind to her; he waits for her each night after practice and walks her home in the darkness, often without speaking. She wonders every time she is with him if he knows, and if he *does* know, how he can be so gentle with her, so forgiving. How terrible—and yet, how much worse if he *doesn't* know and somehow finds out. Because, she thinks, the fact is that I would do it again in a minute. If David showed up at my door one night, even after all this, I would let him in . . . and yet *Jan* is the one who cares for me. Jan is my friend. It isn't fair—I should tell him.

But she can't. She *can't*. When he leaves her at her door each night, she is filled with guilt.

One thing, however, has changed; she never cries these days—not for joy, not for sorrow, not for Beethoven, not for herself. Not even, in spite of all her guilt, for Jan. She does not know what has happened to her— why, after all these years, she should have lost her tendency to weep at the slightest provocation—but she chooses to look upon this development, at least, as a sign of maturity. What is there, after all, worth crying for?

Does Jan know? If he does, he has never said so, never even hinted. She is grateful to him, as a cat is grateful to the steady legs of its owner. She takes what she needs— the soothing voice, the comforting presence on the long walk home in the dark—and leaves the rest behind.

Only once in a while, when she cannot avoid it, she

looks directly into those sad, beautiful, patient eyes and wonders, What does he *really* think of me?

Moon Ja is home, the Asian tour behind her. She managed to escape L.A. without her mother guessing that something was wrong, though she got some speculative glances, particularly when she went to her room each day to take a nap. She is very tired, bone tired, and now that she is home, she can allow herself for the first time to give in to some honest fear.

Her good old friend Katerina picked her up at the airport, gave her a hug, installed her in the ancient Peugeot, and is now driving in companionable silence, letting her readjust to the Washington landscape. And waiting, no doubt, for her to open up; being on tour always intensifies the public Moon Ja Koh and diminishes the private one.

"Seoul was really something," Moon Ja says finally. "I didn't think it would hit me that way."

"How so?"

She stares out the window at the brushy winter trees along the river. "The fact that I didn't recognize it, I guess. I kept thinking it would look like home, but it didn't."

Katerina nods, gripping the wheel. Not a relaxed driver, especially on the Beltway, where, she told Moon Ja once, she has nightmares about smashing into some congressman or vice-president. How old *is* she now? Moon Ja wonders. Well, over sixty, for sure—old enough to be my mother.

"It's a beautiful country, though," she adds. "I did the

tourist thing, visited all the temples . . . I looked for the house where we lived when I was a child.''

"Was it there?''

"No.''

Katerina glances at her. "It's very strange, isn't it? Surreal.''

Moon Ja nods. Surreal. A good word for it.

"The same thing happened to me when I finally got back to Berlin from Geneva. I told you about that, didn't I? My parents sent me off during the war to keep me safe. Only five years, but everything had changed. It was overwhelming. It was like someone had taken away the first sixteen years of my life.''

"The bombing?''

Katerina nods, watching her rearview mirror. "And my parents. They were just . . . gone. And no one could ever tell me what happened.''

"My God, Katerina. You never told me that.''

"Oh well.'' She shrugs and smiles. "There was so much of that back then. People disappearing. Neighborhoods wiped out. You know what I mean.''

"Yes. I didn't feel good in Seoul—I kept thinking about that long freezing winter after the war.''

Katerina has her blinker on now, is edging around an old Plymouth that is going even slower than they are. She is leaning over the wheel, checking the relative position of her right bumper to the Plymouth's left taillight. I should have offered to drive, Moon Ja thinks. "You know what was weird,'' she says when they have safely negotiated the lane change. "What's weird was how I *felt* in Asia. As though there was something I was supposed to be getting and I wasn't. It was frustrating."

Katerina says, "Did I ever tell you about the time I finally got to see Zhmerinka?"

"Where?"

"It's in Ukraine, where my parents were born. They got out during the Revolution and went to Berlin, which is why I was raised as a good little German girl. They even changed our name to help me fit in better." She smiles.

"I don't think so," says Moon Ja. She is suddenly exhausted, longing for her own bed, her cats, her cymbidiums. She stifles a yawn.

"Well, I didn't get to the Soviet Union until, I guess, 1975 or so. And I'd never realized it was that important to me until I was already there. But then I had to see it. I had to see my grandfather's farm, the church, all of it." She falls silent.

Moon Ja is thinking of her piano, the window where she practices, her fabulous view of Georgetown. She was expecting to be more excited than she is. Home. She says, "And what happened?"

"It was gone too. Nobody could tell me anything."

They stop talking. Katerina swerves around a cranberry-colored Mercedes that is chugging to a smoky stop at the side of the Beltway. For a moment they can smell nothing but diesel fumes.

"I made you the appointment," says Katerina. "It's for Thursday—I hope that's all right."

"Fine," says Moon Ja. "Thanks."

"How are you?" Katerina is watching her face. The

Peugeot slows to a crawl. People are braking behind them.

"Drive," says Moon Ja. "I'm fine. Just tired and wanting to be home."

"Really? No other symptoms?"

"No. Just the bleeding. And having to take naps all the time."

"Well," says Katerina. She puts her foot on the gas. They lurch forward. "Well, I think you'll appreciate Margaret. She's wonderful."

Eleven o'clock at night and Sylvia is sitting at the piano, forcing herself to continue with the second movement of Ravel's *Sonatine*. She has played this beautiful minuet through six times already, as though by rote, and though the piece is lovely, she has become deaf to the loveliness. It is an exercise, nothing more; the *Fantasiestücke* and the Scarlatti sonatas have become the same. She has not touched Opus 111 for three days.

So even music has lost its power.

Suddenly, for the first time, she is truly frightened at what is happening to her. If she loses music, what will be left? Music has always been there, the rock on which her life is built. I *have* to get over this, she thinks.

She stops playing, closes her eyes, allows her forehead to come to rest against the piano. The wood is cool and slick. She remembers her vision of Beethoven striding about the messy studio with the terrible ringing in his ears. She raises her head, lets her hands fall to the keyboard and then, without thinking, begins Chopin's Nocturne No. 19 in E Minor, which, she has often thought, speaks more directly than any other piece she knows to the unutterable longing she has always felt in the presence of beauty.

The nocturne does not fail her. Her fingers sing; she feels herself beginning to calm, to soften; for a moment her eyes, so stubbornly dry during these past weeks, actually fill. She thinks of her old friend Chopin dying young. She thinks of herself, a child prodigy under the careful tutelage of Miss Selkirk and her parents, and of how, until the night with David, she has always been under someone else's direction.

The piece moves on under its own power.

He was only seventeen when he wrote this, she thinks. Three years younger than I am, and he already *knew*.

Halfway through she realizes something else, something she has never thought of before: that there are times when playing what she *truly* loves is not a luxury but a necessity. David aside, she has been working too long and too hard on her recital program; she has burned herself up in the daily grind.

Well then, for tonight, at least, she is done with Ravel.

Tonight is for Chopin.

The alley is very quiet; nobody there but Tee. Earlier, there was a poker game; some fool flashed a knife and everybody took off, everybody but him. He's wearing his jacket and Bellyman's old blue hat, but he still feels cold, all the way through. How many winters has he been on the streets? He's lost count. The older he gets, the more he dreads them. The long cold nights, and him hunched up alone with his back to the bricks.

He stares out from under the brim of the blue hat into the darkness, thinking about the girl with the wild hair who lives in the apartment above.

She took the roses; he watched her. She didn't know *what* to think. Don't be scared, girl, he was saying to himself. I ain't no rich man—jus' wanted to *give* you somethin'. Don' mean nothin' but a thank you.

By the time Jan leaves Sylvia at her door it is almost 1:00 A.M., but the hour and a half with Chopin has left her invigorated, as though it is morning instead of the middle of the night—as though, perhaps, she is beginning to awaken from a deep slumber that has gone on too long. She tiptoes down the hall; Colette's bedroom door is cracked open, her room dark; she must have been in bed for hours, but it is hard to tell. Unlike Marushka, Colette is a silent sleeper; she rarely even turns over during the night. Sylvia listens . . . yes, she can hear a gentle, regular breathing coming from the bed.

She moves quietly back down the hall to the kitchen, finds herself an apple and puts on the kettle for tea, then sits down at the table to think. You are a talented girl, Toft told her, but you do not know how to think. Well, she has certainly proven *that* these past few weeks; she has not had a rational thought in her head for days—nothing but grief or sickness or whatever it is you call this kind of suffering.

For the first time since David, she would like to talk to someone wise about what happened. Peter, of course. He has been out of town looking for an apartment in New Jersey and is now in San Francisco visiting his family—the same people who are pulling him away from music. She wonders how he does that—visits, with love, the parents who are forcing him to give *up* what he loves. But Peter is phenomenal; he always has a way to do what other people can't; he has a way of looking at life that makes him strong.

Does she have his phone number in San Francisco? She gets up from the table, still chewing her apple, and searches her address book—yes! And it is only—what?— ten o'clock there? She dials.

He answers. They talk. And though he is three thousand miles away, she can imagine him lying on his back on a futon—does he have a futon in California?—eyes closed and one hand behind his head, and she suddenly realizes how much she has missed his dispassionate calm in the midst of this emotional storm she's been living through. Yes, she will tell him, but first they will catch up.

She says, "My recital's almost here. One more month."

"Are you ready?"

"Are you kidding? Toft won't even speak to me anymore. He just comes in and stands there shaking his head when I play."

"But I thought you figured out some stuff with Opus 111."

"I *did*. But I can't do it in front of *him*."

"Why not?"

"I don't know."

"Syl," says Peter after a long pause. "What's up?"

She bows her head, searching for the right words,

calm words, but nothing comes to her. "It's hard to talk about it over the phone," she says finally.

Peter is quiet, waiting. He's like that, she thinks. Careful not to interfere. When she remains silent, he says, "I'll be back soon."

"I know."

Another long silence. The refrigerator kicks on, humming in the darkness. She twists a curl around one finger, cutting off the circulation. The fingertip turns bright pink.

"Someone sent me dead roses the other day," she says.

"Congratulations."

"I think it was him—the big bald guy, Tee; Bellyman's friend."

"Are you okay with that now?"

"Pretty okay." She does not want to talk about Bellyman, or about Toft, or Colette, who is still so shy and sensitive—Colette, whom she is probably hurting at least once each day without even knowing it. I'm *sorry*, Colette, she wants to say sometimes. But I can't quite concentrate on things these days. I can't quite *be* here, if you know what I mean.

They fall silent again.

"Peter," she says finally. "Have you ever . . . gone to bed with anyone?"

He snorts. "What do you think I am—a eunuch?"

"But you're always so calm!"

He laughs out loud. "Syl, you're too much. What do you want to know? Ask, ask."

She laughs too, surprised. Somehow she has never

thought of Peter as a sexual being, someone who might enjoy touching, might enjoy . . . she is flooded with images of David, the bed on the floor, the dim light, and she closes her eyes quickly, willing them away. "When? How old were you?"

"Fourteen."

"Four*teen*?"

"Eighth grade. I was seduced by a junior. Scared the hell out of me."

She exhales, a long breath. "And since?"

"Didn't you know I was living with someone, Sylvia? Before I got to Baltimore?"

"No," she says. "I didn't. I feel so stupid."

"Why?"

"I thought I knew everything about you, Peter. I thought . . . I thought I was the only woman in your life." She giggles suddenly, feeling cheered.

"Jesus, I'd *really* be in bad shape then, wouldn't I?"

"Was it hard? Breaking up?"

"It's always hard, Syl." He stops. He's trying to decide whether to give me advice, she thinks. And in a moment, sure enough, he says, "Whatever's going on back there . . . well, just be glad you had what you had, you know what I mean?"

"I'll try." For a few seconds her throat aches in the old way, and she waits for the tears to rise, but nothing happens. She hears one of the bedroom doors open and Colette padding down the hallway to the bathroom.

"Take care, babe."

"You too."

She puts the receiver down, full of thought. *Am* I glad

it happened? she wonders. Or do I wish I were still . . . well, the way I was before? Naive? A child?

As she thinks the word—*child*—she realizes, with a start, that little Sylvia is no longer running behind her, that she has vanished for good, and that she herself never even noticed when it happened.

CHAPTER SIXTEEN

Sylvia and Jan sit down together in the eighth row of the Library of Congress hall just as the lights begin to dim and the audience begins to hush. There is always that moment, she thinks, between the talking and the clapping, when everybody is just waiting. When some performer is standing backstage taking deep breaths and waiting, too. And then the spot comes on, and the little figure moves shyly into the circle of light, applause shattering the expectant silence.

Here they are together, she and Jan, waiting for Miss Haupt to play. For a while Sylvia thought of cancelling their date—she feels guilty enough about his walking her home from *practice* each night—but then she decided that she really did want to see Miss Haupt perform, that for some reason she is becoming more and more curious about the sweet-faced woman with the coiled blond braids.

Miss Haupt comes out now in her green dress and green-and-gold scarf, and the audience begins to applaud. She nods at the light, her hair looking unnaturally golden, her plain dress suddenly incandescent. She seems a little confused; the audience loves her. "She is beautiful tonight," says Jan.

"Mmmm," Sylvia murmurs, not listening to him. She has never seen Miss Haupt looking so . . . magical. Like a character out of a fairy tale, she thinks—the drab house-drudge who becomes . . . not a princess, no, not in this case, but maybe a queen of some kind. Somebody old and regal and elegant, not at all like the kindly Miss Haupt who dozes in her easy chair and bumbles between the potted herbs in her crowded apartment.

She has never actually seen Miss Haupt perform. She's heard the recordings, of course, and they're good, especially her Chopin, but so many years ago. She settles back in her seat, glad that she has come, prepared to be surprised.

"Sylvia," whispers Jan as Miss Haupt sits down and adjusts the bench. "Thank you so much for . . . accompanying me."

She is embarrassed. Every time he is kind to her, she feels worse—she feels like a liar. She pats him on the arm without looking at him.

Miss Haupt's hands are now suspended above the keys, her head slightly bowed, and her eyes are no doubt closed besides. That long, long moment when you draw everything in, all the power within you, Sylvia thinks, fascinated as she always is when she watches someone perform—and collect it in your hands and fingertips. And then Miss Haupt's hands rise even higher and come down again and the first notes begin to pour out over the audience. A Field nocturne—and already she is doing it beautifully. She has the same kind of stylishness with her hands and wrists that Sylvia has seen in other German players . . . and that she remembers in Miss Selkirk.

She closes her eyes. It has been a long time, she thinks. A long time since I let myself just be. . . . The music is achingly beautiful; she cannot resist it; in seconds she is far away, watching herself, at ten years old, perched upon a needlepointed pillow on the enormous mahogany piano bench at Miss Selkirk's house. The prow of the shining black piano extends into a corner of windows; outside are a pair of immense spruces, a cascade of white roses, curving pathways and arbors through masses of spring flowers.

Miss Selkirk, who is as much gardener as she is musician, sits beside her in a thin voile dress, her white hair pinned up in a French twist and her gnarled, blue-veined hands lying open in her flowered lap. She smells of gardenias and Lapsang souchong tea.

Sylvia's back is sore from too much playing and she yearns to leap up, to run along the curving pathways of the garden, to fly on her swift feet to a place far away from music. But she has a recital soon at the public library; there are printed programs and newspaper articles coming out; Miss Selkirk is not yet entirely satisfied with her program.

She stares longingly out the window; somewhere in Miss Selkirk's beautiful garden is a place she can hide, a spicy bower, thick with mist and hung with petals. But Miss Selkirk pointedly ignores her yearning look at the trellises, the arbors, the benches, the brick pathways lined with flowers, as though a child in such a place would be a sacrilege. Instead, sighing, she goes to the kitchen and brings back a small white bowl filled with water and holds it so Sylvia can see the blue dragon painted inside. "I want to give you a flower, child," she says, and though her voice is perfectly kind, though she is being perfectly patient about it, even at such a young age, Sylvia knows she is being cheated of something. "Come stand by the window and show me the one you would like."

But Sylvia, suddenly and shockingly stubborn (she had forgotten this! why is she just remembering it now?) clings to the edges of the bench, shaking her head and swinging her legs. I want to play in the garden, she chants to herself. The garden, the garden, the garden.

Her father, if he could see her, would be horrified.

She has the deliciously frightened feeling that she might be spanked, though not by Miss Selkirk, certainly not by her. Not by her mother or father, either—by whom, then? Who would ever spank her? She's not a child who needs spanking; no one thinks of her that way; she is always perfectly behaved, perfectly sweet, perfectly grown-up, in spite of being only ten. She swings her legs, humming defiantly under her breath.

No, Miss Selkirk would never spank her, has never even touched her. "*Sylvia*," she says now, and the voice is quiet, commanding, faintly disapproving. She can feel herself giving in; she allows herself one last kick, her throat swelling hotly, and then stares down at her lap, shamed. "What is *wrong* with you today, Sylvia? Are you ill?"

Sylvia shakes her head, still looking down, as her moment of rebellion fades away. And then, though she longs with all her soul to make a wild, harebrained dash through the garden, she rises and stands obediently by the black piano, looking through the window glass at the white roses she can see but not touch, waiting for Miss Selkirk to find her gardening shears.

"That one," Sylvia mouths finally, pointing to a creamy blossom. And when her mother comes to pick her up, Sylvia goes out the front door carrying the bowl carefully in both small hands, for she is a careful girl, not a rebel after all; she is studious and polite and always very careful. Inside, the white flower floats above the blue dragon, a kind of miniature garden, all that Miss Selkirk will allow her.

She opens her eyes, appalled. How could she have forgotten this? But she truly has not thought of it in years—though now that it has come back to her, she can remember exactly how it felt, that single moment of defiance in an otherwise perfect childhood.

Miss Haupt has finished the Field nocturne and is pushing back the bench to stand while the audience claps and claps. For one moment, she smiles into the crowd, squinting against the lights, then seats herself once again. Sylvia forces herself to pay attention; Miss Haupt is about to begin Busoni's "Variations on a Chopin Prelude."

After the concert, everyone milling around in the foyer, talking and laughing and smoking before they brave the chilly air and the long walks to their cars or the train,

Sylvia, still muddled by her upsetting vision of the past, nevertheless hangs back, wanting to talk to Miss Haupt, to shake her hand and congratulate her. It was *wonderful*, she would like to say. Especially the Scriabin sonata.

She stands on her toes, straining to see over people's heads, and spots a number of students from the conservatory, though not Colette, who has gone to New Orleans for the weekend to stay with her famous father. But there, by the door—oh how terrible!—is Francine, the long dramatic dark hair and the perfect profile, and Sylvia ducks back out of sight, suddenly breathless. Francine. Which means that David is somewhere close by. Though she has imagined him a thousand times, Sylvia has not seen him in person since the morning he left her house. And now he is *here*. What will she do?

Instantly, her muddled head begins to throb; she is swept into panic; her knees shake; she clutches Jan's arm. This is *crazy*, she tells herself fiercely. You are *crazy*, Sylvia. Straighten up. You are making a *fool* of yourself. . . . But all she can think of is the door, the cold sidewalk outside leading away from this room, the train taking her miles and miles away from this place, where hidden somewhere in the crowd he moves and breathes, unaware of her presence, uncaring, unloving . . . like a *snake*, she thinks, a beautiful green deadly *snake* waiting to strike at me. . . . Panic rolls over her in shuddering waves.

Before she can spot him, a murmur rises from the crowd. "Look," says Jan, who has taken her elbow in the crush of people. "It is Miss Haupt and Miss Koh."

"Moon Ja Koh?" Sylvia says, stunned. "You're kidding!" She stands on her tiptoes again, balancing herself against Jan's arm, and catches a glimpse of the two women moving slowly through the crowd. Miss Haupt is smiling broadly, nodding left and right to people as they offer their congratulations, stopping to hug a student or a friend here and there, and Miss Koh, slender and elegant in black silk, follows behind her, head slightly bowed as though she is not, Sylvia thinks, one of the most famous concert artists in the world, as though she is not . . .

"Jan," she says. "I can't *believe* this. When did she get to town? I thought she was touring in China or something. I can't believe we just . . . bumped *into* her like this." She can hear herself squealing like a teenager, half hysterical with leftover panic and fresh excitement at seeing her idol, and laughs out loud. "Wow. Wait till I tell Peter. Wait till I tell my dad."

Jan, much taller, is staring across the sea of heads at the two women. A reporter has arrived. Cameras are flashing. "She looks very tired," he says, bemused.

"Who? Miss Koh?"

"No, Miss Haupt. She looks—how do you say it?— drained."

"Jan, I swear," Sylvia laughs giddily. "You are so funny when it comes to her . . ."

She goes up on her toes once again, hoping to catch another glimpse of Moon Ja Koh, and instead finds herself staring at a dark ponytail, a shoulder in a black trenchcoat—David, scanning the packed room. She reels, then catches herself sternly. So now I've seen him, she thinks. So what? Big deal. She is breathless but not crazy, not out of control as she was only minutes before. And then she realizes something new: It's not even *him*, she thinks. It's not him at all; it's *me*. I do it to myself.

Cornelius Toft in a tuxedo, Brandon at his heels, is moving irritably through the crowd now, headed for the women. He stumbles in the crush of people, and Brandon takes his arm, policing the room like a bodyguard. The three stars are standing together in a small cleared space, greeting one another with kisses on both cheeks, and Toft, with one hand in Miss Koh's and the other in Brandon's, is drawing his favorite into the circle.

Sylvia goes hot and cold at the same time. Toft never even asked her if she would be at the concert. And he and Brandon probably arrived in a white limo, in a manner fitting a future star. Brandon is so tall, so boyishly handsome. He is shaking Miss Koh's hand now and saying something charming. Miss Koh, who is very slender but not small, has to crane her neck to look up at him.

Jan tugs at her arm. "Miss Haupt wants us to come over," he says. "She has signaled to me."

"No!" Sylvia tugs back, feeling frantic. Everything has suddenly gotten to be too much. "You go by yourself."

"But, Sylvia . . ."

"Go ahead. I don't want to."

He is looking down at her, concerned.

"Go," she says. "I'll wait for you here."

He stands for another moment, and she gives him a little push. "Really, Jan." He heads obediently across the room then, and she stands alone, feeling ten years old again, the defiant young child being denied Miss Selkirk's garden.

Five minutes later, Jan returns to her side, beaming. "Miss Haupt wishes to invite us to a reception," he says. "At the home of Miss Koh in Georgetown."

"What?" She gazes up at him, stunned.

"Tonight," he says. "She truly wants us to come."

"Oh my God," Sylvia whispers. "Jan, I can't go there. I can't."

"And why can't you?"

"To Moon Ja Koh's *house*? With Toft and Brandon there? And besides, Miss Haupt didn't invite me, she invited you."

"She has invited you, too. 'Bring your friend,' she said. 'The one with the amazing hair.' "

"Oh, Jan," Sylvia says. "This is unbelievable. I can't..."

"You must," says Jan simply. "Miss Haupt wants you to come."

"Jan," she says despairingly.

"No more thinking."

The crowd parts, opening a pathway for the three stars, trailed by Brandon. They move out into the night, where, no doubt, the white limo waits for them. Sylvia stands frozen, watching them go.

"Sylvia," says Jan. "Come now, or we will never get a cab."

Katerina Haupt is feeling the mixture of exhilaration and exhaustion that is so common after a performance. It has been a long time—she'd forgotten what it takes out of a person. She is very happy, however, in a flushed, somewhat giddy way; she feels twenty-two again, as though she has just made love.

Moon Ja's apartment looks lovely—fresh orchids on the black glass table, a new painting from Korea in a black lacquer frame, the cymbidiums all back in their places. Katerina can smell baked artichokes and parmesan, one of her favorite hors d'oeuvres, and she watches fondly as Moon Ja, looking uncharacteristically domestic in a white lace apron, checks the oven. It is not that Moon Ja cannot cook—she is a wonderful cook. They became friends, in fact, back in Moon Ja's student days when she shyly asked Katerina for her Swedish meatball recipe. No—Moon Ja can certainly cook, but doesn't often choose to reveal the fact. "I have my *image*," she told Katerina once, laughing. "Think of my *image*."

For this reason, and because Moon Ja is looking somewhat wan and tired, there is a small catering crew hard at work in the kitchen unveiling quiches, plates of shrimp, antipasti, fruit platters, warm sourdough bread. Champagne is being chilled in silver buckets on the counter.

The apartment is not large, but neither is the reception. Cornelius Toft, a reviewer from the *Post*, another from the *Sun*. Cornelius's unctuous manager, Larry. The assistant secretary of commerce—or is it agriculture? she can never remember—who comes faithfully to every one of Katerina's concerts and has in fact been courting her in his own way for years. The assistant secretary's wife, a very nice woman who, she imagines, nods off during the music. A slippery-looking Wall Street broker who has been after Moon Ja for years. A select handful of students: that handsome weasel Brandon, poor lovesick Jan, Sylvia of the wild hair . . . too bad Colette is out of town tonight; she would like to see *her* reaction to all this—and to the recital itself. Sometimes she suspects that Colette does not really believe her old teacher can play.

It is a small, mismatched group if she ever saw one. She settles back in one of Moon Ja's white silk chairs, relieved. She will not have to do anything: they will, with their complete lack of common ground, separate themselves into tight, self-defensive knots, and she can simply move from cluster to cluster being properly gracious.

She did not do badly tonight, not badly at all. It was almost like the old days, a fairly credible facsimile of the passion that was her trademark when she first began concertizing in Berlin after the war. Her parents had vanished; the old house was gone, bombed out; her mentor Cornelius had slipped away to America. She was angry during those days; she still thought that happiness was a reward one could wrestle out of life and that she was somehow failing to do so. That passion came out in the music.

"Miss Haupt?" Jan is kneeling beside the arm of her chair in a supplicant's position. She smiles at him, still musing. "You played exquisitely tonight, Miss Haupt. The Scriabin in particular was wonderful."

"Thank you, Jan," she says, restraining herself from ruffling his hair. "I'm glad you could make it."

"Oh, it was a privilege. I mean that!"

"Where is Sylvia?" She glances around the room, wondering what it was the girl did to wound him so and how they have managed to get back together.

Jan blushes. "Sylvia is extremely sensitive, Miss

Haupt. She is not convinced she was truly invited. She is here, but I believe she has chosen to conceal herself in one of the bathrooms."

"Oh for heaven's sake." Katerina shakes her head. Such self-consciousness. "Go find her, Jan—she's missing out."

He gets to his feet, looking uncomfortable. "I will try," he says doubtfully, "but she is very . . . fearful, for some reason."

Across the room the two journalists, both holding glasses of white wine, have their heads together over something. Katerina can hear their chuckling, and an occasional "No!" The secretary's wife is standing in Moon Ja's kitchen watching the caterers cut the quiche. The caterers are nodding and smiling at everything she says.

Cornelius, flanked by Brandon and his manager, is holding court from the other white chair. He looks particularly frail tonight, his cheeks sunken in as though he has forgotten his teeth, pink scalp winking through his hair. His neck, in the tight tuxedo collar, looks wizened—but his eyes flash, his thin nostrils flare; he gestures angrily. Still a handsome devil. Old Cornelius, she thinks fondly. He has a red rosebud in his lapel.

Jan emerges from the hallway with Sylvia, looking a bit wild-eyed, behind him; he leads her to Katerina. "I have recovered her," he says.

The girl's cheeks look feverish; her eyes glitter. But she puts her hand into Katerina's—strong fingers—and says, "I loved your recital, Miss Haupt. I almost cried during the Field—Schumann, too. And the Scriabin was just . . . incredible. Congratulations."

Katerina smiles up into her eyes. She is used to post-concert flattery, but this is sincere; there is no doubt in her mind. The girl is both lovely and frazzled at the same time. Her amazing hair floats above her shoulders, shifting like something live when she moves her head. No wonder she is uncomfortable—Cornelius is holding court in the opposite corner. And, of course, like any young pianist, she must be overwhelmed at the very idea of being in Moon Ja's apartment. She looks like a white rabbit dropped into a roomful of panthers. You must get over this terrible burden of awe, young lady.

"Sit down for a moment," Katerina says. "I want to talk to you about something."

Sylvia sinks obediently to the floor at Katerina's feet, tucking her slender, coltish legs beneath her skirt. Jan, with a whuff, lowers his long body to the floor beside her.

"Tell me about your recital," Katerina says to Sylvia. "Are you playing any Chopin? I've heard your Chopin is wonderful."

"I love Chopin," she answers a bit breathlessly. She has put one hand beneath her ribcage. "I had a teacher who let me play him when I was very young, so I just kind of . . . grew up with him." She stops. Her cheeks are a fiery red. Then she adds, "But I'm not doing anything by him for the recital—I'm playing Scarlatti, Schumann, Ravel, and Beethoven instead."

"Schumann? Which one?"

"The *Fantasiestücke*."

"Ah yes—a good one. What about Beethoven?"

"Opus 111."

Katerina goes silent. "My," she says finally. "Cornelius must have great confidence in you."

Sylvia drops her eyes, clearly embarrassed, and Katerina, to spare her, changes the subject. "I wish more students could have come," she says. "But we knew how small the apartment is. And Moon Ja has not been home for very long—I didn't want to overburden her." She gestures toward the kitchen where the secretary's wife is now arranging triangles of toasted pita bread on a silver tray and the caterers are ladling some sort of exotic-looking dip—that wonderful bell-pepper puree?—into a crystal bowl. "I insisted she get help for this—she was actually thinking of doing it herself." Sylvia looks very startled, as though it has never occurred to her that a creature like Moon Ja might eat, much less cook.

"Have you met her yet?" Katerina asks gently.

"No." It is a shy no; her eyes are downcast.

"Will you let me introduce you?"

"Oh . . . well . . . of *course*. Of *course*."

"Let's go, then," says Katerina. She pushes herself out of the chair, wincing at the pinch of her girdle—she never wears a girdle, only for performances, and this one must be at least twenty years old by now—and gets to her feet carefully, so as not to hitch a rib. Sylvia has already risen gracefully—youth, thinks Katerina—and Jan is standing too.

"Well," says Katerina, feeling as though she is leading a battalion. "Shall we go find her?"

Sylvia follows Moon Ja Koh through the crowded living room, carrying the silver tray with its toasted pita bread points and a basket of French-bread cubes. Miss Koh! Here she is in Miss Koh's apartment, carrying her silver tray! But how sweet she is—how natural. "Sylvia," she had said, taking her hand. "What a beautiful name. Cornelius told me all about you, how well you play."

Well, of course she hadn't believed *that*, but it was kind of Miss Koh to say it. "And this must be Jan," Miss Koh added, looking up into his wildly flushing face, still holding Sylvia's hand in her own. With her other, she reached out for his, and the three of them stood that way for a moment, a triangle linked by Miss Koh and the press of their hot fingers against her cool ones.

"Yes," he managed finally, his Czech accent suddenly thickening. "I am that very he." Oh God, Sylvia thought, and smiled weakly at Miss Koh to let her know that they were not a couple, not in any way.

"Do you know, Jan, I honestly believe that Katerina thinks of you as a son?" Her smile flashed stunningly— Sylvia could imagine her onstage in blue silk, the beautiful inky-black hair shining under the lights—and she winked—had she *really* winked?—at Sylvia as if to say, You know how female teachers are. They can't help themselves. They are always adopting their students.

Jan ducked his head and stood confounded until Miss Koh herself broke the silence by saying, "Would you mind helping me get the food out? These people look hungry."

So Jan had been put in charge of wine and is now bumbling through the crowd, holding tightly to the neck of a crystal carafe while Sylvia follows Miss Koh's slender back, shimmering in the black silk. If she can remember this moment forever, she thinks. Ross and Anne will never believe it—their own daughter serving pita bread at the apartment of Moon Ja Koh.

If only Peter were here! One last concert together before he is gone. But he is still in San Francisco, and she wonders how it will be when he has truly moved away. Will they call each other long-distance at night to talk about their days? Maybe, for a while, but then it will become too expensive and they will allow themselves to forget to call and the habit will finally die.

Miss Koh says over her shoulder, "Just set it down here, Sylvia. Thanks," and at that moment, Brandon steps forward and takes the tray from Sylvia's hands and places it on the glass table.

"There," he says, smiling down at Miss Koh. "You're working too hard tonight."

Sylvia, cut off, stops, confused and empty-handed. What is Brandon doing now? Doesn't he ever relax? Somewhere in the room. Toft barks angrily and the reviewer follows this with another, "No!"

"Thank you, Brandon," Miss Koh is saying. "Do you know Sylvia?" but he has taken Miss Koh's arm and is already leading her away, saying, "I'm thinking of entering the Tchaikovsky next year . . . what do you think?"

Jan, still gripping the crystal carafe by the neck, is now hovering solicitously by her side. "Wine?" he asks, raising the decanter as though he will pour its contents into her cupped hand.

She shakes her head. Toft breaks into peals of harsh laughter—she has never heard him laugh before. The assistant secretary of something turns and gives her a mild, disinterested look before glancing over at Toft on the sofa. Charles Mingus's *The Black Saint and the Sinner Lady* is playing softly on the stereo; Colette has the album; her father once played saxophone with him. Sylvia feels herself begin to faint.

"Jan," she whispers. "I'm sick or something." All she can think of is air, the cool night air outside this small, beautifully decorated apartment, with its endless chatter of the rich and powerful. Even the exotic Miss Koh looks wan, almost emaciated, in this light, the black silk too much against her pale skin.

Two uniformed drivers—Toft's and someone else's— sit silently on a pair of Queen Anne chairs in the foyer, each of them holding a delicate china cup and saucer. One of the reviewers slaps the other on the back, delighted. Toft's manager is writing something on a small tablet for the strange-looking man with the slicked-back hair—a lawyer? a stockbroker? not a musician, she is sure of it—and all she wants is to be home, safe in her bed. She swallows hard, feeling the blood leave her head.

"Jan, I'm going outside," she says, but he has already taken her arm, is hustling her through the room, nodding left and right to people as they cut through the small crowd. "Will you tell her I had to leave?" she whispers to him as he opens the door.

"Of course," he says. "But first we must get you some air, Sylvia. You have become extremely white in the face."

Later, after they have gone down the elevator, she waits just outside the lobby door while he goes back up to call a taxi, to make their goodbyes. The doorman nods at her once and she nods back without smiling. The Georgetown evening surges past them, headlights flashing, people in evening dress laughing as they stroll, arm in arm, past cafés and elegant bars. Whatever is wrong with her came upon her during the concert—during the Field, in fact, when she was caught up in the memory of Miss Selkirk—and she wondered then if she were coming down with something. Her head seems to float above her shoulders, disconnected from the rest of her. Her movements are languid, as though she is swimming underwater. She feels faintly nauseated.

A thought crosses her mind, horrifying and alien. Could she be. . . . No, impossible, not after only one time. But her hands are trembling; she thinks, bleakly, I would have to kill myself. She takes several long, slow breaths, calming herself. Perhaps, instead, she is getting the flu.

She floats in place, thinking briefly of Opus 111, Miss Haupt's Field, the way the headlights sweep across the sidewalk as the traffic makes its turn. Where are they all going, everyone in their cars and taxis? Where will any of them end up? Why can't anyone just stay still for a moment?

Oh my God, what if I'm pregnant?

CHAPTER SEVENTEEN

*I*t is 3:00 A.M., and Sylvia feels once again normal—in fact, ravenously hungry. I'm fine, she thinks. It must have been food poisoning or something. In the kitchen she fills the copper pot at the sink and then tries several matches before she can get the burner to sputter to life. "Stupid stove," she says.

Colette, who arrived by cab from the airport an hour ago, sits shivering in the blue afghan at the tiny kitchen table. "He should give us a break on the rent."

"Yeah, right," says Sylvia. "And it's a she."

Colette seems deeply and mysteriously depressed tonight. Sylvia watches her for a while, trying to figure out what to say. Sometimes they can talk; sometimes they can't. But their relationship is never like hers with Marushka; both Colette and she are, at bottom, too shy and sensitive to maintain an easy friendship. Something always holds them back, and she wonders now, as she often does, what it can possibly be.

Suddenly, she remembers that somewhere in the cupboard is a package of Pepperidge Farm cookies she has been hoarding. She pulls out their little stool and climbs up, feeling around behind the vase on the top shelf. There. "Look what *I've* got, Colette. Double chocolate and pecan."

"Wow," says Colette lifelessly.

They wait in silence until the water boils and then they sit at the table eating cookie after cookie and drinking tea from the wafer-thin blue and white cups that Miss Selkirk left Sylvia, along with her enormous black Steinway, when she died. "Mmmm," Colette says finally, sleepily. "Good."

Sylvia clears her throat. All she can think about is crawling into bed, but if they don't talk about things tonight, they probably never will. And she has too many other, larger, concerns hanging over her head these days; she and Colette cannot continue to poke along in this pseudo-friendship, sometimes intimates, sometimes strangers. If she has wounded Colette in some way these past weeks, she needs to find out. "Is there something, well, *bothering* you, Colette? Something I'm doing, maybe?"

Colette sighs and looks away. "What do you mean?"

"I don't know. I just feel . . . uncomfortable sometimes. You know—with the two of us. What about you?"

"I'm fine."

Sylvia stares at Colette, perplexed. She wants to tell her about Moon Ja Koh, about seeing David and Francine after the recital, but nothing sounds right, not with Colette in this whatever it is. This funk. Suddenly, she feels herself getting angry. She takes another gulp of tea, then says, "I wish you'd just go ahead and tell me. Whatever it is I'm doing wrong. This is getting old, Colette."

"It's not you."

"Well then, what?"

There is a long silence. "*Shit*," says Colette finally. "What do you *think* is wrong? How do you *think* it feels to be the only black in this place? I miss my dad. I miss all my friends, you know?"

"I guess you would. I never thought of that. Sometimes I miss Minneapolis."

"It's not the same, Sylvia. Not at all. And sometimes I get so tired of it."

Colette has the blue afghan pulled over her head like a hood, and her face looks delicate and elfin and remote beneath it. Sylvia feels herself floundering. Who is this person she lives with? What does she really know about her? "Tell me . . . tell me what it's like to have a famous father," she says. "Tell me what it's like to live in a place like New Orleans."

Colette gives her a weak smile from beneath her hood. "I like you, Sylvia," she says. "Don't worry. We're friends."

Sylvia smiles, embarrassed. "You're going to get mad all over if I ask you this."

"What?"

"Sometimes you talk different. You know—more black. And sometimes you sound as white as my mom."

Colette laughs out loud, her rich Colette laugh. "You little ol' boojie thang," she says. "You mean, sometimes I don't sound like Scarlett O'Hara?"

Sylvia nods.

Colette stares at the far wall. "I grew *up* black, you know. That's New Orleans—that's my dad's world . . . even though my mom was white." She looks sharply at Sylvia. "Did you know that?"

Sylvia shakes her head.

"Nobody does—they got divorced years ago. And then she went off somewhere and disappeared. I can't even remember her—just the pictures he has."

Sylvia holds herself very still, listening, though her feet are freezing. "What did she look like? Like you?"

Colette gives an odd little laugh. "Not much," she says. "She was a redhead with freckles, for one thing." She shrugs. "Pretty, I guess. But she looked a little crazy, if you ask me."

"Do you know where she is?"

"Nope. But I think she's probably dead."

"*Dead*? Why?"

Colette shrugs again.

"Have you ever talked about it with your dad?"

"When I was little. When I'd be crying because she wasn't there. But not for a long time. I'm not that interested anymore, to tell you the truth."

Sylvia is silent. I'm going to have to get some blankets out here, she thinks, or we're going to freeze to death. "Do you have a good dad?" she asks.

Colette smiles. "Yeah. He's great. He's one of the smartest guys I've ever met." She reaches out for the empty Pepperidge Farm package, turning it over and over in her fingers. "But he never has gotten it, you know? Here he is, this famous jazz musician, and he doesn't realize that the doors just don't open for most people the way they do for him.''

''For you?''

Colette sighs. ''When I started competing, I was only about fourteen. And I won in a statewide competition and got to go to regionals—there were probably three or four hundred kids there from twenty different states.'' She pushes the empty package away from her. ''I was the only black person there, Sylvia. Out of a few hundred competitors. And nobody understood me when I talked.'' She pulls the afghan closer. ''Or at least that's what they said.''

''Jeez, Colette.''

''So I went home and learned how to speak white.''

Sylvia pushes back her chair and stands stiffly. Her feet are numb. ''I'm going to get us some blankets before we die out here.''

''Okay.'' Colette is gazing down at the table, pushing at a cookie crumb with one finger.

When they are both wrapped in blanket cocoons, Sylvia takes a long breath and says, ''I'm sorry.''

''What for?''

''I don't know. For being so stuck on myself, I guess. I've been in a dream world lately.''

Colette makes a little motion with one shoulder, shaking her head. ''Oh well,'' she says. ''You've got a lot on your mind. And besides, it's my problem, not yours. Sometimes it just hits me harder, that's all. Like when I've just been home.''

''Home. That sounds so good.''

''You miss it too?''

"Right now more than anything. But I can hardly stand to talk to my parents when they call every week—isn't that weird?"

Colette smiles tentatively. "No—I know what you mean. You think about how great it is, how everything used to be, and then you get there and all they want to do is stick you back in time. Turn you back into their little girl."

"*Yes*," says Sylvia. "It's dangerous to even talk to them sometimes—they make you feel like you can't do things yet. Like you're going to automatically screw up without them."

"What's your mom like, Sylvia?" Colette's voice is wistful.

Sylvia folds her hands inside the blanket. Her feet are finally thawing out. "Well, she's great. She really is. It's just that . . ." She stops, shocked at what she is about to say: "Well, she shouldn't have ever married my dad, that's all."

"They're not happy?"

"Well sure, but . . ." Her stomach feels odd; she feels awash in disloyalty—but, she thinks stubbornly, it's *true*; it's always been true. They're not *any*thing alike. He drives her nuts, but she's too weak to leave him. She is astonished, never having uttered the words before, not even in her own mind. My perfect parents. Our perfect house. The lake. Everything . . .

"Do they fight?"

"Oh no, nothing like *that*. They never fight—or hardly ever. They *lie*." Again she stops, amazed. But they *do*. They *do* lie. They pretend. "I've thought for a long time that the only reason they stay together is me. Well, I didn't really think it out in those words, but I felt it. Because they both love me—I know that. And you know, Colette, they're both good, they're good people . . . but they came from different planets or something. And the only way they can connect is through me." She is astounded.

Colette is watching her, her brown eyes deep and empathetic.

"God. I can't believe I said all that."

"It's okay, Sylvia."

"Well, anyway . . ." says Sylvia. She sighs, then smiles at her friend. "May I go with you to New Orleans sometime? Would you get your dad's autograph for me?"

Colette laughs. "Sure," she says. "You boojie white chick."

The White Tower is open all night, but they don't allow vagrants; people who want to sit at a table better be drinking coffee, at least. Tee can't sleep—it's cold tonight and he's thinking too hard about everything: Bellyman, getting himself a job . . . and now, after all these years, his son Raymon is on his mind and he can't shake him off. So he takes out one of his dollars and buys himself a cup of coffee and sits staring at the bright walls.

These days, the questions keep coming, questions Bellyman used to ask him before he got so bad. How did you get here, living on these streets? Where's your little boy now? Tee's never seen his boy, not since he got out of the joint ten years ago. How old would he be now, Raymon? Twenty? Twenty-one?

Tee thinks of Chicago, Cabrini Green, the projects he grew up in, the broken-down chain-link fences. His sweet mama, who always trusted luck more than she trusted herself. Just letting all her kids run loose in the streets until they wound up like their daddy, the whole mess of them in the joint. How he was going to be another Sonny Liston. Coming home every night with his eyes swelled shut, his ears smashed flat, the sweat dried and stinking on him from the gym where he boxed his guts out every day.

Oh, he was big; he was a big boy. Tall and strong, with heavy shoulders. A boxer for sure. And his mama was proud—she cried when she saw his bloody face, but she was proud of him. "Tee," she said, taking a sponge to his face. "You the only one amounted to a thing."

I *could* have, he thinks. I could have fuckin' *made* it, too.

He was headed up, he had the money together and then—*shit*. Tee puts down his coffee cup and runs both hands over the top of his smooth head. Bellyman, where you now? I miss you, brother.

He's making the waitress nervous, he can see it. She's standing over by the cash register, close by the telephone. Come quick, Mr. Cop, big ape loose in my restaurant.

Too lonely in this city anymore now that Bellyman's gone. Time to move on. Maybe find him his son. Say, Raymon, you lookin' good. Your daddy proud of you, boy. Let me tell you some things. The two of them walkin' off together, arms over their shoulders. Raymon and Tee, a son and his father. Just like Bellyman was for him.

Got to get him a job, get him some money. Time to be movin' on. Time to ask down at the Free Library. Where can a big ol' ugly nigger who can't even read find him some kind of a job?

Moon Ja swims out of a heavy sleep and lies still on her back in bed, staring up at the dark ceiling. What is it? What did she hear?

She waits for a long time. Her heart is beating; she can hear the breath in her throat, the faint rustle of her hair against the pillowcase. But what else? What woke her so suddenly and completely?

An hour passes; she holds her eyes wide and the darkness flails against them. Outside, there are the usual traffic noises, a siren, the sounds of the city.

In time, she drifts off once more, sinking back into the deep warm waters of sleep. And then, just before she is gone, she hears it, the sound that woke her in the first place. The faint and ghostly cry of a distant baby.

Katerina Haupt dreams under her warm quilt, turning without waking every hour and mashing the pillow beneath her. Her dreams are long and complex, filled with memories she has almost forgotten and will forget once more as soon as she arises in the morning. In one of them, she is swimming majestically through a cold northern sea, swimming like a whale, rising and falling through the steep gray waves without effort.

She pushes her bare arms between the cool pillows and bicycles for a moment, half awake, snatches of the Field nocturne sliding past her like fish in a thin gray floating light. And then she is falling backward into sleep again, caught for an instant by one sharp image, clear as life: Cornelius, in a pair of old man's flannel pants, his naked chest rising and falling in terror as he flails with a walking stick at the heavy legs of a black concert grand.

Sylvia wakes in the kitchen chair to a pearl light and the certainty that she is about to vomit. As she struggles to her feet, holding her stomach, she sees the empty cookie package, the teacups, half full, the copper pot—and Colette in the other chair slumped forward across bare arms. The bile rises in her throat, bitter and intense, and she stumbles through the living room, down the hall, one hand over her mouth, for the sanctuary of the porcelain toilet bowl.

Down on her knees, her hands on either side of the white rim, she pours her stomach's contents out into the clear water, a wrenching contortion that leaves her dizzy and shaking. After the first spasm, she rests for a moment, panting, eyes closed and head tipped back. And then it hits her again, and when she finishes, wiping her mouth on the back of her hand, Colette is there to hand her a Kleenex and a cup of water. "Rinse," she says.

"Thanks," Sylvia manages. She lifts the cup to her mouth, hand trembling. The water is warm and salty, though she knows that what she is tasting is the bile, and she is surprised that she feels no better yet, that the ground is still tilting back and forth beneath her knees.

"Better?" asks Colette.

"I think," she says, and vomits again, dry heaves this time that produce nothing but a thin dribble of burning spit. "Oh God, I'm going to die."

Colette takes the warm rag from her hand, rinses it in

the sink, and smooths it over Sylvia's forehead. "Jiminy Christmas," she says. "We didn't eat *that* many cookies."

"No," Sylvia moans. "Oh, Colette."

"Think you can get up from there?"

"Just let me rest a minute." She pants, leaning hard on her arms against the rim.

"Well, at least let me flush this mess," Colette says briskly. "Turn your head, girl."

Sylvia turns her head obediently away from the gigantic rushing whirl. A fine mist falls against her arms and she is sickened at the fact that she is embracing a toilet. I must be getting better, she thinks, to realize that. She gags lightly and swallows hard and feels Colette gently tying back her hair. "There," Colette says. "You're like one of those Afghan hounds with the long ears that get in their food."

Sylvia smiles weakly and tries to get up, bracing herself against Colette's thin arm, but it is hopeless for the moment; the room goes skyrocketing past whenever she moves her head. "I'll just sit on the floor for a little," she says faintly.

"How about I get you a pillow and a blanket?"

"All right," she answers, wanting nothing but sleep.

Soon she is curled on the bathroom rug, two pillows under her hair and the blue afghan tucked around her. She has begun to shiver again; the afghan feels warm; she's leaking tears from beneath closed lids. I'm crying again, she thinks. I'm back. But this is the price. How in the world will Anne handle this? Ross? Toft?

"You okay now?" says Colette softly. "Can I get you anything else?"

"I'm fine," she says through the slow tears. "Thank you, Colette."

When Sylvia wakes again, it is full light. In spite of the hard floor, the rusted underside of the medicine cabinet high above her, she feels much more like herself. She moves a little, gingerly, testing. One foot, then the other. Her arms, beneath the pillow. Finally, she turns until she is lying on her back; Colette, holding a saucer and a cup of tea, stands sleepily above her.

"How are you, Sylvie?"

In the midst of everything, Sylvia notices the nickname—and Colette's softer, more relaxed face. I'm glad we talked, she thinks. "Okay, I guess," she says.

"Can you drink this tea? It's the best thing for. . . ."

"For what?"

Colette gets down on her knees beside Sylvia and the toilet, balancing the saucer. "Tea and dry toast," she says quietly. "My aunt lived on it before my cousin was born." Sylvia sits up and takes the cup. The room goes into a slow spin, then bumps gently to a stop. She takes a sip, and then another. It tastes good.

"Oh God, Colette, what am I going to do?"

Colette reaches out and takes her hand. She is mute. She shakes her head.

CHAPTER EIGHTEEN

$\mathcal{T}$oft is not himself today; he paces about the studio as always, but without his usual smoke and fire. It is late afternoon—almost five—and he crosses bars of light on the floor. His skin looks odd—he is sallow and drawn, almost yellowish. Sylvia, on the bench, waits guiltily for his rage (she is distracted to the point of imbecility; she can hardly play a note today), but he seems, if possible, at least as distracted as she. Certainly, he has missed an excellent opportunity to harangue her.

Finally, he stops, his old face divided by shadow and light, and stares at her somberly. "We are what, two weeks away?" he says. "Is there something you intend to do before then about the way you are playing Opus 111? Some secret you have not shared with me?"

She drops her head. What can she say? I'm sorry, Mr. Toft, but I'm a little preoccupied? I'm sorry, but I'm too busy throwing up to think about Beethoven right now? I'm sorry, but I think it would be best for both of us if I just went ahead and died before my recital?

He purses his lips, bows his head, stares down at his shoes as though they will give him the answer. Then, finally, he shrugs, a hands-up gesture that relieves him of all responsibility forever. "Ah well," he says. "It is your life, young lady. You wish to play this way, then this is the way you play. There is nothing more I can do."

What she hears is the last sentence. So he is releasing her after all, probably the minute her recital is over. She waits for the tears to rise, but nothing happens; she has already cried so much this week that she is completely drained. What good does it do to cry? This is absolute failure: a bad recital, Toft dropping her, and then, while her parents are still recovering, the worst news of all. She stares at him, unblinking, one hand over her abdomen; she has finally, it seems, achieved a kind of Buddhist serenity—but only because she has reached a blank wall and can think of nothing else to do but sit and wait.

Toft holds his own pose for a long time, then sighs and runs one hand through his hair. With the other hand he searches his pockets for cigarettes. "Sylvia," he says. "I heard something in your playing when you first auditioned for me that I have not heard since. Do you know what it was?" He shakes a narrow brown cigarette from a crumpled pack and puts it in his mouth, then searches through more pockets for his lighter.

Upstairs, Colette is playing Poulenc's *Les Soirées de Nazelles*, a work she has been learning for her senior recital in May. In spite of herself, Sylvia cocks her head, listening; she has always been intrigued by Colette's cool, elegant playing, the fact that she never misses a note. And she hardly moves at the bench, either, just the flowing wrists and the long slender fingers that never hit the keys, only press them, which is why her legato is so lovely. So Sylvia was surprised when Colette told her once, "I'd give anything to be able to play Schumann the way you do, Sylvia. With all that fire you have."

What would she have done without Colette this week?

Toft has found his light and, eyes closed, is drawing smoke greedily into his lungs. He has moved back to his favorite place by the window and she has a long moment to study him in his private rhapsody. His nimbus of white hair, his delicate old blue-veined hands, the manicured nails—he is a man in a state of fastidious decay, she thinks.

"What was it," she asks quietly, "that you saw in my playing then?" She had been seventeen, not yet out of high school, with a secret crush on Mr. Binder and a happy, stressless existence in Minneapolis. And playing the piano was nothing more for her than a great pleasure. She can hardly remember being that young.

He is staring at her from across the room, the smoke from his cigarette climbing lazily through the long afternoon light. He sighs. "When I first heard you play, I did not hear a girl who occupied herself with young men or love or whatever nonsense is in your mind these days. I heard a pianist, do you know what I am saying?"

"No," she says, swallowing. What is he telling her?

"This is the truth: I heard a pianist who was willing to efface herself for the sake of the music. Somebody neither male or female, do you see? Someone who was—

how shall I put this?—too innocent to give in to the demands of the ego."

She stares at him. Innocence: so *that* is what he saw in her. And for some reason innocence was important to him . . . "Is that what you think I'm doing? Imposing myself on the music?"

"Let us say this: You are not pondering what it is you are doing. You have been given the privilege of playing one of the most profound sonatas ever written, but what do you do? You try to *feel* your way through it—your little moods, your fits of pique—don't you understand? You are not worthy to come close to this work; men much greater than you have spent lifetimes with it. Ah, what is the use . . ." He makes a gesture with his hand, almost obscene in its disgust, and turns away from her.

"Why . . . why did you give it to me, then?"

"It was a mistake," he says to the window.

She is hit with a sudden wave of vertigo and grabs on to both ends of the bench, closing her eyes. Is she going to be sick again? In a moment, though, the dizziness passes and she takes a long breath and straightens up.

"Sylvia," he says, and now it is *his* eyes that are closed. "I am exhausted. You must forgive me if I leave you now."

"No," she says, shocking herself. His eyes fly open; he cannot believe she is answering him back. "I mean, I need to ask you some questions first, if that's all right."

He inclines his head, neither speaking nor smiling— she has really done it this time—and she says, quickly, "Why *did* you give me the sonata? People my age don't play late Beethoven, not usually, anyway. I don't understand what you were thinking—why you thought my innocence was so important. Maybe it would help if I knew.'' She falters to a stop.

He sighs and she thinks, He's not going to tell me, I'm never going to know—but then he says, ''Some people think Opus 111 is impossible, did you know that?''

''What do you mean?''

''I mean, there are people who think that no pianist can play both movements. If he can play the first, he is bound to fail at the second, or vice versa.''

''Well, yes—I've read that.''

''I wanted to see what you could do with the arietta, in particular. It was an idea I had . . .'' He tosses his cigarette out the window and comes across the room toward the piano. She waits, hardly breathing, as he opens the score and points. ''Of course you are looking now at one of the more complex movements one could ever play. Yet, here—do you see it? He brings back the opening figures of the theme—yes?—and then we have a brief exchange here, hardly noticeable, between tonic and dominant. And thus, amazingly, we end in utter simplicity.''

He is looking down at her, waiting for her response.

She nods. She *does* see it—but what is he getting at?

''Simplicity, Sylvia. Utter innocence. And this is his last sonata, the summation of all he had learned during his twenty-six years of writing them.''

She stares up at him—she *wants* to understand, but she is still not sure what he is talking about . . .

''The movement is indescribable. You cannot get a musical quotation out of it—yet look at how it ends.

Listen, Sylvia." He sits down on the bench beside her; she gets to her feet quickly, giving him room; this is unprecedented; when is the last time Toft has played anything for *any*one, much less for a student? He's too old—his hands shake—she watches, amazed, as he begins with the soft triplets in thirds and sixths and goes on to play the entire movement through without stopping.

Silence, except for his labored breathing. She does not know what to say; he is still, in spite of the trembling of his shiny old fingers, incredible. "Mr. Toft . . ."

"That movement," he says, panting, "can only be played by a master or a child."

"Do you mean because it is so . . . pure?"

He nods.

"And you thought I was like that?"

"I thought," he says sternly, "that you, at least, had not yet been contaminated. That your heart might be innocent enough to approach such music without guile."

She drops her eyes; if he even sus*pect*ed how innocent she is not . . . But something is bothering her, something that has to do with all the Beethoven books she has read. Well, of *course*—she is thinking of the composer himself, his personality. "Mr. Toft," she says. "Beethoven wasn't exactly . . . humble, was he? I mean, it seems to me that he thought quite a lot of himself and didn't he have a temper, too? How could he be that way and still be innocent?" She can't believe she is *ar*guing with him.

He says, "It does not matter what he was like personally. We are not looking at the psychological man here but at art. And Beethoven's art raises him above the rest

of us. Beethoven as individual is not important; Beethoven as composer is. Hegel, I believe, would go so far as to
call him 'hero.' "

"Who *is* Hegel?"

He glares at her. "Hegel was a philosopher," he says.
"A German, naturally. Why do you want to know?"

"Because," she says, fast, "you mentioned him to me
once. And I was wondering why. I was wondering if it
might, you know, help me with my playing. With Opus
111."

"I doubt that."

"Well . . . couldn't you try anyway? Just to see?" She
cannot believe her stubbornness, that she is actually
holding him in this room against his will. But he owes
her more, much more, than he has given her; he is her
teacher; she cannot help it if he is old and tired and disil-
lusioned. He owes her what he knows.

He begins to cough, and she flinches as he doubles
over, his handkerchief against his face. This is probably
her fault—she's upset him once again. She waits quietly
while he struggles for breath, but she can't help herself.
She is thinking about Bellyman, his head rolling in Tee's
arms, the old chest wheezing. . . .

"You should quit smoking, Mr. Toft," she adds when
he has finally stopped. "That's a terrible cough you
have."

He clears his throat, his eyebrows raised, and she has
the feeling that one by one she is chopping the supports
out from under herself. What does she think she is
doing? On the other hand, what does she have to lose?

"Hegel," he says finally, reluctantly, "believed that
the individual *as* individual is of no importance—the

only thing that matters about any of us is our place in the broad sweep of history. Which, of course, is heresy here in America, where everyone is a small god, so I do not expect you to accept this." He glares at her as if daring her to disagree.

She does not speak.

He says, "Obviously, there are exceptions—men like Beethoven or Napoleon, who change the entire course of history with a single remarkable life. But most of us do not matter so very much. When you play Scarlatti, for example, it is not you, Sylvia, playing as an individual musician. No—you are deceiving yourself if you think so. For the line goes straight back through almost three hundred years of pianists and harpsichordists to the composer himself. You see?"

She nods.

Toft rises, straightens, clasps his hands behind his back. In another minute, she thinks, he'll start pacing. What have I done? She needs to sit down. She feels an enormous yawn rising; she is exhausted from the many long nights of the past week; suddenly, the full horror of her situation, like some cadaverous grinning apparition, rises up before her once again. I'm pregnant, she says to herself. Me. Sylvia.

Pregnant.

"Hegel," Toft is saying, "put all his faith in something he called the Absolute. And he believed, further, that this Absolute may at times be apprehended through beauty—do you understand what I am saying?"

She nods again.

"So that something like Opus 111, if it is performed perfectly, without contamination by the individual ego—of course, this is quite impossible, but one is to always strive for it—becomes, as it were, a moment in the mind of the Absolute.''

He is actually beaming—she has transformed him by her question. She struggles to listen more carefully.

"The score, Sylvia. Take that score in your hand and look at it.''

She reaches out, confused, and picks up Opus 111.

"Now, *read* it. Read it the way Beethoven did, with no ears to hear it played. Listen to the music in its purest form, before you have distorted it with your moods, your temperamental nature. *This* is what you are after— to play it the way it was first conceived by the Absolute Mind.''

She gives him a weak smile. It is very quiet. The moment drags on and on. "Thank you," she says, finally. What else can she say?

He drops his hands. He nods curtly, then turns on his heel and heads for the door. "Objectivity," he says over his shoulder. "That is your watchword, Sylvia.''

"Yes," she says, "I'll try—" but he is gone.

The Absolute. She looks down at the score in her lap and reads slowly through the first eight measures of the arietta, waiting to see what will happen. Purity. Innocence. Is it possible? Is it even remotely possible that she can play it this way *now*?

But she knows he has finally given her something. That she must take all this inside herself and *think*, in spite of everything else going on in her life. Because what he said, in an odd way, sounded familiar.

What he said sounded like Peter.

CHAPTER NINETEEN

*U*sually after a lesson with Toft, Sylvia practices diligently for several hours, hoping to grasp with her fingers what her mind has missed. Today, however, she gathers up her things and heads downstairs, knowing it is hopeless to sit in front of the piano any longer.

Outside, the air is winter brisk; she feels a little less nauseated when she has taken a great gulp of it into her lungs. Should she go back to the apartment? No, Colette is probably at school, practicing—the apartment is lonely and dark. Should she go sit in the park? Should she get on a plane and fly home to Minneapolis, give up music, jump out a window?

I'm *pregnant*, she thinks.

She is walking down Centre and she turns a corner, blindly, walking fast, and then another, until she realizes she is heading for the Free Library; she relaxes a little and takes another big breath of cool air. The library. An enormous, musty place with dark corners and dim bulbs, not anything like the elegant old library at the conservatory, where she usually does her studying. In the Free Library, nobody knows her; she can roam through the stacks or find herself a chair someplace; she can read and forget everything for a while. However, as she walks along the front of the building, heading for the door, she passes a row of homeless men propped against the library wall. They watch her, unblinking, and she pulls her coat closer and hurries on past without going in.

Should she find a telephone and call home? Her father would be at his office in town; her mother would be alone, cooking or reading or whatever she does when he is not there. Sylvia could say, "Mom, I'm pregnant and I feel like dying," and Anne would listen quietly and then tell her what to do.

She stops in the middle of the sidewalk. There is a pay telephone inside the library; maybe she should go back.

Her heart begins to hammer; she can hear it pounding in her ears. She *can't* call her mother. There *is nobody to call*, nobody—*face* it, Sylvia—who is going to make the decision for you. She stands shaking under an icy deluge of panic. Walk, she tells herself. Just keep walking.

In a few minutes she figures out where she is going after all. Miss Haupt's apartment is on the next block— of course. Miss Haupt understands things like this; she *must;* she could not play the way she does without knowing what it feels like to be half crazy over life. And she is so kind. So Jan was right—Jan has been right all along. Miss Haupt's is where she belongs. Miss Haupt will know what to do. Miss Haupt is where she has been headed all the time. She smiles in relief, walking along, breathing hard, imagining what she will say. Hello, Miss

Haupt, I was just in the neighborhood. Hello, Miss Haupt, how would you like to adopt my child?

Before she can plan her words, or even smooth down her hair, she is there. The same front steps where she first saw Tee and Bellyman that snowy, freezing night, the night of Jan's amazing Liszt. She stands for a long time, looking up. Potted plants sit in the windowsill—of course. And probably a cat somewhere. And there will be tea and fresh cookies and Miss Haupt to listen to her. What is she waiting for?

She stands locked in frustrated indecision, her neck knotting up, the cool evening breeze lifting tendrils of hair from her face. What if Jan is up there? What if Miss Haupt takes one look at her and guesses? For she doesn't want her to know, after all; suddenly, she only wants hot tea, a place to sit that is quiet, someone to watch her while she rests and cries a little.

She rings the bell before she can stop herself, and then, in an instant, changes her mind and turns to leave. But Miss Haupt is already opening a window on the second floor, calling down to her, "Who's there?"

She could keep walking. Evening is near—the light is getting bad. She could pretend it was not her—it must have been someone else you saw, Miss Haupt. Someone who looks like me.

But instead she stops and turns slowly until she is facing the high window. "Yes," she calls. "May I come in for a moment?"

"Certainly," calls Miss Haupt. "I'll pop down and open the door."

• • •

Miss Haupt's living room is just as she remembers it, cluttered and confused, so Sylvia is doubly shocked to see that Moon Ja Koh is there, lying quietly like a sick child on the sofa with a book. She does not know what to do or, more important, what to say. "I'm sorry," she begins. "I didn't know you had company . . ." but Miss Haupt pats her arm and murmurs, "Don't worry, it's nothing—right, Moon Ja?"

Miss Koh looks up from her pillows and smiles a fragile smile. "Don't mind me . . . is it Sylvia? I'm not feeling very well these days—I'm letting Katerina baby me."

Sylvia is miserably embarrassed—to have stumbled in on Miss Koh!—but now she is here, red cheeks and all, and what can she do? She stands frozen in the middle of the room, nodding and smiling and wishing she could disappear, in spite of the wonderful smell of baking that drifts into the room. This is all just getting worse and worse.

"Come, come," says Miss Haupt. "Over here to the table, I have something to show you."

"Okay," says Sylvia obediently, nodding one last time at Miss Koh on the sofa before she turns and follows Katerina Haupt into the kitchen. She moves gingerly; everything in Miss Haupt's apartment seems precarious, as though a strong breeze could tip it all into a tinkling chaos. There are pots on the floor, stacks of books against the walls, pictures hanging crazily. Sheet music is everywhere, and photos and magazines and half-burned candles. A bell hangs from a red ribbon; six or eight bouquets of flowers sit in vases and bowls and cups. On the wall over the kitchen table is a *National*

Geographic map of Africa. No cat, however. She sniffs hungrily at the warm air; it's either coffee cake or some kind of sweet bread. "Here," says Miss Haupt, shoving aside a stack of forms. "My taxes—I'm just getting started for this year. I hate them."

Sylvia smiles and sits in the chair she has been offered, though she is still regretting the impulse that has brought her here. What will she say? How will she explain herself?

"Coffee? Some tea, maybe?"

"No, no," Sylvia says. "I'm fine."

"But you're cold, I can see your cheeks are red. Listen, I've got some great Burmese tea, a little like Lapsang souchong, if you've ever had *that*."

Lapsang souchong. Miss Selkirk. Instantly, Sylvia sees once again the gracious old house, the white faces of the roses bobbing outside the enormous window, Miss Selkirk in her printed voile dresses.

"No tea," she says. "But I'll have a little coffee if it's made."

"Good," says Miss Haupt. "And some lemon poppy-seed cake too, in just a minute. Moon Ja's favorite."

"She's using me as an excuse to bake," Miss Koh says primly from her sofa.

Sylvia smiles and smiles, feeling strangled. If only she'd escaped down the street when she had a chance.

Miss Haupt has opened the oven door, is bending over and gazing intently at the lemon poppy-seed cake. She is wearing an apron—of course—and her gray-blond hair is wound in a loose knot at the back of her head. Warm clouds of butter and lemon scent rise in the room, and other smells too, very faint. Dill? Sylvia recognizes the aroma and then notices the row of drying herbs in the back corner of the kitchen.

In minutes, the lemon cake is sliced, the coffee, with whipped cream melting over the top of it, is steaming in a mug in front of her and, teary-eyed with gratitude, she is ready to confess everything. But Miss Haupt is still bustling, serving Moon Ja in the living room from a wooden tray, changing the music on the stereo to a Schumann song cycle—*Frauenliebe und Leben*, Sylvia is pretty sure—and pulling the curtains against the gathering night. She turns on one small lamp over the piano; the light ripples along the rich old wood.

Finally, she comes back to the table, pulling something from her apron pocket and setting it down in front of Sylvia. "Now," she says. "Look at this."

Sylvia reaches for it curiously, taking it up in her hand. It is a pipe made out of pine: satiny smooth, an aged maple color, and almost weightless. She turns it over and over, stroking the wood with one finger. A faint sweet tobacco smell sifts through the air. "What is this?" she asks, smiling.

"Some old friends in Kentucky," says Miss Haupt. "Relatives of people I knew in Germany. They grow tobacco on a small farm outside of Brownsville, if you know where on earth *that* is." She pulls a pair of wire-rimmed glasses out of another pocket and slips them on; they slide down her nose as she leans forward. "Look at this," she says, running one finger along the stem of the pipe. "Can you believe it? It's all hand-carved, every bit of it. And over a hundred years old now—it was made by the grandfather while he was a prisoner during the Civil War. In Andersonville, I think it was."

"They gave this to you?" It sounds blunt, though Sylvia does not mean it to.

"Well," says Miss Haupt, smiling almost shyly. "I've always loved it and . . . well, today is my birthday."

"Oh, I'm sorry," says Sylvia. "I didn't mean to stumble in. . . ."

"No, no, no," says Miss Haupt, laughing. "This is wonderful—lemon cake, two friends, and I lived through the concert." Behind her on a shelf is a blue and white teapot filled with a sunburst of yellow daffodils. "You never know if you really will," Miss Haupt adds, "no matter *how* long you've been playing."

"I've got a recital in only two weeks," Sylvia blurts out, hoping Miss Koh cannot hear them, that she has fallen asleep beneath the quilt with her empty plate, her fork, a few crumbs of lemon cake left on the tray beside her.

"Oh yes," says Miss Haupt. "You must be working hard these days." The light from the little lamp sparkles on her glasses.

Sylvia starts to nod, then drops her head. "Not really," she says, and then, like that, she is crying helplessly, the tears pouring out of her eyes and splashing onto her folded hands.

An hour later, they go downstairs together and get into Miss Haupt's old Peugeot, parked on the street. Miss Koh is still asleep on the sofa upstairs, her black hair fanned out across the pillow, her mouth making small motions and her fingers flickering against the edge of the quilt. "You cannot walk home alone at this hour," Miss Haupt said when Sylvia tried to leave. "Let me drive you." Too exhausted to argue, Sylvia simply nodded and followed her downstairs.

What has she done? She never meant to tell Miss Haupt—to tell *anyone* besides Colette—but now the news is out and there is nothing she can do about it. "Are you sure?" Miss Haupt asked her. "Have you taken a test?"

"No," said Sylvia. "But I know."

"Well, I would like to take you to a friend of mine. Just to be positive. Would that be all right?"

"Sure. I guess."

"Her name is Margaret. She's a very kind woman, an old friend. Will you let me make you an appointment?" They were still sitting at the kitchen table; they were speaking in near whispers, for Miss Koh had fallen asleep long ago. Miss Haupt's glasses had slipped down so far they were teetering on the end of her nose, and her hair on one side had fallen loose from the bun. The daffodils on the shelf suddenly vanished into the gathering darkness.

Sylvia nodded, bleary-eyed. "Okay. Sure."

Now they are driving slowly through the dark streets. Miss Haupt is not a good driver. They pass parked cars, the Free Library, bare trees, the statue of George Washington. The conservatory looms ahead as Miss Haupt makes her turn along the little square. "Next block," says Sylvia. "Right in the middle."

They pass the alley and park across the street from the

brownstone. Upstairs, three windows are lit. Miss Haupt switches off the engine, which ticks for a moment, then gives a long ghostly sigh and shudders into quietude. "Poor old car," she says. They sit for a long moment, Sylvia beyond thought. "You know," says Miss Haupt, "*I* was in trouble once when I was very young."

Sylvia turns her head. Miss Haupt's profile is rimmed in pale yellow—the streetlight above the car.

"Not this kind, but bad enough," Miss Haupt adds.

Sylvia is silent, not knowing what to say.

"And even though it would have been a disaster, I was devastated when I found myself once again safe." She turns to look at Sylvia. Her face, in the dark, already seems familiar, like that of a mother or an old friend.

"I know what you mean," Sylvia says finally. "I think." She looks down at her abdomen. "In a weird way, having a baby would make life . . . simpler."

Miss Haupt chuckles. "Oh, Sylvia—haven't you found *that* out yet? Life is never simple."

Sylvia sighs and reaches down for her bag of music. "Well, thanks," she says. "I'm glad I came to see you, Miss Haupt."

"Oh for heaven's sake—Katerina. Call me Katerina. Please."

"All right." She feels languid with exhaustion, compliant. All she wants is to crawl into her own bed and sleep the night away. "Good night, Katerina," she says. "I appreciate . . . you know—everything." She opens the door, slides from the seat out into the cold night, shivering a little, when suddenly she thinks of something and leans down to look into the open window. "Is Miss Koh all right? She looked like she might be sick or something."

"No, no," says Miss Haupt. "No, she's fine—just exhausted from touring. She'll be as good as new in just a few weeks. You get some sleep now."

Sylvia nods obediently and starts off across the street. When she has reached her front steps, she turns to wave at the car. Miss Haupt rolls down her window. "Listen," she calls softly. "Will you call me tomorrow? I want to stay in touch about this."

"Sure," says Sylvia. "Good night."

Book
FOUR

These three take crooked ways:

carts, boats, and musicians.

—Hindu proverb

CHAPTER TWENTY

*M*oon Ja wakes suddenly several hours before dawn, throwing off the quilt that is too warm. She feels flushed and feverish, though not weak at all; she feels energized and in need of cold air. She sits up carefully on Katerina's creaking old sofa and swings her feet to the wooden floor, which is early-morning freezing but feels good against her hot toes. Cold rarely finds its way into Katerina's house. At certain times there is nothing better than Katerina's warm and kindly mess, her soft comforting motherly presence, and at other times, Moon Ja has to admit, she finds all of it stifling. She has never been able to understand Katerina's ability to move so easily between the mushy complicated warm hell of human relationships and the cold ice of music; how can such a distracted grandmotherly creature play the piano at all?

Moon Ja pats around on the floor with her bare feet, searching for the shoes she pulled off the night before. She is still wearing nylons and her skirt and rumpled blouse; she's a sight, no doubt about it. Katerina and her influence: "Moon Ja, come on now. You're in no shape to go anywhere, just hole up here for a few days and let me take care of you until we get the word."

She finds her shoes, pulls them on, stands up, tucking in her blouse and smoothing down her skirt, which is indeed loose. So she has been losing weight, all through the tour. She'd been shocked on the scales at the doctor's yesterday: ten pounds in a little over six weeks. She combs her hair with her fingers and rubs her eyes; she feels like a small feral creature with her leg in a trap. She needs food. And none of Katerina's sugary baking, either; she needs protein, big chunks of it.

She walks lightly across the floor, her shoes clicking, trying to avoid crashing into things in the semi-darkness. Katerina is snoring comfortably in the bedroom, turning in her sleep; Moon Ja can hear the bedsprings give.

No protein in the refrigerator except a package of bacon, which she takes out and turns over in her hands. Mostly fat. She puts it back and begins opening cupboard doors, taking down cans and reading the labels. This is probably nothing, Margaret the doctor told her. Lots of women your age bleed off-schedule. It's usually just some kind of hormonal imbalance—premenopausal stuff. But how long have you had these swollen glands under your arms?

Suddenly she finds protein: three small cans of Vienna sausage, cold little pink fingers of meat. Ugh—she rarely eats beef, but she is desperate. She tears open the ringed top on one of the cans and pulls out two sausages, chewing slowly, eyes closed, imagining the protein passing into her bloodstream and moving directly to the rubbery lymph glands she's noticed but ignored for quite some time.

I'm going to do some blood work, Miss Koh. And maybe, depending on what we see, a biopsy of these glands and possibly a lymphangiogram. But let's get the blood panels back before we get too excited, all right? As I say, this is probably a combination of harmless symptoms we're seeing here.

Moon Ja moves to the window. The sky vibrates with suppressed light; the buildings are black against it. Suddenly, she wants to walk and walk, though she has been so fatigued for weeks. We can't take any chances, Miss Koh; try not to worry. We'll know more in a day or two, when we get word back from the lab.

The streets are dangerous; Katerina would be upset if she knew Moon Ja was out walking in them, so she is very quiet as she finds her coat and opens the door to the stairway. Her face is still flushed; the coat feels much too hot; she holds her hair impatiently away from her neck. The first wave of icy dawn air, damp and salt-laden, feels wonderful. She could probably walk forever, but where she heads (like Lassie coming home, she thinks wryly) is the conservatory. Her hot face tingles in the cold air; she jams her hands in her coat pockets; she is forty and she's never felt more achingly alive.

Sylvia is back in the practice room before 6:00 A.M.

She slept very hard for three and a half hours—the sleep of the dead, as her mother used to say—but woke absolutely by one-thirty and lay staring into the darkness for the rest of the night, thinking, of all things, about Opus 111. She could not shake Toft's words out of her mind. What had she missed in all her practice, in her books about Beethoven? What important key had eluded her?

In spite of her wakeful night, she felt fine—no nausea, no dizziness. Was she crazy after all? Had she jumped to a ridiculous conclusion after a week of the stomach flu?

At five she rose quietly, dressed, and slipped down the hallway past Colette, asleep in her bed, to the kitchen, where she had half a banana and a piece of toast before it hit her. Colette, of course, heard her vomiting and handed her a wet washrag and patted her on the head before stumbling back to bed. When Sylvia finally stood up, she was looking directly into the mirror over the sink: astounding. In less than seven days she'd become hollow-eyed, fox-faced, mad. Her hair, always wild, now writhed like snakes around her head.

She had to look away quickly; she frightened herself.

Now she is here, back on the bench, watching through the window as the sky turns a roseate morning gold. It is a clean, ancient color, like the gold on the domes of the Ukrainian Orthodox cathedral she saw once on a long Easter morning walk with Marushka; just as they passed the big church, hundreds of small doves came tumbling over the old buildings in a cloud that expanded and contracted like breath. They flew inland, away from the sea, and the sun glinted on their white wings.

Sylvia looks down at the piano keys, runs her left hand lightly up and down them. Her eyes burn; she feels sweaty and unwashed, though she took a long hot bath last night. She cannot at this moment connect the act she committed with David—the softness, the warmth, the shine of skin—with the heaviness that has settled in on her. And yet they are inextricably connected; they are one and the same thing. But in the first part of the act, there was a man; in this, she is alone. There is only herself and the tiny pink thing that is blooming and buzzing within her.

She begins the Beethoven sonata without any new ideas, keeping in her mind the words *innocence* and *purity*, but her fingers are stiff and sore, her hands unresponsive. My body knows more than I do, she thinks. Without making any kind of decision about it, she stops playing in the middle of a bar, gets up from the bench, walks to the great French window in its mahogany frame.

The two panels are locked tight against the cold night air; she reaches up, unlatching them, and swings them wide open. The smell of the sea—sometimes it is so strong at dawn—seeps into the room and billows over the piano, leaving behind a faint patina of mist. She can feel the ocean—dead fish, floating garbage, tenacious oozing mussels—playing in her hair. She steps up onto the sill.

Miss Haupt—Katerina—had helped, and so did the lemon cake and the dim, warm kitchen. But only for an evening. For the answer here—she sees it very clearly—is that she's alone in this. No succor anywhere. No mother who will not be devastated by the news. No father who will not be cut to the core. She clings lightly to the edges of the window frame with both hands, her feet sturdy on the wide sill, and looks down.

There is nothing there. A long, long drop—five stories—and the sidewalk below, still in gray shadow, not yet touched by the rising sun. The little park, the benches. The wrought-iron fence, the street. The brownstone across the square where her life takes place. Her friends, asleep. No one to see her, to wonder what she is doing, what kind of craziness is at work in her this moment.

Someone else is up, too; she can hear a cello, faintly, and another piano—maybe Brandon, maybe Jan. Everything is very clear, yet miles away; she recognizes all of it, the pieces that both instruments are playing, the sections of each composition, but it is as though they are playing in San Francisco or on the moon—they are not playing in her life, anyway. Her life has been distilled to several simple things: the windowsill, the dawn wind lifting her hair, the hint of mist in her nostrils.

So go ahead, she taunts herself. You always wondered if you could. What had Peter told her, standing like a stone Buddha above the city? If you can do this, Sylvia, you can do anything. Though *this*, of course, is not what he meant.

What would happen? She imagines the easy step into air, her arms rising of their own volition, the futile attempt at flight. Tumbling through showers of white feathers from a cloud of frightened doves, and bells all over the city breaking out in a jubilant clamor: she has fallen, she has fallen.

Lying on her back on the cold concrete, arms outflung, eyes wide open and staring at the dimming sky. If you can do this, Sylvia. . . . Toft crying out in terror from the window above, Katerina Haupt calling down to her, Jan sobbing, Colette keening like an old woman. The faint, high wail of an ambulance weaving its graceful, futile way through the early morning streets to where she has already vanished.

She closes her eyes for a moment. What a simple ending; how clean and final. No music, no sex, no baby to be dealt with. No need, ever again, to decide anything.

And then she realizes what has been bothering her about Opus 111.

Something Beethoven said; she had written it down—it was in one of his letters, perhaps to a woman, she can't quite remember—but it had struck her then as important, even though she had not connected it directly to the sonata. What *was* it? And where are her notes?

She opens her eyes, thinking, I'll go home and find them, I *know* I've got it written somewhere—and then she sees that someone has come out into the square. He is standing in the long shadow of the conservatory building, staring straight up at her. She looks at him for some time, wondering what he is doing, who he is, and then the sun finally crests over the top of the building and light pours down upon his shining bald head and she sees that it is Tee.

By the time Moon Ja gets to the conservatory, she is thoroughly chilled, the restless heat having left her like a flame going out. She can hear a cello playing—some eager young student, beating the rush. She stands shivering, looking up at the old building that was her home for four long years, thinking of Cornelius Toft, the way he pushed her into excellence. Every time she plays, she has to admit, old Cornelius is in the audience judging her, even now when she is more famous than he. Well, he was her father in a way that her real father, not being a musician, could never be.

She hugs herself with her arms, feeling the loss of weight, the fragility of her bones. The building looms darkly above her like the huge stone Buddha in Kyongju, and she remembers her own hubris, the way she'd stood there before the sunstruck god in all her implacable arrogance and pride. There's something I'm not getting, she'd told herself smugly. She can still taste the salty sausages; she tucks her hands into her armpits and then withdraws them quickly.

I might die.

She looks up and down the street, swinging her head like a slow, wounded animal—is there nobody coming to help me? am I really here alone?—and then, with a small sound close to a sob, she walks toward the kiosk with its old guard beside the conservatory door. Maybe he'll let me in, she thinks, humbly. If I tell him I used to be a student.

As Sylvia climbs back down into the practice room, still thinking about Tee staring up at her that way, how odd it was, she hears a piano, close by, playing Schubert. The Sonata in B-flat Major: Who's working on that one? She's never heard it being practiced before; whoever it is, is playing it perfectly. She stands by the window, entranced, waiting to see how long this will go on, and then, when it is clear that this is a performance and not a practice session, she moves quietly to the hall door and opens it, following the music.

Moon Ja plays with her eyes closed, in a deep trance. No audience to think of this time; just the battered grand piano, the early light flooding the room, the music. She is playing the long, slow, ravishingly beautiful andante sostenuto and behind her closed eyelids moves a haze of images: burnt gold, Gothic stone archways, blue and scarlet stained glass, Flemish paintings dark with age, narrow winding streets, cobblestones, fishermen, goblets of ruby-red wine, heaped clouds, masses of deep yellow roses. All the lovely places in the world she has ever performed. She can smell blossoms; the scent blows through her hair; she sways, sometimes singing to herself in a crooning voice. Her face is cool and wet with tears.

Intolerable music.

When she is finally done, she sits, head down, her hands flat against the bench, taking deep breaths. The tears well and well within her; how few people on this planet, she thinks, know what this gift is like? For she is aware, in sudden deep humility, of how unusual a creature she is, how wonderful and strange her ability . . . and in the same moment is struck with a terrible sadness at her own inadequacy and shallowness. No one can ever do this the way it is meant to be done—nobody, not even Schubert himself. We are so far off the mark, even the best of us.

Tears spill over, making runnels down her cheeks; she wipes them away with the flat of her hand and wipes her nose, too, thinking of the glands beneath her arms, the fatigue that is making her shake, the great yawning pit lying just below her feet. If only there is music there, then I think I can . . .

But of course there is no music; that is why it is called death.

She sighs, rising, feeling empty, scoured out. Her legs shake; she imagines glands throughout her body glowing with a merry, poisonous light. Music is still melting in the air and the scent of yellow roses billows around her. Monks are chanting in a monastery, striking gongs. The wooden fish clacks in the cold dawn light of Kyongju.

Auntie Lee, she thinks, how can you bear it?

Sylvia watches, stupefied, from the hallway. Miss Koh, playing alone only two rooms down from her! Miss Koh, up at dawn to practice! The Schubert is perfect, unbelievable. She watches with her hands clasped before her, the fox-faced girl in the mirror forgotten, the lingering nausea banished. She has never heard anything like this, never in her life. She thinks again of the Easter doves, and now they are rising, fluttering small and free, blowing out over the ocean. Miss Koh!

But when the music ends, Miss Koh bows her head and sits for a long time smoothing her cheeks with one hand as though she is crying. Sylvia is caught, not wanting to be seen, yet not able to leave. What is wrong? What if Miss Koh is ill or in pain? Should she go get help?

And then Miss Koh rises and Sylvia is shocked at how thin she looks, how old. There are lines in her face; her hair is limp, her blouse rumpled, her skirt askew. She looks both terrified and helpless, and Sylvia moves first toward the door—may I help, Miss Koh? is there anything I can do?—and then steps backward, uncertain. Would she want anybody to see her this way? Looking like a street person? Crying? Well, of course not, Sylvia thinks. Of course she wouldn't.

She turns and hurries away down the hall to her own room, where she slips inside and closes the door against Miss Koh's spectral image. She cannot believe how shaken she is, how naked Miss Koh looked just then. How weak. Toft's most famous student. The famous, elegant Moon Ja Koh. Amazed, she goes back to her own practicing, forgetting all about her Beethoven revelation, though Miss Koh's anguished face floats before her for hours.

At three she remembers that she was supposed to call Katerina Haupt. She has not eaten since she threw up the half a banana and dry toast; her hands are trembling from her hunger and fatigue, but she feels stronger somehow—perhaps the vision of Miss Koh in her weakness has something to do with this—and she has worked hard today. The *Sonatine* is getting there, Scarlatti is in pretty good shape; she has always been good with the *Fantasiestücke*. Opus 111—well, she will work on it more tomorrow. She has not thought of her pregnancy in hours, though now it comes flooding back to her, the huge, knotty, unsolvable problem. I'll think of *something*, she tells herself, dialing Katerina's number.

"Hello," says Katerina cheerfully. "How are you doing?"

"Okay." She is leaning up against a cold wall in the hallway, the receiver of the pay phone pressed to her ear. "Better, I guess. A little more settled, anyway."

"Good. That's good," says Katerina. "I just wanted you to know that I've made the appointment with my friend. No need for you to go on wondering, right? We might as well get it confirmed?"

"Thanks," says Sylvia. Her own voice sounds dead to her. She clears her throat, and suddenly she is asking, "Why me? You don't even know me, not really. I'm just somebody in trouble." Her voice catches. For some reason, she is thinking of the ambulance attendant in the alleyway that night, his cloud of angel hair.

Katerina is silent. Sylvia hears her sigh into the receiver, not a frustrated sigh, but one without any explanation in it. "I honestly have no idea," she says finally, apologetically. "But it seems like the thing to do."

"Okay," says Sylvia, nodding dreamily. "What time?"

"Thursday morning," says Katerina. "I'll pick you up at eight. And, Sylvia—just try to forget it for a while, okay?"

"Sure." She is feeling very obedient now; someone is telling her what to do. She will go home, try to eat something, work a little on her term paper. And she'll go to bed early tonight and make herself sleep.

Tee has been sitting on the park bench for hours pretending to read the newspaper while the day grows warmer and warmer and finally almost hot. He is sweating and nervous; he doesn't like just sitting out in the middle of everything this way.

The girl finally comes out, late afternoon. And she's not even making a straight line down the sidewalk; her music bag is pulling her whole shoulder down and her hair hangs in her face. She's thin and white as bones.

He sits where he is on the bench, the paper up in front of his face, watching her over the top. Big trouble, he can see it. The way she's slumping along like that, and her standing in the window that way. Five stories up—holding on to the frame with just her fingers, staring off into the sky.

All he could do was stand there looking up at her with his mouth dropped open, waiting for the big thump. Nobody around, nobody but him. He'd seen it before, people jumping. Once off a tier in prison, once from an apartment building when he was a kid. Nobody as young as her, though.

So all this restless moving around, this thinking about money and Raymon—all this stopped today. He's got a job now, a new project. He's going to watch out for her. Everywhere she goes, he follows. Everywhere she sits down to cry, he's behind her somewhere. And if she climbs up in that window again, he goes to the phone booth, calls the cops. He'd do that for her—he'd even call the cops.

Who *you?* they ask him.

Jus' a friend, he tell them. Jus' somebody who care. No big *deal.*

• • •

Moon Ja is back in the apartment before Katerina, an early riser, is even awake. She sits at Katerina's table with her cup of tea, blankly watching the day take shape. You have to get yourself together, Moon Ja, she tells herself once.

But she has been undone.

CHAPTER TWENTY-ONE

S ylvia has not been to a gynecologist since she was fifteen. That time it had been a short, well-fed man with faded red hair and freckles like red pepper over every visible part of his body, including his eyelids and fingers. The nurse and her mother had both been in the room too, the nurse busily taking notes as though completely unaware of the fact that the doctor's freckled fingers were embedded deep inside of Sylvia. He had pushed down on the outside of her at the same time he pushed up from the inside, asking, "Does that hurt?" She remembers panting with shame. Where would his fingers go next? What kind of instrument on the little tray would he try to put inside of her?

Anne, she remembered, had stood off to the side, looking pale and brave. Every time she caught Sylvia's eye, she nodded encouragingly.

He cured Sylvia's cramps with a little pink pill she had to take every day—estrogen. What will this doctor—Margaret—do? she thinks now. You can't cure pregnancy with a pill.

She strips slowly, folding her skirt and blouse and placing them on a stool in the corner. She saves her shoes for last—her feet are already cold. When she is naked, she stands for a moment on her tiptoes before the small mirror that hangs at face height on the wall, trying to see down the length of her body. There is not much to see. Her hips look like her protruding cheekbones; her belly is not only not round yet, but concave. However, her breasts, never much, are larger, the nipples more . . . authoritative somehow.

She grimaces at herself and reaches for the paper shirt lying on the table. It is flat, with big armholes, like a paper-doll dress; she can feel the cool air circulating against her skin.

At least there is not much of her to examine—just a rack of narrow bones and white skin stretched taut over it and those swelling breasts, which, she has to admit, are completely foreign to her and really almost beautiful. Women's breasts, for the first time. How large will they become for the baby? Will her belly stretch like a blown-up beach ball?

She sits, pondering, her hand over her abdomen, and then Margaret knocks once and comes in, a chart in her hand, her stethoscope swinging. "So," she says. "Are you plenty cold by now?"

"My feet."

"Put your shoes back on, I don't care." Margaret is gathering things together on a tray, her glasses slipping down.

Sylvia feels her breath catch. She must have been holding it without realizing. Okay, so I'm nervous, she thinks. So anyone would be.

"Been to a gynecologist before?" asks Margaret, turning. Her gray hair, very tough and shiny, springs up from her round forehead like a small crown made of wire. Katerina said that Margaret lived for years on a kibbutz in Israel, where she delivered hundreds of babies out in the middle of the desert; looking now at her scrubbed and competent hands, Sylvia can believe it.

"When I was fifteen."

"Fun experience?"

Sylvia snorts.

"Okay, well it never is, no matter how gentle the doctor is, so just lie back and try to relax if you can. Here, put your feet in these and slide forward . . . that's good." Sylvia's knees are bent and far apart; the cool air swirls against her.

Margaret washes her hands. "First, we'll take a peek in there with the light." She dries her fingers on a paper towel and tosses it into the trash. "How many weeks since possible conception, Sylvia?"

Sylvia is quiet, thinking. Everything has been moving so fast, she has actually lost track. "Five?" she says. "Almost six?"

"Okay. I'm going to take a look at your cervix—sometimes at this stage there'll be a beautiful bluish tinge to it that's a pretty good indicator."

She sits down and swings the light beneath the paper drape, snapping it on. Sylvia can feel the heat immediately, like rays from a small sun. "This'll be weird for a minute," Margaret says. "I've just got to slip this speculum in here so I can see."

Sylvia feels something enter her, hard and unyielding; her muscles clench against it. She looks up at the ceiling.

A sign in fuzzy writing says, "Too much sex blurs the vision." Relax, she tells herself. Relax. It's just a little tool.

But whatever Margaret is doing, Sylvia can feel up to her stomach and down to the bottom of her feet. "Ah yes," she hears Margaret murmur. "Mmmm*hmm*." The light goes off, the warmth fades quickly, and Margaret's head appears above the drape. "Okay," she says. "You're blue all right, though as I say, that's not a definitive sign."

Now she is pulling on plastic gloves, dipping her fingers in something that looks like Vaseline. She moves to the side. "I can tell a lot more by whether or not your uterus is enlarged. At this stage it should be about the size of a lemon." Sylvia winces as Margaret's fingers enter her.

"Hmmm," says Margaret. "Yes indeed." She is traveling deep inside, her face tipped toward the ceiling, her glasses set sternly in place. She pushes up the way Sylvia remembers the red-haired doctor doing, then pushes down at the same time, finally pulling her fingers out and stripping off the gloves. "Well congratulations, my dear," she says. "You're going to have a baby."

Sylvia's stomach clenches. "You can tell just like that?"

"Let's say that after all the pregnant women I've seen in my life, I'm pretty damn good at recognizing an enlarged uterus when it walks up and says hello." She tosses the gloves in the trash. "But I'm still going to have you pee in a cup for me."

"How . . . how big is it? The baby?"

"Very small. And it's called an embryo at this stage."

"Could you tell it was a baby if you saw it?"

"In a couple more weeks I'll be able to see it moving on an ultrasound. Listen, why don't you get dressed and meet me in the office? We can talk better there."

Sylvia pulls on her clothes in slow motion, pondering the now-official fact of her pregnancy. Her arms and legs feel heavy, as though she is moving underwater. Congratulations, you are going to have a baby. A baby. A baby. Her ears are ringing, her knees feel weak. She has to touch the wall several times for balance as she walks down the hallway.

She sits down before the cluttered desk. Margaret is on the phone—it sounds like a doctor-to-doctor conversation—and then she puts down the receiver and looks at Sylvia over the tops of her glasses. "So," she says. "What's next?"

This is what Sylvia has been dreading more than the exam, more than knowing for sure. Somebody coming out and asking her what she is going to do about the pregnancy. For what *is* she going to do, after all?

"It's not that I haven't thought about it," she says finally, apologetically. "It's just that I don't know yet."

Margaret waits. She does not smile—she looks very stern, in fact—but she generates a solid warmth. Whatever I tell her, Sylvia thinks, she'll accept.

"If I decided to have an . . . abortion," she says, feeling her throat close over the word, "could you do it?"

Margaret nods.

"And how would it be? What would you do?"

"It's really very simple, especially at this stage." Margaret sounds brisk. "It's an outpatient procedure. I'd need you to come in the morning, early, but you'd be out of here before noon. A few days of lying around, and you're back to normal."

"What do you . . . how do you get it out?"

"Vacuum. I'd insert an instrument—nothing bigger than what you felt today—and suck out the tissue. At this stage there's not much." The light shines on Margaret's glasses, making her look both blind and wise.

"And how much will it cost?"

"Three twenty-five. But we can work out payments if you need to."

Sylvia swallows. "Do you do this very often?" The question seems rude, but she has to know. How many women, how many babies? Is it an everyday thing? She's never known anyone who had one. Not anyone who admitted it, anyway.

"Very," says Margaret. "And you won't find a bigger fan of babies anywhere."

Sylvia stares at her; the room is very quiet. This woman thinks I am an adult, that I can decide on my own, she thinks. So why can't I? "Do I need to do it right away?"

"Not immediately. You've got a couple more weeks in the simple stage. But the sooner the better."

"I have a recital coming up. Next week. If I decide, could I wait till after then?"

"No problem at all. Just let me know."

Suddenly, Sylvia's eyes are filling. She blinks hard and looks at a spot on the wall above Margaret's head. "I really have thought about it. I have. But it's so hard."

"You have a good family?"

"Oh yes."

"They'd take you in?"

"Of course."

"But you don't want to?"

Sylvia shakes her head. "It wouldn't be fair to them. They're not . . . that happy together."

"And the young man?"

"No way."

Margaret laughs. "Well, *that* sounds pretty final."

Sylvia smiles too, shakily. "It *is* final. It would never work in a million years."

"Adoption?"

"I don't know if I could. But I'll think about it."

"Okay, Sylvia." Margaret rises, and Sylvia gets to her feet. She towers over the older woman. Margaret holds out her hand. "Hang in there," she says. "This is hard stuff, very hard. Just let me know."

Sylvia takes her hand. It is small and dry and callused, a hand that has worked long hours. A gardener's hand. Margaret gives her a double squeeze—one, two—and then releases her. "Try to eat more," she says. "I know it's hard with the vomiting, but you're pretty thin. Dry toast or crackers the minute you open your eyes in the morning. Weak tea. Works like a charm. And don't forget to pee in that cup on the way out."

"Thanks," says Sylvia.

When she finally gets back to the waiting room, Katerina is looking frayed. "How are things?" she asks.

"Fine," says Sylvia. "Really." She tries to smile, but she is thinking of the vacuum, the tiny embryo. She has been vacillating for so long between the tiny blooming buzzing thing inside her (which, in an odd way, she is growing to love, or at least care about) and the possibility of nothing at all that it is difficult to think clearly. Well, at least she finally knows one thing for sure.

"I'm pregnant, Katerina," she says. "No doubt about it."

Sylvia lets herself in the downstairs door with her key, thinking about her lesson with Toft in forty-five minutes—she will have to hurry now; she'll have to grab a piece of fruit and a sandwich or she'll be sick again—when she catches sight of Tee in the park, sitting on the bench, reading a newspaper. Lately, it seems as though everywhere she goes, he is somewhere close behind. Oddly, however, he does not frighten her, not even when he leaves old boxes of candy, obviously out of the trash, on her front stairs. He means her no harm; she is sure of that. What he does want from her, she cannot tell.

She pushes the door open with her foot and rushes upstairs, pulling herself along by the hand railing. Halfway up, she is hit with a cloud of sleepiness—she will die if she doesn't fall straight into bed. It happens all the time these days, these sudden terrible spells of narcolepsy, as Colette calls them. One minute she will be awake and functioning, the next she is asleep.

She climbs two more stairs, stopping to rest again. Okay, she says, but just for ten minutes. Just ten minutes on her cool sheets with the pillow under her head.

"You are still losing color in the upper registers," Toft snaps. They are poring over Opus 111, as usual. "You

need to voice the subject in your fifth finger. And allow
the dissonances to come out, for God's sake—that is
what we are listening for." He is agitated today; his old
cheeks are flushed, his fingers trembling. "You are too
passive when you are quiet—you must not lose the direction of the phrase. Look—here, and here, and here."
He stabs his finger at the score. "Listen to me—bwa da
da de, bwa da—do you hear what I am saying? *Think*,
Sylvia. You must concentrate, where are you? Listen—
they will come in laughing; they will not believe a creature like you can possibly play this. You must prove
them wrong."

A creature like me? she wants to say. What does that
mean? I'm too young? Too thin? My hair is too wild? But
she does not ask; of course she does not ask. Toft can say
whatever he wants.

She was fifteen minutes late for this lesson; never, in
her entire two years with Toft, has she been late before.
In fact, it has been a phobia with her, the possibility of
walking in and finding him already seated, waiting for
her. So she comes early, always. If she can't please him
with her playing, at least she can cater to his demand for
punctuality.

But today she slept like the dead for three quarters of
an hour and then woke in a panic, heart pounding, and
grabbed her music without stopping in the kitchen. Oh
God, oh God, she was saying—he's going to *kill* me.

When she finally burst through the studio door, he
was sitting in his chair reading a book. "I'm sorry," she
started to wail, but he held up one hand without looking
at her and read slowly to the end of the page, where,

sighing heavily, he marked his place, closed the book, and finally gave her his attention.

"So," he said before she could explain. "I thought this would be a good afternoon for reading since I have no students who are interested in seeing me today." His mouth was puckered; he looked like a cruel elf; he seemed to be perversely delighted at her wrongdoing. He's going to torture me forever, she thought.

"I'm sorry," she said. "I've been sick. I had to go to the doctor this morning. And I got back later than I thought."

"You are ill?" He drew back in his chair, looking horrified, at the same moment she remembered his fabled aversion to germs.

"Nothing catching," she assured him. "It's a female disorder."

"Oh I see, I see." He looked no less horrified—she could imagine what he thought of *female* disorders—but at least he did not cancel the lesson. "This is very . . . inconvenient. Your recital . . ."

"I can do it. I'm taking medicine."

"Ah yes." He patted around for his glasses, perched on the top of his head and tangled in his white hair, and then got up slowly and moved to a chair by the bench. "I am very tired, Sylvia," he said, almost as an afterthought.

Now they are huddled over the music, so close she can smell him, a musty old man's smell, a combination of smoke and mouthwash and denture cement. And, of course, cologne—dim and spicy and eighteenth-century. But there is something else about him—something sickish and old he cannot cover under the cologne and mouthwash. Under normal circumstances it would not bother her much, but her sense of smell these days is so acute . . . she feels herself becoming nauseated.

"In the allegro," he is saying, "you are not balanced enough—you are not bringing out the voices. I was not persuaded by it, not in the least."

"All of it?"

"From the first transition"—he points to the nineteenth bar—"to the development, and then you are losing something again in the coda, do you see?"

She nods. Mr. Toft, she wants to say, I'm going to throw up all over you. She nods again, briskly, as though he has told her everything already and the lesson is over.

"So play it," he says. "Let us *hear* if you understand." He cocks an angry eyebrow at her and marches to the center of the room, where he poses with his hands over his flat belly.

She shifts nervously on the bench. Well, she will fail him once again, that much is sure. Her stomach is churning, her hands icy cold—perhaps she should just get it over, the abortion.

Abortion? What has she just said to herself? Is this her decision? She goes absolutely still, shocked.

"Tut, tut," says Toft, clapping his hands together. "I do not have all day."

She lifts her wrists above the keys and holds them there, panic-stricken. Abortion. Is this truly what she will do? She begins to play without thought, her hands in charge of the music. Beethoven fills the studio. Inside, she is shaking. Abortion, abortion. A vacuum, Margaret said. And it is an embryo, a tiny pink . . . thing. Not a child yet. Or is it?

She plays and plays, and Toft stands somewhere off to the side, like Napoleon, with his hand in his shirt. She cannot remember a thing he said about the allegro, not a thing he punctuated with his stabbing finger. But the music is coming from somewhere anyway—all the hours of practice, she thinks. All the late hours, and Jan waiting by the door . . .

She feels the music swelling and listens, suddenly amazed. What is happening without her? What are her fingers and Beethoven doing on their own? This phrase, always her nemesis, and this one here . . . she glides through them, as close to perfection as she ever hoped to get. And not only this, but it is suddenly achingly beautiful, the movement she always thought so ugly.

So this is being a musician, she thinks; this is it. Playing the best you've ever played when everything is falling to pieces around you. Her heart rises; she is light and empty and filled with a surging power. What a thing to know—you can live through almost anything this way.

By the time she gets to the epilogue of the arietta, she is transported; she has never in her life played like this; she listens in happy shock to the last chords leaving the air. And when behind her Toft says grudgingly, "Not quite as bad this time," she laughs out loud. I *know*, she wants to yelp. Isn't it *wonderful*?

When she leaves the studio, finally, she is ravenous and filled with an electric excitement. She's gotten through the sonata! In the middle of everything, she's gotten through it!

When she is at the end of the hallway, however, she hears Toft's faint voice from the open door of the studio. "Sylvia," he is calling. "Do not gloat."

She stops, waiting.

"Do not presume to gloat, Sylvia. You cannot count on it being there the next time, you know what I mean? It is only a gift, and gifts can be taken away like"—he snaps his fingers—"that."

CHAPTER TWENTY-TWO

*M*oon Ja can't believe what she is doing—but what else is there to do? She and Katerina are waiting for Margaret's phone call, the results from the lab, due back today. Neither of them feels like eating lunch at the table next to the silent telephone. Instead, Katerina has brought out her boxes full of photographs—she's never gotten around to putting them into an album—and she and Moon Ja, sitting beside one another on the sofa, are slowly perusing the haphazard stack of pictures that make up Katerina's life. The apartment is dim; outside, the day is gray and muzzy; on the stereo, low, are Gregorian chants.

"Oh, look at *this* one—these are my parents," says Katerina in a tender voice. Her head, with its thin coiled braids, is down; she holds the picture up for Moon Ja to see. "Mother was twenty-three here, and Father must have been thirty-four or so, I suppose." They each take a corner of the black and white photo and stare silently at the handsome blond couple fated to die—still, perhaps, holding hands—beneath the rubble of their bombed-out house. He wears a watch chain; his thick hair is parted in the middle; she is a graceful ship in full sail with her billowing white skirts and upswept pompadour. Katerina touches her mother's tiny face with one finger, then lays the photo aside.

Moon Ja reaches into the box for a fistful of pictures and spreads them out on the coffee table like playing cards. "Oh my," she says. "Weren't you the cute one?" Five Katerinas, all twelve or thirteen, all in long blond rag-curls, stare back at her. In each of the photos is a piano; the young Katerina sits with her hands in her lap, or her hands resting on the keyboard, as though she is playing; she stands somberly with one hand flat on the piano case; she stands beside a large plant, the piano in the background, with hands folded in front of her.

"Publicity shots," says Katerina. "I was starting to do my first little recitals."

"May I keep one?"

"Oh, of *course*. What am I going to do with all these, anyway?"

On the stereo the Benedictine monks chant, *"In velaménto clamábant Sancti tui, Dómine: allelúia, allelúia, allelúia."* Moon Ja has not studied Latin since high school, but she has never forgotten it. "Hidden in the cloud, O Lord," she silently translates, "thy saints cry alleluia . . ."

She does not want to think about saints, or about God, either, for that matter.

"Look at this one," she says, instead, laughing. Her laughter is weak, compressed by the enormous fear that neither of them talks about. She holds up a picture from the late thirties; in front of a massive stone building stands a hatted and overcoated man with an austere face and sharp, irritable eyes. "No, Katerina, this can't be . . ."

Katerina nods without speaking.

"I'm glad I didn't know him then," says Moon Ja thoughtfully. She holds the photo closer to her eyes, studying Cornelius's younger face. "He looks so . . . unforgiving, I guess."

"He's never been an easy one."

"But I love him, don't you?"

Katerina doesn't answer; Moon Ja wonders what she is thinking. The monks chant, *"Spíritus et ánimae justórum, hymnum dícite De nostro . . ."*

The doorbell rings.

"Now, who can that be?" Katerina pushes photographs from her lap and rises, moving to the window, where she can see down to the street. "Oh no," she sighs. "Moon Ja, I've got problems below."

"Who is it?"

"My student Jan."

"Oh, let him come up, Katerina—it'll take our minds off it."

"You're sure?"

"Really. Go ahead."

On the stereo, the monks chant, in Latin, "The righteous will shine as the sun in the presence of God." The sky brightens for a moment, then goes gray.

Sylvia has not been inside this particular kind of clothing store since she came to Baltimore. Gloria's, it is called. The sort of place where, if she had gone to her high school prom, she might have found her dress. A serious expensive place, devoted to serious endeavors: weddings, formal dinners, recitals. The burgundy carpeting is soft and thick; the very air sparkles with mirrors. Vivaldi pours out, a pleasant waterfall in the background. Women with silver-white hair and glasses' chains move smoothly into place beside the clothing racks as Sylvia and Colette wander past blues and blacks and greens and shimmering roses. One of the silver-haired saleswomen has attached herself to the girls and every so often darts to the hangers, plucking out something and holding it up against Sylvia while Colette studies the effect.

"That's good, I like it," Colette says finally. "Try that one on."

"Okay." Sylvia wishes her mother were here instead; Anne has always known, instantly, what looks best on her. It's because we have the same ridiculous hair, she thinks. And we always have to work around that. She yawns, her jaws cracking, and gives the saleswoman an apologetic look. The euphoria from Toft's lesson has worn off. I'm going to have a baby, she thinks.

Finally, when the stack of dresses they have chosen is large enough, they all move to the dressing room, where the saleswoman—Nadine, her nametag says—hangs everything on brass hooks and then backs away, smiling. Sylvia peels off her jeans and sweater, letting them fall at her feet. When she is down to bra and panties, she glances at herself in the mirror, then at Colette, sitting on a spindly gold chair beside the dressing room door. Colette looks shocked.

"What's the matter?"

She shakes her head.

"Come on."

"You're so *thin*," she says.

Sylvia turns back to the mirror, studying herself dispassionately. It is true; she looks bad—scrawny, almost, with knobs of bones showing everywhere and her skin a translucent bluish white in the all-seeing light of Gloria's. Her weighty new breasts ache. My mother will know, she thinks, the minute she sees me. She pulls a dress from the wall and lets it fall over her head, thinking of the phone call a week before. "You haven't gotten something to wear for the recital yet? What's wrong, Sylvia?" Anne's voice had an uncharacteristic edge to it—not anger, exactly, but something more like exasperation. All the unreturned phone calls, the feeble excuses of the past few weeks—by now, they have to know *something* is up. "Do you need money for the dress?"

"No, no, Mom," she'd said quickly. "That's not it— I've just been really busy. I've got enough saved—don't worry." Later, she'd thought: Maybe I should have taken the money. For . . . in case I decide to go back to Margaret. Why was it so difficult even to think the word? *Abortion*, she'd said to herself. It sounded awful.

Colette, her head cocked, is studying the dress on Sylvia, frowning. "No," she says. "It's not the one."

Other voices come into the dressing room, talking and laughing. The dressing room door next to theirs opens and closes; dresses are hung on the brass hooks. Sylvia pulls a red wool with a full toreador-cape skirt over her head. Why had they chosen this one? No one wears red for a recital; Toft would flip. But the dress falls into swirling folds around her ankles; she swings her knees to the left; the skirt turns, turns, and settles. Her hair, in its usual cloud, lifts and lands. She looks . . . not beautiful, but something else. Something unworldly. Ethereal— that's the word. She turns toward Colette, mute, her eyebrows raised.

"*Yeah,*" Colette says slowly. "That's it, Sylvie. You look great."

The voices next door have fallen silent. Vivaldi has become Albinoni.

The dressing room door opens. Francine, her white face set, stares in at them. "I thought so," she says.

Colette stands up and moves over beside Sylvia. No one speaks. Francine looks as bad as I do, Sylvia thinks. Like she's been sick and almost died. Oh God. "I wish . . ." she begins, but the door is already closing, soundlessly, and the door to the other dressing room, too. After a minute, Colette goes out to check.

"They're gone," she says. "Don't worry."

Sylvia's stomach aches. She hunches over with her arms across her belly, shaking her head. "What am I going to do, Colette?"

Colette takes one of her hands, opens the palm, strokes the fingers. "Sylvie," she says thoughtfully. "You really have to get all this straight pretty quick, you know. You can't just keep waiting for something to happen. That little baby is growing in there."

"I know, I know. Oh God, Colette, I know."

"Have you told David?"

"Are you kidding? I haven't even talked to him since that night."

"Well, he should know."

"Why?"

"He should pay, if you do it."

"Why?"

"Because it's his too."

It's his too, Sylvia thinks. Of course—why hadn't she thought of it before? She is not alone in this, after all. He has some kind of responsibility here, doesn't he? He may not want her, but surely he won't abandon his own child? The tiny, dark-haired child—a little boy with melting eyes like his, exquisite skin, perfect fingers and toes? Little Benjamin, she thinks. Benjamin, with his Israeli grandparents on one side, his Minnesota roots on the other. A genius of a child—a born musician with two musician parents. She tries to imagine herself in a hospital bed, a blue bundle in her arms, and David, like a character in an old Doris Day movie, bending over them both, his Madonna and child, radiating paternal pride.

Oh stop, Sylvia, she thinks.

But Colette is right—he should know what he did.

Jan sits stiffly in Katerina's rocking chair, deeply embarrassed by the fact of Miss Koh's pale presence, the fact that he has interrupted their exploration of the photograph collection, the fact, Katerina thinks, that he is here at all. Sylvia is driving him crazy. I wonder if she's told him yet?

"I'm off to the bedroom," Moon Ja says lightly. "Time for my afternoon nap."

Good old Moon Ja, Katerina thinks. Here she is, waiting for the call, and she can still notice that Jan is falling apart in front of her, desperate for a chance to talk with me alone. "Go ahead," she says to Moon Ja. "Close the door so we don't bother you, why don't you? We won't be long."

Moon Ja gets up and moves away, and as she disappears behind the closing bedroom door, Katerina feels a sudden tightness in her throat. This can't be, she thinks. She can't be sick—not that way. She clears her throat and gives Jan a fainter smile than she means to.

"I'm so sorry, Miss Haupt," he says. "But I must ask you a question—it is a matter of life and *death*." He sucks in his breath on this last, and she sees that his sweet blue eyes are once more rimmed in red, as though he has been operating without sleep for weeks.

"Jan, you have to take better care of yourself. We talked about this last time."

"I know, I know," he says impatiently, "but it is not me who is sick."

"Is this about Sylvia?" She almost adds "again," but stops herself at the last moment. The whole thing is becoming too much for her.

"She is losing weight, Miss Haupt. She looks very ill. She must see a doctor."

Katerina sighs and looks around her apartment, the usual comfortable mess. Her taxes, untouched for weeks, still lie on the kitchen table. Crumbling dry herbs hang from the ceiling. Candle wax spots the piano and— she has to admit it—one can stir up dust clouds by simply walking across the room. Laziness, she thinks guiltily. Utter sloth—maybe I should make bread today? Fresh bread and wild-rice soup for dinner? . . .

"Miss Haupt?"

Katerina sighs again. "She's been to see a doctor, Jan. She's perfectly healthy."

Jan looks puzzled. "She's been? . . ."

"Yes, with me, just a few days ago." Shall I tell him? she wonders. Do I have the right? No—but I can't lie to him either. She holds up her hand. "Jan—this is Sylvia's private business we're discussing here, do you know what I'm saying to you? She'll have to tell you or not tell you herself. But you don't need to worry—she's really fine."

He pushes his fingers through his hair, pondering, and Katerina thinks, he's so damn innocent. He probably won't get it, even now. Finally, he rises and goes to the window, where he stands looking out for a long time. Katerina waits. His long fingers move on the window ledge as though he is playing. You need to get back to your music, she thinks. You need to give up this cause, or whatever it is, as a bad job. You can't help that girl— she's on her own in this one.

Finally, he turns to her. My God, she thinks, startled. He looks ten years older in that light.

"Is Sylvia going to have a child, Miss Haupt?" He stares at her, his mild blue eyes burning, and she has to look away before she answers.

"She's making a hard decision right now, Jan. You'd better leave her alone with it."

He gasps out loud and she looks back at him quickly. "Are you all right, Jan?"

He nods, but she can hear his quick, strangled breaths. His eyes have grown very large and he is staring at something in the far corner of the room. "Jan . . ." She rises and walks to his side, putting her hand on his arm. It is trembling. "Listen to me, Jan." He shakes his head, turns away from her. She comes around the other side and puts an arm around his waist. He lets her give him a quick squeeze, but she can feel the way something is tearing at his chest and throat. He might cry, she thinks. Poor sweet kid. He didn't do anything to deserve this. She has an urge to stroke his hair, as she would a son's, but something tells her not to. Instead, she stands beside him in the window, waiting for a long time until his breathing slows and he is almost calm again. Finally, he sighs, a ragged sigh, and puts out his hand to her.

"Thank you once again, Miss Haupt. You have been wonderful to me."

"What are you going to do, Jan?"

The apartment is very quiet, and Katerina imagines Moon Ja lying in the bedroom, her narrow shoes off, her palms crossed on her chest, waiting for the phone to ring. What in the world is going *on*? Katerina thinks. Why all this at the same time?

He shakes his head without speaking, and she can see, even up close, the new older face that she thought was merely a trick of the light. He gives her a shaky smile; the crooked tooth flashes; she wishes she could make him young again, but she can't—he's launched himself into the world now, and there's nothing she can do about it. Just be careful, she thinks. Protect yourself a little, Jan.

She pats his arm once again; he takes her hand and lifts her fingers to his mouth, kissing them, then turns and hurries toward the door.

The phone rings.

Tee loiters on Charles Street, waiting. She's in the clothes store, she and her friend. They've been in there a long time and he doesn't know why he's hanging around. She ain't goin' to do no jumpin' *now*, he thinks. She buying *clothes*, man. But he stays on anyway, maybe out of habit, keeping watch out of the corners of his eyes for cops on horseback, for anyone telling him to move on.

He's been thinking about Raymon again. It's like he can't stop thinking about him; he wakes up, there's Raymon; he goes to sleep, he dreams about Raymon; he finds some good food in the trash, he thinks of Raymon, first thing. Where *is* that boy now? What he *doin'*? He in trouble? And there ain't, thinks Tee, no damn body to ask. Gotta go find him my*self*—ain't *no*body goin' to look out for him 'cept me.

But where would he even start? Chicago? Cabrini Green? Could be *any*where by now.

And meantime, he's growing up, learning how to fight, getting himself into trouble, and no daddy around to show him how to be. Good-lookin' Raymon, straight and tall. Tee paces back and forth on the corner. How'm I even get a bus ticket? he thinks. Can't even do *that*.

But Raymon and Bellyman—both—are haunting him now: won't let him go.

The girls come out. She's carrying a big bag over her arm. She doesn't look happy, but she doesn't look sad. Looks, instead, like she's going somewhere important.

He waits until they move down the block. When they are almost out of sight, he follows them. Don't do no good, he thinks, to let her see. Just be scare out of her mind, see big ol' Tee slouchin' along behind her.

I'm keepin' you *alive*, girl, he wants to tell her. Just in case you *in*terested.

CHAPTER TWENTY-THREE

Sylvia sits on her front stoop. Late afternoon, not near darkness yet, but night is coming soon enough. Perhaps she shouldn't be sitting here alone, but she is careless about such things these days.

The stars are already in the sky, waiting; she tips up her face, thinking of Minnesota and the way the light dies over the lake each evening amidst the calling of the loons. She has not just sat, in silence, for a long time—not, perhaps, since she left home for Baltimore. As a child she craved it; she would go off into the woods behind the house and lie on a towel on her back, swatting insects and staring up at the swaying canopy of spring leaves, the rolling of the clouds across the sky. Or, in the early mornings, would get up before her parents and bundle into her jacket, slip out of the house, and go down to the edge of the lake, where she would watch the black water turn silver, then faintly pink, then bright silver again as the sun came up over the trees.

The city is full of noise and the hot breath of other

people. She strains after silence for a moment; she hears cars and an airplane and birds in the park, a burst of laughter down the street. A couple strolls past her on the sidewalk. No silence in the city.

She is waiting for David.

What will I say to him? she asks herself. She still does not fully believe that she called him, that she has made her demand upon him in this bold, tough-sounding way.

She'd gone straight to the telephone after Gloria's, not even hanging the new dress in the bedroom closet first. "What are you doing?" Colette asked, seeing her set face, the way she was hurrying across the living room, but Sylvia waved her off and quickly dialed the number she'd memorized weeks before but had never been brave enough to use. Don't think about it, she kept telling herself. Just do it.

By the time he answered, she was taking short hard breaths and holding to the back of a chair for support. "David," she managed to get out. "I need to talk to you right away—I'll meet you outside," and then hung up before he could either respond or refuse.

Will he come? Why should he? He's smart enough to know it can't be good news, she thinks. I wonder if he'll guess? Well, if he doesn't come *here*, I'll have to go *there*. She can't believe how suddenly angry she is—filled with a shaking rage. And it's not the baby, she thinks—it's how he has haunted me all these weeks, how he's messed up my life. I'm not even the same person; he's killed the best part of me, the part that could love people without being afraid.

Her eyes fill with this realization; she shakes her head angrily, wiping the tears from her cheeks with the flat of her hand. *Damn* him. I never wanted *this*, I just wanted . . . well, what *did* I want? The strange sad yearning sweeps over her once again, and is gone. It's *that*, she thinks—whatever *that* is. The same thing I hear in the music sometimes. The terrifying, beautiful *some*thing . . .

Someone is coming along the sidewalk, slowly. She straightens, peering down the street. A man, not large, with sunstruck dark hair—yes, it's him. She's strangling, suddenly; she can hardly swallow; she leaps to her feet and backs up against the doorway. I won't let him in the apartment, she thinks. He's not going up there, ever again.

"Sylvia?" He is standing in front of her now, looking young, nervous, tentative. He smooths his hair back into the ponytail and gives her his self-confident smile, but his fingers are shaking a bit; she closes her eyes for a moment and then opens them again. His jaw, as always, is shadowed in blue and he stands with his feet apart. He's wearing tennis shoes and his black trenchcoat; his hands are jammed in the pockets. For the moment no one else is on the street.

"Hello," she says.

"How *are* you?"

She shrugs (blunt and tough and cool, she thinks, the way they do it in the movies) and shakes her head.

"I've been meaning to call . . ." he begins, and she cuts him off.

"Don't say that. Don't lie to me, I can't stand lying."

He looks surprised. "Okay, Sylvia. I was just trying to be polite."

"Polite."

He nods. "I don't believe in being weird about this kind of thing."

"What kind of thing?" She can't believe she is doing this. She can't believe she is pushing him this way. All the lies she has ever heard come flooding over her. She thinks of her parents, horrified. Lies, lies, lies.

David sighs. He no longer looks tentative, merely resigned. So *this* is the way it is, she can see him thinking. This time it's *this* way—next time, maybe another. Women. He is chewing his upper lip, considering. Then (she can almost see his mental shrug) he reaches out and takes a handful of her hair, shaking it loosely. "This hair," he says, "is so incredible." He smiles at her, a flash of white.

"I think I hate you, David." Her voice breaks when she says this; she is shocked by her hissing vehemence, as he is too. He drops her hair, takes a step backward, looks down the sidewalk. He will walk away any moment; she can see him making the decision.

"Don't you dare run away," she says in the same ragged voice. My God, she thinks, startled, I sound like my *father*.

"Hey," David says, and for a moment his voice is as thin and angry and young as hers. "You don't own me, babe. Don't even think it. What happened between us . . ."

"Nothing happened between us," she hisses.

"Look, Sylvia . . ."

"How's Francine?" she says deliberately.

His eyes shift. "She's okay. We're fine."

"That's not what I asked."

One of his thumbs is hooked through his belt loop. He taps his fingers against the belt, as though marking time. He sighs again. "Look, Sylvia, I'm a big boy, you're a big girl. We know what we did, so let's not make a huge thing out of it, okay? All right?"

She stares at him; she can see the flash of his eyes against the late, slanting sun; how cool he sounds, but how angry he is. She thinks, I *do* hate him. "Right," she says.

"Guys don't appreciate this kind of shit, you know what I mean?" He is beginning to sound on top of things again. He slides his hands back into his pockets.

"Sure," she says. "I can see that." She feels something rising inside of her, something strong and dangerous and solitary.

"Okay," he says, and she can hear the relief in his voice. "So . . . is this it? Because I've got some practicing to do . . ."

"This is it," she says with a hard smile. "Thanks for coming by, David." And you'll never know any of it, she is thinking. I wouldn't tell you now for a million dollars—not if you begged me. It's not your baby; it's mine.

And whatever I do, I do on my own.

Katerina, finally, is the one who takes the call. The bedroom door behind her opens and closes: Moon Ja, of course, who will be standing there, her shoulders hunched forward, her hands clasped in front of her, waiting.

"Hello?"

It is Margaret. "Good news," she says.

"Oh my God," Katerina says, sinking down into a chair. "Really?"

"Really—is she there?"

Katerina turns, holding out the receiver, a silent gift, to her friend. Moon Ja comes forward slowly, her eyebrows raised, and Katerina nods at her, smiling, feeling as though she might sob. Good news.

Margaret and Moon Ja talk for a minute and then Moon Ja hangs up the phone and goes to another chair and sits down slowly, her hands against the armrests. "She says I'm fine."

"I *know*—isn't it wonderful?" Katerina takes a deep shuddering breath, wanting to get up and gather her friend into her arms, but holding still, giving her time to absorb it.

"She says my blood panel was normal, except for anemia. She says . . . iron supplements."

Katerina nods, smiling. The skin over Moon Ja's cheekbones is leaping. And *now* she's going to fall apart, Katerina thinks. Now that she doesn't have to worry. Iron supplements. All this, and then iron supplements. Life is just too funny. She chuckles, coughs, and then the chuckle becomes a fast bright sob, cut off.

Moon Ja gets up then and comes over to her chair where, putting a hand on Katerina's shoulder, she squats down until their eyes are level. "This has been hell for you, hasn't it?"

Katerina nods mutely, her eyes wet, and laughs again as Moon Ja leans in and kisses her on one wet cheek. In all the years they have known each other, Moon Ja has never made such a gesture; she is not an affectionate person. "Thank you so much, my friend," she says in a new voice. What is new about it? Katerina wonders. And then she realizes it is a kind of music she's hearing, something complex and infused with sorrow momentarily deferred. I love her, Katerina thinks, surprised. I never knew how much. She waits, but the jealous little worm has vanished, burnt away by three days of fearful waiting.

Later, much later in the evening, as they sit with wine goblets in the half-darkness listening to Mozart's *Sinfonia Concertante* with its delicious partnership of violin and viola, Moon Ja says, "I think I died anyway."

"What do you mean?" Katerina whispers, so as not to disturb this most beautiful of second movements.

"I don't *know* what I mean. Maybe that *is* what I mean. I'm lost, Katerina."

They are quiet. Katerina's heart aches; she feels drained. She has not practiced, alone, in days, and this has not happened since she lived in Switzerland during the war and there *was* no piano. What might she have been without those lost years and all the lost time in between? What might she have been if she'd had the discipline to hold back and hoard her talent to herself, to hone it and polish it and harden it in the way Cornelius had, in the way Moon Ja always has? But why think of it? She has lived the way she has lived.

"I don't know what to say."

"I'm very thankful, Katerina—I'm very glad that it's nothing. That's not it. It's what comes next. It's what comes after you . . . *look* at it."

"At what?"

"At *it*—the fact that you aren't going to go on, and that you're all alone in this. *It*. Death, I guess, though it's worse than that. I can't even explain it."

"Don't try," says Katerina, hoping she sounds wise. "You'll figure it out." I know nothing, she thinks to herself. I know nothing, but I'm always in the middle of other people's lives. They depend on me, and they shouldn't. I'm not wise at all.

"Oh, I will," says Moon Ja, and her voice, for the first time in days, is firm. "I *have* to, Katerina. Or, you know, everything stops meaning anything. My life, everything I've done. Poof. Like it never was."

Katerina stares at her friend in the semi-darkness. Candles on the table make wavering gold lines on the windowpane behind her. Katerina suddenly remembers her dream of Cornelius, half-naked, beating at the massive black legs of a concert grand with his cane.

I'm tired, she thinks.

After David leaves, Sylvia sits back down on the stoop, alone with the baby. The baby. She cups one hand over her abdomen, thinking, her mind seared bright with anger. Inside me, she thinks, is a tiny child. And what am I going to do about it? What am I going to do about you, little Benjamin?

She could go home, in spite of what she told Margaret. Her parents would take her in—of course they would. And Benjamin would learn to toddle across their polished wooden floor; he would climb the stairs on his hands and knees, and her mother and father would take hundreds of pictures of him, of everything he did. And she herself could still practice on the old grand piano in the sunroom and everything would be almost the same as when she was growing up.

At first, naturally, it would be difficult; Ross would be enraged—not at her, of course, but at the boy, whoever had done this thing to his daughter and then left her to fend for herself.

But is that how it was? Something was *done* to me, against my will?

She sits frowning for a long time, thinking this through, then straightens, easing her back. It doesn't matter anyway, not in the long run. It doesn't matter if David seduced her or whatever old-fashioned term her mother might use. She went along willingly; she loved it; she had been exquisitely happy that night in a way that no *child* could ever imagine.

Ross would be a problem, but he would come around; he would eventually even come to love little Benjamin, his first grandson. She can imagine the two of them, her youthful, powerful, compact father, her beautiful son, playing catch outside the kitchen window. She can imagine Ross and Benjamin on Cedar Lake, leaning over the side of the old rowboat, searching for bluegill, and the dog racing down the hill to meet them at the dock.

But what about her mother? Sylvia frowns again, and pulls her hair back over her shoulders. What *about* Anne? What would this baby mean to *her*?

She tries to imagine Anne old, and she can't. Because when she thinks of the house in twenty years, the green lawn, the lake, she can see Ross tossing the ball for some new dog or sitting on the porch in the evening watching the sun go down, but she can't find Anne anywhere. Not working in the kitchen, not sipping her coffee, not watching for cardinals out the dining room window. Where *is* she? Sylvia thinks, chilled. Is she dead?

No—not dead. But somewhere else, a new place, where Ross isn't. Oh my God, Sylvia thinks. But yes—she has always known it, hasn't she? They're waiting for her to grow up, to be all right, before they go through with it. They're waiting for her to become an adult, and then they'll say goodbye. So how on earth—Sylvia's hand, cupped over her belly, grows icy cold—how on earth can she possibly arrive on their doorstep with a baby?

She bows her head. The picture is shrinking. No Minnesota, no parents—just the two of them, she and little Benjamin.

Could she raise him herself? Drop out of school, get a job, find an apartment of her own? An old brownstone, like this one, close enough to the conservatory that she can still come to recitals? But, of course, who would watch Ben when she is sitting in the audience? Who will watch him when she goes to work each day? And what will it be, this job of hers?

Well, she can play the piano, after all. Perhaps she can play in a restaurant at night, an expensive restaurant where wealthy lovers come to linger over French food in the candlelight. She will have to have a number of good dresses; she will have to wear makeup and control her hair somehow. She will have to look much older than she is. And people, no doubt, will be startled at how good she is—though without time to practice, that won't last long.

For there will come a day, without practice, that she begins to slip, to forget, here and there, to interject her own emergency phrases. Most of the diners, who are not listening anyway, but are fully absorbed in the handsome faces of their lovers across the table, will not notice. Once in a while, however, someone will, someone who is also a musician. And he will see clearly how it is with her: He will see that she is a young mother with very little money and a child to raise, and that she has sold her considerable talent for a meager paycheck. He will see that at twenty-two, twenty-three years old, she has already lost the promise she had at eighteen, that without a teacher, she has become sloppy, impatient, plagued by bad habits. That she has lost her devotion to music, and that someday she will be a thin nervous brittle woman with a handsome son she cannot trust.

Sylvia sighs and gets up slowly. Only two days ago she was sitting in front of Toft, playing Beethoven's last sonata as if for the first time. Only two days ago Toft gave her the first grudging compliment he'd ever given. "But don't ever take it for granted," he'd warned her. "It's a gift, and a gift can be taken away like that." I *do* have it, she thinks. I do. I have the gift, in spite of everything.

But now I have a baby, too.

CHAPTER TWENTY-FOUR

———◆———

*A*t midnight, flushed and furious and sleepless, Sylvia climbs out of bed and goes down the hall to the dark living room. Guys don't appreciate this kind of shit, she hears David say for the thousandth time. Oh, thank you so much for the tip, she thinks. You bastard. She paces back and forth across the wooden floor, her robe clutched to her throat.

She has never been this angry in her life—not at her parents, not at Toft, not at the man who wrenched her throat to the sky. How can someone *be* like that? How can someone touch you all over in tenderness and then throw you away as though you never existed? This is the worst, she thinks—the absolute worst. To pretend to honor something and then to crush it.

She walks to the kitchen window and peers out, her hand falling, by habit, to her belly. Nothing. Nothing inside that means anything—only the seed of a baby that nobody loves. Nothing outside but blank brick. Tee, maybe, asleep in the alley below, dreaming of Bellyman.

Tee and his worthless life. She hates him too, the way he is always skulking along behind her—oh yes, she sees him, though he doesn't know it. She hates him, she hates David, she hates Toft, she hates her father . . . my God, what's happening to me, she thinks, suddenly terrified. What is *happening*?

She whirls and looks at the clock. Colette? No. Poor Colette; let her sleep. Peter? He just got back to town; she hasn't even told him yet. She's all alone; she has to figure out some way to get rid of this anger—it's like an animal chewing on her heart; she hurts—and then she thinks: Jan. He'll be up—he always is; he stays up half the night with his composing. I'll just go there; I won't even call. Jan loves me; I can . . . well, I can talk to him about this *whatever* it is. This hatred, this poison David has put in me. She feels like howling. She hurries to the bedroom, throws on her clothes without turning on the light, grabs her coat, shivering. Be home, Jan, she is chanting in her head. Be home, be home, be home.

Moon Ja sits at her piano in the dark, the curtains open over her wide windows and Georgetown glittering below her. She has no idea what time it is, but certainly very late; she's been up for hours, ever since Katerina dropped her off in the evening, gave her a hug, and wished her well. What a three days, she thinks. Poor Katerina has aged ten years, and look at me—I'm like a corpse. She shudders.

She's gone through fifteen Chopin nocturnes in order by key, an exercise that usually calms her, but not tonight. Car lights play across her window and along the black mirror of the piano; down below are crowds of late-night celebrants. Celebrants, she thinks. What an odd thing to call them. But it's true—they are all at a party they think will never end. They don't *know* yet. They haven't seen *it*—or maybe they have and they're trying to forget.

On her answer machine, when she got home tonight, were a series of messages: three from her manager, with tentative dates for a European tour; one from the amorous stockbroker; one from *Newsweek* requesting an interview; and one from her mother. "Moon Ja, I don't like to leave this on a machine, but we have many people to call. Your Auntie Lee died this afternoon, very peaceful. Don't worry about the funeral; everybody will understand."

Very peaceful. She thinks of Auntie Lee, the dishes in the sink, the white puff of hair and the tiny smiling bird's eyes. She'd known. Eight months to go, Moon Ja, she'd said. Gypsy lady read my palm.

What have I done with my life? Moon Ja thinks. Seriously, and not in false humility? Have I ever loved *anyone*? Have I ever felt anything bigger than my own strong will? Well, music, of course. I've felt *that*; I've been swept away on *that*. Isn't that enough, damnit?

Knowing that it is not, that it is not even close to being enough, she rests her hands on the keys once more and begins a new nocturne, number sixteen. Halfway through, she begins to ache—I'm aching for Auntie Lee, she thinks, not myself—and she plays and aches and plays, thinking of Kyongju and the peasant pilgrims huddled in the cold dawn light in the wet grass, waiting with such terrible hope for the rising of the sun.

• • •

Jan opens the door after Sylvia has knocked frantically for some time and, looking shocked and sleepy, pulls her quickly inside. "Sylvia!" he says. "What are you doing out on the streets at this time of night?"

She shakes her head, unable to speak, unable to explain to him the impulse that made her rush through the darkness to his door. He takes her by the shoulders; she looks up at him, her face burning with vestigial anger and the frightening run through the silent streets. His hair is everywhere, his eyes naked; she has never seen him without glasses before, or in red-striped pajamas, for that matter. He's like a large, frightened owl; in spite of herself, she laughs up at him. "I can't believe I'm here," she says, breathless. "But I just had to . . ." She shakes her head again, then puts her hands on his shoulders, and they stand that way, hands to shoulders, just inside his closed front door. He looks terrified, embarrassed, drenched in light and hope. He starts to speak. She moves her hands to the back of his neck, pulls his head down, sees his wide blue eyes come seeking toward her. And then they are kissing, hard, and when he tries to pull back, to look at her, she pulls him in closer, kissing his face, his throat, his ears.

He makes an odd noise; she closes her eyes determinedly, holding him close with one hand and pulling off her coat with the other, then ripping at her own buttons until he catches her hand, saying "Sylvia!" against her teeth. She is panting; the rage is all back; she wants nothing more than to destroy someone the way she has been destroyed. She bites his lip—not hard, but hard enough to let him know she means business. This is not a game, Jan, she thinks. Grow up. She pushes her body into his, forces him to feel her against him, and then she moves back and forth until he takes her by the shoulders, hard, and holds her away from him.

She can't look him in the face. She feels the tears, hot and full of poison, rising behind her closed lids.

"Sylvia," he says hoarsely. "What in the world . . ."

"I'm sorry," she whispers. "I'll go now."

"No, you will not," he says, and gives her a shake.

She opens her eyes. His face is flushed and gleaming with sweat; his hair is stuck to his forehead. "No, you will not," he says more gently. "Come and sit."

She follows him, head down, drained, finally, of everything but the deepest shame. He leads her to an old sofa—she has never been in his apartment before, she realizes—and then he goes into another room and brings back a crocheted quilt, which he lays across her shoulders. "I will make you tea," he says. "You wait here."

She sits on his sofa, nodding off once, as he bustles in the kitchen. She is already far away from him, floating, distant. Don't you know, Jan, she wants to whisper, that anyone can do anything to anyone? And that none of it means a thing?

He comes in, finally, with an old-fashioned wooden tray, the kind her grandmother in Hitterdal would have. On it is a china pot with tiny pink rosebuds, and two china cups on china saucers. The sugar bowl is tarnished silver; resting beside it are a pair of tiny silver tongs for the sugar cubes inside it. She notices all these details dispassionately, as she does the rest of the living room, and the fact that everything—the tray, the cups, the sofa, the pictures on the wall—look like the possessions of a nineteenth-century man.

"Cream?" he asks her.

She shakes her head and takes the cup he lifts from the tray. She drinks. The tea is hot and sweet—with two or three sugar cubes at least—and it reminds her of the honeysuckle bush beside her parents' house, the drop of nectar she would lick from the stamen. After three swallows, she feels more like herself. She looks at him, sitting in a chair across from her, and smiles shyly. What can she say? There is nothing that will make it any better.

He has been watching her, and when she smiles at him, he smiles back. "There," he says. "Okay."

The "okay" in his Czech accent makes her smile more broadly. What an odd character he is—hardly older than she, but so different! "I'm sorry, Jan," she says. "I'm really, really sorry."

He puts up his hand. "There is something I wish to say, Sylvia. Something I had already decided before you came here tonight."

She waits, humbled.

"I think that you may already know how I feel about you, Sylvia." He leans forward earnestly, his hands on his pajamaed knees. His eyes, looking blind and stunned without his glasses, strain toward hers. "And I know that we are young, but I think we could live happily together, Sylvia—I think we could, if you could love me as I love you." He stops, abashed, and drops his eyes. She floats far away from him, far off in space, alone. The anger is gone, the murderous passion spent, and now what will happen?

He looks up at her again, and this time the mild eyes are burning. "We can marry, Sylvia. We can. I will drop out of school, get a job—I will support you until you graduate. And then you can help me finish my own courses—we will be fine, I promise you. It will all work out."

She stares at him: This young man in red-striped pajamas whom she hardly knows is offering to give up his life for her.

What would it be like? She has to consider it; she has to consider *everything* these days. She has to consider the baby before anything else.

They are twenty and twenty-three, she and Jan, and they have a child. But it is not even their baby. It is a little boy, a small version of the handsome David, and its name is Benjamin. And Jan is a good, if bumbling, father; he holds the black-haired infant in his arms, burps it after she has nursed it, changes its diapers. The baby watches him with its shiny black eyes, and Jan traces the curve of its cheek with his finger. But of course every time he touches its skin, he is touching David—he can never escape that terrible fact—and no matter how he tries to love this beautiful foundling, he grows to hate it more and more each year.

And her? How does she feel, watching her son being raised by a man not his father? Little Ben—he will be intelligent, but in a quick flashing brilliant way, not at all like the sensitive and passionate Jan. He will be very talented, extremely so, but he will also be a rebel, and before he is ten, he will have rejected the music of his three classically trained parents. He will have, instead, a small and growing collection of blues recordings; he will listen to Muddy Waters and practice his saxophone every day after school.

Each year from the time he is three or four and first realizes that the man he calls Daddy is not his real father, he will demand that she take him to see David, whoever and wherever he is. He will demand love and attention from someone incapable of giving it, and finally, when he is sixteen, he will repudiate his patrimony; he will become closed and angry and secretive, and she, his own mother, will never be able to trust him again.

She sighs. She cannot rely on her own imagination; it is so powerful that she believes almost everything it tells her. But is she right or not this time? Of course she is. And Jan has no idea of any of this. She could pretend to love him, say yes, marry him before he found out about the baby. No one would ever have to know.

She puts out her hand toward him, blindly, shaking her head. He straightens in his chair. "What, Sylvia?"

"I'm pregnant."

He is quiet for a moment, a delicate silence. Then, "I know," he says.

"You know?" She cannot believe it; she cannot believe Miss Haupt—Katerina—would tell him, how could she have trusted her, a stranger! . . .

"Nobody told me. Sylvia," Jan says. "I guessed."

He guessed. So then anybody might guess; anybody might know what is going on. Toft, even. She shivers.

"I . . . watch you, Sylvia. I watch out for you. I saw that you were ill, losing weight, preoccupied."

She stares at him, a new harsh thought crossing her mind. "Did you ask me to marry you because of *that*? Because of the *baby*?"

He looks away uncomfortably. A cuckoo clock announces the hour—2:00 A.M.

"Well," he says. "I would have asked you anyway, Sylvia. Though not, perhaps, at this very moment."

She is quiet, her pride wounded to the quick. He feels sorry for her; he's a good person, he goes to mass every morning, he is doing a good deed—nothing more than that. She cannot even look at him; how, how, did she come to be in this position, sitting this way on someone else's old sofa in the middle of the night, pregnant and trapped?

"No," she says finally, stiffly. "I mean, thank you for the offer, but I can't."

"Sylvia . . ."

"No, Jan. Thank you. I have to go now." She rises and places her empty china cup on the tray beside the sofa. She looks around for her coat, lying on the floor near the door, where she tore it off, and blushes deeply.

"Wait," says Jan. "Oh, Sylvia, at least let me walk you home. I will be dressed in one moment."

"Okay," she says, but when he disappears into the bedroom, she moves to the door, opens it, and darts out into the night.

At five, Moon Ja finally falls asleep on the bench, and wakens suddenly two hours later with sun in her eyes. She is stiff, exhausted, hungry, but also . . . something else. Alert, perhaps. Ready. Waiting. Alive again, she thinks. I'm finally back to life. Though there is no real joy in the thought, just an urgent sense of her own blood coursing once again through blue veins. A certain anticipatory tingling in her arms and legs. I'm back, she thinks. I'm back, I'm back—though there is a shadow just behind her now, a shadow that moves when she moves, turns when she turns. Something new.

She eats hungrily, a poppy-seed muffin with cream cheese and a tall glass of icy orange juice. She makes coffee. She has a peach, and then a banana. She strides from room to room, checking her cymbidiums, stroking the cats. I could plan, now, she thinks. I could get to that tour schedule. But every time she sits, she rises again in nervous agitation.

The sun floods her apartment; the sky is very clear and blue today, windswept.

Tomorrow, in California, they will bury Auntie Lee beside the other relatives in the cemetery with the odd name. Flowers, she thinks. I've got to order those right away. She starts to write this down, then gets up again and goes back to the window by the piano. There is nothing on her schedule for today; she cancelled everything during the wait for Margaret's call. She could go anywhere, see anyone. Who? Who shall I see? Not Katerina, poor thing. She's got her hands full already between me and that poor pregnant kid—what's her name? Sylvia? A twenty-year-old Toft student with a baby—my God, he'll flip when he finds out.

Katerina didn't tell her; she'd overheard the conversation between Katerina and Jan. Later, when Moon Ja brought it up, she and Katerina had talked about Sylvia and then babies in general, the plain fact that neither of them had ever had children—never married, for that matter—and how these decisions had affected their lives. Katerina quite frankly admitted it made her sad at times—that at times she could feel herself mothering her students, substituting them for the children she'd never had. Babying Cornelius like a husband. Moon Ja had shuddered; she'd never been tempted that way, nor did she feel any sadness now over the fact that she'd never been swept off by love.

No—what she's been feeling in the past three days has little to do with any of *those* decisions, much more to do with music and everything she's asked it to bear. And, of course, there is only one person who could ever understand *that*—that business of putting your entire self into art: Cornelius Toft, her old teacher and beloved friend.

Well, of course. Cornelius. She hasn't even seen him yet, she's been so wrapped up in all this other. Of *course*. She'll take the train into Baltimore; they'll have lunch; they'll talk . . . about what? She moves, and the shadow moves behind her. Her apartment, in spite of the flooding sunlight, suddenly looks somber.

She pauses for a moment beside the phone, thinking. Well, for starters, perhaps we'll talk about death.

Sylvia wakes at 9:00 A.M., vomits, has her tea and toast, then reluctantly returns a call from her parents. She is very calm on the phone, very mature. Her father comes on the line briefly to confirm their arrival date and time—next Thursday, the morning of her recital day. Then Anne comes on the line.

"You sound funny," she says. "Are you okay, sweet-heart?"

"I'm fine."

"Getting enough sleep?"

"Oh yes. I've lost a little weight, though. Just so you won't be surprised."

"Yes?" Her mother's voice is carefully light, but Sylvia can hear the worry. Teenage girl under stress—anorexia, bulimia, diet-pill addiction. Anne keeps up on the latest societal dilemmas.

"I'm fine, Mom—just working too hard. I can put it back on after the recital."

"Sylvia?"

Sylvia is quiet for a long moment, her eyes closed and her hand clenched around the receiver. Suddenly, she wants nothing more than to tell her mother everything, lay it in her lap, break down and confess, but she does not. She waits until she can speak clearly, then says, "What?"

"Did you get a good dress?"

"Yes," she answers. "Colette helped me pick it out."

"That's good. We can hardly wait to see you, honey! We're all looking forward to this so much!"

"I love you, Mom," she says, and hangs up crying, a bout of fierce quick tears that passes as suddenly as it came. I *have* to make my decision, she thinks. I *have* to. I have to make it before they come.

And then she remembers Peter. He's been back in town for three days, but—yes, she has to admit it—she's been avoiding him, secretly resenting his cool sanity, re-senting the fact that he's leaving her life just when she needs him the most. I've been weaning myself away, she thinks. Without even knowing it. But now is the time—I need his cool head—now when I have to be strong, to decide once and for all.

She picks up the phone and dials his number. In the background, when he says hello, she can hear his love-bird screeching.

CHAPTER TWENTY-FIVE

$\mathcal{P}$eter is sitting at the round table in the kitchen playing solitaire when Sylvia comes in the front door. He is wearing a blue bandanna, his black hair falling loose beneath it, and she is amazed at how relieved she is to see him. A gray-and-white bird paces restlessly on his shoulder. She can feel herself loosening, and she sighs happily, plopping herself into a chair and looking around as though she is on vacation and has just checked into a nice hotel.

"Hi," Peter says mildly.

"That's not Fred."

"Nope." The bird stretches its wings at the sound of her voice and screws around to see her. A long crest rises from the top of its head. "This is Al," says Peter. "Al, Sylvia." The bird makes a clacking noise, then gives a wolf whistle.

She laughs. "When did you get him?"

"Couple days ago. He's a cockatiel. Fred hates him."

She walks across the room to Fred's cage. The yellow

lovebird is huddled in the far corner, long feet wrapped around his dowel perch, looking morose. She bends down until she is on the same level as the steady round eyes. "Hi, Fred," she says. "*I* still love you."

The new bird fans its wings again and gives a loud squawk. "*Damn,*" says Peter. "Watch that right next to my eardrums, bird."

Sylvia is smiling; she can feel herself already letting go of things. Peter is like that for her, though she has never been able to figure out why. Perhaps it is the way he concentrates so on whatever he is doing. He has not gotten up to greet her, for instance, though she knows she is perfectly welcome. Instead, he is frowning at the cards laid out on the table, taking his time over his next move. And he will finish the game—she knows this absolutely—before he turns to her problem, which she has finally admitted to him. "I'm pregnant," she said to him on the phone, and it came out more bluntly than she'd planned. "Oh," he'd said. "Well, come on over." In some people, she thinks, I'd hate that. That kind of detachment. It would seem selfish. How come not Peter?

She sinks down on the floor next to Fred's cage. The lovebird sidles along the dowel until he is pressed against the cage bars, as close to her as he can get. "Poor Fred," she croons. "Edged out by the competition."

"Fred's okay. He's got an ego the size of Manhattan."

Peter takes a card from one pile, puts it down on another.

"What about this new Al here? Pretty flashy, if you ask me."

"Oh, Al." Peter shrugs, and the cockatiel rides his

shoulder up and then down again, fanning its tail. "Al's all right, for a baby."

"Oh God," says Sylvia.

"What?"

"That word—*baby*. Everywhere I go, it seems like."

Peter picks up another card, flips it over. "Shit," he mutters. "I needed at least a jack."

"You have any food, Peter?"

"Check the frig."

She gets to her feet, surprised at how tired she feels. Not narcolepsy-tired, not pregnant-tired—just bone-dead tired, as though she could sleep for three days. Well, this has been hard, all this. And the recital coming up on top of it—what does she expect? She's in the middle of a full-fledged crisis. Eggs, she thinks. A huge omelet with cheese and peppers in it. And orange juice, if he has some.

She moves around Peter's small kitchen, edging behind his broad back, the gray-and-white bird, to get to the stove. She knows where everything is, not because she has spent so much time in Peter's kitchen, but because she knows Peter. Things are where they make most sense; there are no surprises. The eggbeater is in the drawer by the refrigerator, for example, just where you'd expect it to be. The frying pan is beneath the oven.

She cracks six eggs into a bowl and whips them with the beater. "Help," mutters Al in a robot voice. "Help, help, help, help."

"They warned me about this," says Peter. "Shut up, Al, we're trying to think here."

If I did have the abortion, Sylvia is thinking, what would it mean? Would it mean I was killing a real baby?

She cracks another egg into the bowl; the yolk slides out whole, floating in its clear jelly. She stares down at it, eggbeater poised. Somewhere in that yolk, maybe, is the beginning of a chicken. The smooth yellow surface gleams up at her in the kitchen light, unwinking, mysterious, impenetrable. Alive, perhaps, but alien and inert; she can see no evidence of chicken-ness; she can hear no song from the heartbeat of its yellow mass. She plunges the beater down into the center; the yolk bursts, bleeding into the clear jell around it.

"Damn," says Peter. "Lost again." He pushes back his chair. The new bird spreads its wings for balance, dancing along his shoulder. "You want a beer?"

"No," she says automatically. "I'll throw up."

He gives her a look, then opens the refrigerator door and takes out a bottle of Japanese beer; it is very cold; she can see the condensation forming on the brown glass. She watches as he pries off the cap and takes a long swallow, sighing. Peter, Peter, she thinks, why are you leaving me?

"You all packed?" she asks him.

He shrugs. The bird rides up and down. "Look around," he says. "What do I have to pack? The futon, a few clothes, Fred and Al, the eggbeater. I'll do it the day I'm out of here."

"Which is?"

"Friday. Day after your recital, babe."

She watches him steadily, the eggs bubbling in the pan beneath the suspended eggbeater in her hand. He watches her. "I don't know if I can do this," she says finally.

"What?"

"Say goodbye to you."

He drops his eyes for a moment, the first time she has ever seen him flinch in a conversation. It is what she loves most about him, she thinks—the way they can talk about anything. Nobody else in the world is like that for me. But now he won't look me in the face.

He sighs finally. "We'll make it," he says. "Don't worry. We'll be in touch."

"Yeah." She stirs the eggs, obscurely angry. What does she want from him anyway? This isn't David, she thinks. He doesn't have any obligation to me. And this isn't Jan, either. This is my friend, Peter, the brother I never had. So what am I waiting to hear from him? She can feel the tears, her old nemesis, rise to her eyes.

He takes three steps toward her; she looks up just as the bird makes a frantic, flapping leap into her hair. She drops the spoon into the eggs; the bird is whirling, tangling itself tighter and tighter in her wild curls. "Peter!" she cries.

"Slow down, Al," he is saying. "Come on now, bird. Let me get a hold of you here."

Peter's hands are in her hair, his fingers surrounding the thrashing bird's body. She holds perfectly still, watching him. Total concentration; he is hardly aware of her, only her hair, which has now become a deadly net. The wings beat loudly against her ears. She has to force herself not to reach up and grab them. She can see tiny white feathers—bits of down—whirling in the air. One of his fingers brushes her temple, and she shivers involuntarily.

Who is Peter, really? They have been friends for two years; they have gone to concerts and jazz bars together; they've drunk from Peter's flask. They've had their arguments; she's been angry with him, but she's always felt perfectly . . . safe. Peter is Peter, a calm mass, like a mountain. What they've always shared is an absolute love for music, Marushka, the piano. She's never thought before of questioning their relationship; she's never thought of Peter as . . . a man. She blinks, surprised. Well, of course he is. He lived with someone, didn't he? He's been in love . . . why hasn't this ever occurred to her before?

The back of one of his hands is warm against her head; he has the bird now, is gently untangling long strands of her hair from its tail feathers. What would it be like to kiss him? she thinks, and blushes. What would it be like to lie down with him on that futon? Oh, what's *wrong* with me? First David, then Jan, and now I am thinking about *Peter*? But this would be different, wouldn't it? We're friends; we trust each other. Maybe he could make me myself again. Fix what David broke.

Has she ever thought this before? She does not remember if she has, but the idea of sleeping with Peter does not, somehow, seem foreign to her. Maybe she has dreamed it, and maybe it is the dream she remembers when she is with him. Maybe, she thinks, it was *I* who was the sexless one, not him. And I never thought of him in that way because I didn't *know;* I didn't know anything about any of this.

The bird is wildly clacking its beak. She feels it nip at

her earlobe. She clenches her hands at her side, willing herself into stillness. What if he asked me? she thinks. What would I do? And if we did, could we ever be friends again, or would it be like with David—would I get that sickness about it?

A terrible smell rises around them. "The eggs!" she cries, and grabs for the hot pan. The bird, almost free, goes crazy again, thrashing and scratching at her with its claws.

"Dammit, Sylvia, hold still. I almost had him."

"But the eggs."

"Fuck the eggs. I got more. Move over here so he doesn't land on the stove."

She flips the burner dial to off and moves slowly and obediently away from the burning pan. Sleeping with Peter . . . well, it doesn't mean anything anyway, she tries to tell herself, but she doesn't believe this; she knows it isn't true. Not after Jan. Her face still burns when she thinks of the way she tried to . . . whatever she tried to do.

Touching people means something. And touching someone you already love, someone you trust . . . wouldn't it have to be better? Or maybe it would ruin something, maybe it would make things worse.

Peter, with his long black hair, his cigarettes, his whiskey flask. I don't know one eighth of who he is, she thinks. As completely as I think I know him. So maybe that's all it is, sex: wanting to know someone better. Thinking you can find out if you lie naked beside him. But it isn't true—look at David. A total stranger to me, no matter what we did together.

She's swept again by longing, the mysterious yearning

that has haunted her ever since she first heard music. It *aches*. She feels herself turning every which way, seeking blindly in the dark for something that is never there.

Would I know my son any better? Would I know Benjamin? She has seen mothers with their babies, the way they bend their heads down to stare into the marble eyes. She has seen them nursing in restaurants sometimes, bent over their babies' heads, their heavy breasts shielded with yellow blankets. And even though they are talking to some adult across the table, their bodies are busy with their babies, shifting, adjusting, enfolding, as though the baby is a loosely attached part of them. Those mothers—she has noticed this—are absolutely confident; they do not seem to be yearning for something they can never have.

Peter has the bird now and is holding its wings closed, soothing it with one hand. The little chest is beating; the head plume rises, a beacon of distress. "Okay," Peter is saying. "Nothing can be *that* bad, bird. Just calm down."

He leaves her to take the creature back to its cage; Fred cheeps loudly and furiously for a moment, then subsides. She stands in the middle of the kitchen where he has left her, breathing through her mouth so she won't smell the odor of burning.

"Syl," he says when he has put the bird away. "No offense, but you look dead. I'll make the damn eggs, okay? You take a break."

"Okay." She is speaking in a voice she realizes she has not heard for a while, her small and obedient child's voice. *No*, she thinks—that's not how I wanted it to be.

I didn't come to dump it all on him and have him tell me what to do.

Well, then why *did* you come? she asks herself. What did you think was going to happen here?

After the omelet—they both sit cross-legged on the futon to eat it—it is her time to tell him everything about Benjamin, David, Katerina, her parents—to agonize out loud over the decisions to be made—but suddenly she can't. Something, perhaps, to do with that small voice she hadn't heard in so long, the realization that little Sylvia, who used to run so hard to keep up with her, has vanished for good and can't be gotten back—but suddenly she feels uncomfortable in the old relationship with Peter. It no longer fits. She is not his student; he is not her mentor, though that is how she has always thought of the two of them together. Peter is my *friend*, she thinks. And that's all he's ever wanted to be. Besides, he already knows all these things I came to tell him—he's too smart not to. He *knows* what kind of decision I need to make. I don't have to spend half the night explaining it, like I used to. She yawns and shakes her hair, then yawns again hugely, helplessly, her bone-deep fatigue suddenly too much.

He looks away for a moment, then back at her, then down at the quilt they're sitting on. "You're gone," he says. "You take the futon—I'll crash on the floor. We'll talk in the morning."

She yawns again. "I admit it—I couldn't even make it down your stairs right now. Colette calls this my narcolepsy."

"So stay. No problem."

"Peter," she says, determined to ask him this single question only. "If you were me, what would you do? About this baby?"

"If I were you," he says. He is not looking at her, he is looking at the ficus in the big pot across the room. His black eyes seem odd to her; they are filled—that's it—with some kind of emotion. Peter the detached. Peter the calm. Maybe he's sad, too, she thinks. About going away. About giving up music.

"If I were you," he says finally, "I'd do the thing I could live with the best. Whatever I could wake up with in forty years and not feel shitty about."

"Well, either way . . ."

"But one of them is better, Sylvia. One of them is. You just have to figure out which one."

"How?" There it is again, that voice. Small, helpless, dependent. It comes back so quickly if she is not careful. Tell me what to do, Peter. Save me. Take care of me. I'm so selfish, she thinks. I'm only thinking about me, what he can do for me. And this has nothing to do with him—this isn't his problem.

"Well," he says, "*thinking* about it ain't going to do it. You've been thinking about it day and night ever since you found out, right?"

She nods.

"Well, now you have to let it go."

Let it go? The biggest decision of her life? "What do you mean?"

He looks uncomfortable. "I mean you just give it up. You just say, I can't do this myself—somebody's going to have to help me. And then, after a while, you'll know."

"Somebody? Who? You?"

"Not me, Syl."

"I don't get it."

"Don't try. Just do it. Just let it loose."

She sits staring at him. Let it go. Little Benjamin, growing inside her. This isn't what she thought she'd hear. This isn't why she came. "Peter . . ."

"Shhh," he says. "Just sit. Just close your eyes and wait."

She shudders and pulls the quilt over her lap. Peter is beside her—she can feel his warm presence in the very air she is breathing—but he is far away, too, off somewhere in his own thoughts. Let it go? I *can't*, she thinks. Her mind is crazy with thoughts. Could she have this child and give it up to someone else? Watch this baby grow, touch the perfect face, the dark hair, and then, *knowing* it is hers, hand it over to a stranger? No, she thinks, no, no, no.

Well, then. Abortion? She shudders again at the word; it makes her feel physically ill. And would I spend the rest of my life wondering about him, who he would have been?

The apartment is dim. Earlier, she lit the candle stub on Peter's round table; it flickers steadily in the darkness. Peter, sitting across from her, seems very large, but he does not breathe like a large person, she thinks. She cannot even hear him; he is just there.

Could I spend my life thinking I'd killed my own child?

She can feel her face going white; she clutches the edge of the quilt with her fingers. There—she has said it.

The unspeakable. It is not a . . . what did Margaret call it? An embryo? It's a *baby*.

She looks around, blinking. Fred and Al are in their cages, covered by old sheets. The frying pan sits soaking by the sink. The deck of cards is stacked on the table. Peter's transient life—is this what she wants? The life of a single and celibate artist? In three days this room will be empty—not one scrap left to show a marvelously talented young man ever lived here, or that a terrified young woman came to this room to decide the rest of her life.

She looks at Peter. He sits facing her, his legs crossed, his hands on his knees. He is wearing baggy cotton pants, white, with a drawstring. His shoulders are broad and sloping, like a bear's. His hair falls over his shoulders, halfway to his waist; he has untied the bandanna. He watches her quietly, concentrating, and suddenly she feels something—a blue rush of cold fire through her feet and hands, along the extremities of her body and deep into her chest—wave after wave of something joyful and electric.

She remembers the night David knelt on the floor by her steaming bathwater; she remembers the bed he made by the radiator and their hot skin kissed by the cold night air. She remembers the time she first heard Jan playing Liszt. And just the other day—she remembers it now, the strange feeling, like cold fire racing along her arms into her shoulders—just the other day, sitting at the piano with Toft glowering behind her and Beethoven pouring out into the room.

She takes an enormous, shuddering breath and smiles weakly at Peter. "Let it go," she says. "Well, I don't know. But you don't have to sleep on the floor tonight. And we don't have to . . . well, you know. It's not anything like that."

Peter shakes his head. His hair ripples in the faint light. "Sylvia, you're too much. Get under these covers."

She slides down, pulling the quilt up over her shoulders and turning away from him onto her side. She can already feel her eyes closing, though her body is still tingling from the rush. Peter, almost without sound, slides in beside her; she feels the quilt being drawn up. They lie for long moments in stillness and then the candle stub on the table gutters and goes out.

I could put back my hand, she thinks, and touch him. I could *make* him want me; it would be the easiest thing in the world. He's leaving; he is already missing me. And he hasn't made love in a long time.

She does not move, however, and soon, though they are not touching, a steady heat envelops her: their bodies, together but apart, beneath the same quilt. She still cannot hear him breathing, but she can feel the quilt rising and falling and she can picture him flat on his back staring into the darkness, his hair spread out like a black fan against the pillow. What is he thinking? she wonders. What is Tee thinking, down there on the street? What is anybody thinking? And then a strange progression of colors and lights and creatures passes before her and she realizes, very briefly, that she is almost asleep.

Moon Ja lies in her bed, thinking over her day, trying to rid herself of a heavy sense of sorrow. What had she expected from Cornelius? What wise words had she planned on hearing? After all, he *had* been glad to see her, giving her his rare twinkle, even taking her hands for a moment, squeezing them. And she could tell that he'd actually been worried about her; he'd even asked, entirely uncharacteristically, several fumbling questions about her health.

They'd gone to a good French restaurant near the Sterling—she could tell he wanted to stay close to home—and they'd talked in the way they can never talk in front of Katerina. Hard-hitting questions back and forth at one another like Ping-Pong balls. She never spares him because of his age, as Katerina does, and he never spares her either—not because of her relative youth, not even out of consideration for the student-pedagogue relationship they once had. We are equals, she thinks. And that is why we refresh each other. And both of us know somehow that poor Katerina has always been jealous of that.

They'd had onion soup with a thick crust of cheese, fresh brown bread, glasses of Chardonnay. On the white linen tablecloth were tall stalks of bluebells in a glass vase. The waiter spoke French and carried a white towel over his arm; over the speakers came a Marcello bass and harpsichord duo. Cornelius, as always, ate with gusto, patting his mouth frequently with an enormous linen napkin and indulging himself in two glasses of the very good wine.

They'd had fun. And when the opportunity arose, when he actually broached the subject himself, she hadn't had the heart to tell him about her scare after all—not about the bleeding or the swollen glands or the three days of terrified waiting. Why should she? He looked too frightened of what he might hear, for one thing. And, she thought, he's eighty-*four*. Death must be on his mind all the time these days. What can I tell him that he hasn't already thought of?

After dessert—coffee and lemon tarts—he had cleared his throat and given her an odd, beseeching look. "One of my students," he said gruffly, "has a recital next week. I would like you to come." At first Moon Ja was affronted—he *knows* how I feel about student recitals, she thought, exasperated; I've already agreed to go see that insufferable little preppie Brandon play; what more does he *want*?—but then she realized with a shock that Cornelius was talking about Sylvia's recital, poor pregnant Sylvia. Does he know? she wondered. Could he possibly know?

"You are fully aware, dear Cornelius, of my policy on student recitals," she'd said sternly.

"Hmmm," he'd growled. "Ah yes. But sometimes it is worthwhile to make an exception."

She'd sighed. Nothing beneficial, she'd decided years ago, could ever come out of her presence at the performance of some inexperienced, gangling adolescent shaking with stage fright, no matter how talented the student might be. "She's that good, Cornelius?"

"You know her?" he asked in surprise.

"I met her at Katerina's reception."

"Ah yes." He paused, then said firmly, "She is the most exasperating student I have ever had, but I see in her the same possibilities I once saw in you."

Oh God, she'd thought. If only he knew—poor Cornelius. He's going to be crushed; he won't be able to handle it. "All right then," she'd said, patting his hand. "I'll come if you really want me to."

And then she had stared at him long and hard, remembering Katerina's photograph of that austere and irritable young man in front of the conservatory in Berlin so many decades ago. He was invincible then, she thought. He was young and healthy and bursting with talent—and look at him now: he can hardly control his fork, no matter how he tries to hide it.

So she lies sorrowfully in bed, listening to the thought that comes to her over and over again: And also me.

Sylvia is sitting in a red chair she has never seen before. She feels odd—a bit stiff. She looks at her hand: it is white and thin—the same hand, but the veins stand out, prominent and blue. A blanket covers her lap.

The door opens. A young boy, five or six years old, comes into the room and walks across to where she is sitting. He is a beautiful boy, dark, with a head of shining curls and a white smile. He puts his hands on her knees. She smiles back at him. He leans forward, takes the back of her neck in his small hands, pulls her toward him. She can smell the clean hair, the dark, milky skin, like coffee. He kisses her on the lips. And then he says, his voice like a flute, "Goodbye," and turns and walks quickly away from her, vanishing through the door.

She calls after him, struggling to make a sound, the blanket heavy across her knees. And then she is awake and sobbing and someone is hushing her, stroking her hair, her neck, and she looks around wildly in the dark for the little boy.

"It's okay, Sylvia," says the voice, a deep hum in her ear. She can feel hair, long and coarse and not her own, lying across her cheek. And the mattress, too, feels odd.

"Oh, Peter." She turns over, into his chest, and he wraps his arms around her. She is still crying, but these are tears like she has never cried before, tears of absolute anguish, deep and body-shaking and salty as blood. He holds her close to him, the whole length of him against her, and she tries to tell him about the little boy, the feel of his soft lips against hers, the voice, how it had sounded, and that word, *goodbye*.

In time she calms, though she still shudders when she breathes. Peter does not speak, but strokes her back, long, firm strokes. It feels good—all of him feels good—and she notices, almost in passing, that he has grown hard against her legs and that he is choosing to ignore this.

She lifts her face, tries to see his eyes in the dark. Her own are so drenched, so swollen, that it is like being underwater. "Peter?" she says.

He puts his fingers over her lips. "Hush," he says. "It's okay. I mean it."

She sighs, nestling close. The night, after a long time, becomes dim and formless, soft as a warm bath. And she lies there safe in the arms of her friend, hour after hour, and finally, close to dawn, when she knows absolutely that the beautiful little boy is gone forever, she is able to whisper the word to herself.

Goodbye.

CHAPTER TWENTY-SIX

When Sylvia awakens, the sun is already streaming through her white window. She lies still for a while, hardly daring to stir, while the huge realization comes slowly to her: Today is my recital.

The light settles on the wall where her Thelonius Monk poster hangs. He smiles brilliantly at the wooden floor, her stacks of books, the round rug, the radiator under the window. She follows his gaze through the gauzy curtain to the dim rosy bricks of the building across the alley. She can hear pigeons strutting throatily upon the rain gutters and a spoon falling in the kitchen. Somewhere in the brownstone water rushes through a pipe.

I love this room, she thinks.

Her parents will be here in two hours. She has to practice, to take a long walk, to bathe, to dress. Well, little Ben, she starts to say, we'd better . . . but no, I can't think about that anymore.

What will Ross and Anne think when they see her? Will they know?

She can't worry about that, either—only about playing tonight. She sighs, a long exhalation, then sits up and stretches, waiting for the hot rush of bile into her throat. Nothing, however—and she is curiously light this morning, as thought the procedure has already been done.

She is calm, but her skin is tingling. Is she ready to play tonight? Well, of course not. But you do it anyway—isn't that what Katerina told her? You just do it in the best way you can. Like everything, she thinks. What else can you do?

For some reason, this sounds familiar—and then she remembers Beethoven's letter, the one she'd thought of that morning as she stood, pregnant and terrified and thinking of jumping, on the windowsill above the sidewalk. Where are her notes? She climbs out of bed and goes to the pile of books on the floor beneath her window.

Katerina is sitting in her studio watching Colette play. A bright morning, and the room looks dramatically white, like a room, perhaps, on the Aegean Sea instead of the Baltimore harbor. She is glad she brought flowers this morning—hothouse lilies from the shop three blocks from her apartment; they stand tall and yellow and exotic on the black Yamaha by the window.

Colette is playing Satie's *Trois Gnossiènnes*. She is thinking about something else, which is the danger when you are playing Satie, Katerina thinks. I should wake her up. Instead, she sips her coffee and contemplates the scene before her: the red silk scarf Colette is wearing in her hair, the yellow lilies on the piano, the girl's dark slender fingers, the light walls.

Colette is such a mystery. But, Katerina has to ask herself, has she ever taught the child of a famous musician before? Well, there was . . . but no, not really. His mother was well known in the classical world, true, but certainly not a household name like Colette's father is.

Has it spoiled her? Katerina watches her play, admiring, as she always does, the wonderful fluidity of her wrists. She is very self-possessed, which some people—students have told her this—read as snobbishness. There is the tendency to be impatient. A certain moodiness that sets in without warning. And at times she is obviously lonely. But spoiled? No.

Colette finishes the piece and drops her hands in her lap, sighing. "Sorry, Miss Haupt. I'm out to lunch today."

"I noticed."

"I'll do better next week. I promise."

They could, right now, talk about Colette, her life, her wishes, her dreams. What she fears and what she desires. They could talk about Sylvia, the traumas and heartaches of life, but this, thinks Katerina, is not the relationship they have. Instead, they are carefully pedagogue and student, the way Colette seems to want it.

She smiles at Colette, stretches, and rises, setting her empty mug on the cane seat of the chair. "Oh well," she says. "I guess I'm out to lunch today too. It must be catching. Why don't we call it quits?"

Colette gives her a relieved look and begins gathering her things together. Katerina goes to the other side of the piano to see, once again, what the yellow lilies look like up close. They are exotically beautiful, like orchids, with their deep brown throats and the spray of bronze freckles that fades into the petals.

When she looks up, Colette is standing by the door, the two ends of the red silk scarf hanging down over her shoulders and her music bag slung from one arm. "Well, 'bye," she says. "Thanks."

"Goodbye, Colette. I'll see you tonight at Sylvia's recital."

Colette nods and goes out the door. Maybe she just doesn't like me, Katerina thinks. It's possible, isn't it? She considers this proposition for a while—somebody doesn't like me—and then rejects it. Impossible, she thinks. I'm just too damn wonderful.

She picks up the empty mug by the handle and moves slowly toward the door. As much as she hates to admit it, even to herself, Colette gets her down—well, not Colette particularly, but the whole fact of her own age and childlessness, the way she insinuates herself into the lives of her students whether they want her there or not.

Oh now, that's not true either, she thinks. I'm being too hard on myself. Yes, I do get involved with people, but not in any kind of obnoxious way—at least I don't *think* so. Look at Jan—he came to *me*. And Sylvia, too. And Moon Ja and Cornelius, besides—I don't *ask* for all this, do I?

Katerina glances once more around the studio, her beautiful old studio, then pushes open the door. From somewhere upstairs she can hear, very faintly, a late Beethoven piano sonata. Sylvia. And how will *she* be tonight?

There I go again, Katerina thinks. She's out of my

hands, damnit. I've done what I could. And if I've done the wrong things, then . . . Well, the plain fact is that in two years I won't remember her face. They move on, these students of mine. Even the ones like Jan, the ones I grow to love—even *they* move on.

So what's the point? she thinks. Why do I ache for them this way?

Moon Ja has decided that she is simply lonely. That in her three days of facing death she'd come to realize she'd never lived, not really, and that what she needs to do now is try love. She pages through her address book, a hundred names of strangers—not a real friend, except for Cornelius and Katerina, among them—until she comes to one that makes her smile. Nathan. An ill-fated suitor she'd nonetheless not forgotten.

She dials the number before she can think about what she is doing. A man answers.

"Hello, Nathan?" She rarely blushes, but she can feel her cheeks throbbing with embarrassment.

"Who's this?" His voice is much the same—warm, a little broken at the edges. He sounds relaxed, friendly, curious. She has a vision of him with wet hair, a white towel around his waist, bare feet. The mist is still dissipating from his shower; he is standing in the bedroom, holding the phone to his ear and looking out at . . . what? What kind of place does he live in now? And is there a woman sleeping in the bed beside him?

"Nathan, this is Moon Ja," she says, and gives a little coughing laugh. "Long time no talk."

"*Moon* Ja," he says happily.

But *is* he happy to hear from her, or is he feigning it? He's nice enough to fake it, she thinks. But he doesn't *sound* fake. Her hands are shaking a little, holding the phone. This is why I've never gotten into love—too paranoid. Too damn proud.

"How are you, Nathan?" she asks him, striving for dignity.

"Well, I'm great," he says. "I'm really good. How about yourself?"

Not only nice, but hearty. She'd forgotten that—really, she didn't remember all that much about him when it came right down to it. Only that he had been very sweet, very good looking, sexy. And that they had slept together at least three times after some complicated dating, and that she had never returned his calls after that. Why not?

"I'm fine too, Nathan. Getting older"—she had not meant to say that—"but doing pretty well. Just got back from a long tour, as a matter of fact"—what, is she trying to impress him?—"in Asia."

"Wow," he says happily. He is an anthropologist, and if she remembers correctly, he specializes in bones. Skulls and jaws and such. So—presumably a serious person. And nice and hearty, too. Why hadn't she ever called him back? And what will she say to him next?

She clears her throat. "Look, Nathan, being gone for so long . . . well, when I got back, I just felt like seeing people, you know? Old friends? And you came to mind. And I wondered . . ."

A long pause. Help me, she says silently. Say something.

Now *he* clears *his* throat. "Moon Ja," he says finally. "Guess what? I'm married now, isn't that great? I've even got a little girl—she's two."

Moon Ja closes her eyes, drops her head, raps herself lightly on the cheekbone with the receiver. You fool, she is thinking, what did you expect? A nice, sexy guy like that?

But it is getting worse. "Would you . . . would you be interested in coming by for dinner sometime? Barbara, my wife, loves music; she'd get a real kick out of meeting you. And Brandy—my little girl?—she's something else, she really is." Another pause. And then, lamely, "What do you say, Moon Ja?"

Well, at least she is smiling now, though ruefully. Is this going to be her new life from now on? Calling old, happily married boyfriends, stirring up their lives? "No thanks, Nathan," she says, laughing a little. "You're sweet, but that's not what I had in mind."

"I know," he says sheepishly, as though it is somehow *his* fault, the fact that she dumped him long ago and left him free to pursue his own kind of happiness.

"Hey," she says, and she means it: "I'm glad for you, Nathan."

But when she hangs up, having raised a ghost from the dead, then put it to rest once again, she feels flattened. Not from disappointment—what did she think could possibly happen, after all?—but instead because she is caught once again in the somber fact of her own aloneness.

• • •

One of the mothers is turning thirty-three today, the same age her own mother was when she had her fifth child. Thirty-three! she thinks. But I still feel twelve.

She has not yet been out of bed, though it is nearly ten; her children and husband (who has taken the day off from work) are holding her captive with breakfast on a tray, cups of coffee, and both the *Sun* and the *Post* tumbled on the end of the bed. She can hear the kids on the other side of the door. They are whispering loudly in the hallway, about to have a fight. She should get up before one of them hits the other. But she does not, though lying in bed this way, imagining what the kitchen must look like by now, is not exactly relaxing.

She has propped her homemade cards on the night-stand, along with a little man made of toothpicks and grapes and a half-empty goblet of Champagne and orange juice. She is supposed to be choosing what they will do tonight—her "birthday event." Her husband has hired a baby-sitter, she has a new dress, and he is only waiting for her command.

So—now she knows what it is she wants to do, something they did together long before they had kids. First, dinner at the Sicilian place downtown by Washington Square, then a stroll through the bookstore, then over to the conservatory to see if there are any recitals tonight.

And afterward, a drink at a pub, perhaps a little dancing, and home late, very late—home hours after the kids are asleep, when the house is dark and quiet and mysterious in the old, sexual way.

• • •

Tee is hungry. He's trying not to think about it. His four-teen dollars are long gone; the Dumpsters are empty; the shelter is full. Time to move on, Tee. Time to find you someplace better.

He walks down the street toward the corner where the music school stands, where the White Tower, full of good cooking, sits without him in it, swinging his arms, trying to confuse his belly. He takes in bites of air. Eatin' air—he learned it from Bellyman. Sometimes they didn't have food for two or three days. Got fe store de food up, Bellyman say. I tell you, mon, got fe eat him while you can. And when dere none of him, you got fe gulp-gulp some good air.

Katerina goes back to her studio for a lily and then downstairs and out into the balmy spring morning. The park, she can see, is full of transients—they lie on benches or on the ground, soaking in the sun. She tips her face upward, takes a big breath, looks at the park once again. Who are all those men, and where did they come from? Why do they lie that way, helpless and sprawling, clutching their old wine bottles to their chests?

She has sometimes wondered about them in the way she wonders about her students. She asks herself, What are they good at, those thin dirty men? Are they artists in disguise? Geniuses? Saints? Musicians?

She looks at the men in the park and thinks, What would you be if you were not here? Who would you become?

If she had a hundred thousand dollars she could go from corner to corner collecting them, the young and apathetic, the poverty-stricken, the drunks. And then she would gather them into her home and cook for them, a meal they would never forget, a meal of tomatoes and basil and steaming pasta. And afterward she would take them to the piano and they would begin at the beginning. This, she would say, pointing, is called middle C. This is where you start.

One of the men is passing the park slowly, coming her way, and she squints into the sun to see him better, for he looks familiar. A big man with sloping shoulders, but shuffling as though he hurts. Where has she seen him before? She stands in the middle of the sidewalk, staring, and then her arms begin to tingle, for she recognizes him after all. The bald one, the one who sat on her front steps that night in the middle of the snowstorm while his friend coughed beside him.

She feels her throat closing—so much trouble in the world, so much suffering—and she watches his ravaged face coming closer and closer, his bear's shoulders rolling forward in slow motion. What is he thinking? She cannot even begin to guess.

He is only feet away from her—he's monstrous!—and she stands planted in the middle of the sidewalk, caught there by something she can't control, prepared to be asked for money; he swerves to miss her, however, goes past silently, glancing down for half a second, and she sees that his eyes are exquisite with pain, his forehead wrinkled with worries she cannot fathom. He drags on by her like something wounded and takes her breath with him; she stands shivering, overweight, aging, a good pianist, true, a good friend to one and all . . .

If I gave him everything I had, she thinks, helpless, it

wouldn't be enough. If I gave him my car, my apartment, my talent, even . . . Life has *hurt* that man; how can anyone even *begin* to help? And if I tried, if I asked him about all of it, pushed myself into the middle of it like I always do, then what? Do I know anything, really? I'm not wise; I've never even been married; all I know is teaching and music . . .

She turns and watches him shambling away from her down the street, past the school, headed inexorably toward some destination she can't fathom. Where is he *going*? she thinks. Where does he think he's *going*? The very air around him vibrates with suffering; she shivers again, feels herself begin to move after him, says to herself, frantically, Katerina, what do you think you are doing; are you crazy? But this is all I am, she thinks, digging into her purse, pulling out her wallet, emptying a fistful of dollars into her hand: This is all I am—just love, just somebody who can love people; there's nothing wrong with that.

She has to run to catch him, a shuffling, clumsy gait that has her panting and holding her chest when she finally gets close enough to reach out for his sleeve. He whirls, stares down at her wild-eyed, his hand raised, and she thinks, My God, he has no teeth and look at his *nose*; somebody's beaten him; what kind of life has this man *lived*? . . . then thrusts the roll of dollars at him, $236 or $237, she can't remember, but it is all she has in her purse, and he spots the money right away and steps back, startled, his hands falling to his sides. She pushes the roll at him, saying, "Here, this is for you," and he finally, cautiously, reaches out and takes it, still staring down at her. His forehead is like black silk, the whites of his eyes caramel-colored. She cannot tell how young or how old he is, if he is sick or well, good or bad. She is breathing very hard; she puts a hand under her ribs and leans over for a moment, and it seems to her in that position that the air around her is vibrating with gold.

She sees him open his hand, look at the money, then he slides the whole roll slowly into his front pants pocket, patting it once to make sure it is there, and touches her very lightly on the shoulder, nothing more than a breath of a fingertip. "Thank you," he says, and turns and is gone.

Sylvia and her mother and father stand together in her favorite practice room—she is showing them her world—and though they have both toured the school before, it is different this time. Now she is not a young student, fresh from Minneapolis, who can only imagine her new life. She looks at the old piano, the battered legs. How many hours has she sat at that bench? Her parents are quiet, both of them, although they have been full of talk since they arrived.

Her father turns and looks at her, a long look; he doesn't smile, only watches her somberly with his handsome blue eyes, and she wonders what he sees. A too-thin Sylvia, a Sylvia with enormous unhealthy dark rings around her eyes. A Sylvia who cannot quite meet his gaze. A Sylvia he probably does not recognize.

He says, "Nice view."

She nods.

Her mother slips an arm around her waist. Anne feels

the same—slender, made of hollow bones, with warm and freckled skin that smells like flowers. Sylvia wants to lay her head on her mother's shoulder, rest against the thick cushion of their mingled hair, but she does not, only stands quietly watching her father assess her life. What does he see? she wonders, glancing up at him once again. What does he know? And why do I feel so separate from him all of a sudden?

And then she notices his eyes, how they are shining with something fierce and Ross-like; icy terror washes over her; any second now, she thinks, he will ask me what is wrong, what I have been up to . . . but then he clears his throat and says, "You work hard in this room, don't you?"

She nods, thinking of the long nights, the late walks home, the bars and measures she has played over and over again until they are as natural to her as breathing. Thinking of the way, sometimes, her back aches like a tooth and the times she's worn down the tips of her fingers. Thinking of the wrenching morning sickness he doesn't even know about, the way she's had to force herself simply to get out of bed each day, much less work on Beethoven.

"I'm proud of you," he says then. He shrugs, embarrassed, and turns away, too late to hide the tears standing in his eyes.

Book
FIVE

What if the man could see Beauty Itself,
pure, unalloyed, stripped of mortality
and all its pollution, stains, and vanities,
unchanging, divine, . . . the man
becoming, in that communion, the
friend of God, himself immortal; . . .
would that be a life to disregard?

—*Plato*

CHAPTER TWENTY-SEVEN

*S*ylvia can hear the audience muffled behind the heavy old curtain, a friendly group, it seems, who are murmuring to one another and occasionally breaking into laughter. Who is out there? She wants to know, but she doesn't. She thought earlier about walking around the building, spying from the back, but they would spot her right away in the red dress. And that would be terrible luck, like the groom seeing the bride before the wedding.

She could peek through the curtain if she wanted to. Or she could send Colette out for a report. But does she really want to know? Especially about whether or not Miss Koh is actually there? Her father, when he heard the rumor that Moon Ja Koh was coming, turned pale; tonight he is almost sick with anxiety.

She stands quietly in the wings in her red dress and a pair of fur-lined gloves to keep her fingers warm. Colette, in raw silk the color of sand, her hair pulled back in a complicated and delicate knot, stands beside her. She looks like a woman all of a sudden, not a girl.

Sylvia found the Beethoven note, a letter to Countess Erdödy, and while she was floating in the bathtub, she thought of the vision she'd once had: the messy studio, the anguished deaf man with the ringing in his ears, the glorious music he would never hear pouring out into the empty air. Opus 111—his hymn to wisdom gained through sorrow. She'd memorized the passage, and now she thinks it through one last time: Man cannot avoid suffering; and in this respect his strength must stand the test . . . he must endure without complaining and feel his worthlessness and then again achieve his perfection. Yes. She closes her eyes for a moment, thinking of what Toft once said: You are only one in a long line of pianists going back through history to the composer . . .

Suddenly, the lights go down. Sylvia and Colette stare at one another in the dark, then Colette reaches out and touches her lightly on the shoulder. "Break a leg," she whispers.

Out beyond the curtain, everything has fallen silent. Sylvia takes a long breath and peels off the gloves.

Well, here she is, Katerina thinks. And, my God, look at that red dress!

The audience, which stirred a little when Sylvia first came wobbling out on her high heels, applauds as she makes her way to the piano bench. They are hearty, supportive—mostly students and a smattering of strangers—city folk who drop in for the odd recital. But Katerina also spots Jan in the front row, his hair ruffled in lovesick dread and anticipation; close behind him sits the handsome young Israeli violinist—the father of Sylvia's child!—with his dark-haired girlfriend.

Just then Sylvia turns and squints into the spot; her mass of curls, tied back with a red ribbon, suddenly lights, a brief and luminous halo that is extinguished when she looks down at the keyboard. Katerina thinks of how difficult it is to be up there alone. How each time you must force yourself once again into the belief that it can be done. Just concentrate, she urges silently. Don't let anything in but the music. She can feel herself flowing out toward Sylvia on the bench, an outflowing of love, to help her get through it, and her own eyes feel hot with something suppressed. She is still shaken by her strange encounter with the big bald man, by her wild impulse to give him everything she had. And yet she feels lighter, freer, dangerously spontaneous—a guiltless giver, for the first time in her life. Who knows what I might do next, what I might offer someone? There's no rationality to this, true, but why should there be? How can there be, without killing it . . . whatever it is? The strange compelling spirit that sometimes passes through me.

On either side of her sit Cornelius and Moon Ja, Cornelius wheezing, his fingers drumming on the armrest, and Moon Ja nervous as a cat. Moon Ja does not want to be here, poor thing—that much is very obvious. She's even come in disguise, though it fooled no one; tonight she's not exotic, but instead a slender, girlish-looking woman in a soft blue sweater and black skirt. When they came through the door, a kind of sigh swept through the audience, though most people kept their eyes determinedly ahead so as not to stare. She belongs onstage, thinks Katerina. She's not used to being out here, surrounded by real humans. I wonder how on earth Cornelius ever got her to come. And then: Thank God she's here beside me and not in some hospital tonight.

She glances at Cornelius; his breath is whining through his nose and he's cleared his throat at least four times in the past minute. Will you stop? she thinks. He sounds like a very old dog, dreaming angry youthful dreams beside the hearth. But of course he is agitated; he stuck his neck way out on this one; what if Sylvia fails miserably and he's invited Moon Ja Koh to hear her play? Moon Ja doesn't go to student recitals; she won't even judge competitions; she's only been back to the school two times in twenty years.

Cornelius harrumphs and Katerina glances down at the fingers he is tapping on the armrest. Old, very old—shiny, with nails of horn. They tremble, an old man's dance, and she remembers in a quick flash how she used to study those famous hands so many years ago in Berlin. How she had once worshiped them. Why, he's living on borrowed time, she thinks. He could have been dead years ago, and look at him—shaking, wheezing, agitated . . . what keeps him going? She pats his nervous hand with hers, then leaves her hand there resting on top of his, letting her warmth and love and, yes, forgiveness, flow into him. For whatever he's done all these years, she thinks, that's bruised my heart and made me jealous. His fingers are cold and move under hers.

Just then Sylvia begins a trio of small Scarlatti sonatas, and Katerina leans forward to listen, her head cocked to one side. Stiff, she decides after the first minute. No mistakes yet, but the balance is precarious, the audience nervous. The girl is walking a tightrope, and audiences don't like not being able to relax. They want you to take

them in your hands—concentrate, Sylvia, or you're
going to lose them.

Cornelius, his hand twitching under hers, has gone silent, his eyes riveted on the stage.

The mother who is turning thirty-three today sits in the
audience beside her husband feeling faintly self-conscious. After all, these people are all musicians, and she
is . . . what? A mother. Old. Thirty-three already. But
still having fun, she thinks defiantly, taking her husband's arm. Going out for dinner, sitting at the little
table, eating slowly by candlelight. Slinking around in
her one good dress. And then the long walk through the
warm evening to the conservatory, not thinking, for
once, of the kids, what trouble they are getting into at
home without her.

No, she is not a student any longer. She is living her
life now, and she is happy. But this—this slender young
girl with the amazing head of hair, sitting at the piano
bench, making music—is beautiful.

The young mother, self-conscious, self-satisfied, sits
watching the girl in red, sometimes closing her eyes as
she has seen people do at concerts. I'm no musician, she
thinks, but this is wonderful. And congratulates herself
for feeling only the faintest touch of envy, almost negli-
gible, at what life must be like for the pretty girl onstage.

Oh God, thinks Moon Ja, thoroughly miserable. What
the hell am I doing here? And I have to say something
afterward, and she's a nice kid, too. How did I ever get
talked into this? Thanks a lot, Cornelius.

• • •

The Scarlatti sonatas are terrible—jerky, wooden, un-feeling. Sylvia is flushed with shame when they are finally over, and even though they clap for her, some of them hard, to be encouraging, she cannot look at them. Sweat is running down her ribs inside the red wool dress; she feels like crying, like leaving the stage and never coming back. All of this for *this*? All these years, all the lessons with Miss Selkirk, Mr. Binder, Toft? The money her parents are paying?

What, what, what are you doing, Sylvia?

The polite clapping fades away; she can hear two or three people still applauding loyally: Jan, she thinks, and probably Colette . . . She takes a quick glance at the audience but is blinded by the light. Who is out there? Her friends, her family, Peter of course, Toft—Miss Koh? David and Francine? She swallows hard, her stomach churning, sure, somehow, that David is there, unable to stay away from a Toft recital, the way she will not be able to stay away from Brandon's. The Toft mystique: What potential genius is he nurturing along in his madman's laboratory?

At the word *genius*, she begins to shake—her legs, her shoulders, her arms, her hands. Great waves of shaking that make her jaw rattle. What's happening to me? she thinks, terrified. She clasps her hands together in her lap, but her thighs are thudding against the bench, her heart humming . . . panic attack. She takes quick sips of air, wild-eyed, and her father's face floats above the piano, white with anxiety and expectation. She feels a slow and insidious nausea rising; will she be sick? Little Benjamin's last revenge?

She searches desperately for something, anything, to think about besides her certain failure, anything that will help her get through Opus 111, when, teeth chattering, she remembers the whirring of wings, the gray and white bird thrashing in her hair. What had Peter said that night? *You just have to let it go, Sylvia.*

Immediately, she takes four deep ragged breaths, forcing herself down, down, as though she is going underwater, away from the audience, the heavy expectant air that is gagging her. All is quiet there and she feels lighter immediately; she floats. *Beethoven,* she says to herself. *All these months of work. Think, Sylvia. Concentrate.* But her mind keeps slipping away, swimming like a fish through the silent watery world, and suddenly she recognizes it, the place she has come to rest: she is in a white bowl, shallow, and beneath her is a blue dragon with blind eyes and huge blue open jaws. Something with great white ruffled wings floats above her—an egret? No (she feels herself suddenly and deeply moved)—not a bird at all. A white flower, the one she chose from the rosebush on the other side of Miss Selkirk's window. And she is suspended between them, the dragon and the flower.

With a long sigh, fixing her concentration on the petals above her, she begins to play a deaf musician's last sonata. In a few minutes she can hear that it is going to be all right after all.

Katerina straightens in her seat, surprised. What has happened? Sylvia is moving differently at the piano; her eyes are closed now and her face is shining oddly in the light. But the big chords are tense and powerful; it seems that someone else entirely played the wooden Scarlatti sonatas.

So, thinks Katerina. She has *that* problem, does she? One of those flighty, inconsistent, incredibly gifted types—no wonder Cornelius gets so wound up about her.

She glances over at him. He is leaning back in his seat, his eyes closed. The nasal whine is gone; he is breathing like a baby, though he looks old, fragile, exhausted. Does this make him happy? she thinks curiously. Vindication? Or is he simply relieved he has not made a fool of himself in front of Moon Ja? Eighty-four years old, and not the slightest shred of wisdom, in spite of all his talk of Hegel, the spirit moving through time, etc., etc. In fact (poor Cornelius) he is being dragged off to death now like nothing more than a stubborn toddler being carried off to bed. And he doesn't want to leave the party yet; he's been the center of attention for too long. She pats his hand, still lying obediently under hers.

She looks at Moon Ja: Her back is straight; her hands grip the end of the armrests; she watches the stage unblinkingly. She's caught too, Katerina thinks. She's caught in the spell. Oh, good for *you*, Sylvia.

Moon Ja can hear the rush of her own breath past her ears. Not the music, which is stern, unforgiving, majestically Beethoven, but her own breath. I'm alive! she thinks. Not sick after all. Spared!

Ice is melting somewhere inside her, seeping along through the channels of her heart, her veins and arteries, her tendons and ligaments and muscles. Freezing water, painful, stunning, courses through her as she watches the girl at the piano in her young, tremulous beauty.

So will this happen to me the rest of my life? she thinks. Will I keep realizing it over and over like this?

Here's a wonderful passage. She drops her head and closes her eyes, listening, thinking of the man, deaf, with all this music in his head. Silent choirs, frozen symphonies, sonatas worked out in mute solitude—what kept him going? What great vision? Oh, in spite of the bad Scarlatti, Sylvia is doing this well; Cornelius was right about her . . .

Alive. In her head she cannot escape Kyongju; she keeps going back, over and over, to the crowd of pilgrims at dawn, the great Buddha, the sun rising over the brilliant green valley, and everyone turning toward the jewel . . . she had not looked. She *could* not.

She twists in her seat, eyes still closed, and the music pounds at her relentlessly. You have to get through this movement, she thinks, and then comes the beautiful stuff . . . but Sylvia and the piano are not what she sees before her. She is still in Kyongju. She cannot escape. The jewel must be looked at: You must at least see if it is true, Moon Ja, what they say about the light streaming out of it. The pilgrims had gasped out loud, but still she refused to look.

All right, all *right*, she thinks, and stares straight at it, the clear spot in the great stone forehead, empty of light, water-colored . . . and then the sun is rising; she can feel it on her back, feel the pilgrims around her stirring in anticipation, open-mouthed, and she holds her eyes on the jewel. A pulsing silence, then suddenly it bursts into flame, a brilliant, colorless flash that pulls her out of herself, plummets her into a luminous stream, washes her up on the shores of . . . what? She sits up slowly, weak and shaking, and stares out, terrified, at an immense ocean of light.

Sylvia's hands fall into her lap; the hall is still ringing with Beethoven, and the clapping—a hollow pounding—rises to meet the dissolving music in the air. She opens her eyes, panting a little, smiling, her cheeks still wet. What is happening? Suddenly, they are all in love with her and she is in love with them; she can feel the love rising around her, lifting the enormous piano on its sturdy legs, the bench, her floating red skirt. She holds on with both hands, out at them, her hair bouncing gently off her shoulders as she turns her head. For a second, from habit, she cups one hand over her abdomen— do you hear, Benjamin? do you hear them clapping for your mother?

She looks out at the audience in a happy daze, loose and unfocused, and thinks, this isn't what Toft says. This isn't nothing.

They are still clapping and she stands up slowly and nods, thanking them, and then she is walking offstage, thinking of Schumann's *Fantasiestücke* and Ravel's *Sonatine*, the pieces she still has to play. She pulls her hair away from her hot neck, gulps the glass of water Colette left for her. How can I do it? she thinks.

But I have to.

• • •

Afterward, they bring her flowers, four or five bouquets while she is making her last bow, the red dress swinging around her ankles. Red roses from her parents—her father brings them to the stage himself, his eyes shining—and pink gladiolas from Katerina, and yellow anemones from Marushka—Marushka, all the way in Kiev!—and a gardenia corsage from Colette. She holds them all in her arms, smiling, shaking her head, and then, suddenly afraid of breaking into tears, hurries offstage. It's over! she thinks. It's over, it's over, it's over!

She already knows how she did; no one has to tell her. The *Fantasiestücke*, her favorite, was fine, nothing more and nothing less. Although "In der Nacht" was very good, she could hear it herself.

By the time she got to Ravel, however, she was totally worn out, the surges of power beginning to dissipate into nervous jittering, and so the piece was not nearly as good, even, as in practice, but they forgave her because she had already done what they wanted her to and they understood, being musicians, how tired you can get.

She stands alone for a moment on the other side of the big curtain, quiet; then suddenly there are voices and laughter and she is engulfed in someone's thin arms—Colette—and passed from hug to hug as people make their way backstage. For a long moment Peter has her and he is hugging especially hard—he is leaving in the morning, and they will never again have what they are losing—and she is laughing and tingling with leftover energy and trying to touch everyone, her mother and father, Katerina, shoulders, faces, arms.

Someone taps her shoulder and she turns from the

happy tangle of her friends and finds herself standing face to face with David, who, without speaking, gives her his hand. She freezes, holding his fingers, the fingers of a stranger, really, though absolutely familiar to her in every cell, and then, neither of them smiling, she shakes his hand as though they are old business acquaintances, people who, though they do not particularly like each other, have some respect when all is said and done. He wants to say something, she can see it, but he is incapable of it, and she—flushed with triumph and the resonance of love—forgives him for this on the spot, and then goes on, recklessly, without thinking, to forgive him for everything else, all the sickness and heartache and worry, which, she can see, he did not and could not suspect. He just wanted to touch me, she thinks. After Bellyman dying like that in front of us—we *did* share that, that awful frightening wait in the alleyway. He never asked me to worship him like that—so all right, David, you are absolved, I absolve you of all your crimes, here and now. No more sickness. She squeezes his fingers, a strong squeeze with her tired hand, and he squeezes back, then turns and vanishes into the crowd.

Brandon, across the room, catches her eye and gives her a grudging nod (he is already scanning the room for Miss Koh, who seems to be gone) and Sylvia nods back generously, still caught up in the spirit of forgiveness.

Colette is back. "I'm so proud, Sylvie," she says. "I'm so damn proud of you." She seems unfamiliar—light and giggling, like a glass of Champagne.

"What's with you?" Sylvia asks, half kidding. "Have you been drinking?"

"Yes," she says. "No." She does a half spin on the toe of her high heel.

"Colette?"

"I loved it, Sylvie. I loved you getting up there and *doing* it."

"Hello?" A woman stands in front of them, someone Sylvia has never seen before. She smiles nervously, as though she feels uncomfortable, and she is wearing a black cocktail dress. A tall man stands behind her, kind-looking, with graying hair at the temples.

"I just want to say," the woman begins, and then stops, flustered, and runs her hand through her hair. She's pretty, Sylvia thinks. You can see what she used to look like.

"Well," the woman says, and laughs. She puts out her hand and Sylvia takes it. I guess this is what you do, Sylvia thinks. After performances. "I just want to say how much I enjoyed your recital. It was wonderful. You see, it's my birthday . . ."

But just then Toft comes into the room, and Sylvia cranes to see the expression on his face. What is he thinking? Her skin begins to tighten in the old frightened way—he looks as stern as ever, and petulant, too, but maybe it is the crowd, maybe he just can't handle being around so many students at the same time—so when he is stopped in his tracks by Brandon, she almost sighs in relief.

"What?" she says, turning back to the dark-eyed woman, but the woman is gone, has disappeared along with her husband into the crowd, and Sylvia's hand is empty and aching from all the music; she is wondering whether she will like this part too, the aftermath of performing, or if she will long to escape, to relish what happened on the stage. She is exhausted and exultant all at the same time.

Katerina turns back to her now, and before Sylvia can think of what to say to her—thank you for helping me, I wouldn't have been able to play tonight if it weren't for you—she is enveloped in another warm hug. Katerina pats her, saying, "Well done, well done," and Sylvia wants to say something back, something profound they will both remember in ten years, but she can think of nothing and instead grins foolishly. "Moon Ja wanted me to give you her congratulations and apologies," Katerina adds. "She wasn't feeling well and had to leave before the second half."

"Oh," says Sylvia, embarrassed. "Well, I can't even believe she really *came*. People have been telling me, but . . ."

Toft is back on track now, steaming toward them, and Sylvia's throat goes dry. What had he told her she needed? *Gründlichkeit*. The discipline of thoroughness.

"You again," he says to Katerina. "What are we doing out at such an hour, eh?" And then he turns to Sylvia. For a long moment he is silent, sizing her up. His color is high, his eyes particularly hard and bright. Just as she begins to feel panicked, he says gruffly, "The Scarlatti sonatas were an embarrassment. And the *Sonatine* was very weak, very passive. But you already know that."

She nods, swallowing. He's right.

"The *Fantasiestücke*, however, was quite competent, especially "In der Nacht." He coughs, turning his head, then clears his throat several times. She waits. "Opus 111," he says. "Yes. You have learned something this year, have you not?" And then, for the very briefest moment, he smiles at her from under the hooded eyelids and she catches a glimpse of what he must have been when Katerina first met him in Berlin years and years ago.

She stands in awkward silence. He has never before given her a compliment, after all. And he looks so small there beside the ample Katerina, a wizened little man who has to draw in his chin to stand up straight. Across the room she can see her father on tiptoe, straining to see what is happening. Sure that he is missing something important. Without thinking, she walks forward and kisses Toft on the cheek beside his puckered mouth. "Thank you," she says simply.

He steps back, his hand at his face. "Well," he says. "Yes." But he suddenly looks old and tentative, not at all the cruel wizard she is used to, and in a few more minutes he makes his hasty goodbyes and shuffles off in the direction of Brandon.

Katerina laughs. "It will take him two weeks to recover."

Sylvia is smiling, shaking her head; her cheeks—she can feel them—are flushing over and over. What has she just done? Kissed *Toft*? But it felt like the thing to do. She can't explain it any other way.

She starts to say something to Katerina, and then suddenly thinks *Jan*. Where is he? Surely he was at the recital. She looks over the crowd—no Jan. But she has to talk to him—she has to. She has to tell him about what she felt onstage, the strange . . . *love* that bore her up; she has to tell him that she understands, now, why he made his loving offer. She has to apologize; she *has* to.

Tee has not been on a bus since he left prison, but he is riding one now, headed for Chicago, for Raymon, for that old life.

In his pocket is his bus ticket, bought with the blond lady's money, and a candy bar to last him through the night. A moonlit darkness has already fallen, so he can't see much when he turns around to give Baltimore one more look. Just lights, the bare trees with new leaves—Bellyman would have liked that—and, in his imagination, the dark water of the bay.

He never saw the girl all day; he'd thought about telling her goodbye somehow—getting the guts to go up to her, say thank you for Bellyman, but she never did show up. Finally, before the bus left, he took three of the blond lady's dollars and bought a yellow rose—a real rose, this time, not one from the trash, and laid it on her front steps. Then he walked through the alley one last time—I won't be back here ever again—and on to the bus station.

Goodbye, Baltimore, he thinks. That's all I got to say.

CHAPTER TWENTY-EIGHT

*E*ventually, the group backstage breaks up, and everyone heads out to the street for the walk to the apartment. Colette has been cooking for most of the afternoon—Creole food. Sylvia discovers that she is now ravenous and urges the group along the sidewalk, laughing and newly bold.

Dark has fallen, though the air is still faintly tropical —the day was very warm, very springlike after all— and the group, which was hot and pressing to Sylvia inside the building, now feels small and strangely vulnerable moving together along the street.

Katerina and Anne trail behind everyone else, talking like old friends. Her mother fits here, Sylvia can see, in a way she never has fit in at home. She could be a student with her long slender freckled legs, her white wool dress, her crazy hair in a thick braid down her back.

Where is Ross? She looks around for her father and finally recognizes him up ahead, side by side with Brandon. They are talking earnestly—probably about tennis, she thinks—and look like a couple of fraternity brothers on their way for a beer. Next they'll be pulling out business cards. She can't help feeling a faint stab of jealousy and disappointment—how can her father not see what a jerk Brandon is?—but tries to stifle it with relief. At least her dad has something to concentrate on besides her; she can't handle too much more of his intensity tonight.

And then they are in front of the brownstone, her very own front stoop, and Sylvia looks up at the place they live, the lighted windows, thinking of how it appears from the outside (she has never thought about this before) and what kind of people lived there before and who will live there after her. The building is at least a hundred years old, which is not so old, really. But whoever lived there first is dead now, and if this place is still standing in another hundred years, well, I'll be dead, too, just like Bellyman and little Benjamin. We'll all be dead. And so what if I *was* a pianist? The thought is dark, and she pushes it aside quickly, laughing over her shoulder at something Peter says.

"Look at this," says her father. "Someone left more flowers." He hands Sylvia a single yellow rose, long-stemmed. "It was lying on the steps."

She takes the rose, puzzled, thinking that it must be Jan who left it, Jan, who has still failed to make his presence known, though a number of people have told her he was at the recital. If he doesn't come to the reception, she'll have to call him; she can't go to sleep tonight without making things right between them.

"How beautiful," says her mother. "I love roses." She takes the flower from Sylvia and holds it to her face. Ross turns away and heads up the stairs.

• • •

The small apartment has been transformed into something delicate, floating, ethereal. Flowers are everywhere, and Colette has lighted fifty candles; the white walls are luminous and wavering. Colette herself stands in the middle of the living room welcoming people, a lace apron over her raw-silk dress; Thelonius Monk plays "Epistrophy" in the background. People sit down on the sofa or floor, talking quietly, and soon there are wineglasses out and the perfume of wine is filling the candle-lit room.

This is perfect, Sylvia thinks, suddenly so happy she could cry. This is exactly the best thing that could have happened, having everyone here this way. She goes over and stands by Peter in his usual place beside the fake fireplace. He drops an arm over her shoulder and she gives him a thankful squeeze.

"I wish Marushka were here tonight," she says, "but I'm glad you stuck around till this was over."

"No big deal," he says.

"How was I?" She can't imagine asking anyone else this question, but she knows Peter will tell her the truth.

"Not bad, Syl. You had Beethoven wired."

"I know," she says smiling. "It felt *great*." She stands for a while with Peter's arm across her shoulder, indulging herself in private self-congratulations, then feels someone's eyes on her. Her father, from across the room, where he is still talking with Brandon, is giving her a stern and somber look that flusters her until she figures it out. And when she does, it makes her angry. He's upset about Peter. Peter, with his long black hair, his boots, his faint aura of cigarettes and whiskey and jazz. He's worried about *Peter*, she thinks, amazed. He can stand there and talk for hours to a jerk like Brandon and then be worried about *Peter*?

"Your dad doesn't like me," Peter says mildly.

"Oh, I don't think . . ."

"Look at him."

"Well, you know, he must think we're . . . going out or something. He's figured out something's wrong with me, anyway, and he's trying to find out what—or who— it is."

"Are you going to tell him?"

Am I going to tell him, she thinks. The big question. If I tell him, what will he do? She can hardly bear to see him glaring at her from across the room that way. He's so strong, so compact, so tanned and healthy and mus- cular and *right*. And he has always known what is best for her—the best concerts, the best teachers, the best schools. So of course he'll also know what's best in *this* situation too, no matter what *I* want. And he'll be wrong this time.

"No," she says.

"Good girl."

They stand facing the crowd, and she can feel the great calm of Peter's presence descending upon her. He only spends time on the important things, she thinks. He never wastes a single minute.

"You've taught me a lot," she says, looking straight ahead.

"Me too."

"Let's not lose touch, Peter."

He gives her a squeeze and pulls his arm away. "No way," he says. "Now, you'd better go take care of *that*."

She looks up, startled, to see Jan edging through the door with an enormous flat pink box; her heart contracts in relief.

"Jan," cries Colette. "Where have you been? I was about to give up on you!"

"I am sorry. I locked the door of my house, leaving the key inside. And then the apartment manager had to come, but he was at work . . ."

"But the cake is all right?"

"Oh yes, yes." Jan, his young cheeks flushed, his mild blue eyes shining, nods vigorously, still balancing the enormous bakery cake, and Sylvia thinks, why, he could have been my husband. He really would have married me, in spite of everything. He would have put the whole rest of his life on the line over *my* mistake. And I don't even know him, not really. I don't even know why he left Prague, what kind of sorrow *he* is living with—I've never asked him about his Catholicism, what he meant that time. I've been so focused on myself—how can he even *like* me?

She crosses the room, humbly, and puts her hand on his arm in front of everyone. "Thank you, Jan," she says. "Thank you for bringing the cake, and for . . . everything."

His crooked tooth flashes at her; his wild mop of hair bobs nervously. "I was happy to do it," he says. "And I will still be happy to . . . be of assistance. You may count on that, Sylvia." His breathing is quick and shallow, but his words are firm.

People are watching them curiously. She can see her mother's face turned in her direction, and Katerina's beside her. Jan is still holding the cake. She stands on her tiptoes and removes his glasses, which are so clouded he cannot possibly see. Tenderly, she cleans them on her skirt, then reaches up and puts them back on his nose. "There," she says. "And you don't need to worry any-more—things are under control."

He raises his eyebrows; she nods back at him. "Come on," she says. "I want to see what this *cake* looks like."

Hours later, when everyone has gone home but Anne—Ross decided to go back to the hotel, where there is a spa and a weight room, open all night—Sylvia and her mother are alone for the first time. When they finally say good night, Anne will sleep on the sofa, but for now they are sitting together on Sylvia's bed, a mother and daughter who look like sisters, and Anne, somewhat drunk, somewhat flushed, reaches into the pocket of her white dress and pulls out a small package. "For you," she says. "I love you, honey."

Sylvia takes it and turns it over in her hand, trying to imagine in what way her mother will commemorate this occasion. The package is very light, almost insubstantial, and Sylvia feels light too, light with relief that decisions have been made, that the recital is over, that Toft, obvi-ously, is not going to drop her after all. "What is it?"

"Open it and see."

Sylvia tears off the silver paper and opens a small white box. Inside is a gold ring, ornately old-fashioned, with a large ruby in the center that flashes in the light. Why, it must be worth a fortune. She takes it out slowly, turning it over in her fingers. This isn't the kind of pre-sent her parents would give her; she doesn't understand. "Mom?"

"It was Miss Selkirk's. She gave it to me when you were only ten. It belonged to her grandmother. Do you remember her mentioning her grandmother to you?"

Sylvia shakes her head. She remembers very little about Miss Selkirk, actually, besides those long hours of music.

"She was a pianist, too—English. Born sometime back in the middle 1800s—I think she told me 1840 or so."

Eighteen-forty. Thirteen years after Beethoven's death.

"She wanted you to have it, but not until you had grown up. Not until you had shown the world what you could do, she said."

Sylvia feels an enormous ache rising in her chest; she opens her mouth, on the very edge of confessing everything—oh, Mom, you don't know how close I've come to giving it all up, how hard this has been, how I've wanted you—but something stops her at the last second. She blinks and puts her hand to her throat, massaging the ache, then gives her mother a smile. "Thank you," she says. "I never knew . . . well, I never knew that Miss Selkirk had any feelings for me. You know, beyond the piano."

Anne looks surprised. "Really?" she says. "Why, you were the apple of her eye. She'd never had a student like you—what made her saddest is that she knew she'd never get to see what you were like as an adult."

An adult.

Sylvia stares at her mother, the young-looking shoulders, the slender legs tucked beneath the white dress.

Suddenly, she has to know. "May I ask you something, Mom?"

"Of course."

"Did you *have* to get married?"

"What?" She gives a startled laugh. "Now where did you get *that* idea, Sylvia?"

"Did you?"

Her mother reaches over and takes her by the chin, the way she used to when Sylvia was a child, and turns her face gently back and forth. "No, I did not. I just fell in love, that's all. And I got married too young, and then pregnant long before we planned to, after your father already had his orders and was practically out the door." She pauses. "Why would you ask me such a thing?"

Sylvia tries to meet her stare, but can't. "No reason," she says. "Just that you and Dad don't seem . . . well, I've kind of worried about you. Over the years."

Anne laughs, a laugh clearly meant to be reassuring. "Oh, Sylvia—that's just marriage, don't you know that? That's just two people grinding each other's edges off."

She's lying to me, Sylvia thinks. Even though it's out of love. And someday, when she finally leaves him, she'll have to tell me what *really* happened.

"Is something wrong, honey? Is there something you need to let me know?"

Sylvia raises her eyes until she is looking into her mother's face, which, though still flushed, has gone quiet and concerned. Now is the moment, she thinks. Now is when I give her the truth.

"No," she answers, and it's not a lie after all, not in any sense of the word, for this burden is *hers*—this *life* is hers—and from now on, she must carry them both in her own way. "Everything's fine," she says. "You can stop worrying."

EPILOGUE

Sylvia is standing on the ledge of the practice room window, watching the pigeons congregate on the winter grass in the park five stories below. They bob and weave like tiny people in a dance, and she can hear, though she is far above them, the gurgling joy of their gathering.

No one is up yet, no one but Peter, who is at least an hour north of Baltimore by now, driving the old Ford sedan he bought last week for the move. She stands with her feet planted on the wide sill, looking out over the city, over the pink sky, the vanishing mist, the buildings, still wet from the night, already missing him. It will never be the same, she thinks, no matter how we try. I know that now, from Marushka.

For a moment she is filled with sorrow, then thinks, Miss Koh came to my recital! Moon Ja Koh! and wonders why she doesn't thrill in the old way, the way she did even six months ago, just thinking about her idol. Maybe it was seeing her that morning, Sylvia thinks, after she did the Schubert sonata when she was crying.

She looked so old and sad then, not like her posters. And I felt sorry for her, the way I did for Toft last night.

She straightens. Sorry for Toft? Well, I was, she thinks. He seemed so small and . . . harmless all of a sudden. Maybe *that*'s why I had to kiss him. To prove he was still real.

A car turns onto the street below her, moving slowly past the park. From where she stands, it is a ridiculous thing, squat as a beetle and shiny green. Someone worked hard for that car, she thinks. It's a nice one. She watches as it searches along the edge of the wrought-iron fence, halting and starting again, and she wonders who is at the wheel. A stranger to the city? A young boy learning to drive?

When it comes to the corner, it sits for a long time, though there are no other cars in either direction, and finally, tentatively, turns right, away from the statue, and disappears, though she can hear the throb of its engine for minutes longer.

Somewhere out at sea a foghorn is calling. It reminds her of Lake Superior, Minneapolis, the big house on Cedar Lake. She thinks of the dense dark pines edging up against the acre of lawn. When I go home again (in her mind she can see her father in his workshop, her mother reading on the porch in her black-rimmed glasses), nothing will be the same.

She has let go of the frame with one hand, is cupping her abdomen again. Thinking of the other time she stood up here, half crazy, and of Tee's dark face tipped up toward hers. I'm *glad* I did that, she thinks. I'm glad I thought about letting go. She remembers as clearly as if it had happened the step into air, her arms rising like an angel's wings, and the showers of white feathers—the Easter doves. And bells—she had heard bells from all over the city as she tumbled through the frightened white doves to the ground. And then, afterward, not having done it after all, the fact that she had chosen to go on and how important that became.

Do you understand? she says to the tiny creature inside of her. That's all of it, what you see out there. All those people, struggling along, trying to be happy. Look hard, little Benjamin. And forgive me.

From somewhere in the building she can hear a piano. Someone doing scales, over and over. Some student, perhaps someone she has never met, up with the sun, who will practice for two or three hours before a slow walk to the White Tower for coffee and eggs and . . . pancakes? She sniffs the air. The ocean, yes, and the grime of the alleys, the stench of traffic, starting now to flow, but something else, too, something beautiful and crisp frying in a pan somewhere—breakfast.

She takes a long hungry breath of it, still listening to the piano, and steps carefully down from the sill onto the floor. Behind her is the old Steinway, scarred in the morning light, and beside it is her canvas bag of music.

About the Author

PAULA HUSTON lives on the central California coast with her husband and four children and teaches writing and literature at Cal Poly, San Luis Obispo. She is a National Endowment of the Arts recipient, and her short stories have been selected for *Best American Short Stories'* 100 Distinguished Stories of 1993 and 1994. Her story collection *A Misery of Love* is forthcoming from Random House. *Daughters of Song* is her first novel.

About the Type

This book was set in Berling. Designed in 1951 by Karl Erik Forsberg for the Typefoundry Berlingska Stilgjuteri AB in Lund, Sweden, it was released the same year in foundry type by H. Berthold AG. A classic oldface design, its generous proportions and inclined serifs make it highly legible.